QUANTICO

Other Books by Greg Bear

Science Fiction

Collections

Fantasy

Edited

QUANTICO

Greg Bear

MADISON
PARK™

NEW YORK

Published by Madison Park Press, 15 East 26th Street, New York, NY 10010.

ISBN: 1-58288-217-7

Printed in the United States of America

To those who put themselves in harm's way to save us from madness, greed, and folly.

PART ONE

Brewer, Baker, Candlestick Maker

They have moved me to jealousy with that which is not God; they have provoked me to anger with their vanities; and I will move them to jealousy with those which are not a people; I will provoke them to anger with a foolish nation.

—KJV, Deuteronomy, 32:21, cf. Romans 10:19

. . . make the town see that he was an enemy of the people, and that [the guerillas] shot him because the guerillas recognized as their first duty the protection of citizens.

—CIA Manual: Psychological
Operations in Guerilla Warfare

CHAPTER ONE
Guatemala, near the Mexican Border
Year Minus Two

From the front seat of the Range Rover, the small fat man with the sawed-off shotgun reached back and pulled the hood from his passenger's head. "Too hot, *señor*?" the fat man asked. His breath smelled of TicTacs but that did not conceal the miasma of bad teeth.

The *Nortamericano*'s short sandy blond hair bristled with sweat. He took a deep breath and looked out at the red brick courtyard and the surrounding lush trees. His eyes were wild before they settled. "A little."

"I am sorry, and also it is so humid today. It will be nice and cool inside. *Señor* Guerrero is a man of much hospitality, once he knows he is safe."

"I understand."

"Without that assurance," the fat man continued, "he can be moody."

Two Indians ran from the hacienda. They were young and hungry-looking and carried AK-47s across their chests. One opened the Range Rover's door and invited the *Nortamericano* out with a strong tug. He stepped down slowly to the bricks. He was lanky and taller than the fat man. The Indians spoke Mam to each other and broken Spanish to the driver. The driver smiled, showing gaps in his tobacco-stained teeth. He leaned against the hood and lit a Marlboro. His face gleamed in the match's flare.

The Indians patted down the tall man as if they did not trust the fat man, the driver, or the others who had accompanied them from Pajapita. They made as if to pat down the driver but he cursed and pushed them away. This was an awkward moment but the fat man barked some words in Mam and the Indians backed off with sour looks. They swaggered and jerked the barrels of their guns. The driver turned away with patient eyes and continued smoking.

The tall man wiped his face with a handkerchief. Somewhere a generator hummed. The roads at the end had been brutal, rutted and covered with broken branches from the recent hurricane. Still the hacienda seemed to have suffered no damage and glowed with lights in the dusk. In the center of the courtyard a small fountain cast a single stream of greenish water two meters into the air. The stream splashed through a cloud of midges. Small bats swooped back and forth across the blue dusk like swallows. A lone little girl with long black hair, dressed in shorts, a halter top, and pink sandals, played around the fountain. She stopped for a moment to look at the tall man and the Range Rover, then swung her hair and resumed playing.

The fat man walked to the back of the truck and opened the gate. He pulled down a quintal bag of coffee. It thudded and hissed on the bricks as the beans settled.

"Mr. Guerrero uses no drugs but for coffee, and that he drinks in quantity," the fat man said. He squinted one eye. "We will wait for you here." He tapped his platinum watch. "It is best to be brief."

A small old woman wearing a long yellow and red cotton dress approached from the hacienda and took the tall man by the hand. She smiled up at him and led him across the courtyard. The little girl watched with a somber expression. Beneath a fine dark fuzz, her upper lip had the faint pink mark of a cleft palate that had been expertly repaired. The bronze gates before the hacienda's patio were decorated with roughly cast figures of *putti*, little angels doing chores such as carrying fruit. The angels' eyes, sad but resigned, resembled the eyes of the old woman and their color was a good match for her skin. Beyond a serious iron door and then a glass door, the hacienda's centrally cooled air stroked the tall man's face. Music played through the broad white rooms—light jazz, Kenny G. The old woman showed him to a white couch and pushed him back until he sat. She knelt and removed his shoes, replacing them with sandals from a pouch concealed in the folds of her dress.

Mr. Guerrero appeared alone in the doorway to the dining room. He was small and well-formed and he wore a yellow and black Hawaiian shirt tucked in and white linen pants and a rope belt. His hair was thick and dark. He looked like a well-to-do man pretending to be a beachcomber.

"Mr. Santerra, welcome," Guerrero said. "I trust your ride was sincerely terrible."

The tall man, whose name was not Santerra, held up a small cloth bag. Glass vials jingled softly inside. "At least nothing broke."

Guerrero's cheek jerked. "It is done, then?"

"Proof of concept," the tall man said. "Pure and lethal. Try it on someone you no longer need."

Guerrero held up his hands. "I am not that kind of man," he said. "We will test it in a lab, with animals. If it is what you say, you will be given your next money at a place of our choosing. Money is not safe here or in the islands. Terrorism has forced your nation to pay too much attention to world banking."

A large balding black man in a black suit entered from the kitchen and walked around Guerrero. He stood in front of the tall man and held out his hand. He received the bag and opened it carefully. Three vials filled with fine powder tinkled into his pink palm. "You realize this is not the final product," the black man said in a reedy voice with an Austrian accent, to Guerrero. "It proves nothing."

Guerrero waved his hand, dismissing that concern. "You will tell me if they have proven good faith before the next payment. Correct, *Señor* Santerra?"

The tall man nodded.

"I may never see an end to this trouble," Guerrero said. He had not taken a step closer since the tall man held up the cloth bag. "But I hope my children will. Have you viewed the movie *M*, *Señor* Santerra?"

The tall man shook his head.

"The underworld of Germany seeks out a child molester and puts him on trial because he is bringing down so much *heat* on their operations. It is so here. If you keep your promise, we will give those thoughtless monsters what they deserve." He paused, allowing the black Austrian to leave the room with the bag. Then he sat on a heavy wooden chair. His face was lined with years of worry. "You have a dangerous quality. It makes me want to trust you."

The tall man did not acknowledge this compliment, if it was one.

"I appreciate that you have come in person. When can I expect news?"

"Within three months, at most six." The tall man held out his hand to shake on their deal.

Guerrero looked down at the hand. His cheek twitched once more. He looked decades older than his forty years. "Now you will go," he said.

The old bronze woman hustled into the room again and knelt to replace the tall man's shoes. He stood and walked to the door.

In the courtyard, they had kept the engine running. The little girl had gone inside. The driver extinguished his cigarette and deposited the butt in a tin he drew from his pocket.

The fat man opened the door to the Range Rover and dangled the hood from one hand, smiling. "There are too many bats around here," he said. "I suppose it is because there are so many insects."

CHAPTER TWO
Iraq
Year Minus One

The red plastic beads on the curtain rattled like finger bones in a cup.

The man who stepped down into the coffee house had yellow hair. He wore sunglasses, as did almost every man in Baghdad, a city of thieves, killers, and merchants. Fine dust swirled from his shoes as he pushed them through a double brush set in the bricks. For a moment, he turned up his nose and frowned as if possessed by some noble doubt, and his temple and cheek were lit by a false hope of rubies. A hero, obviously—an Englishman perhaps—tall and slender and possibly strong, though that was difficult to judge beneath the baggy cut of his linen coat.

Ibrahim Al-Hitti watched from the small round table and pulled in his polished black shoes, not wishing them to be trampled. There was little room in the basement, few tables and fewer customers. A one-eyed cousin of a cousin owned the establishment and had been persuaded it could be used on occasion as a place of personal business, not to be asked after. He would literally turn a blind eye to any activities. That plump and ill-dressed relative now stood behind the small black bar surrounded by a rising cloud of steam from an old espresso machine imported, so he boasted, from Italy. The steam frightened two horseflies seeking refuge from the outer heat. They buzzed and batted until settling on the plaster wall beside a small fogged mirror. The air in the basement café was humid and hot like the rest of Iraq this time of year, a climate fit for sordid talk and deeds.

Al-Hitti had been born in Yemen but had spent most of his youth in Egypt and England. He had no love for Iraq and he did not like Iraqis in general. This part of town, near Firdos Square—allegedly cooled by breezes off the Tigris—was frequented by businessmen mostly and the secretaries and office workers of Shiite clerics. Businessmen he despised. Of clerics he held no opinions.

Though a Muslim and a Sunni, Al-Hitti was of that pragmatic sect that had proliferated in the Middle East in the last century—a nonaligned brotherhood most interested in diverting the rivers of power. Religious passions had divided Muslims for too many centuries and only made them weak. What would bring them together and restore lost glory were the cool efforts of the mind, working to enact difficult, some would say sordid deeds.

The tall man removed his sunglasses, unafraid to reveal his face. Al-Hitti saw immediately that he was American, not English—they were as different in step and behavior to his discerning eye as Ethiopians and Somalis. So this was the one whom he was scheduled to meet. It was an appointment he had not looked forward to. A *disappointment*.

He enjoyed playing with English words.

And he was even less happy now that he saw that the man he would have to kill was in fact a decent-looking fellow with strong features and even a respectable *tan*. That English word, *tan*, appeared in his head, surrounded by half-naked women. This irritated him.

The American caught his eye and stepped forward, walking lightly around the tables to the rear of the shop. To Al-Hitti he offered his right hand and in low, mellow tones introduced himself. His name was John Brown. He was from Massachusetts—a silly, sneezing sort of name for a place. His Arabic was of the Cairo variety and surprisingly good.

"You are just as I imagined you," Al-Hitti told the American, a lie. He had imagined instead a small, furtive man wearing loose clothing.

"Is it so?" the American said, and pulled back a flimsy wrought-iron chair to sit. They both measured out tiny smiles.

The cousin arrived to take their orders. He pointedly ignored the American, turning his good eye from that part of the room. John Brown did not seem to mind.

As Al-Hitti waited for a glass of thick sweet tea, he examined the American closely. Their silence drew out. His first impression had been one of quiet strength, a man who would appeal to women. But Al-Hitti's deeper instincts made him less certain. There were telling lines in the American's face and a determined sadness that reminded Al-Hitti of an old fighter—not a soldier, who could be casually cruel and blame others, but a mountain guerilla, used to working and living alone for months and having no one to blame but himself.

John Brown's appearance was made more striking by the fact that he had one blue eye and one green eye. Al-Hitti had never seen such a thing.

The American put his hand to his chest. "Before you decide whether or not to kill me . . ." He reached swiftly into his coat pocket and pulled out a heat-sealed plastic packet full of beige powder.

Al-Hitti reacted as if stung by one of the horseflies. He pushed back, eyes wide, and his chair banged into another chair. "What is this?"

"A sample," the American answered.

"Complete?" Al-Hitti asked, his voice rising in pitch.

The American raised his chin. "Not yet. Soon."

Al-Hitti refused to handle the package until he saw his courage was in question and that the American was rapidly losing confidence. It was probably fake, anyway. Anything else would be too much to hope for. He took it. The plastic was beaded with sweat from the American's hands, but inside, the powder was miraculously fine and light, clinging and dry.

A handful of a hundred thousand miseries.

"Tell your scientists, or your graduate students at university, to examine it with great care," the American instructed. "It will behave like a gas, penetrating everywhere if not properly handled. They will tell you that it is pure and that it has been genetically modified, but it is not complete. Not yet. Try it on someone you wish dead. Let your subject breathe a few grains, or swallow it, or touch it to his skin. In time, examined in the dark, his lesions will glow green and then red. These inserted genes are proof that we can do what we say."

Al-Hitti could not help avoiding the tall American's gaze. There was something about the blue eye that reminded him of the sky over a desert waste.

Al-Hitti leaned forward. "What sort of proof is this, just a package of powder extracted from the soil of Texas, where a steer has died, perhaps? How can we believe the rest of your story?" Al-Hitti held the package out between two fingers. "I hear this is easy to make. That is what I am told."

"Believe what fools say," the American said, "less the fools they." He brought forth a small knife, pulled open a blade, and laid it on the table between them. "Rub it on your skin like baby powder. Let's breathe it together."

Al-Hitti shrugged too quickly, hiding a shudder. "We are not here to piss up a wall."

"No," the American said.

"When will the final product be ready?"

"When money is made available. I will conduct my own tests and you will do yours. Then, next year . . . Jerusalem."

"There are very few Jews in Iraq. Saddam no longer protects them, and the clerics . . ." He lowered his eyelids. He was *getting ahead of himself,* like *a cart before a horse.*

"Until the gene sockets are filled, as specified, Jews need fear this no more than you or I," the American said. "And no less."

"Who is paying for what you have done so far, a Wahhabi?" Al-Hitti asked with quiet anger. "May he die in the bed of an incontinent pig." Al-Hitti did not like Wahhabis. What they had done to maintain their hold on power had killed many of his best men. Now, all Saudi Arabia was in turmoil. Just retribution had finally arrived.

The American noiselessly pushed back his chair. He looked down on Al-Hitti.

"If I say yes, and arrange for people, and the money is given?"

"Then we will meet next year," the American said.

The cousin's cousin had had enough, and a crack like a tiny shot sounded in the small coffee house. Al-Hitti turned to look. The proprietor raised a swatter besmirched by horsefly.

When Al-Hitti turned back, the American was at the door, parting the beaded curtain. Another horsefly entered with a looping buzz and the American was gone.

The proprietor returned to the table to remove the glass. He stared at Al-Hitti through his one good eye. "Is it that you are taking tea alone today?" he asked.

No one of any importance in Iraq other than himself could remember seeing a pale blond American with the face of a warrior and eyes of two different colors. But there was always the plastic bag. And what was in it was true. Indeed, very true.

Al-Hitti had the powder examined and then tested. It made five kidnapped Iraqi businessmen and two secretaries of the clerics ill and pitiable. In the dark, their lesions glowed first green and then red, so the doctors reported to people that Al-Hitti knew.

And then they died, all of them.

As the months passed, Al-Hitti came to believe that it would actually happen. His hope reflected how bad things had become for his people. Three years ago, the Dome of the Rock had been blown to pieces by a Jewish terrorist to make way for the rebuilding of their Temple. In response, a few weeks later, on October the fourth—thereafter known as 10-4—another blow had been struck against the financier of all things evil, the United States. Thousands had died. Though he had secretly approved and even gloated, it had made Al-Hitti's job that much harder.

The Israelis were now assassinating the immediate families of suicide bombers and leaders of Hamas and Hezbollah. Muslim youth rushed to destruction and did not seem to care that by so doing they were also condemning their brothers and sisters, their mothers and fathers—and then, their uncles and cousins. Back and forth, the slaughter turned all into monsters.

In the late summer or early fall, he knew, Saudi Arabia would be invaded by tens of thousands of anti-Wahhabists working out of Sudan, Oman, and Iraq. Irony of ironies, it was said Americans were financing a number of the insurgents, including Iraqis, in hopes of replacing the House of Saud with a more stable regime. *The enemy of my enemy is my friend. For the time being.*

Once again Muslims were engaged in *Takfir wa Hijra*, condemnation and exile, killing nonbelievers and traitors—Westerners and Muslims alike—to reclaim the holy lands.

The next hot wind would blow from the desert and cleanse the world like a pillar of fire.

CHAPTER THREE
Year Zero
Arizona

Special Agent Rebecca Rose stared through the window of the FBI Econoline van at the dark desert along the highway. Brian Botnik from the Phoenix Field Office looked sideways at Rose in the front passenger seat. She rubbed her hand nervously over her knee—gray pants, cuff of dark pink cotton blouse protruding half an inch from her coatsleeve, fingers thin and strong, red-enameled nails bitten short and chipped. It was five a.m. and she could almost see the heat of the past day rising slowly into space. That's what happened at night—the Earth shed its heat like a cooling corpse. The sun hid away, nowhere to be seen; maybe it would never return.

"Gerber's a good fellow," Botnik said. "But he hates being kept in the dark. So tell me—why are we keeping him in the dark?" Botnik was a big man with a deep voice, a tight stomach, farmer's hands, and sandy hair—attractive, had she the energy to think about such things. Ten years younger than her, she guessed, but neither inexperienced nor a dummy.

Rose smiled. "Because if I tell him why we're interested, he'll think we're idiots."

"I'm open to that possibility," Botnik said, flashing a grin.

"Hush," Rose said.

Two FBI analysts sat in the middle seat behind them. Both were young, white, clean-cut, and male. Both were respectful and earnest. Little pitchers have big ears. The younger, whiter, and more clean-cut the male agent, the more likely he would talk behind her back.

After the flights and the drive from Tucson, she was bone-tired and on the edge of hallucinations; her science and most of her sense had fled. But she had to stay tactical. This would not be easy. Every cop seemed to regard FBI agents, especially senior agents, as short-timers going down for the third time in a flood of politics. Some felt sorry, others exhibited a parochial gloat.

It was getting harder and harder to focus on work even when she wasn't exhausted.

The headline of the newspaper folded across the divider read:

FBI "PATRIOT" FILES KEPT ON
6 DEM SENATORS, VP:
"Traitors to the Nation," Dossiers Claim

Rose was acquainted with the agents who had prepared those dossiers. Two were clowns; she had thought that the other six were good men. Now they were buried in the depths of Headquarters or testifying before a federal grand jury. One and all, they had messed their britches.

Screw that. Just do your job.

The first sign of happy times along the highway was a single-vehicle set of peel-out marks. Sixty yards further on, deep truck-tire gouges marred the right shoulder. In the blink of an eye, a second pair of smudges like strokes of artist's charcoal extended for thirty feet. A half-mile beyond that, multiple curving conga lines of laid-down rubber—some parallel, some crossing—played with the divider for a hundred yards. Those tracks ended at an overturned and battered big rig trailer.

Patrol officers were stationed to flag drivers through the single open lane. At this hour of the morning there was almost no traffic.

Botnik steered the Econoline to the side of the road, parking behind a gray Suburban marked with Arizona's rising sun. As Rose stepped out and stretched, the young agents pulled aluminum cases from the rear of the van. Botnik introduced her to three Department of Public Safety officers. Lieutenant Colonel Jack Gerber, the Deputy Director of Criminal Investigations, had been dispatched from Phoenix along with two analysts. They had been waiting at the scene for three hours. Remarkably they were still willing to pretend not to be teed off.

Gerber was a tall lean man in his late forties with straight black hair and a brown boyish face lacking any trace of a beard. Multi-racial, Rose judged: American Indian, Anglo, and some black. America's future. His eyes were brown and his large fingernails curved around the upper half of each fingertip, rounded and neatly manicured.

Rose walked with Gerber and Botnik back along the highway and studied the scene from the beginning of the skid marks. Gerber was explaining what little they knew. "The chase must have begun about ten miles back.

Patrolman Porter queried the truck's RFLM—Radio Frequency License and Manifest transponder—and got a bogus authentication. When the truck's driver ignored his lights and siren and the truck failed to respond to Cop Block, the patrolman became aware he might have a situation. We get a lot of drug traffic. Patrolman Porter was an excellent officer, very keen on his job."

All cars and trucks in the U.S. were now required to have Cop Block. A patrol car could radio a coded signal that slowed and then shut down the engine. Workarounds were illegal and the fines were expensive, plus real jail time.

The rig had jackknifed and the trailer had flipped and twisted the truck along with it, corkscrewing the rear frame and tires a quarter turn. The International 9200 had then split off from the trailer and skidded on its side for fifty-two yards, leaving a broad scrape of paint and sidewall rubber and lots of fresh gray grooves in the asphalt. The trailer's rear doors had sprung open and about a third of the contents had tumbled out, depositing a trail of white boxes along the road, most of them intact.

They were all inkjet printers.

Rose held back an urge to request that the trailer and the boxes be marked off and tested by a HAZMAT team. Too early and too obvious, a tipping of her hand. She had yet to bring out her WAGD—pronounced Wag-Dee, for Wright Assay Germ Detector—a biohazard analyzer the size and shape of a large Magic Marker. She carried two in her coat pocket. Some in the field called the WAGD the Death Stick. Others had corrupted the acronym to "We're All Gonna Die."

One of the white boxes had ripped open. She pulled back a flap and bent to peer inside. The printer had fallen out of its foam packing. Its top had broken off, exposing the metal tracking bars and ribbon cables within. The cartridge wells were empty.

"We're still not sure what happened after that," Gerber said. "Porter must have been ahead of the truck when it flipped—it's our procedure to park behind an accident and switch on all lights, to warn traffic. At around eight p.m., the officer was shot three times. He had not called in the wreck, and he did not call in his situation. He must have been surprised. We think there was another man, perhaps hiding in the trailer. The officer did manage to get off two shots. Neither of them hit the truck."

"Patrolman Porter's Infodeck—when did it last make its uplink?"

"Seven forty-one," Gerber said. "Nothing unusual. He was at the Bluebird Tall Stack, a truck stop. You passed it on the way here."

"We did," Rose said.

The reflecting tape between the lighted mobile cone barriers flapped in the early morning breeze. A patrolman waved through a small silver Toyota. It drove slowly around the scene, well clear of the rippling tape, its middle-aged female driver goggling.

Colonel Gerber was being straightforward and professional, and for that Rose was grateful. She reached into her coat pocket and pulled out a WAGD, hiding most of it in her palm and up her sleeve, then swiftly uncapped it, bent over the open printer box, and ran the moist gel tip along the inside and across the printer carriage. She capped and pocketed the device, then moved on with Gerber.

Twenty yards further on, the patrol car was a blackened shell hunkered on the right shoulder and facing the wrong direction—east. It had been set on fire with gas siphoned from its own tank. The patrol car's tires had burned to the steel belts. Melted aluminum traced shiny rivers down to the roadside gravel. Whatever onboard data—video, officer commentary, the contents of the patrol car's orange box—that had not been transferred by satellite link from the car's Infodeck had been destroyed.

A small grass fire had been extinguished by a quick light rain minutes after the wreck.

The officer's body had been found on the north shoulder of the road, ten yards from the burnt-out patrol car. The body had been removed by the Pima County Medical Examiner but a silver marker line still recorded its outline. A rain-diluted smear of blood pointed in the direction of the cruiser, about thirty feet away.

In the center of the outline, a small spherical projector sitting on a hammered peg threw out grainy patterns of blue and red light.

"Glasses?" Rose asked.

Gerber offered a pair from his pocket. She unfolded the temple pieces and slipped them on. The officer's body came into clear view, frozen in place and lit all around by multiple strobes. Legs straight, arms limp and angled.

"The body was moved before we got here," Gerber said.

She walked around the projector and stooped. Patrolman Porter's body looked perfectly solid against the black pavement. *Had he been closer to the cruiser, he would have burned. Someone dragged him across the highway. A bystander? The killer?*

Why have empathy for a dead or dying cop?

Projectors were good but the emotional assault of seeing an actual corpse always heightened her senses. Death so close, injustice everywhere.

Still, the photographer had done a good job. The 3-D image was clean and sharp. In a few hours, no doubt, the ME and the CID would merge their data and she could call up the same projection and see a reconstruction of the officer's stance, the lines along which the slugs had traveled, his reaction to the force of tons of accelerated mass hitting his shoulder, his chest, his neck.

The FBI evidence techs had fanned out along the road and were busy taking pictures, checking the interior of the truck's cab, scraping paint and rubber off the road, setting up survey poles and lasers, repeating much of what Gerber's people had already done.

"You still haven't told me why the feds are interested in a few hundred gray-market computer printers," Gerber said. "Obsolete models, too."

"We're curious where the truck was going. Whether it had any escorts."

Gerber flipped his hand at the International. "There's no driver log, no valid license, no bills of lading or any of the records required for interstate transport. The truck seems to have been modified in Mexico and driven across state lines about two months ago—we have a video of a rig with that federal ID number crossing the border at that time, with all its papers in order. But the last registered owner claims he sold it in Mexico six years ago. Still, the truck had a Grit Mitt and seemed to be trying to meet current highway standards—other than Cop Block, of course. Nor are there any signs of these printers being a dummy cargo—our K9s just looked bored. We're still pursuing the trail . . . but backwards, not forwards. I have no idea where this rig was going, and if we don't catch the second man, or woman, we'll probably never know."

"Second man or woman?"

"Just a possibility. Someone gave our perp or perps a ride. Between here and the next town it's fifty miles of nothing. Long walk. We've looked. And no hospital here or across either border reports anyone with gunshot injuries." He rubbed a light stubble on his chin. "We're done. Let us know when can we clear our highway."

"Thanks for your patience. I need another hour."

"Porter was a smart patrolman. Nobody could have just got the drop on him," Gerber said. "This whole thing is an awful mess."

"Amen," Rose said, getting back to her feet. She folded the glasses and returned them to Gerber. "Was Porter married?"

"I don't think so," Gerber said. He called to one of his analysts, a short, plump man with a dapper mustache. "Earl, was Porter married?"

"No, sir," Earl said, glad to get in on the conversation. He had been checking out Rose. "Never married. Patrol was his life. Well, he liked to drive to Vegas once a year."

"Eager?" Rose asked.

"The best always are," Gerber said. He sniffed and peered around the highway and the distant hills. His irritation was about to break through. "As long as you're here, I'd be fascinated to hear your take. I'm sure it's filled with exceptional, FBI-level insight."

Sometimes, cops let other cops reel out a little rope. Whoever went first was eager to jump to conclusions. Earl backed off and returned to his group.

Rose said, "I'm curious as to how your cruiser ends up spun around in front of a jackknifed semi."

"A curious situation," Gerber agreed.

"You've had problems with escort vehicles that can interrupt communications. Are you looking for a jammer?" Rose glanced up at Botnik, ten yards off. He could hear their conversation. He gave her a quick nod, out of Gerber's sight.

"Should we be?" Gerber asked innocently.

"There could have been two vehicles," Rose continued, "one traveling a few minutes behind the other. The first, our International and its trailer, must have attracted Porter's attention. He decided to bird-dog the rig and look for an excuse to pull it over."

"Okay," Gerber said, and stuck his hands in his pockets. They were walking side by side now, the best of chums.

The WAGD was still quiet.

"The second vehicle could have followed at a discreet distance," Rebecca said. "Porter lit up and pulled the rig over for inspection. Maybe the driver couldn't produce the right papers. He called for backup but didn't get a response."

"We received no request for backup," Gerber said, but he wasn't disagreeing.

"Porter's Infodeck told him he was off the grid and he couldn't make direct radio contact. His display told him he was being jammed."

"All right."

"With the rig pulled over, the occupant or occupants of the second vehicle decided to make a run for it. Porter suspected this was the jammer, got his wind up, ordered his first quarry to stay put, and took off after the second truck."

Gerber looked thoughtful. "Evidence?" he asked pleasantly.

"Nothing, really," Rose said. "Unless we count tire marks a few miles back, two vehicles peeling out, not far from a long set of truck tracks in the gravel."

"Mm," Gerber said, and his smile broadened. She wasn't ahead of him yet. He knew about those marks. "Jammers work for hire and don't carry contraband. Porter knew the drill. He would have let the little one go."

"But you said he was a gambler," Rose said. "Right? Unmarried, eager, a Vegas kind of guy. Patrol was his life. For just a few seconds, he couldn't think past the glory of making a twofer—of pulling over a rich cargo, and grabbing a jammer besides."

"Are we about to cast aspersions on an officer who can't defend himself?" Gerber asked. His face was professionally blank but his pupils had widened.

"Not at all," Rose said. "Happens to the best of us."

Gerber squinted. "Tell me, why would any driver risk a chase and the hoosegow for a load of old printers?"

Gerber had spent a lifetime figuring out what people were really interested in. Rose walked back toward the burnt-out patrol car. "Porter reacquired his perspective after a peek in the rear view mirror. He saw the rig get underway and quickly decided to give up on the jammer. He and the rig played a little chicken. Risky, but maybe not out of character. He got in front and tried to brake the rig to a stop—got tapped, spun out . . . and the rig jackknifed and flipped. Porter ended up by the side of the road, reversed."

She stood beside the distorted, blackened curve of the cruiser's driver's side door. "Porter squatted behind the door and drew down on the truck cab. Based on chase maneuvers and the spin-out, his Infodeck would have automatically attempted to re-connect and call for urgent backup, and he probably surmised the jammer would soon be out of range."

"All right," Gerber said. "Now explain to me, how did he end up getting shot? Did the jammer return? Was he caught in a crossfire?"

Botnik and Earl approached. "No fingerprints or blood inside the truck cab," Botnik told Rose. "No food items or cups or urine jugs. Nothing much at all. We're fuming and dusting the exterior, but I'll bet the driver was wearing gloves."

Rose stood behind the burnt-out cruiser door, looked back at the rig, drew sight-lines. Then she and Botnik crossed the highway and walked along the south side. Gerber and Earl glanced both ways for traffic—the road was almost empty—and followed. "Did you work the ditch here, off the shoulder?" she asked.

Gerber turned to Earl. The younger man shook his head, uncertain whether he was admitting to a mistake.

Botnik caught on right away. "Jesus. Sounds like some sort of combat vet."

Gerber was now the one short on rope. He looked along the length of the ditch and saw how a man could have exited the International and crawled along the ditch without being seen. His face wrinkled. "Shit."

"After the wreck," Rose said, "Porter may have called for the driver to get out or shout if he was unable to comply." She took two steps into the ditch, put her hand on her hips, raised her right arm, then lined up her eye and her pointing finger with the position that Porter would have assumed beside his cruiser. "From this angle, the shooter could have watched and waited until Porter got impatient and stood up. The first shot passed over the hood and between the door and the window frame and hit Porter in his left shoulder. Porter may have been knocked half about, then lurched forward and hung on to the door. The second shot could have passed through his neck, spinning him around again, and the third impacted the chest. The neck wound, was it from the side or rear?"

Gerber pointed to the right rear of his own neck.

She stepped gingerly along the rocks. "Rough crawl, but someone well-trained could have done it in thirty seconds or less. Your shooter pushed up . . . Here and here." She pointed to the rain-softened remains of two gouges, one shallow, one deep in the gravel and dirt. "Knee mark. Toe of shoe or boot digging in. No sole imprint. He shot your patrolman three times, then walked across the highway and made sure he was dead or dying. The assailant then dragged Porter away from the car."

She finished with, "Our shooter unplugged the Infodeck, removed the officer's data vest, tossed it in the car, set the car on fire and cooked the memory so there wouldn't be any record. But for some reason, the assailant was squeamish about letting an officer burn. Even a dead one."

Gerber's jaw muscles flexed. "All that, for old printers?" he asked.

Botnik gave Rose a hard stare.

"I can't see it," Gerber said. "Too many holes. I think we have drug runners getting creative. Maybe this time, the escort vehicle carried both contraband and jamming equipment, with the International truck, full of a dummy load, acting as decoy. Hell, you could pack ten million dollars worth of Tart in a suitcase. Maybe Porter saw the printers, surmised the rig wasn't carrying, and went after the jammer. That explains the tire tracks."

"Then why would the driver of the rig light out?" Rose asked. "Why not just stay put, act innocent, plead to a misdemeanor and get a ticket?"

Because he did not want anyone to learn about his printers.

The bastard knows I'm looking for him.

"I believe in the competence of our patrol officers," Gerber said, his face flushed. "We're done here, Agent Rose."

"Mm hmm." Rose knelt in the gravel and rocks and looked hard at the ground around the knee imprint and the toe mark. *Didn't feel right torching an officer. What sort of smuggler . . . ?*

A former cop?

Rose pictured the driver of the International biting on his glove's fingers to pull it off. It could have dangled from his teeth as he fired at Porter. She got down on her hands and knees. Urban cops tended to wear close-weave protected gloves, to reduce the chances of cuts or needle pricks during pat-downs. Many wore Turtleskins. Rose preferred Friskmasters. "Did anybody find a glove?" she asked.

"No, ma'am," Gerber said.

Rebecca measured the distance between the toe marks. A smooth stone in just the right place had been pressed down and twisted, the dirt scrunched up around its perimeter. She picked it up. A fleashit speck of rain-washed blood had fallen on the tumbled-smooth surface. She palmed the stone, and then saw another drop of blood, unmistakable, on a pebble nested in a patch of sand. "Something here," she said. The young analysts joined her in the ditch. As they worked over the area, she pocketed the larger rock, unseen.

"Could be a ground squirrel or a coyote," Gerber said with a sniff.

"I'd like to be copied on any human DNA results."

"Of course." Gerber knelt beside her. "It's a golden age of cooperation."

Botnik walked beside Rose back to the Suburban. "Gerber's a good guy. He won't stand in our way if we need something. And don't get me wrong. If Hiram Newsome shows an interest in inkjet printers, I'll be there for you with bells on."

"Thanks," Rose said. "Has your Minitest been certified recently?"

"Not in the last month," Botnik said.

"Can I borrow a plastic bag?"

One of the young agents gave her a baggie. She pulled the rock from her pocket and slipped it into the baggie, inspecting it to make sure the blood speck was still there.

"Jesus," Botnik said, and whapped the steering wheel with his hand. "This is just the kind of federal arrogance that's killing us."

"They have blood evidence, we have blood evidence," Rose said, deadpan. "Pima County ME lost its board certification again last year. Arizona CID is backed up for days or even weeks. And you haven't even primed your Minitest. What's a poor girl to do?"

Botnik turned a fine ruddy shade. "All right," he said. "You've got it figured out. But you still have a problem. You still have to learn where the suspect was going. Maybe somebody around here can help. To that end, I'm hoping you'll spread at least a little enlightenment."

"Thanks again," Rose said. "But we have reasons to keep it quiet."

"Quiet?" Botnik chuckled. "This is the worst-kept secret in the FBI. It's got something to do with Amerithrax. The only question I have is, what the hell's the connection?"

Rose took a shallow breath.

"I do crossword puzzles," she said. "Sometimes, when I can't solve one right away, I put it aside. Some of my puzzles have been waiting for years."

"Secrecy is most of why we're boots up in a pile of shit," Botnik said. "What if there's another anthrax attack and you could have prevented it by sharing?"

Rose stared straight ahead.

"*Is* there going to be another attack?" Botnik asked.

She climbed into the truck. The WAGD in her pocket buzzed. No *squeeee* of alarm, just a little warning buzz: all done. "Keep the rest of the boxes sealed and make sure nobody pokes around the open ones. Take along a HAZMAT team. I'd like a thorough fingerprint check and PCR on all of them. If HAZMAT clears them, I'd like them quietly removed from state jurisdiction and impounded as federal terrorist evidence. Send them on to Frank Chao at Quantico."

Botnik shrugged. "You got it." The two field agents climbed into the seats behind.

"You're investigating jammers, right?" Rose asked.

"We are," Botnik said.

"What priority?"

"Moderate."

"Push it higher. Let's spread the theory that jammers might have killed Porter. And if you find our particular jammer, let me know."

"Anything to help."

The sun was coming up. "Could we drive west for a few miles?" Rose asked. "Slowly. Before we return to Tucson."

"I hear and obey," Botnik said, and salaamed lightly over the steering wheel. "Looking for something in particular?"

"Just being thorough." She leaned her head back, mouth gaping, pulled down one eyelid with a finger, and deposited a drop of Visine. She treated the other eye, returned the Visine to her coat, and removed the marker-sized analyzer. Reading small print was becoming harder and harder. The narrow LCD panel flashed happy zeroes. No WAGD biohazards were on the printer or inside the box. No anthrax. She hadn't really expected any. They wouldn't use the printers and then pack them up and ship them. Nobody was that stupid—nobody still alive.

Half a mile down the road, she spotted something crumpled and black on the gravel shoulder. Botnik stopped to let her retrieve it.

"Hatch Friskmaster, right hand," she said as she climbed back into the Suburban. Botnik pulled out another Baggie. She slipped it in and he sealed it.

The earnest agent sitting directly behind her looked impressed. He held up a Thermos. "Coffee?"

"Christ, no thanks," she said briskly, her cheeks flushed. "I'd jump out of my skin."

Her slate buzzed in her pocket and she jerked. Botnik lifted the corners of his lips. "Just like that," she said, then answered the slate.

"Rebecca, it's News." Hiram Newsome—News to friends and close associates—was Assistant Director of Training Division at Quantico. He had taught Rebecca most of what she knew and had long supported her work on this unfinished puzzle. "Tell Botnik to haul your ass back to Tucson. I've chartered you a jet to Seattle. Someone's been ordering medical equipment they have no honest use for. I've told Griff you're coming in. He's irritated, of course."

"Erwin Griffin?"

"The same. Play nice, Rebecca."

"Always," Rebecca said.

CHAPTER FOUR
FBI Academy, Quantico, Virginia

Quantico is cop Valhalla. They say good cops go there when they die. Every day you solve crimes, make arrests, study hard, work out, do target practice, and at the end of the day you get together with your fellow agents in the boardroom, swig back some beers, and laugh. Hardly nobody gets hurt, nobody locks their doors, everyone knows the rules, and the bad guys always lose.

—Note pasted on a bulletin board, Jefferson Dormitory, FBI Academy, Quantico, Virginia

I'm FBI. More beef!

—Apocryphal incident in New York between an FBI agent and a deli sandwich maker.

Hogantown covered twelve acres on the sprawling Academy campus, nestled between copses of pine, maple, and dogwood. The most crime-ridden town in America, possibly on Earth, Hogantown used to look small and quaint, like a backlot movie set—Hogan's Alley. Now it was an entire town with real apartments—for role-players and directors—and real stakeouts and real-time, year-around crime taking a month or more to solve and involving multiple classes of agent trainees. The town had a functioning drug store, AllMed, and a good-sized Giga-Mart that was a favorite hangout for Marines.

Hogantown employed fourteen crime scenarists who surveyed the goings-on—alongside teachers and directors—from hidden walkways. It was the world's biggest training center for law enforcement—even larger than the Gasforth complex at Bram's Hill in England.

Crime and terror had been good to Hogantown.

Invisible flame shot along his arms and legs and up his neck to his jaw. William Griffin gritted his teeth to keep from screaming and clutched his pistol with two spasming hands. Ahead, angular and black against the gray concrete walls, the slammer wobbled on its drop-down carriage like an old dentist's X-ray machine. This was Agent Instructor Pete Farrow's last word on screw-ups—a quick, sharp blast from the shoot house's microwave pain projector.

Farrow had just blown the last of his meager reserve of patience.

William jerked off his helmet and stepped away from the test track. Still trembling, he lowered his weapon and switched off his Lynx. There was blood in his mouth. He had bitten halfway through his tongue.

Hogantown's Rough-and-Tough had just gotten him killed—for the third time.

"Mr. Griffin, you are a *pissant*." Farrow came around the corner of the observation deck and descended the metal stairs into the shoot house with quickstep precision. He stood six and a half feet tall and weighed in at two hundred and thirty pounds. With a bristle-fuzz of blond hair, a dubious squint, onyx eyes, and a face that seemed always on the edge of a cruel grin, Farrow looked more like a Bond villain than an FBI agent.

"Sorry, sir." William had been second in a team of four going into an apartment. All his partners had been virtual. They had waltzed through the rooms with precision and then there had been gunshots and smoke and confusion. Dripping red letters across his visual field announced that he had taken two in the chest and one in the head. To emphasize the point, Farrow had unleashed the slammer.

Even before the pain, the simulation had been so real that William could still feel the acid in his gut and the sweat under his body armor.

Farrow took William's Glock and with the click of a hidden switch removed it from the grid of computer tracking and control. "You heard shots. You saw Agent Smith go down. Then you saw Agent Wesson go down. Then you saw a miscreant come from behind the fridge."

"There was a child."

"The murdering SOB was right in front of you. The child was not in your line of fire."

"I'm not making excuses, sir." He could barely talk.

Farrow hitched up his pants. He had the kind of build—barrel chest and slim hips—that precluded getting a good fit anywhere outside of a tailor's shop. "Your squeeze and firing patterns are daggers, same height, all in a row, just fine—whenever you're shooting at a target. Otherwise, you're a complete, balls-to-the-wall pissant. Have you ever gone hunting, Mr. Griffin?"

"Yes, sir," William said, his shoulders falling about as low as they could go. "I mean, no, sir."

"Your daddy never took you hunting? That's a disgrace."

"Sir, I do not understand what you mean by 'pissant.'"

"Look it up. A useless, insignificant creature. It means you're not worth your native clay. It means in a situation of self-defense, with clearly defined antagonists whose mission in life is to put you down like a mangy dog, you *cringe*. To me, specifically, it means you have buck fever. Put anything living at the end of your nine mil and you start to shake like a cup of dice. Your teeth click like castanets, mister."

"Yes, sir. I would like to try one more time, sir."

"Son," Farrow said, his face an ominous shade of pre-heart-attack red, "this shoot house consumes twenty-five thousand watts of electricity. I will not waste any more of our nation's valuable energy. I brought you here this late to see whether you could acquire your live target skills if we subjected you to a little less peer review. You have not done me proud. Nobody gets through the Academy without passing Rough-and-Tough."

"I need one more chance, sir."

Farrow stood with hands on hips, the perfect figure of fitness and power. "Buck fever, Griffin. Some people just cannot kill. Your father was a Marine, right?"

"Navy Seal, sir."

"Did he ever talk to you about killing people?"

"No, sir."

"Did he ever kill people in the line of duty?"

"He did not talk about it, sir."

"I know for a fact that as an FBI agent he has killed three people. How does that make you feel?"

William swallowed. At times, Griff had been hard on his family—irrational fits of anger, silent drinking, and one awful night, wailing and shrieking long into the morning. His mother had grabbed William's shoulders, pulling him back to keep him out of the den. He had so much wanted to comfort his father.

William had been nine years old.

Griff had sung an awful song in the den, twenty years ago, the words slurred by a pint of Johnny Walker: "Bullet to the thorax, cried the Lorax. Bullet to the brain, what a pain. Bullet to the gut, then you'll know what's what, and mister, you'll never be the same, *all the dead are in your head*, not the same."

Had Special Agent Erwin Griffin killed a man that day?

William had spent five years in NYPD and not once had he drawn his weapon while on duty—and he had been grateful for that. He closed his eyes and recalled Griff's face on the morning after that bout, puffy yet still hard, a face that had once again learned how to hide what was inside, to tamp down the hopefulness that it could not get any worse.

After William's mother and father had finalized their divorce, Griff had moved to Washington state. He currently worked out of the Seattle Field Office.

William felt like he wanted to throw up. "For my father's sake, sir."

Farrow did not look pleased. "Last chance, Griffin. One more bout of buck fever, and the blue is not for you."

CHAPTER FIVE
Washington State

Special Agent Erwin Griffin—known as Griff to practically everyone—removed a pair of wire-rim sunglasses from his faded blue eyes and slipped them into his pocket. The snow-dusted mountains to the east caught the last of the daylight like blunt rock fingers with flaming tips. The interior of the fire tower cabin was quiet, just a soft, stubborn whistle of wind through the boards and occasional creaks and groans, like a boat caught in a slow wash. Rising forty feet above the ridge, supported by a slender lattice of iron beams and cedar planks, the cabin peered over the listless crowns of the second-growth hemlocks and gave a good vantage on the valley to the east.

Griff had occupied the cabin for two days, tending a telescope, two pairs of high-powered binoculars, digital cameras, and a small computer. He wore jeans and a zipped-up Navy blue windbreaker with "FBI" printed in yellow on the back.

The windbreaker had a pinky-sized hole to the right of the "I," just below his shoulder blade.

It had been a peaceful time, mostly alone, with a Port-a-Potty and an ice chest full of sandwiches and canned ice tea. Time to think. Time enough to wonder why he hadn't worked for the Forest Service or become a hermit. It seemed all his life he had been chasing and catching. He had hundreds of felony arrests and convictions to his credit. He had helped lock up bad guys and sometimes judges and juries threw away the keys but it never seemed to do a damned bit of good. There were always more.

Tides of crime, sweeping in, sweeping out, always leaving the bodies behind. So many bodies.

Griff wiped his eyes and prepared to move things around in preparation for the coming darkness. At night all he had was a single red lantern mounted under the lookout's north-facing window. It made him look like a submarine captain.

"Penny for your thoughts," Cap Benson said, pushing up through the hatch with a whuff of steaming breath. Benson was with the Washington State Patrol, thirty-seven years old and a twelve-year veteran of their SWAT team. Griff had known Benson for ten years. Benson owned a mobile home on a two-acre lot twenty miles down the road. He had a slender, pretty wife who liked to wear aprons and bake bread, and a white scar crept down his neck—terminating, Griff knew, at an unnatural notch in his clavicle. He was in better shape than Griff, who was pretty fit for his age, and the whuff was just an expression.

They had last seen each other at a big drug lab bust in Thurston County the month before.

"I'm going crazy up here," Griff deadpanned. He twitched an eyebrow, held a stick of Doublemint gum between his front teeth, pulled back his lips, and waggled it. "Hey, look," he said. "I'm FDR."

"You need a long black holder," Benson said, unfazed.

"For gum?" Griff fixed Benson with a squint. "That would be silly." He pulled the gum in and started chewing.

"Any luck?" Benson asked, walking toward the window that faced the valley.

"Today, a couple of women. A few kids. No animals. It's quiet. They've been burning trash in barrels."

"What about the Patriarch?"

"Not a sign."

"Your Jewish law center guy should be here in a few minutes. He's wearing snow pants. Looks like a cheechako."

"Maybe, but he knows everything there is to know about Chambers."

"You sure you don't want to just hand this over to us?"

"Thanks, Cap, but I guarantee you don't want it."

"We're awesome and eager, Griff."

"Right," Griff said. He called up the stabilized image on the computer screen and showed Benson what he had been looking at all day. Three and a half miles away, green spruces, loblolly pines and sapling cedars spotted the seventy acres around a big gray weather-battered farmhouse. Sixty yards to the east stood a large barn. Right now, the farm looked deserted. No visible cows or other livestock. No dogs.

"Nice," Benson said. "Kind of place I might like to retire. I'd paint the house, though."

It *was* a pretty place, a mile from the nearest road, serene and quiet on a chilly but clear April evening. Nothing like the Old Testament desert where sun-dazzled, long-bearded patriarchs stashed their wives and ruled their tribes. Though there *was* a fire on the mountain—the high snows looked as if they were burning.

Judgment light.

"You sure it's him?" Benson asked.

"We'll have a positive ID soon enough," Griff said. "Pass me those binders, will you, Cap?"

Benson reached across to the small table and handed Griff three thick white binders filled with photographs. Griff laid them out under the binoculars and opened each one to a good photo or mug shot, for his next visitor. They could hear his footsteps on the narrow stairs.

A shaved tanned head crowned by a plain black yarmulke poked up through the hatch and swung a green army duffel bag onto the floor with a thump. "Ahoy there. Anybody home?"

"Come on in, Jacob," Griff said. "Good to see you."

The small, skinny man stood up from the step below the hatch, climbed onto the cabin's rough board floor and brushed his baggy black snow pants with one hand. He wore a sleeveless purple down vest over a spotless and pressed white business shirt. "Always good to hear from you, Agent Griffin," he said. "You have such interesting things to show me." He grinned at Benson, who nodded back, polite but noncommittal, a seasoned cop greeting an outsider who was not himself a cop.

The hatch creaked again, making them all jerk. Griff was not disposed to like whoever climbed up through that hatch, not now. Three was already a crowd. Worse still, this one was female: thin strong hands with chipped nails, hazel eyes, mussed auburn hair, high cheekbones, and a goddamned gray power suit.

"Pardon me, gentlemen." The female stood up straight and wiry on the drafty wooden floor and pulled down her jacket. She wore black running shoes and white socks, her only concessions to the woods and the climb.

Griff scowled at Levine. Levine lifted his brows.

"Apologies for interrupting," she said. Griff hadn't seen this woman in over ten years and it took him a moment to go through his memory, age a face, and place her name.

Griff introduced them all. "Cap Benson, Washington State Patrol SWAT team, this is Jacob Levine from the Southern Poverty Law Center. And this is Special Agent Rebecca Rose. She investigates bioterror. That was what you were working on the last time we met."

"Still do," Rebecca said.

"Pleasure," Benson said. They firmly shook hands, but all three men looked like boys whose tree-house club had been violated.

"What brings you here, Rebecca?" Griff asked.

"Someone down in that valley has taken delivery of contraband biotech equipment. Fermenters, incubators, some driers."

"No shit," Griff said. "And . . . ?"

"Don't mind me," Rebecca said. "I'm just an observer." She whistled at the array of binoculars and the telescope. "There must be two dozen guys loafing around at the trail head. What have you got down there?"

"Ant farm," Griff said.

"Sonofabitch," she said. "Can I see?"

"Be my guest."

Rebecca applied her eyes to the biggest pair of binoculars. "Your ant farm doesn't have any ants," she murmured.

"Just wait," Griff said.

The operation had begun a week ago, following a complaint about illegal fireworks. Intense white flashes like giant morning glories had bloomed in the middle of the night over the hills around the farm, letting loose echoing booms, two a night for three nights in a row, bright enough and loud enough to wake up the nearest neighbor—a sleepless old codger who lived with his Airedale four miles away.

Two days after the complaint had been filed, a Snohomish County sheriff's deputy had driven down the long dirt road to the farm to investigate. He had found a hidden homestead with a concrete and wood-frame barn, one large old house, and a newer, smaller house at the rear, almost lost in the trees. A polite knock at the door of the main house had roused a gray-bearded, broad-shouldered, proud old man with brilliant green eyes. The old man had two middle-aged women, slender and worn-looking, living with him in the big house. Six kids had come around from the back and stood in the yard, ranging in age from three to seventeen, all well-fed, conservatively dressed, and well-behaved. Respectful. The deputy had asked about fireworks and been met with puzzled denials and the offer of a hot cup of coffee and fresh sourdough biscuits. He had been invited into the house. The deputy had removed his Smokey hat and held it to one side, leaving his gun hand free. Taking it all in.

The bearded old man had asked one of the women to get coffee. They had waited in the living room, the deputy's brown uniform wrinkle-free, his equipment and holster shiny black, shirt tucked tight over a young patrol car paunch: a good and reasonable defender of the peace, standing straight and a little awkward on the throw rug in the living room; the old man tall and erect in a loose white shirt and denims, dignified and relaxed. The house inside neat and spare, with handmade shelves and a big antique oak table. Red curtains on the windows. Yellow daffodils in a big vase on a mantel over the stone fireplace.

The old man had seemed amused by the idea that he might be setting off fireworks. People around here, he had told the deputy, tended to be a little dotty. "It's the air. Too pure for some, not pure enough for others."

The deputy had drunk one cup of good strong coffee poured by one of the tired women from an iron pot. Two kids, a boy and a girl, both about nine, had sat quietly side by side in a big rocking chair near the fireplace.

To be polite, the deputy had eaten a sourdough biscuit slathered with homemade jam and fresh sweet butter. He had found it very tasty.

The woman and the kids had let the old man do all the talking. The deputy was welcome to come back any time. His presence made everyone feel protected, watched over. "The Lord God provides for those who heed the necessity of strong arms," the old man had said.

The deputy had paid his respects and returned to his car. He could not begin to figure why a stern but hospitable old man with a biblical grip on his large family would be lobbing starburst fireworks in the early morning darkness.

But something had stuck up in the deputy's memory like a log rising in a smooth river. Back at the office, he had looked up the NCIS and NCIC files on one Robert Cavitt Chambers, AKA Bob Cavitt, AKA Charles Roberts. Chambers had last been seen in Texas in 1995. A computer artist at FBI headquarters had updated an ATM security photo taken that year to show Chambers in his sprightly eighties.

The aging trick had worked.

The deputy had recognized the biblical old man at the farmhouse.

"We lost track of Chambers years ago," Levine said. There was only one folding chair in the fire tower. He did not want to occupy the one chair, not with Cap Benson watching him like a hawk. Levine smiled, showing large, even teeth, lightly speckled. He had been raised in Texas on naturally fluoridated water and his teeth were colored like turkey eggs, but strong. "You sure this is him?"

"Positive ID from the deputy," Benson said.

"Too good to be true," Levine said. "But if it is true, we could be in a world of trouble."

"Why is that?" Benson asked.

"Who do you think we have down there?" Levine asked. Now it was Levine's turn to give Benson a look, and slowly shift that look to Griff, then to Rebecca. At that moment, Levine owned the fire tower.

"Bank robber. Abortion clinic bomber," Benson said.

"Ah." Levine pressed his lips together. "That's all?"

"That's enough for me," Benson said. Griff let Levine have his fun.

"Well, I wouldn't want you to underestimate him. If it *is* him. Because the Patriarch has lived a life of almost uninterrupted criminal activity since 1962. Before that, he was an altar boy for St. Jude's in Philadelphia, a predominantly Irish parish. In the seventies, he committed at least five bank robberies in Oklahoma and Arizona. One arrest and trial led to a hung jury. The Oklahoma County prosecutor's office refused to try Chambers again. I quote the DA, 'We will always have some trailer-trash slattern with damp panties sitting in the jury box. Just get him the hell out of my state.'"

They all looked to see if Levine had offended Rebecca. He hadn't. Levine continued.

"Chambers moved to Ireland in 1979. He became an expert in IED— improvised explosive devices. His specialty was nasty booby traps. Don't hold me to it, but he may have been the guy who actually set the charge in Margaret Thatcher's toilet in a Brighton hotel in 1986. He returned to the United States later that year, when things got too hot in the UK, but he couldn't stay out of trouble. In 1988, Nevada State Police caught him at the tail end of a barroom brawl, drunk out of his mind, with a broken pool cue in one hand and a perforated buddy bleeding out on the floor. Chambers was convicted of manslaughter and sent to prison in 1989. Sometime the next year, he broke from his Irish roots, swore off drink, and converted from Catholicism to the Aryan Church of Christ Militant. White supremacists."

"I am aware of that," Benson said.

"In 1992, his conviction got thrown out on appeal. Turned out an FBI technician didn't conduct the tests he said he did. Chambers was released in 1993. After that, from 1995 to 1999, he robbed banks from Oklahoma to Alabama. They called him the Proud Poppa because he was assisted by two pre-adolescent males whom he referred to as 'my strong and righteous sons.' He then organized the bombing of three Planned Parenthood Clinics in Bos-

ton and Baltimore in 1999, resulting in two deaths and six injuries. He's been
on the Post Office hit parade for the last twenty years."

"All because of an FBI screw-up?" Benson asked.

"Uh-huh," Griff said.

"If that really is his family down there," Levine said, "and he thinks
we're on to him, he's going to fight like a cornered bobcat. He will not go
back to prison. How are you going to handle this?"

"We're still working on that," Griff said.

Levine looked doubtful and took his turn peeking through the big binoculars. "Well, looky here. Ants."

The day after the Snohomish County sheriff's department had passed the
deputy's information along to the FBI, Griff had driven from the Seattle
Field Office and taken over a seldom-used Forest Service fire tower with a
pretty good view of the farm. Without asking permission, he had instructed
two agents to chainsaw the single obstructing tree. He had then set up his
surveillance. Seattle Field Office Special Agent in Charge John Keller had put
Griff in command of the operation, but provisionally, in case it threatened to
turn into another Waco.

FBI headquarters wanted to be very sure of their footing before they
made a move.

Other agents had worked their way into Prince, the nearest town: a gas
station, hardware/feed store, three churches, and a diner. They had learned
that three women and at least seven children picked up groceries and sometimes their mail in Prince. Less frequently, the citizens saw four men ranging
in age from seventeen to thirty-five. The family or families also drove into
Prince for church services. Chambers himself never ventured into town. The
best guess was that Chambers had about twenty men, women, and children
living on his farm.

Their church was a thorny cane of the original Seventh Day Adven-
tist bush known as The Empty Tomb of God Risen. Tombers, FBI files said,
showed strong anti-Semitic tendencies, often associated with Christian Identity types, and were allied in some northwestern states with Aryan Nations.
Their ministers were banned from visiting federal prisons.

Upon learning this, Griff had contacted Jacob Levine.

They took turns looking through the binoculars while the computer used a
satellite link to try to make facial comparisons with National Security Service records in Virginia.

"What are all those posts and clothes lines for?" Rebecca asked.

Griff shrugged. "You tell me."

"Looks like an antenna. TV, maybe?"

"Even Jed Clampett has a dish out here," Benson said.

Two women stood on the porch. One was knitting and the other just stared out over the long span of weedy lawn in front of the main house. They were talking but there was no way of knowing what they were saying. At this angle and that distance, the lip-reading software on the computer wasn't much good.

"They look nervous," Benson observed.

"Chambers starts out charming but in the end he rules by force," Levine said. "He picks women who want nothing but guidance and routine, but that doesn't mean he makes them happy. Though he does provide, in his way, and he loves his kids. In his way."

"They're all his?" Rebecca asked.

"Chambers has never shared his harem," Levine said. "He teaches his sons to be crack shots but forbids his wives or daughters to use guns, ever. When are you planning to make a raid?"

Griff winced at the word "raid" but he did not answer in the negative. Something would have to be done and he would likely be at the tip of the spear going in. "Not until we know all there is to know," he said.

"There could be an opportune moment," Levine said. "That is, if what the guys in town have found out is true—about them being Tombers."

"Do tell," Griff said.

"It is likely the women and children will all go to Easter services at the church, and that could be a good time to find Chambers home alone, or at most with his eldest son in attendance. He insists on piety but I've never heard of his entering a church, not since he was a kid. He needs to be top dog wherever he stands, and that includes before God."

"No way we're going in at Easter," Griff said. "Besides, people in town are alerted. We can't afford to wait."

Levine smiled. "You're in luck. Tombers are Julians. They believe Easter comes before the date commonly observed by you *goyim*. They're eleven days off. The Gregorian calendar is the work of the devil, you know."

"Scout's honor?" Griff asked. He was looking through the scope now. A Coleman lantern had been slung on a beam inside the porch overhang and the two women were setting up folding chairs.

"For them, Good Friday is tomorrow."

Then, down in the valley, the old man finally came out and stood watching the twilight. His face was clear in the bright white glow of the lantern: an aquiline, craggy profile. The old man appeared thoughtful. For a moment, Griff thought he might be watching them.

Rebecca folded her arms. "Just the kind of fellow to need a microbial incubator."

Griff set the digital cameras humming and backed away. "Is that him?" he asked Levine.

Levine peered. "I hope I look that good when I'm his age."

"Whenever you're sure, Jacob."

Levine spent a few more seconds on the binoculars. "It's him," he said.

CHAPTER SIX
Quantico

William Griffin jogged across the lawn to join the group of nine students standing in front of the Biograph theater, on the edge of Hogantown and just across Hoover Road from the towering dorms and walkways and the squat tan bulk of the Academy.

"All right, listen up," Pete Farrow called out. The recruits—two women and seven men: two blacks, one Asian, one Middle-Eastern, five shades of white—stopped talking and assumed parade rest. Compared to the instructor they were a motley bunch, spread over the range of physical specimens: plump and skinny, tall and short, dark-haired and light.

Farrow walked along the loose line. "All right, agents, this is it. Today, you will be using equipment worth about two hundred thousand dollars. Try not to break it. Only about twenty percent of our field offices have all this stuff. It is rare. It is valuable. But it is the future—and you will get used to it.

"If you are a sadist, you are shit out of luck. Some of this new stuff threatens to turn you bloody-minded SOBs into kinder, gentler peace officers." Farrow winked in the general direction of William Griffin. "Out on the street, if you do this right, nobody has to die. Though I do expect a few sprained ankles and wrenched necks, and we have been known to break arms and even legs. Understood?"

The class nodded in unison.

Three men in gray suits passed behind the students and entered the Bank of Hogantown. They were carrying bagged sandwiches from the Pastime Deli. One turned and said, "Farrow's litter. What do you think? Blood in the gutters?" The others flashed evil smiles and pushed through the swinging glass doors.

William watched Jane Rowland scratch her ribs under her suit coat and the white FBI Academy golf-style shirt. His underwear itched, too. Something about the diagnostic sensors embedded in the bulletproof weave or the fluid piping that smoothly wrapped around the torso.

Medium-sized piles of equipment lay at their feet. They would soon put on masks and special network jackets. More weight, more wires.

In their holsters they carried blue-handled revolvers filled with paintball rounds. The Academy cars were equipped with pump-action shotguns with blue stocks that discharged a nasty, smelly pink spray, and mock H&K MP5 9mm carbines that fired nothing but made a horrible racket—all networked training weapons. Everything they did with these guns showed up on monitors somewhere in the recesses of Hogantown.

"You have made your case," Farrow said. "You are now about to arrest four suspects who are transporting an illegal substance for sale. This is no longer the good old days of cocaine or heroin. Neuraminoline tartrate, known on the street as Tart, is colorless, odorless, and tasteless—but it is the most dangerous and destructive GM drug on the market today. Loser users tell themselves that Tart is a harmless organic performance enhancer. It produces long-lasting feelings of angelic well-being. But in five percent of its devotees, Tart leads to a degenerative neuromuscular disease called Kepler's Syndrome. You end up in a wheelchair, drooling, unable to control your bowels and in constant pain. But that's not the end of Tart's charms. In an estimated seven percent of users, Tart binds to chromosomes in sex cells—eggs and sperm. It causes distortions that can be passed on to future offspring, who, if they survive beyond the age of two, will suffer the agonies of the damned. Tart makes babies into monsters." Farrow slipped on his grid-linked gogs—short for goggles, but actually more like a thick-framed pair of glasses. "If that doesn't psych you for this bust nothing will. Remember—if you screw up, your classmates could get hurt. I do not like to have my heart flutter. I do not want to grieve for lost ducklings. Stay tactical. Use all the skills we've taught you. Ready?"

"Ready!" they shouted.

"Suit up and get your Lynxes on the grid. Today we're all top code, to keep the bad guys from knowing who and where you are, so line up and get your numbers." He began handing out strips of paper.

William Griffin put on his gogs and field jacket, labeled with a strip of silver tape with his name on it. He ran his index finger along the bumps and ridges on the forearm Lynx keyboard, logging on to the team server and inputting his number and five fake numbers and positions that his node would disperse like chaff, should someone hack in. The others did the same. They all stood clutching their paintball masks, clear visors with plastic headbands. Cheeks, temples, and ears were no longer protected—hadn't been for years. Pain was a teacher, a tool.

They then clipped health stats boxes to their belts and arranged their shoulder-mounted holsters. Farrow checked them over, as solicitous as a mother hen.

"Keep boxy stuff away from your mid-back. Clip everything to the side. If you fall backward on a hard surface, you could injure your spine."

They sheepishly readjusted. This was basic stuff and already they were screwing up.

Farrow checked his slate. "Mr. Al-Husam, you're not on the grid. Get your numbers."

Fouad Al-Husam, a small man with beautiful black eyes and a round, almost feminine face, touched his keyboard, trying to find the bumps. Farrow approached him and patted his jacket sleeve. "Here," he said, and lifted Al-Husam's arm to the right place. "Follow the guide ridges." Al-Husam smiled but his face darkened with embarrassment.

"Still not there," Farrow said after a few seconds. "Reboot your pad. I have eight Lynxes on the grid, all healthy and happy. I see code in action. Good scatter. Ms. Lee, are you happy?"

Lee was the shortest and lightest person in the group but that did not faze Farrow. He was running her hard through her paces. "Yes, sir, I am happy," she called out.

"Happy to be here at the Q?"

"Sir, I am very happy to be here at the Q."

"We are not Gyrenes, Ms. Lee. Academy mandates snappy repartee. Show me your FBI beef."

"Happy as an aardvark under a full moon . . . at the Q, sir."

Farrow's grin was tepid. "Is wit truly dead?" He glanced around the group, raising his shoulders in a long, sad shrug.

They all laughed.

"*Focus*," Farrow shouted. "You've been working toward this moment for three weeks. You have the bastards in your sights. Remember your training. You ARE ready."

William quietly sucked in his breath. He was far from sure of that. Standing beside him, Jane Rowland looked confident—hard as a piece of glass and about as brittle.

"Okay—Al-Husam, you're on the grid. You can stop fiddling with the keys."

"Yes, sir."

"You are knights in high-tech armor," Farrow said. "Make the flame-tormented shade of Mr. Hoover proud. Let's go."

"Right, coach," William Griffin said under his breath as they fanned out.

They dispersed as four teams in four vehicles. William and Jane Rowland had drawn chits and were partnered for the bust. They climbed into an unmarked tan Caprice from the last century. Rowland took the wheel. "Ready?" she asked William, face forward.

"I am *icy.*" He grinned.

Rowland rotated and poked her finger. "Don't mess up," she instructed. "We have our docs, right?"

William held up his steno pad and a plastic folder full of paper-copy warrants and mug shots. The actors in the shots looked tough and bored.

"We'll do fine," he said. "You'll do great."

Rowland gave William a *don't patronize me* scowl and cinched her seat belt. A helicopter blew overhead. Rowland flinched. Hostage Rescue Team personnel dressed in black and armed to the teeth hung out of the chopper doors like commandoes, waiting to abseil down to a roof. Hogantown could get crowded and noisy. Ten or twelve practicals could fill any given day.

"Yeah. Right," Rowland said. She started the Caprice, pulled out onto Hogan Boulevard and drove around the corner and down Ness Avenue to their stake-out, just across the two-way street from the Giga-Mart parking lot. The suspects had been sighted shopping there this morning by an alert police officer, who had traced one of the men back to the Dogwood Hotel and the other to the Tolson Arms apartments. The Dogwood was across the street from the Giga-Mart. The Giga-Mart was small but functional. Its shelves had been stocked with goods that agents and Marines could buy but its clerks doubled as actors in Academy scenarios.

William put on his gogs and waited for the display to come up. The data and graphics looked greenish blue in the daytime, red at night. A little bell dinged in his earnode. He heard his own pulse magnified. He sounded nervous. He checked the pong sensor that detected human stress chemistry. The watch displayed three green lights, one yellow. Yeah, he was nervous. So was Rowland.

William glanced up at the Eyes in the Sky—cameras jutting out over the intersection from a power pole on the corner. A red light was on—surveillance was underway. The Masters of the Universe, agent instructors in the second floor command center above the Bank of Hogan, were waiting to pass judgment. MAVs—Micro Air Vehicles equipped with cameras—buzzed overhead.

William and Rowland were to take point once the suspects had been spotted. Team two and team three would serve as reinforcements and back-up as each arrest was made. Team four would stand ready to intercept fleeing vehicles if necessary.

"Team one to all teams," William said. Their grid lights blinked in his gogs. "Are we set?"

"Team two in rear view of your position," came the response through their earnodes. That was Matty's soft drawl—George Matty and Al-Husam had been partnered, almost certainly to Matty's displeasure. He was a deep Mississippi boy and generally kept quiet around Al-Husam, but so far had played things professionally. And well he might. Al-Husam was special, they all knew that. Bigger judges than the Masters of the Universe were looking down on Quantico this year.

"Team three here. We're at Tolson Arms." Team three was Errol Henson, Nicky Di Martinez, and Carla Lee. They were in the dark blue engineering van, equipped for surveillance and carrying the Lynx server.

"Team four setting up on State Street." Team four was Finch and Greavy, heavy-set men with bulldog expressions and quiet, efficient manners. "We'd like video hookups as soon as possible. Let us know which way they're coming, gang."

"Apartment twelve at Tolson has motion," Lee said. "Lights are on."

"What's parked out front, team three?" William asked.

"Five cars and a pickup," Errol Henson responded. His voice trembled. They were all high with excitement, like a brace of puppies chasing ducks for the first time.

William glanced at Rowland. She pressed her lips together.

"Our suspect, Geronimo del Torres, is driving a 1959 Chevy Impala, primer gray with mottled paint, tinted windows, a work in progress, according to our sheet," Lee said.

"We don't see it," Henson said. "I like Impalas."

Someone else said, "I catch and eat Impalas."

"Identify, joker," Farrow growled in all their ears, his voice like an angry God.

"Team two, that's me, Matty, sir."

"Tongues in neutral, team two."

"Yes, sir. Wit, sir."

"Team three here. A man and a woman, both Hispanic, are leaving unit twelve. They're getting into a late model blue Camaro, license plate Wonka MF8905. Neither resembles del Torres."

Hogantown police activities involved residents of five fictitious states: Graceland, Oceania, Sylvania, Wonka, and Numbutt. White-collar criminals usually came from Sylvania, smart crooks and contraband dealers of any stripe from Graceland; violent crooks from Wonka; drug dealers and dumbasses from Numbutt. Profiling on that basis, however, was discouraged.

Matty pushed his head back against the neck rest. "I watched you in Rough-and-Tough. Very impressive."

"Thank you," Fouad Al-Husam said.

"Natural born killer instinct."

"Not so killer," Al-Husam said. "They are images and cutouts, not people."

"Felt real to me. I wanted to throw up."

"Perhaps so did I," Al-Husam said.

"Arabs don't naturally like killing? That's kind of news, isn't it?"

"I am not Arab," Al-Husam said, and he looked out of the car side window to avoid showing his irritation.

Matty glanced at Al-Husam. "I always feel like praying before going into practicals. How about you?"

Al-Husam nodded. "A little prayer," he said.

"You pray five times a day, don't you?"

"Of course."

"I hope you don't need to get down and pray right here," Matty said. "That would be inconvenient."

Al-Husam took a shallow breath.

"Five times a day. That's more than my grandma used to do. She and my mama put me off praying. They were always asking for little things. 'God, make my garden green. God, let me grow the prettiest roses, the biggest tomatoes. God, I hope the pot roast doesn't burn.' See what I mean? But going through Quantico, I totally get it. 'God, don't let me screw up.' Where *do* you pray when you have to?"

"Wherever there is room. Shall we concentrate?" Al-Husam asked.

"I *am* concentrating. Got it. Hoo-ah!" Matty exclaimed, and touched his gogs.

Al-Husam jerked in surprise, that this man should proclaim *Huwa*, the name of the essence, *Qul Huwa Llahu Ahad—Say, He is God, He is One.*

"That plate was on the board," Matty said, triumphant. "Let's run a check before the others catch it."

"Of course," Al-Husam said.

*　*　*

William twitched in his worn bucket seat. "We had a bulletin on that vehicle," he said to Rowland. "I saw it in the briefing room." He pulled out his notebook and flipped through the pages, then resorted to the button pad hidden in his sleeve, to bring up the case on his gogs. Before he could find what he wanted, in his ear he heard Matty saying, "We ID that as belonging to a Constanza Valenzuela, registered guest worker from Honduras, no criminal record, nothing on VICAP."

William frowned intensely at Rowland. "I'm sure there's more," he said. Both worked their keypads. William's face brightened and he parted his lips.

Al-Husam broke in before he could speak. "We have info that Ms. Valenzuela has gone missing in Wonka and that her car has not been located."

"What's a stolen car from Wonka doing here in Virginia?" William asked, muting his headset. "Highly suspicious."

"Confirm with a case number, Al-Husam," Farrow instructed. "Give the other teams all you have so they can log in and exercise their own judgment."

Now it was Al-Husam's turn to be slow.

Rowland butted in and read out an FBI Crime Index Case Number, issued to the Wonka Department of Public Safety. "VICAP not yet filed," she added.

"Why no VICAP, Ms. Rowland?" Farrow asked.

"Recent missing person report," Rowland answered crisply. "Wonka authorities do not yet know whether a violent crime is involved, sir. That could be a car filled with buyers or partners. Or a mule's car. It could lead us to the Impala."

"We're on it, team three," said Matty. "Will follow."

"Team three will backup," Henson offered.

"Negative," William said. "Team two is sufficient. Let's head toward the Dogwood and see if we can find that Impala on our own."

"Roger that, team one," Henson said.

Rowland nodded and turned the old Caprice around in the middle of the street, heading toward the Dogwood Motel.

Team four reported they had bubble gum at the ready.

"Just relax," William said. "We're doing fine."

Rowland narrowed her eyes.

If the Impala suspected it was being tracked, then eluded them and left Hogantown—which, of necessity, had few real escape routes—then Farrow would be very disappointed.

A map of the area around the motel popped up on William's display. His eyes were tearing up—the image in his gogs was too bright. The map began to wriggle. None of the students had been fitted—these were generics and his tended to slide down his nose. He blinked and looked far left, then back. The view cleared. He saw two red dots moving south on Rosa Parks street—team two and team three. A small video square in the upper right corner showed what the van was seeing: team two's Ford Crown Victoria and the suspect blue Camaro with Wonka plates. Traffic was light in Hogantown today. It would almost certainly get worse once they made their stop. Farrow liked to keep up the pressure and the presence of too many civilians in the line of fire would certainly do that.

Griffith dimmed the display in his gogs and concentrated on the street. "There," he said. The Impala was parked in front of the motel about a block and a half away. Two men were loading boxes into the open trunk. Rowland slowed. William touched his hand to his holstered pistol. It lightly buzzed approval—instantly recognizing the keycode in his Lynx. Some field agents resorted to surgery to hide their small cylindrical keycode units.

Rowland kept one hand on the wheel and reached down to connect with her own gun.

The men by the Impala glanced over their shoulders and spotted the Caprice. They slammed the trunk and rushed to the open car doors. William compared them to the mug shots. One matched the description: Geronimo del Torres, bulky, dark, denim jacket with cholo markings and baggy pants. The other was a younger male, ID unknown.

"Team one here. We have Impala and suspect del Torres in sight," William said. "There's two in the front seat, one's a possible juvenile. I see no one in the back seat."

The doors of the Impala slammed and the car's tires squealed.

"They're fleeing the scene!"

The wide, heavy car peeled out from in front of the motel and took a sharp left down Ness Avenue, the longest street in Hogantown.

"Gives him room to pick up speed," Rowland said, spinning the wheel and turning left as she lit up the dash lights. "He's going for the Freedom."

If the Impala made it to the Freedom Highway, they would have to change their plans, not a good thing. Highway pursuit was not desirable since it was always rush hour and the next off ramp—so they had been told—led directly into Gangsta City. In fact the onramp led nowhere and the nonexistent Gangsta City meant a forfeit.

Rowland gunned the Caprice. A few wary pedestrians jumped to the curb and flipped them off. Heads leaned out of windows on second-floor buildings.

"This is fun," she said. "Like playing Vice City when I was a kid."

"My dad never let me play that," William said.

"Makes you smarter," Rowland said.

Then, abruptly, team three's van roared into the intersection ahead. The Impala skidded to a halt, tail wagging, tires smoking. They were a block from the onramp. Lee got out and drew down on the fugitives.

The blue Camaro came to a stop at the cross street ahead. Two people got out, one male, one female. Both put up their hands. From William's perspective, both cars were in a line—and the engineering van was moving slowly onto that line, a bad situation for putting colleagues in jeopardy.

Team two came out of Melvin Purvis Boulevard and pulled up behind them. Two unknown vehicles joined the tail of the procession, honking. William and Rowland unstrapped their holsters. Rowland pulled up to the curb twenty feet behind the Impala, parking at an angle so that the engine block provided maximum protection. The visor cam blinked red. "We're on the record," she said. "Let's do it."

William exited first and squatted behind the door with gun poised to gauge the situation. The two occupants of the Impala faced forward, hands out of sight.

"Exit your car!" Rowland shouted.

"FBI," William prompted. "Tell 'em."

Fuck. "This is the FBI!" Rowland called out. "Get out of the car with your hands in plain sight."

William repeated the command in Spanish.

They did not respond.

"Get out of the car, hands in plain sight, *now.*"

Smoke puffed from the tailpipe. The driver, presumably del Torres, stuck out his arm and waved as if giving them permission to go around. "Joker," William said.

Team two angled their car and blocked the street behind them. Matty exited with a pump shotgun and positioned himself behind the Caprice's right rear bumper.

William tried to focus on the corner video image in his gogs but sweat was dripping in his eye and he could barely make out anything.

"Team three in place," Henson announced in his ear. "We're at the corner of Hoover and Grand. We're going to block their escape."

William instructed, "Pull around and hem them in, team two."

"Roger that," Matty said. "Fred, stay with team one. I'll block."

Al-Husam exited the car, pistol drawn, finger resting on the trigger guard. The Glock had no safety, merely a little flippy switch on the trigger itself that went down way too smooth and fast. Matty drove the Crown Victoria around the Impala and wedged the right front wheel against the curb, almost slamming their bumper into a blue mailbox.

"They're eyeballing and grinning," Matty said. Al-Husam walked up behind William.

"It's my collar," Rowland said.

"Quaint," Al-Husam said.

"Just, you know, throw down on them, with your guns," Rowland said. Her face was slick with sweat. Beneath the jacket, William's shirt clung damp as a washrag despite the coolness in the morning air.

Rowland approached the left bumper of the Impala, parked a generous three feet from the curb. She assumed a classic Weaver stance and trained her mock SIG on the heads in the rear window. William stayed in a crouch behind his door, also aiming at the Impala's rear window. Al-Husam took a stance behind the Caprice's driver side door.

"Yo, lady," said a youngish voice from the Impala. The window rolled down in jerks.

Rowland stopped. "Exit the car *now*," she called out. "Show me your hands." She would have them out and flat on the street in seconds.

"Lady, we are just hangin'," the young man said. "Just drivin' and chillin'. No hassles?" Arms covered with crude gang tats, tiny goatee, hennaed lips smirking, he looked like the real thing, a true murdering scumbag.

In Hogantown, he is real, William thought. *He can kill your career.*

William moved to the rear bumper. He took another step. The young man hung his head out the window, and his hands, both empty. He was grinning like a happy whore, more than a little obvious. The driver stared straight ahead, hands still on the wheel. William wondered if all those hands were real. Rubber hands had been used in the past; you walk up to the window and *blam*.

"Exit the vehicle. Get out now and lie on the ground face down with arms and legs spread!" Rowland ordered. "Both of you!"

"Tell us what you want, bitch," the young man said. "We doing nothin', we got nothin'."

They weren't complying. They were going to force the issue. William sidled around the bumper. The car had been through nine different kinds of hell, a mottled patchwork of paint and primer, but it was still chugging along, still being targeted by naïve recruits. *What would they really throw at you? Think icy. Stay tactical.*

William glanced left to see where Rowland was. Suddenly, his shins exploded in pain. His legs flew backward and out from under him and he came down on the left rear panel of the Impala, then toppled into the street, barely breaking his fall with his right hand. The pistol discharged a paintball and flew from his grip. Rolling to one side, he saw a rubber bar waggling from a spring-loaded hinge below the Impala's rear door.

In the texts they called it a cop blade. A cholo trick. In real life it would have been made of steel and honed as sharp as a sword. It would have sliced off his feet.

Rowland saw William go down. Inside the Impala, both heads ducked. Her partner was writhing on the asphalt, trying to roll up onto the curb. In real life they could—they *would* back over him.

Al-Husam and Rowland aimed and fired. Paintballs exploded red and purple across the Impala's rear window.

The car's engine roared and the wheels spun, throwing rubber smoke all over William. The Impala barely grazed the bumper of team two's Crown Victoria, making it rock, and accelerated down the street. Matty and Lee blazed away, scoring more paintball hits on the side windows and door panels. Puffs of purple and red trailed behind the Impala as it sprinted toward freedom, belching gray smoke. It had reached thirty miles an hour when loud bangs and ear-piercing shrieks echoed between the brick buildings. Long ropes of steaming pink shot from both sides of the street. Team four had efficiently and quickly dropped flares to halt traffic on the side streets and set up bubble-gum pylons at the end of the block. The gum net wrapped around the Impala, sizzling and popping. Its trailing edges grabbed at the asphalt and stuck, spinning the car around, while the span of the net slapped across the windshield and gelled to the consistency of tire rubber. The car jounced on its shocks and rolled on for fifty feet, dragging both pylons sparking and clanging down the street.

The Impala's engine died.

Matty and Al-Husam gave chase on foot and took up positions on both sides of the gummed car. Pistols poised, they ordered the occupants to stay where they were and keep their hands in view or they would shoot. Finch and Greavy joined them, happy as larks at having expended precious FBI resources, and with such a loud bang, too.

The actors, barely visible through the pink strands and paintball splat-ters, raised their hands. They would have to be cut out with box knives. Right now, they weren't going anywhere. Al-Husam kept his gun trained on them.

Rowland stood by William and watched as teams three and four joined Al-Husam and Matty, taking up front and rear.

"Goddammit," William said, over and over, rolling back and forth, clutching his shins.

"You okay?"

"I should have seen it. I should have seen it coming. Fucking cholo car."

"You need a medic?"

"Christ, no, it was just a rubber hose. I'm fine." He glared up at her. "Don't you goddamn laugh at me. It hurts." Tears streamed down his cheeks.

"Nobody's laughing," Rowland said solemnly. She sat on the curb beside him.

"I'm toast," William said.

Farrow seemed to come out of nowhere. He was trying hard to hold a grim face. Clearly he was enjoying this. "You all right?"

"I'm *fine*," William said, pushing up to his feet. The whites of his eyes showed like a skittish horse.

"It ain't over until it's over," Farrow said in a low growl. He held up a box-cutter and thumbed out a length of blade. "Get those bastards out of that vehicle and make your arrest. Pick up your pieces and finish your job. Tonight, meet me in the motor pool garage. You're gonna buff and scrape my car until it *shines*."

CHAPTER SEVEN
Washington State

Griff looked over the map he had drawn. It showed places on the property where they had seen children playing or people walking. Little x's peppered the paper, safe places and paths to the houses, the barn, just in case. He drew lines, boundaries.

The children tended to stay away from the barn.

Everybody stayed away from the barn.

Only a crazy man would mine or booby trap the yard where his own children and grandchildren were playing, right?

After all the years Griff had been tracking the Patriarch, he still could not say, with certainty, that they could rule out that possibility.

They had been ready to move out when edicts had come down simultaneously from FBI headquarters and the Attorney General—no big raid, no massive force maneuver, on any date that anyone by any stretch of the imagination could say was Good Friday. If something had gone wrong—or even if they had done their jobs perfectly, and nobody had died—then the headlines could wreak havoc with federal law enforcement in general. The whole country was on edge. It had been on edge for over thirty years, worried and challenged and bitten from without and within. America was half-crazy with suppressed rage.

They didn't have much time. The Patriarch would surely find out something in the next couple of days, and there were any number of ways he could slip out of the farm and get clean away.

A small white bus drove onto the farm during the mid-morning. While Griff notified the incursion team at the trailhead, Rebecca counted the women and children boarding the vehicle, parked just yards from the main house's front porch—two middle-aged women in long dresses and six younger children dressed in their best church clothes. The children boarded the bus with cheery energy.

Griff played back the digital video record and counted heads again, to be sure.

Cap Benson, Charles Sprockett of the ATFE, and SAC John Keller, Griff's Seattle boss, climbed into the tower at ten thirty and looked over the evidence. They conferred briefly.

"Are we sure that's all the dependents down there?" Sprockett asked.

"No," Griff said. "Jacob thinks there might be two young adult males, and so do I, based on those bank robberies. They're not on the bus. There might be two more kids, and we've been talking over the possibility that the males have girlfriends or wives. We haven't seen the kids all together to count them, but—"

"There's a redheaded girl, and maybe a white-blond boy of five or six. We did not see them get on the bus," Rebecca said. "Younger than the others. They may be the Patriarch's grandchildren. They may all be living in the rear house."

"Why wouldn't they go to Easter services?" SAC Keller asked.

Levine shrugged. "Some sort of sharing of familial power. Training his sons to be heads of households. Or, they're just figments of the light and our imagination."

"Well, his two sons are certainly not on that bus," Keller said.

"What if they start firing back? The kids, I mean," Levine said.

"You think they'd do that?" Sprockett asked. "You think he's trained them all to fight?"

Levine rubbed his forehead with two close-spaced fingers. "Chambers is hard core. The Big Time's coming, and a White Christ out of the north is going to scourge the ungodly and drive the Mud People into their graves, from which they will be resurrected as the zombie slaves of true Aryans everywhere. Anybody who doesn't defend themselves will be raped and eaten alive by the Mud People."

"No shit," Cap Benson said.

"He's off the main sequence, philosophically speaking."

Keller said, "Griff, you've tracked him for two decades. This may be the best opportunity we've got. We can't afford to lose him to old age . . . or let him bomb a few more clinics, if he's so inclined."

"Or worse," Rebecca said.

"Are you seriously thinking there's a bioterror operation going on down there?" Levine asked. "I have to say, that just isn't the Patriarch's style. He's classic. He loves to blow stuff up."

Rebecca smiled sweetly. Keller said, "Washington doesn't want a raid. They're afraid we'll hurt some kids down there."

Griff rubbed his cheek stubble. "Obviously, I'm going to have to go in alone and reconnoiter."

"The hell you say," Keller commented dryly.

"It's worth a shot. We've never actually met. He let the deputy go in and out—offered him coffee and biscuits. I think I could go in and take a closer look, ask some questions, and come out alive."

"On what pretext?" Keller asked.

"I'd have a better chance," Rebecca said. "A social worker. Census-taker. I look less like FBI than any of you."

"The Patriarch hates social workers," Griff said.

"She might try for the harem," Sprockett said. No one seemed to think that was a good idea.

"Can you make me look like an aging yardbird?" Griff said. "I already have a few tats."

Sprockett and Keller stared at him.

"Time's short," Griff said.

"Shit," Sprockett said.

Keller got on his cell phone to issue instructions. Sprockett and Rebecca, working different phones, told the agents in town to let them know when the bus arrived.

Griff took a deep breath. He hated wearing body armor—especially the new reactive stuff. It was thin but it wriggled whenever you walked. Made him feel like he was in a living straitjacket.

"You are what you eat," Rebecca told him as she followed Griff down the steps to the first landing. "What'd you have for breakfast this morning?"

"Flakes," Griff said, grinning back at her. He then paused to look through the trees. His eyes were wide and he had difficulty taking a cleansing breath. What would it be like after they suited him up?

Over the next few hours, they procured a beat-up Ford pickup, a pair of denim dungarees, a T-shirt, and three quick forearm tattoos, on top of the two he already had, courtesy of one of Cap Benson's backup team who moonlighted as a makeup artist. Benson called up Monroe to find out the latest trends in jailhouse art. Ten minutes later, they sent him some scans. Skulls, ripped hearts, Jesus on the cross, scorpions, and chains were still big. For some reason, fat seated Buddhas were having a good run—wearing berets and cradling Tommy guns in their ample laps.

As a last touch, Rebecca shaved Griff's head down to a stubble.

"You look like someone I'd boot out of town," Benson said.

Rebecca was less sanguine. "Twenty to one he'll still peg you as FBI."

"All right," Griff said. "Tell me what I should look for."

Rebecca pulled a lab catalog from her travel bag.

The mile down the dirt road in the noonday sun was long and bumpy. The trip would have been pleasant, but there was no way he could know what waited at the end.

Fresh to the FBI, he had carried a folded file card he would read whenever he ventured into a dangerous situation. On that card he had printed his own little set of mantras:

You can relax and trust your training. You know you're good.
You can count on coming out of anything alive, you're so damned good.
Say it to yourself: I will live and prosper, and the bad guys will rue the day.

He had lost that card on the day his team had encountered the Israeli gunbot, but he knew the mantras by heart. They still had juju.

Griff steered a slow curve around a big cedar stump, found the less bouncy part of the road, slowed, then glanced down at a black lapel button, a small camera that would feed video to the team forming at the main road and the smaller team working their way through the woods from the fire tower.

Hidden in the bagginess of the dungarees was his SIG, strapped to his waist and available through a large side pocket. Someone hadn't positioned the Velcro fasteners properly. One of them was chafing.

"SIG's nothing," he reminded himself. "SIG's a peashooter."

The gunbot . . .

A team of fifty agents from the FBI and the Secret Service had stormed the Muncrow Building in downtown Portland two years before, preparing to arrest ten Serbian counterfeiters. They had been met by seven guys and two women in body armor, expecting no mercy and wielding a savage array of automatic weapons—but what lay hidden in the corrugated steel shed that blocked their only exit route—what had brought down nearly all of the team within twenty seconds, cutting them into bloody gobbets—had been an Israeli Sholem-Schmidt D-7, a self-directed, insect-carriage auto-mated cannon. None of them had never seen one outside of *Popular Science* magazine.

Before it had run into a brick wall, jammed, and blown its super-heated barrels into shrapnel, the D-7 had all by itself killed forty-three agents. Griff had come out of the Muncrow Building alive, not a scratch. He had had nightmares for weeks.

Still did.

And in the mess, he had lost his file card.

The last U.S. President had privately threatened to bomb the Sholem-Schmidt factory outside Haifa. That had put a strain on relations for a few months, until Israeli intelligence had discovered D-7s being exported to Iran. Mossad had finally done the job themselves, arresting the owners and workers and dismantling the factory.

Wicked old world.

The barn came into view and then the farmhouse. The farmhouse was unpainted. Griff guessed that both had been assembled from the local trees. The exterior boards had warped slightly under the weather and the cedar roof shingles were rough along their windward edges like the scales on an old lizard. The trees that had once covered the farm had been probably been downed with cross-cut handsaws. He tried to picture the long old trailer-mounted sawmill hauled in by a stoop-shouldered truck and smell the fresh-cut wood and hear the *wik-wik-wik* of the boards being planed by hand and fastened together with mortise and tenon and square blacksmithed nails.

Rustic, independent, living off the land.

He drove by one end of the apple orchard, peering under the windshield visor at the thin forest of two-by-four studs arranged through the dead-looking trees and around the barn and house. The studs were newer than other wood around the property. Between the studs, someone—presumably the Patriarch and his sons—had strung a high checkerboard of wires at a uniform height of about six feet, sometimes in parallel, sometimes wrapped around each other, like someone's crazy idea of a network of clothes lines.

Through his side window, he saw the spring leaves on a few of the apple trees. They were streaked with pale dust. There hadn't been more than a drizzle of rain in a couple of weeks—perhaps the leaves had been coated with fine dirt from the road. The pines around the barn and the trees all around the old farmstead had all been lightly and uniformly powdered.

Griffin pulled out his handkerchief and blew his nose. The dust might be tree pollen. He kept an eye out for any sign of surveillance within the house. The truck made a few last bumps, and then he pulled up in the middle of a dirt parking area marked by a line of four creosoted railroad ties. Griff glanced at his watch. It was eleven. The truck's noise hadn't brought anyone to the front door or the porch but he saw a shade flicker in a window.

The old man had structured his life to a fare-thee-well, and no doubt he had prepared for a moment like this. But for a few minutes, at least, Griff was pretty certain he could convince Chambers he was just a wayward visitor.

It was a myth that crooks could always tell when somebody was a cop. Donnie Brasco—Joe Piscone—had been an excellent example and there were plenty of others. Criminals were not the shiniest apples in the barrel when it came to understanding human nature. If they were they'd be CEOs and they'd be making a lot more money, with fewer chances of landing in jail.

As he reached to pull on the emergency brake, he wondered how William was doing back in Quantico. Third generation. He had never wanted that even before the divorce, even before they had been reduced to seeing each other only once or twice a year.

He straightened and opened the truck door, pushing everything out of his mind but his story, his act. As he stepped down from the truck, he consulted a map and then turned, squinting at the house and the trees and hills.

His arm hair prickled when his back was to the house.

When he finished turning, he saw the old man on the front porch, standing with a slight stoop, hands by his sides. Up close he did not look so good. He had long thick white hair, leonine might be the description, but his mustache was darker, almost black. He might have been wearing a wig but where he would get that sort of wig, Griff did not know. A Halloween store, maybe. The old man's eyes were wide, bright and observant and his face was neither friendly nor concerned. He did not look like he wanted company but he did not look terribly unhappy about it, either.

"Hallo!" Griff called out. "Is this the Tyee farm? I hope I've come to the right place."

Someone had parked a jug of sun tea on the edge of the porch, away from the steps. It was a big glass jug with a cap and yellow flowers painted on one side.

"This homestead used to be known by that name," Chambers said. "What's your beef?"

"I've been looking for a place to stay, maybe get work, and some folks in town said you might be able to help me. I'm a traveler in a dry land, friend."

Chambers remained on the top step of the porch but his lips twitched. "You're probably in the wrong place."

"Well, I see the trees are dusty," Griff said, trying for a joke. "They look dry."

The old man's face settled into concrete. "Have to spray all the time, kill the damned insects. Let me know your intentions or move on."

Griff tried to look unnerved. "What I'm saying is, I hear there's a church around here and some people I could sympathize with. It's kind of lonely for that sort of company where I live."

"Where do you live?"

"Multnomah County."

Chambers grimaced. "Queer place. Liberals and queers. Just right for each other."

"Exactly," Griff said. "Don't know why I ever moved there. Niggers and Kikes. Crawl right up your pants leg. Have to squash them or they'll nip you in the jewels." He slapped his pants and shook one foot. Levine had coached Griff on this dialog.

"You're somewhat of a clown, aren't you?" Chambers asked. His eyes had wandered casually to the truck, then to the barn, and finally to the northern hills, and his lids drooped for a moment along with his shoulders. "Show-offs and clowns always bring trouble."

"I apologize. I sure could use some good old-fashioned preaching, whatever you can offer, sir," Griff said, hoping for the right amount of awkwardness, out-of-stepness. Chambers was the brightest and most experienced of a sorry lot. He had instincts born of fifty hard, ambitious years. Margaret Thatcher's loo. Griff could hardly believe it. Right here in Snohomish County.

"You been in prison until recently?" Chambers asked.

"Yes, sir, Monroe. I did not want to let on right away."

"Did they tell you about Tyee at Monroe?"

"Yes, sir."

"Who told you?"

"We'll need to get better acquainted, sir, before I reveal that."

"Well, come closer, let me get a look at you."

Griff took a few steps forward.

"My God, boy, you have arms like pig thighs. Pumping iron?"

"Yes, sir. Weights kept me sane."

"Some almighty tats. Come on up here. Where you from before Monroe?"

"Boise."

"Why don't you tell me some names."

"Jeff Downey, he used to be a friend. Haven't seen him in ten years. Don't know if he's still alive."

"He isn't," Chambers said, and sniffed. "Which is convenient."

"Mark Lindgren. His wife, Suzelle." Again he was working from Jacob Levine's script.

"You talk with Lindgren recently?"

"Nosir, but he knows me."

"Mind if I do some checking up on you?"

"Nosir. But right now I'm very thirsty."

"For word or deed?"

"Beg pardon?"

"Will my words quench your thirst, or are you here for deeds? Because I'm not much in the way of deeds these days. Kind of staying quiet out here, like those volcanoes you can see from the road."

Griff nodded. "I understand, sir. Just wanted to make your acquaintance and get some preaching. Find a church where I can feel comfortable."

"Well, that's all right. What's your experience with weapons?"

"Knives kept me alive once or twice. Know guns pretty well. Used to collect shotguns. The wife sold my whole gun rack on eBay. Ex-wife." He jammed a load of masculine resentment into that. "Nigh on fifty thousand dollars' worth, some my granddaddy had back in North Carolina. French-made, German, beautiful things. She just . . . sold them." He waved his hands helplessly, and tightened his throat muscles to make sure his face was red.

Chambers said, "We all lose earthly things. Time comes when we make others lose earthly things, that's the balance." Chambers liked this display of anger, the red face. "I've got sun tea out there on the porch and ice in the kitchen. Want a glass?"

"Nothing harder?" Griff asked, twitching his right eye into a wink.

"I do not allow alcohol. I do excuse that request, coming as it does from a Monroe man. Still, you could have been worse off. You could have done your time in Walla Walla."

Griff grinned and shook out his hands. "Yessir."

They sat on the steps of the porch and drank tall glasses of sun tea sweetened with honey. Chambers was surprisingly limber and got down on the front step with barely a wince. His legs were long and skinny within the faded dungarees. His bony ankles stuck up from oversize and well-worn brown leather Oxfords. The sun was high over the farm and the dusty trees cast real shadows. It was the sort of bright day rarely seen up in these foothills at any time of the year and there had been many more of them recently—a long dry spell. They chatted for a few minutes about global warming and what it might mean.

"Fuck, we'll all get suntans," Griff said. "Then we'll be closer to the Mud People. Might even marry one of them."

Chambers chortled deep in his beard. "I do wish you would clean up that prison language. I have kids here. They're off celebrating Easter. Good Friday."

"That's not till next week," Griff said.

"We worship to God's calendar," Chambers said. "All the world's calendar brings is grief and worse luck." A little bit of old East Coast had crept into Chamber's tone. "It cannot keep going on the way it is."

Griff peered at the Patriarch, respectful, even worshipful, nodding his head. Taking it all in.

"Prophecy's a crock," Chambers said, his voice low and crackling. "Revelation is a Jewish fantasy. Israel has nothing to do with prophecy. It is a political entity. It brings disgrace down upon the white races. Jesus was not an observant Jew. His people came from the north, Northern Italy, maybe even Germany. None of the apostles were Jews except Judas. Defending the so-called homeland of the Jews has brought us to this. Brother against brother. 9-11, call the cops, and now 10-4. Roger and out."

Chambers stared out across the scrubby grass of the big front yard, then fixed on the barn.

Eyes betray. Where they look is important.

"It's so bad, Jesus should have returned long ago," Griff said. "Don't you think?"

Chambers squinted to the north and stuck out his arm, a lean finger pointing. "He isn't coming. He's disgusted, all these Mud People building places they call churches . . . He's not going to help *you* until you help *Him*. You got to believe what is in your heart. What's in your heart?"

"I don't know. Anger. I'm mad. I want things better. I want things to go down easy."

"Things are not in the habit of ever being easy, my man from Monroe. I know that in my heart, always have." Chambers thumped his chest with a knuckly fist. "Circumstance has a way of sneaking up on you, just when you're ready to sink into old age and enjoy the grandchildren. You have to prepare." He pulled down an eyelid and cocked a clear gaze at Griff over a clever grin. "Every week or so I hunt deer and take treks around the homestead. I can still get off a straight shot. My eyes are still sharp." He leaned forward and swung his right arm out in a point. "You see that low ridge? Just in front of the triangular peak. There is a fire tower up on that ridge. See it?"

Griff tracked along the long arm. "Nosir."

"Used to be a tree up on that ridge," Chambers said. "A few days back, someone chopped it. Just took it right down."

Griff put on a dumb face. "Those towers are all around up here."

"I hiked by that one six months ago. It's the only one. This time of year, most often it's rented. Campers use it. Campers don't cut down trees. Someone's in that tower."

"Maybe the rangers moved in early. Warming and all."

Chambers shook his head. "They're up there, watching me. But that's all right. I'm prepared."

"I could scout for you," Griff said, giving the ridge a fierce scowl.

"No need, Monroe man. It's over. I took a few risks, even risked my family, but it's going to be worth it in the long scheme." He did not look at Griff as he spoke. "I told my sons to go out by the back trails, follow the bus, get to a real church somewheres and pray for me."

Griff looked puzzled. This was being transmitted back up the road. Another ambush was the last thing he wanted. "Why leave?" he asked. "It's beautiful here. I could live here and be happy." He studied Chambers' dingy white shirt, trying to contour the skinny ribs beneath, looking for padding—any sort of hidden bomb. The shirt was too loose. Bombs could be hidden anywhere.

"The tree hath blossomed in the night, and the fruit it is set. I am an old man, and my family will prosper and do great works after I am gone."

Griff shook his head. "You got a long life ahead preaching and spreading the word."

Chambers took a deep breath through his nose. "Come into my house, Monroe man. I'll show you something glorious and then we'll say goodbye." Chambers pushed himself slowly to his feet; getting down was easier than getting up again. Griff did not like this. Playing a part and being wary all at once had never been easy for him. He followed the old man through the wood-framed screen door with the squealing spring into the neat shade of the snow porch with bundled twigs pushed into a corner and two rusted metal snow shovels, and then into the living room. The oak furniture was sturdy but worn. The big stone fireplace was as described by the deputy, who had eaten his muffin where Griff was now standing.

"I do love my children," Chambers said, "and they love me. I will miss them, but I have through deeds built my mansion in heaven. There will be a sharp correction, Monroe man. The Jews will weep and Jesus will greet me as a brother. Mary will soothe me and stroke my hair and though I am reborn in a youthful body, I will mourn for those that still suffer on this Earth, forced to dwell among the ones bathed in darkness. For surely the dark races are hiding from that cleansing ray. Surely the sun is out today, searching, and they hide in their ghettos and in their holes in the cities, in their black and noisome hives of squalor and brick. Comes soon a time when the pillar of fire shall yet again rise, and a man will carry with him across this world a vessel as virulent as the Ark of the Covenant, and all who come near, all the Mud People and the lying and deceitful Jews, wearing their pubic hairs on their heads, their long curly black hairs, shall reach out to touch the beauty of it, and they shall be smote by the tens of thousands, as it was in olden times. God never did much like the Jews. History proves it. Once more, a pillar of fire shall rise over the land by night, and a pillar of cloud by day."

Chambers' face turned peaceful. He favored Griff with a fatherly smile.

"Hallelujah," Griff said. "That's preaching, Reverend."

"You haven't told me your name, son."

"Jimmy, Jimmy Roland."

The Patriarch held out his hand. Griff shook it: a dry firm grip, no sweat, no worry.

"It is no sin to sweep away the polluted."

"Amen to that," Griff said.

"Now you look a proper wise fellow, Jimmy Roland, no sense playing stupid, you've been around. You know your work, and you know mine." Chambers sat gingerly in a rocker-glider and slowly started moving back, forward, back and forward, up a little, down. "Nobody comes from Monroe without passing me special words. I am certain I smell a Jew on you."

Without being obvious, Griff had taken inventory of the room. Behind and to the immediate right, Chambers had within his reach a narrow cabinet set back to one side of the fireplace, where pokers and shovels might be stored, the door open. Griff could not see the inside.

"You should have been here last month. Nipped it in the bud. You could have had us then. You saw the burn barrels. We cleaned things out. We have cleared the path. The rest is in the hands of the true God. Has been since before you arrived. Just know that the fruit has set, and soon the Jews and their children will bring it to the world's table and eat of it." He leveled a finger at Griff's chest. "They are listening, so let them hear my epitaph." He paused with a wicked smile. "An end to all the evil they have done since time began. Death to the Jews, my friend."

Chambers leaned and thrust his gnarled fingers toward the cabinet.

Griff slipped his hand through the Velcroed seam in his shirt. "FBI!" he shouted.

Faster than he had any right to be, Chambers brought out a sawed-off double-barreled shotgun from the cabinet. In an instant he had it cocked. The blued-steel barrel gleamed as it swung.

Griff's gun was out and he shot Chambers four times. The shotgun barrel swayed and dropped an inch, the old man's finger still trying to pull the trigger. Griff squeezed off two more rounds. Chambers let go of the stock and the shotgun fell. Its butt thumped heavily on the floor. The barrel sang against the stones of the fireplace. The old man's lungs gurgled air through new holes in his chest and neck and his eyes twitched back in their sockets. His voice was liquid and bubbled like a frog's and he said, "Lord, Lord." Then, barely audible, eyes quivering but trained on Griff, "Fuck you."

After that his eyes went flat and he was dead but his movement continued, legs and one arm shivering as he slumped in the chair and finally hung half-in, half-out. His trigger finger jerked like a snake. Stopped.

Griff raised the SIG and with a grunt rolled the old man over, quickly and rudely palped him, then turned out his pockets looking for IED or remotes or timers. He pulled a plastic restraint cord from his pants pocket and cinched the limp, bony wrists. Only then did he check the old man's pulse, mostly avoiding the slick smear of blood around the floor and the last of the flow from the nicked carotid.

He swallowed hard, trying to focus on the remaining danger, trying to keep the nervous crime-comedy voices out of his forebrain and back in the rear cages where they belonged. *Papa has left the premises.*

Suicide by cop. At his age. Preaching and then trying me on. I don't believe it.

Griff quickly moved through the house, swinging along the walls, down the hall, into the rooms. He opened the closets just to make sure; very likely with kids so recently in the house they were not booby-trapped but he was still taking a chance. The house was clean and neat, beds made in each of the four small bedrooms, the single office with its roll-top desk prim in ordered austerity.

He passed the Patriarch on the way out. Erwin Griffin hated dead bodies. He had never admitted that to anyone; agents were supposed to be hard-core. Bodies made him feel sick.

Only then did he remember he was on the grid and that since the shooting, other than shouting out his affiliation, he had said nothing—maybe grunted, maybe cursed. Back up by the main road, they should have heard and seen everything that had happened inside the house and especially the shots and he did not want hordes of people up here or near the barn, not yet.

As he stepped through the door and out on the porch, peering left and then right, he said, "Chambers is dead. I'm fine. Keep everyone back."

He faced north and saw agents and police running toward the house. How long had it taken him to search, two or three minutes? It had seemed like at least ten.

"Get the hell back!" he shouted from the porch, his voice cracking as he waved them off. They stopped. "Get back, you idiots!" They turned and retreated with equal haste.

He had blood on his arm. The tattoos were smeared. He sat on the porch, letting his heart slow from Krupa to oompah, wishing to hell he had a cigarette, before deciding he would have to take a turn about the yard, around the house, just to make sure.

By that time, he saw vans and more people up by the edge of the clearing.

The farm was no longer quiet.

CHAPTER EIGHT
El Centro, California

"I've been thinking about what you were saying," Charlene told the tall blond man. It was past noon. Her eyes were puffy. They had made love and slept a little and then talked into the morning. Now they were having breakfast in a Coco's restaurant. "I just can't be that cynical. I need hope. Even when I know what I'm doing and think about where my husband is, I still want to be a Christian."

The blond man glanced at his skinned knuckles. They had already scabbed over. He had told Charlene that he had barked them while changing a tire. In fact, he had slipped in a ditch after shooting an Arizona patrol officer.

The waitress brought another glass of orange juice. Charlene drank the second glass with equal speed—three quick gulps—sniffed, and looked around the Coco's: Scotchgarded print fabric on the booth seats, scarred oak table top, one knife magnetically stuck to a fork beside a plate smeared with yolk and bacon grease. Outside, bleached by the sun, El Centro, California: warehouses and auto repair businesses and trucks roaring by. The blond man was in his late forties, thin, run-down. He had put on sunglasses after leaving the Day's Inn to hide his eyes—one green, one blue.

"You're so quiet," Charlene told him.

"Sorry. I've probably said too much already."

Charlene had driven the green Ford van from Highway 10, where she had picked him up by the side of the road, to El Centro, stopping at a Day's Inn. They had both taken rooms. She had met him in the lobby after midnight and asked what his name was and he had told her it was Jim Thorpe. Charlene had been needy. Even after she had fallen asleep, Jim Thorpe had stayed awake. He looked as if he had not slept for weeks.

Charlene looked through the low window beside the booth, out to the dry lawn and the street beyond. "I'm ready to believe in Jesus, just give myself up to something that I know is totally good," Charlene said. "I mean, I can see Jesus so clearly and he is beautiful and compassionate and he has a lovely smile—just like yours." She looked at him with real longing. "I do not know why men have to act so tough. You certainly don't need to be bitter . . . I mean, you're an attractive older guy. You can travel the whole world, no responsibilities . . ." She stopped, confused, and looked at the table.

Charlene's husband had gone to West Point. After 10-4, he had signed up for infantry, taking the idiot sticks, the emblem of crossed rifles, over more plum army opportunities. Charlene had wanted him to stay home and be a husband and a father. He had enlisted for a second tour to kill ragheads and stay with his buddies. His name was Jason. She had shown Jim Thorpe a picture. Her guy was upright, young, strong, bullnecked, laser-eyed. He wondered what Jason was seeing right now.

"I think about him being God knows where because the *damned army* won't tell the families anything and I wonder, what is Jesus really up to? What is He thinking, making all of us suffer? But I can't blame Jesus. It's us, isn't it?" Charlene tapped the juice glass on the table. Made it do a little dance. Made as if to smile bravely, but too late. Women liked confessing to him. It was the one thing that they gave him that he would have gladly dispensed with.

But hadn't he confessed to her—just a little, and started her flow? Opened up about his innermost opinions? *If she only knew the half of it.*

"I know you're a good man," she said. "But being so hopeless . . . I can't feel that way. It's just the way the world treats us. We're being tested."

His nerves were starting to jangle. He needed to move on or the grief would slam back and he'd find the brick wall that he had built between him and his lost faces crumbling. "Then maybe it's all taken care of in the end," he offered.

Charlene's eyes filled with tears.

"It is so wrong to have to wait for my husband, and feel . . . so *hungry* to have a man. Just a man to hug me, wrap his arms around me. I have never been desperate, not like this. Never. And my boy needs a father. I need *his* father." Her face hardened. "I have never done this before."

Yes, you have, he thought.

"When is it all going to come right again?" she asked.

"Soon," Jim Thorpe said. He wrapped one hand around her fingers on the juice glass and gave them a gentle squeeze.

Charlene frowned at him, *don't tease.* "I just want my husband home. I want to feel normal, be right with my kids and my family."

"Of course." He stood beside the booth and opened his wallet. "Breakfast is on me."

"No," Charlene said primly. "We're not poor." She laid a twenty next to his. Then she put down another ten and gave him back the twenty he had put down. Bravely, she said, "Your money's no good here."

"You sure?"

"I'm sure, Mr. Jim Thorpe. Or is it James?"

He smiled.

"Such a lovely smile," she said. Her eyes turned quick and efficient, darting around the tables, squinting through the bright windows. "You leave first." Even in El Centro she was worried that people who knew her might see her with another man.

"Thanks for breakfast," he said.

"Thanks for having a patient ear," she said.

As he walked out into the glare she passed him in a tidy hurry. No one could have guessed what they had been doing on thin hotel sheets just a few hours before. He admired that sort of efficiency. Women were good at such things.

He was not. The bricks were falling. There was no mental wall thick enough to block what he had lost. He stood on the sidewalk, hands in his pockets, waiting, shivering despite the heat. He wasn't looking forward to telling Tommy. Tommy did not need to know about the patrolman. His self-important partner was tippy at the best of times. That was how Tommy described himself: tippy, but enthusiastic—when he wasn't Dipsy-Down, as he called it.

Unpredictable—but for the moment, still essential.

The tall man watched Charlene pull the green Ford van out of the Coco's parking lot. She rolled down the window and looked both ways but deliberately did not see him as she drove by.

Five minutes later, Tommy roared up in his battered, cream-colored El Camino. He reached over and pulled the door lock with fat dexterous fingers. He was small and skinny but for his face and his fingers; these belonged to a larger man. The effect was grotesque but Tommy no longer seemed to care how people reacted.

"No luggage?" he asked, his plump face showing an early flush of dismay. "No truck. No printers. God, Sam, what happened?"

Sam opened the door and climbed in, sitting on the ripped seat. "Let's drive," he said.

"What happened to the big truck?"

"There's been a change in our strategy," Sam said.

"Sam, I don't like being *disappointed*," Tommy fluted. "We need those printers. I can't do everything we want without those printers. I don't like *failure*."

Sam was dangerously close to chucking it all. "To the winery, Jeeves," he said with a flourish.

"You're in *fine spirits*. You got laid last night, didn't you, Sam? That's why you're trying to be funny." Sometimes, Tommy's bursts of intuition made him seem psychic—hard to get used to in such a man-child.

"We're okay, really. We'll be fine. We'll get more printers."

"Before you got here and got laid, something went wrong. Don't tell me," Tommy insisted, his face clouded like a baby about to burst into tears. "I don't want to hear it. Really, I don't. I couldn't take it."

"We'll be fine," Sam said.

"Did you leave fingerprints?" Tommy asked.

Sam raised his right hand. His fingers were shiny with clear silicone caulk.

"There's something else," Tommy said, his tiny eyes shifting and wild. "I turned on the radio. I heard it on the way to pick you up." He pushed the radio knob. The big news was the death of the bank robber and abortion clinic bomber called the Patriarch and the ongoing search of his farm hide-away in Washington state. "Is that our guy?" Tommy asked. "Sam, is that our guy? Is that our second factory?"

Sam did not have a quick story to soothe Tommy—or himself. He stared at the radio, then out the window.

Tommy said, "Oh my. Oh my. Sam, oh my."

"All right, Tommy. Pull over and I'll drive for a while."

Tommy's nose was dripping and he was shaking badly. He had entered the land of Dipsy-Down and it was all he could do to stop the car without getting them both killed.

CHAPTER NINE
Washington State

Griff stripped off his shirt and body armor and handed it to the FBI evidence team. They whisked it to their van to offload the data and video contained in the vest. All of the police vehicles, at Griff's request, stayed on the edge of the clearing, about a hundred yards from the house and the barn.

He walked back toward the house with Rebecca Rose at his side. They stared at the barn. Griff's nostrils flexed and his upper lip twitched as if he were about to sneeze. The breeze was cool against his naked upper torso. He slipped an Underarmor T-shirt over his head. Jacob Levine joined them and handed Griff his own purple vest. Griff declined. Even chilly, he refused to go that far.

"Becky," he said, "Chambers kept looking at the barn."

"Yeah," Rebecca said.

"I think you might want to get back with the others."

"I will if you will," Rebecca said.

"Don't be an asshole," Griff said. "I've done this kind of stuff for decades."

Rebecca shook her head. "I'll need to see what's in the house and the barn ASAP. Then we'll know what to do next."

Levine held his ground, too. "Have you heard?" he asked them.

"Heard about what?"

"The bus never made it to town. It stopped and the families loaded into three cars. They diverted at a side road and threw off the tracking vehicles. Some of them may be headed east to Idaho."

Griff rubbed his upper lip, first checking to make sure there was no blood on his finger. "He knew about us all along. He saw us cut down the tree."

"Makes you wonder where his righteous sons are," Rebecca said.

They both stared into the far stands of cedars and larches.

Griff cringed as a helicopter passed slowly overhead. Even at three hundred feet, the steady beat of the rotors thumped the barn and the ground under his boots. Three crime scene techs came around the main house, stringing yellow tape. The tape flapped and curled in the downdraft. There was a news station imprint on the chopper's side—KOMO Seattle. Someone must have radioed the pilot that the scene was unsecured and dangerous, for the helicopter abruptly backed off and swung around, heading west over the woods to the highway, probably to take more pictures of the base camp.

Cap Benson approached bearing in his arms a more suitable blue blazer he had pulled from the trunk of his car. Griff slipped the blazer on over the T-shirt and decided he looked if anything even more ridiculous than he would have wearing Levine's vest.

They all stood in the broad, scrubby front yard of the old farmhouse. Inside, the Patriach still lay sprawled on his stomach in a pool of blood, cuffed, awkward, and bedraggled and not giving a damn one way or the other. Griff could see him like an after-image over the barn. He had killed three times—four, now—in his FBI career. Six or seven times before that, in the Navy. Much more than the average. He did not enjoy the distinction.

From the road, blowing in on a westerly breeze, they could hear the faint sounds of big trucks on the move. Washington State Patrol, FBI, ATF, Homeland Security, whatever.

Dogs running to sniff at the old man's kingdom.

"That's one big barn," Benson said. "Wonder what's in it?"

"Why don't you go have a look?" Griff said. He would have to re-evaluate the entire scene. If Chambers had known he was being watched for several days, who knew what he could have accomplished? What chain of events he could have started by making a few night visits to the barn, or the second house . . . ?

Chances were, with all the kids, there would not have been tripwires or other traps spread around the yard, or in the houses . . . but Griff just could not be sure.

He turned to the north. Several techs in white plastic suits and hoods were swabbing samples of powder off the distant trees. "Your people?" he asked Rebecca. She nodded. "What do you think they'll find? Chambers said they had sprayed for pests."

"I doubt that," Levine said. "He hated pesticides. Called them a conspiracy by the Jews to help feed the Mud People of the world."

Rebecca looked amused. Griff did not know what to think about the world's evil. Another tech closer in had climbed a ladder braced against one of many wooden poles around the property and was attaching a multimeter to the wires suspended overhead.

"How many long arms of the law do you have back there, Cappy?" Griff asked.

"There's me and my boys. ATF has pulled back, I don't know why."

"Bureau asked for primacy. We still have some chips to play."

"I don't see your boss, Keller," Benson said.

"He was called back to Washington, DC," Rebecca said. "He's going to testify before some senate committee."

Griff sucked that back in. Not even collaring the Patriarch stopped the wheels of partisan politics, trying to grind down the FBI. Trying to kill it and hand its responsibilities over to others. No matter. His retirement was secure. One more year and he would cross the boundary of GS-1811—into mandatory retirement.

Benson continued, "There's Sergeant Andrews and four guys from the state inter-agency bomb squad. We got Dan Vogel from the K9 explosives unit. I saw Child Protective Services hanging around with nothing to do, and one black girl in a leather jacket, like a goddamned Black Panther, but I suppose she's one of yours."

Griff nodded.

"And two other feds I don't recognize."

"Homeland Security and Bureau of Domestic Intelligence," Griff said. "They'd love to horn in. I want Dan and his dog to sweep the main house, then the second house, in that order." He waved his hands, drawing a plan in the air.

"Not the barn?" Benson asked.

"Griff thinks the barn is rigged," Levine said. He paced in a small circle, eyes on the ground, sweat on his forehead despite the chill.

"Bots coming soon?" Griff asked.

Benson nodded.

"Send a bot into the barn. And get some more troopers into those woods. His sons could be drawing a bead on us right now." He closed one eye and cocked his finger at Levine.

"Hell, they would have taken you out after you killed their pappy," Levine said. "The sons are long gone."

"Maybe."

Griff did not think the houses were rigged with explosives. Kids had been there too recently; tough to control kids, keep them from setting something off. No one had seen anybody walking outside to the rear house after the bus had departed. Still, it would be necessary to thoroughly check for both explosives and kids in hiding—and the K9 could do that.

He now stood with hands on hips and faced his main nightmare directly. The big sliding barn door had been left open six or seven inches, not enough for a man to easily squeeze through. He did not want to touch that door. It was too much like an invitation.

"The Patriarch would plan for bots, don't you think?" Griff asked Rebecca.

"Sounds like," Rebecca said. "X-ray triggers. Trip mikes tuned to machine sounds."

"All these wires," Griff said. "What the hell are they for? What level of paranoia should we consider unreasonable? He's been at this for fifty years, right?"

"We should wait," Rebecca said. "Less chance of someone clumsy hitting a tripwire."

Griff turned on her but kept his voice low. "What if it's all hooked up to a goddamned timer, Special Agent Becky Rose?"

"Your call," Rebecca said, pursing her lips. Griff was the only agent who called her Becky and she didn't like it much, but in the grand scheme . . .

"Is it? Or is News breathing down my back?"

"As I said . . ."

"Right. It's my call. Well, fuck that, too."

The police waiting up at the start of the clearing were milling about, observing the four of them as they faced the barn.

"He'd know," Levine said. "He'd plan for dogs."

"Our dogs are trained to avoid wires. They work through all sorts of masking scents," Benson said. "I'd rather trust them than the bots."

"No dog I ever met could spot a tripwire in dim light or slip past a motion detector," Griff said. "I think the houses are safest. Dogs for the houses. We'll send bots into the barn."

He was starting to shake. It had been hours since he had shot the old man. Shot him six times in his fucking living room. A man's home is his castle. Deep things were churning in him and making his hands and shoulders tremble. "Well," Griff said. "Let's bring them all forward. Get me Watson."

Rebecca used her comm.

Special Agent Alice Watson pushed through the crowd of police and agents and walked down the road with quick, off-kilter steps. She was a plump woman of thirty-three with one leg shorter than the other, acres of attitude, and the expertise to justify it. Long scars pulled her face on one side. She wore a thick lens over one eye but with the other eye she could still see clearly.

Watson had nearly died two years ago, in Paris. She had made one small mistake dealing with an Al Aqsa handbag packed with a proximity fuse and two charges of T6 Anafex, set to release a vial of osmium tetroxide through spray cans that had once held Raid. The bag had been found in a public park. There had been no time to bring in robots. The main charge had dudded. The canister of tetrox had remained intact, sparing a large crowd—and Watson. But there had been a third fuse buried under the pack, and she had taken the backup charge—just a pinch—square in the face.

Later, in the hospital, she had told Griff, "I met the ghost of that bomb. I put both my fingers up its nose and twisted. That's why it let me go. Next time, it'll share some secrets."

Watson had spent time recuperating with her husband and kid. She had returned to the job after six months but had spent the next four months in a powered walker. The bomb ghost might or might not be a joke. Griff didn't care.

She was the best bomb expert he knew.

Watson shook hands with Rebecca, then stood beside Griff and said, "We're on bombnet at HDS and Eglin. They're feeding it to experts in Los Angeles and Washington. We're going to have about fifteen good eyes on this one, including mine." Her grin was a cruel parody but it bucked up Griff's spirits.

A few steps behind Watson followed a short man with close-cut brown hair, wearing black jeans and a black T-shirt and leading a golden retriever on a glittering chain. The dog whined and dodged, eager to earn her play treat. This would be Dan Vogel and Chippy, Griff thought. Beautiful dog, fluffy and reddish-gold, recently shampooed and totally focused on the red ball that Vogel clutched in one hand. A happy dog with way too much energy. Under one arm, Vogel carried a thick folder filled with scent tabs: a library of bomb ingredients to help Chippy focus. In the last ten years there had been a substantial revolution in both the variety, the compactness, and the strength of explosives. Microreactors—chemical factories little bigger than a breadbox—had put the creation of lethal amounts of dangerous substances into the hands of small groups, and even individuals.

"Chippy's happy," Watson said.

"All my bitches are happy. Where first, boss?"

"That is a big barn," Watson said.

"What's your ghost telling you?" Griff asked.

Watson glared at him with one good eye, the other goggling behind its lens like a blank moon in a telescope. "That was private, Griff."

"All right. What kind of bomb would fill a barn?" he asked. "Fertilizer," Watson said. "But this bastard has used kitchen TAMP, C4, Semtex, Anafex, triminol, passage clay, Poly-S phosphate, and aerosol kerosene—that's a baby daisy-cutter, to you guys—you name it. I really don't know. This would be his *pièce de résistance*?"

"Sounds right," Griff said. "He died proud. He said it was all in God's hands."

"Shit," Benson said, and his face went a shade more pale in the dusk. Levine stopped pacing and shoved his hands in his pockets. Rebecca looked down at her feet, then up again, eyes slitted.

Vogel knelt by the retriever and opened the book to the first page, a stimulating scent. The dog snuffled happily, eyes bright and tail wagging. Then she sneezed.

Watson looked at the network of wires on poles surrounding the house and strung over the dirt road. She took a cleansing breath, let it out, pointed to the edge of the clearing, and said, "Gentlemen, Agent Rose, if you're nonessential, you best move on out. Who knows what you might step in—or on?"

Rebecca said, "I'll stay."

"You're not going in there, Rebecca," Griff said.

"We'll see," Rebecca said. "I've put in my request."

"Shit. We need to reduce personnel and do our search, no crap. I've been involved in tracking this bastard for twenty years."

"No crap," Rebecca said steadily. "I've been working bioterror for longer than that. I'm here, I'm interested. I won't get in your way."

"Becky—"

"Can you identify a minilab, Griff? Sequencers? Fermenters? Do you know what to look for?"

Griff set his jaw. "You could tell me. You're a Janie-come-lately here. You three, bug out."

Benson shrugged. "You've got enough grief, you don't need any more from me," he said, and patted Griff's arm. He and Levine walked up the road, leaving the field and the barn to the experts, and to Rebecca Rose, who had set her jaw and was *interested*.

Levine looked back over his shoulder. Griff did not like having people look back, one last glance; that sort of shit bothered him. He pointed his finger at Rebecca. "You're not even rated for a bomb suit."

She folded her arms.

Watson eyed them both with amusement.

Chippy was whining and tugging toward the barn.

"Is Chippy good on her own?" Griff asked Vogel.

"Got a four zero on the Fairview course last month," Vogel said. "Found ten out of ten devices, including Anafex."

"Is she okay with kids?" Griff asked.

"Loves them. Kids play fetch."

Chippy strained at her leash. She really wanted into that barn. Griff did not want her or anyone else in there. That barn was creeping him out badly. He glared at Rebecca.

"Number one." Griff pointed to the main house. "Then the house behind."

Vogel led the dog away to the first house. He opened the screen door then reached down and unclipped her collar. The golden retriever trotted inside.

A snow-white and freshly waxed inter-agency bomb truck, sporting the odd symbol of a flaming wasp nest, rumbled through the cordon and approached the house. Cap Benson rode the running board, wearing a boyish grin. Inside was the bombot coordinator, a sergeant whom Griff had hung out with in Portland during a training session for local police departments. They had gone drinking together. His name was George Carlin Andrews.

Benson jumped off as the truck pulled up beside them. "No guts, no glory," he said to Griff.

Griff brushed past him without a word. Watson opened the door for Andrews. "The machine gods have arrived," she announced.

"Why, thank you, pretty miss," Andrews said, stepping down with his aluminum box of goodies. "Griff, is that you, all dolled up?" He peeled off a glove and held out his hand. He was tall and thick across the middle but he had delicate fingers, jeweler's hands.

Griff nodded and shook with him.

"What are we hoping not to find? Any clues?" Andrews asked.

"Not many," Griff said. He told Andrews about the way Chambers had looked at the barn and a little more about his history. "He said it was all in God's hands."

Rebecca liked that even less the second time she heard it.

"Uh huh," Andrews said. "Jacob Levine filled me in. We probably can't move back far enough to escape that sort of wrath. We could take time to dig some foxholes. What do you think?"

"If something that big blows, we'd just get sucked out," Watson said.

"Pink clouds," Rebecca said.

Andrews faced her square. "We haven't met, have we?"

"Special Agent Rebecca Rose," Griff said. "She thinks there might be biologicals in there."

"I surely do love this job," Andrews said. "I'm told Homeland Security could have EEOs flown up from Walnut Creek in a few hours."

"It would be wise to—" Rebecca began.

"We don't have time," Griff said.

"I thought you'd say that." Andrews walked around to the back of the truck and opened the gate, then pulled down a rack stuffed with rounded foot-high cylinders, six of them, striped black and yellow like the business end of a hornet. One by one, he plucked four from the rack and let them roll in the dust, inert. "How many of my little beauties do you want?"

"Two for now, one at a time," Griff said. "Best if they can squeeze through that opening without jiggling the barn door."

Andrews opened the aluminum case and pulled out earnodes and gogs. "We're on Lynx with bombnet and HDS," he said. "The bots will relay pretty good pictures. If they find anything, I suggest we just close the roads and blow the whole damned thing. You've got your man, right?"

"I want to see what he has in there," Griff said. "When he tried to blow my head off with his shotgun, he was happy. The last words he said were, 'Death to the Jews.'" *Well, not quite the last words. But it makes my point.*

"There aren't many Jews around here," Andrews said.

Griff stuck his hands in his pockets. Christ, he was tired. He just wanted this to be over, to find out how his son was doing at Quantico, to lie in bed and pull the covers up to his shoulders and breathe deeply of a dark quiet bedroom's home-scented air.

"Exactly," he said. "In his sixty active years, Robert Chambers worked with mobsters, the IRA, Thai smugglers, probably the Russians, and Aryan Nations. Is there anyone here who *isn't* curious about what he really meant, and who else he might be connected to?"

Watson raised her arm. "Me," she said like a student in class. She looked around the group. "Just joking."

Griff ignored her. "Can one of those fit through that opening?"

"I think so," Andrews said. "Armatec 9 D-11s and a D-12. They're smaller and cheaper than last year's models, and so far they're pretty damned good. Each one is a little different, you know. Custom programs, more and more independent. I've named them all." He upended one of the cans and unscrewed the container cover. Inside, folded and strapped into a compact unit, was a cross between a go-kart and a cockroach, with three wheels mounted on springs and pistons and five triple-jointed legs, two in the front and three in the rear. Andrews unlatched the bot and it stretched out with a hydraulic sigh. A pole as thick as a pencil rose from a lozenge-shaped "head" above a three-wheeled base plate. The head looked like the bridge on a toy ship. The pole thrust out two little black eyes on thin flexible stalks. A third eye was mounted on the pole itself, centered just below the stalks. Pressed into grooves behind the head were two retracted arms with graspers and cutters extensible from their tips. Griff, vaguely familiar with Armatec bots, looked for and saw the case that contained the scanner kit—fluoroscope and stethoscope, along with remote chemical analyzer. He also spotted two disruptors, slender barrels mounted behind the head designed to shoot slugs into bomb detonators. Unfolded, the bot was about fifteen inches long, with a wheelbase of six inches.

"This one's Kaczynski. These guys here are McVeigh and Nichols. And this one, the temperamental one, is Marilyn Monroe." Marilyn was bigger than the others.

Rebecca walked up to the nearest wooden post and examined the wires strung overhead. "I'll bet it's some sort of antenna. But it's new to me. No sign of it being wired to the barn, but the wires could be buried." Rebecca patted the post. Griff could not read her expression. "We're at solar max," she said. "Auroras all the way down to San Diego, prettiest I've ever seen— like a sign from God. Was the Patriarch the kind of guy who liked to watch the skies?"

CHAPTER TEN
Quantico

William walked briskly to the library to drop off two texts. Along the way, two agents in red shirts ran past double-time, heading for the lounge, eager to see the bombnet telecast. He was in no hurry. Bombs held little interest for him. Having to wait up long nights as a boy for his father to come home had cured him of any interest in blowing up model airplanes with firecrackers or concocting little pipe bombs to light off in the woods. There had of course been those weeks when Griff had taught him about fireworks . . . Odd, exciting weeks. He'd almost forgotten about them.

He passed part of the Academy art gallery—framed prints lining the walls, all realistic and comforting, landscapes and farms and domestic situations. These he liked well enough. They served as a perfect counterbalance to gory crime scene photos and shoot-'em-ups in training. *Why we fight.* His favorite was of a young blond girl tending a newborn calf in a grassy field. He paused for a moment in front of the framed print. He really wanted to be there with that girl and that calf.

William Griffin was aware he looked nothing like the typical FBI agent, if there is such a person. At six feet four inches tall, he certainly looked nothing like his father, a bluff, stocky bull of a man. Even after five years in the NYPD, William had acquired none of the solid decorum and steady, critical gaze of the good cop. Instead, his brown eyes tended to be sympathetic, humored, and friendly, and beneath a long, straight knife of a nose, his lips wore a perpetual, half-hidden smile.

He jogged up the stairs—PT had put him in great shape—dropped off the texts, and jogged down the stairs again, passing a glass case with some of the Academy's prizes on display. He had studied these artifacts many times in the past few months and knew them by heart: weapons manufactured from household items—including an ice pick with an incised groove for poison—bomb-making materials, dog-eared Arabic printouts of Al Qaeda manuals on killing and conducting terror operations confiscated from safe houses in Iraq, Germany, and England.

A meticulous model of an insect-carriage gunbot like the one that had almost killed his father in Portland.

The cases weren't changed out often. Everyone was too busy to look back over their shoulders. And here he was, in the shadow of legends—including his own father—coming across as a gangling, bright but not too savvy agent trainee who had buck fever and a wicked way with a cholo stick.

Still, he was doing okay. In two days he would graduate—by the skin of his teeth.

He picked up his pace, turned the corner and jogged past the chapel. Then a return loop back by the art gallery. Had these been Hoover's favorites? Not many students had much to say about Hoover. Most didn't remember him.

In the study lounge, chairs and couches had been pulled up in front of an old model plasma TV with lots of missing pixels. Some students were still studying. Others had firmly fixed their gazes on the spotty display.

William walked up behind Fouad, who was sitting straight up in one of the lounge's well-cushioned chairs. "Where's this?" William asked him.

"Washington state," Fouad said. "A farmhouse has been raided. The Patriarch, Robert Chambers, was killed in a shootout. Erwin Griffin, is he your father?"

William let out his breath. "Yeah," he said.

"Well, he is due to go into that barn and discover if there is a bomb. Everyone with bomb expertise is listening. It is very interesting, very frightening."

William pressed his teeth together and sat on the arm of Fouad's chair. *Saturday night at the Griffin household. "Griff's at it again," Mom would say, sitting at the dinner table with her son and an empty chair, a plate set out, on more than one occasion with tears streaming down her cheeks. "I can feel it. Can't you?"*

Then he recognized his father, seen from behind—stocky and poised, of medium height, standing with two others in front of a big barn. A shiny bomb squad truck with *Washington State Patrol* painted on its sides stood a few yards away. He could barely make out some robots arranged on the ground around the truck.

William heard the subdued conversations from bombnet. All the heroes were chitchatting, trying to work out the deadly puzzle, to figure out how his father might die and try to prevent it from happening.

William could not just turn away. Family honor.

"May I sit here?" he asked Fouad.

"I am proud to have you," Fouad said, and meant it. There was respect in his upturned eyes. "Your father shot the Patriarch. He is very brave."

CHAPTER ELEVEN
Washington State

Chippy found nothing in the two houses. Vogel took her back to the edge of the clearing with her tail between her legs, then tossed her a rubber ball for a few minutes before loading her back into her travel cage.

Watson, Rebecca, and Griff hunkered down behind blast shields about fifty yards from the barn—a trivial distance. At the edge of the clearing, more police and agents squatted behind their vehicles. They could all see Kaczynski's—the bot's—progress toward the door.

Griff tapped his gogs. The images from Kaczynski were sharp—better than bomb suit video. The bot paused at the opening, then turned around on its wheels, giving Griff a view of their own position—three black rectangles with heads bobbing behind tiny plastic windows.

Even from outside the barn, the bot's minitrace was off the scale. There was no hint of plastique, Semtex, or any more recent explosives, but the barn's air was redolent with a number of suspicious substances: diesel fuel, urea nitrate, particulate carbon that could have been from recent fires or explosions. There could be alternate explanations for most of these traces, however—it was after all a barn and fuel and fertilizer were to be expected. The particulate carbon could have come from a barbecue.

"Are we ready?" Andrews asked from the back of the bomb squad truck.

"Do it," Griff said, then took a breath and held it, hardly aware he was doing so.

Rebecca moved from a crouch to a kneel behind the blast shield and braced her hands on the ground.

Kaczynski walked through the nine-inch opening, quieter than any mouse. At first, the bot's cameras revealed little more than bouncing splotches and bars of sunlight. Processors adjusted the picture. Details emerged and contrast smoothed.

The barn was big, empty of animals, but most of the stalls and an overhead hayloft were stacked high with containers—bottled water, sacks of sugar and what looked like barrels of wheat, rice and other grains. The Patriarch had been well-prepared for the Endtime.

The three behind the bomb shields listened to the conversation inside the truck. "Can you make a bomb out of wheat?" asked a younger tech, new to the division.

Andrews whuffed. "You ever work a grain elevator?" As he guided the bot, Andrews reminisced about his younger days in Wyoming, when he had witnessed a mishandled load of wheat puff out a dusty fog. A spark from a pump motor had ignited the flour/air mixture and blown the silo cap two hundred feet into the air. Two loaders had been killed and the concrete building had split down its length. "Don't underestimate the calories in a cup of flour, my friend," Andrews said.

Griff tapped his gogs again. After a while, he couldn't see the displays clearly—the problem with aging eyes. With a glance at Rebecca, he whipped off the display glasses and stuck them in his pocket. "The hell with this." He rose from behind the shield—crouching was playing hell with his knees—and hustled across the short distance to the bomb squad truck. Watson followed.

Rebecca removed her own gogs and joined them. The back of the truck was crowded. Watson grudgingly moved aside for her. They stepped around bomb suits arranged in clear plastic packages on the floor.

"Welcome to bot central," Andrews said. "Hope you're not claustrophobic."

Griff was, a little.

The small space stank of adrenaline-pumped fear.

"Don't you guys use deodorant?" Watson asked. Griff knew well the sharp, stewy pong. He had become familiar with the smell of frightened men first in combat overseas and later in many tight stateside situations, and he hated it.

They had all learned to work at peak efficiency despite the fear and the smell.

"Pardon me," Andrews said.

The young technician grinned and moved forward, sitting on a steel box.

Inside the Patriarch's barn, the bot called Kaczynski had paused before what looked like an abstract sculpture—metal tubes welded in bristling clumps on a central steel ball. The bot's cameras angled down. The whole arrangement was mounted on a wheeled platform. A tow bar stuck out from one end.

"What in hell is that?" Griff asked, his voice soft.

"A calliope?" Andrews guessed.

Watson pressed her lips together.

Gray cylinders of pressurized gas thrust up behind the wheeled platform. The bot's camera played over them in up-and-down sweeps. Rebecca was looking for labels. "No color-codes," she murmured. "Could be anything. We're going to have to pull his welding license."

The sensors were negative for acetylene as well as propane and methane. The lack of methane in itself—in a barn—showed that ruminants had not lived there for some time. The bot pulled itself around the abstract metal object and down an aisle between empty stalls. Griff was focused on the display when the image took a jerk. In the corner of their gogs, a red dot blinked.

"What now?" Griff asked.

Andrews said, "The bot's located something moving." He turned up the sound: harsh breathing, frightened little gasps. Then the dot stopped blinking.

"Bot's decided it could be human," Andrews said.

The camera image stabilized long enough on the interior of a stall to show a flash of reddish blond hair, then a small, blurred figure. The figure dashed out of view.

"Did you catch that?" Griff asked.

"Looked like a little girl," Watson said.

They saw quick blue flashes and heard three distant popping sounds in rapid succession. As they all cringed and hunkered, Kaczynski's displays blanked.

It took a few seconds for them to relax. The barn had not taken flight.

Andrews fumbled at controls. "Shit," he said. "Bot's down."

"What, did somebody shoot it?" Watson asked.

Andrews shook his head. "I think we tripped a fryer. I'm getting nothing."

Fryers were clever little generators of electromagnetic pulses, essentially arrays of hundreds of high-powered, needle-shaped electromagnets that would jam out through a molded lattice of nickel and copper when a small internal ball of explosives went off. In the last few years fryers had been miniaturized for use by terrorists in England, Spain, and Saudi Arabia. They shorted out all solid-state electronics within ten meters. It was difficult to shield bomb robots sufficiently to avoid damage.

Fryers were used by terrorists who wanted to force humans to confront their bombs in person.

Andrews looked around the little trailer and raised his hands from the controls. "I can send in another," he said, his eyes sad.

"No need," Griff said. "We all saw her. There's a child in there, probably a little girl."

Rebecca sighed. "Did they forget her?"

"Maybe she didn't want to go to church," Griff said. "It happens. Too many kids and you lose track." He stood up, shoulders and neck bowed to fit under the roof. His booted toe nudged one of the suits. They were Ang-Sorkin Systems EOD-23 models, made in New Zealand and now standard around the world. EOD referred to Explosive Ordnance Disposal. "Time to fit me out with one of these."

"No way," Andrews said. "This isn't your squad." His expression said it all: the FBI agent was older and a bit on the heavy side. Nobody wanted to go in after a guy who'd had a stroke or a heart attack—and if either of these things happened while he was handling a detonator, there would be no need.

"I'll go," Rebecca said.

"Well, hell, if you'll pardon me—" Andrews began.

Griff put his fingers to his lips, let out a shrill whistle that had them holding their ears. He raised a beefy hand. "I'm in charge. And if it means anything, I was once rated a Master Blaster in Navy EOD."

"No kidding?" Andrews said. "Crab and laurels? And how old were you then?"

Griff's lip twitched. "I used to teach at Redstone. That's how I got assigned to the Patriarch. I'm the lead going in, and because I am old and feeble, and may not be up on the hottest new techniques, one of you can come with me." He eeny-meeny-miny-moed with a thick finger around the back of the bomb van between Rebecca, Andrews, and Watson.

Griff's finger stopped at Watson, as he had known it would. He pointed to the suits.

"Oh, goody," Watson said.

Rebecca started to speak but Griff swiveled and cupped his hand over her mouth. She glared over his thick fingers. "You can tell me what to look for," he said. "Tell me what I'm seeing. Okay?"

Rebecca removed his hand with two delicate fingers.

"Sorry," Griff said, brows furrowed.

"Sorry won't cut it if we lose our evidence," Rebecca said.

"Yes, ma'am," he said. "Thanks for caring."

Griff radioed the agents up the road and told them to keep a close watch on the perimeter in case anyone tried to enter or leave. If the girl fled the barn while they were inside they'd pull out and resume robot operations.

Andrews and the tech helped them suit up, a process that took ten minutes. The last step—putting on the aerodynamically curved face-plate and locking it to the chest rig—always made Griff feel like a deep-sea diver. Rip-and-zip could peel them out of the suits in less than twenty seconds if they needed to run away—otherwise, they'd be clumping around like big clumsy beetles.

Griff looked through the thick plastic plate at Rebecca Rose. Her quiet anger comforted him.

"You're my good luck charm, Becky," he said.

"Screw you," Rebecca said, not unkindly.

In the twilight, the bombot approached the barn door, rammed a metal arm against the edge, dug in, and pushed the door back so they could enter. Wheels on the rusty track squealed in protest and the door shivered as it slid open, but that was all.

Through his face-plate, Griff could see nothing in the gap. Just a dark and empty yawn.

"What if there is no little girl?" Alice Watson asked as they waddled toward the barn. Her voice came through his earnode like a buzzing fly. "Wouldn't that be a hoot?"

The bomb truck kicked on a floodlight and trained the intense blue beam into the entrance. A row of stalls and the cart with its strange, bundled pipe sculpture stood revealed in the harsh light. Beyond, like serried paper cutouts against velvety blackness, stood workbenches, cylinders, hanging ropes—a hoist and pulley.

Griff turned and surveyed the farmhouse, the yard, the nearly black ridgelines hackled with trees, the deep blue of the dusk sky with cottony rips of yellow and orange cloud. He tried to find the gap where the fire tower now stood revealed. He could not. It was late, and his eyes were not sharp enough.

No doubt he was missing other things as well.

"Me first," he told Watson. "Stay out of my spray line."

Below glossy nested plates and front pads, the Ang-Sorkin suits were jacketed with water-filled micro-piping that networked around the exposed front surfaces and exited through sealed blow holes along the back. The shock front of an explosion, as it met the smooth plastic curves of the front pads, would find little purchase. Particles carried by the blast, including shrapnel, would dimple the plates and possibly even pierce them—but all but the largest and sharpest pieces would be stopped by an underlying layer of monocarbon fiber. What gaseous force—and force from shrapnel—did not flow around the suits and faceplate—still a major proportion of the blast pressure—would compress the micro-piping beneath those layers and heat the water to steam, which would then jet from the rear of the suit in hundreds of gaseous needles. Within six or eight inches, those water needles would be sharp enough to cut holes in human skin or pierce another suit. You always stayed out of someone's spray line.

Bomb suits had become very sophisticated. But entering the barn at a deliberate plod, Griff did not feel much safer. He might as well have wrapped himself in Kleenex like a Halloween mummy. Or faced a howitzer in a brown paper bag.

Suit cameras—two mounted to face fore and aft, and a third focusing exclusively on a point less then a meter in front of their breastplates—conveyed some of what they were seeing back to the bomb squad truck and the bombnet viewers. Gimbaled lamps mounted above their face-plates silently played beams of light wherever their eyes were looking. A small heads-up display mounted below the chin projected data abstracted from the video the bot had captured before being fried. The bomb squad computers in the truck had already used enhancement techniques to outline and identify the objects recorded during the bot's few minutes inside the barn, and marked them on a floorplan.

Griff found the white and pink map distracting and switched it off using his tongue mouse. Once inside, he could see well enough. The barn had been converted into what looked like a basic engineering shop. A metal-working lathe and drill press covered a wooden workbench behind the pipe sculpture. He was starting to think of the weird shape on its cart as the Calliope, just for reference. "We're passing the Calliope now," he said. "Looks like it might have been made to disperse powder or water—sort of like a big sprayer or fountain." He was thinking of the powder on the trees. "Maybe they used it for pesticide."

"Pipes are too big," Watson said. "They're more like mortars. It could be some sort of hedgehog—a launcher. Could take out a city block if it was lobbing shells."

Griff made sure to pause before each area. "Alice is right. Not a sprayer."

If he didn't make it, someone could use the video to figure out what had killed him. They advanced to the workbench, then turned. The bench was littered with tools—wooden and rubber mallets, split tube-shaped molds lying open, tamping implements, scraps of foil and paper, brushes.

"Not very tidy," Watson said.

"They didn't get a chance to clean up everything," Griff observed. "Maybe we moved in faster than they expected."

But they had been burning trash in barrels all week . . .

The power outlets had been masked off with duct tape and gummy spark-stop plastic. They would inspect all this in detail later, after they had found the girl. Watson took the lead down the broad aisle between the rows of stalls. She called out, "If there's anyone in here, you need to come out. We got to evacuate this barn, honey. It could be dangerous, you hear me?"

The bot stood frozen in the middle of the aisle. Mounted to posts on each side, at knee level, were two fryers. Watson bent to inspect the bot. Griff put his hands on his knees and stooped to look at the fryer mechanisms. His helmet light played over them. They resembled wind-up toys with burned heads. The posts had been charred by the heat of their small charges. They were home-made, possibly with German or Italian parts. The whole world was mad against authority.

He rose and said, "You got that?"

"Got it," said Andrews' voice in his ear. "Are there any more?"

"I don't see any." Griff nudged the bot with the toe of his boot. It slumped like a freshly killed spider.

Watson stood gingerly, hands pushing on her thickly padded knees. "He's dead, Jim," she said.

Griff's heel scraped aside some straw. Beneath the straw, a thin strip of metal tape had been stretched between the posts. He pushed aside more straw. Not only did the tape connect the posts—and the fryers—but a longer strip almost certainly ran the length of the barn. He continued scraping for a few feet to make sure. The tape took a zig-zag course between the stalls.

"Got this?" he asked Andrews.

"Simple enough," Andrews said. "Bot crosses the tape, sets off the fryers."

"And what else?" Rebecca asked.

The stalls were the right size for horses, with metal gates that provided good views of the interiors. One contained large bales of straw wrapped in what looked like oil cloth or some sort of rubberized fabric.

Buffers for observing explosives from a safe distance.

"You thinking what I'm thinking?" Watson asked.

Griff nodded. "Tell the boys back home."

Watson explained what she thought the bales might be.

"Right," Andrews said.

Everything they did here was chancy. If the barn was "alive"—if any more devices carried sound or motion sensors—then they were probably already dead, though still walking around.

The possible presence of the little girl lent some small assurance. Unless, of course, she had entered the barn against express orders. Children were capable of that. Griff wondered what sort of punishment the families meted out to their kids. Perhaps they were caring and gentle. He hoped so. Even bigots loved their children.

He could feel his testicles drawing up, his scrotum shrinking as they approached the last of the stalls. They had found little so far. Maybe the Patriarch and his sons had wired things in the hayloft or up in the rafters. High above, birds flew in and out through the beams and struts, their cheeping faint through his helmet.

Maybe the little girl had come to the barn to watch the birds, to spy out nests. Griff scraped aside more straw to confirm that the tape ran the entire length of the building. It did, in slow, loping curves. Very clever.

Griff pictured taking long lines of clever people with many different faces and expressions, and whacking crowbars over their pointy little heads. Oddly, he included Jacob Levine in that lineup, just because he had ID'd the Patriarch, thereby confirming their suspicions and placing them right here in this barn.

Alice Watson once more called out for the little girl. He could hear Watson's breath in one ear, slow and steady. "I don't think there's any little girl," she said. She had an odd, appealing accent caused by the stiffness in one side of her face. Funny he hadn't found it appealing before now. "I think we're chasing spooks."

"We'll see," Griff said. He was looking ahead three or four meters to a trap door half-covered with old straw, at the end of the aisle in the back of the barn. To the left was a rustic wooden Dutch door leading into what at one time might have been a feed or tack room. To the right, a vestibule that still held an old tractor. Behind the tractor was another door, shut and padlocked from the inside.

"Want to start up that tractor, Alice?" Griff asked.

"I ain't going near it," she said.

"They could use the tractor to haul that Calliope outside," Griff said. "I'm wondering why, though."

"Fireworks," Watson said. They slowly turned to face each other. "Shit," she added, grinning.

"I should have thought of that." Griff held up a thickly gloved thumb. "Hey, listen up, guys. Alice just set off a little light bulb."

"We heard," Andrews said. "Watch for devices triggered by bright ideas."

"Well, why didn't we think of it earlier?" Watson asked. "Portable fireworks launcher. Atta girl," she added quietly. Then, "Why?"

"Any theories, Becky?" Griff asked.

"Keep looking," Rebecca said.

Griff had reached the trap door. It was off its hinges, if it had ever had hinges, and was pushed to one side, leaving open a knife-shaped triangle. He estimated that the door was light enough he could push it aside with one boot if he had to.

At this end of the barn, and probably the other end as well, the floor was made of wood. In the middle, he had been pretty sure he was walking over concrete. At some point, no doubt many years ago, the barn had been expanded on both sides.

Beneath the trap door Griff could make out a wooden ramp leading down into the darkness under the floor. The long strip of metal tape had been glued to another strip that ran down the middle of the ramp.

A small child could have crawled through the gap. But a small child would not have needed a piece of metal tape to guide her.

CHAPTER TWELVE
Temecula, California

The trip west into the hills lasted several hours. Sam drove smoothly and steadily. Tommy slumped in the passenger seat wearing a fixed look of light concern. He chose his faces with care and often wore them for some time.

They approached the winery by a gravel road as the sun dropped below the oak-crowned hills. The air was hot and dusty and smelled of dry brush. The old vineyards stretched to their left, undulating rows of stakes and dead gnarled vines almost covered with grass and weeds—well over eighty acres, left to rot.

Sam turned the El Camino up the long, tree-shaded drive. Half-dead ivy covered the northeast side of the single-story, Spanish-style stucco house. Recent rains had greened some of the overgrown front lawn. Tommy's aunt had placed plaster gnomes out front and they grinned amid the grass and weeds like happy dwarf guerillas. The house's big picture windows were marked by rivulets through a thin layer of dust.

Behind the house rose three winery warehouses and equipment sheds, their gray steel sides catching the last of the daylight.

Tommy turned to look at Sam. "I'm sorry. I overreacted, Sam. I didn't '*think*.'" He fingered quote-marks in the air. "I was taught to be polite, really, but I've been alone for so many years. You know that."

"I know, Tommy."

"I'm supposed to ask, '*were you hurt?*'"

"Not really. I skinned my knuckles."

"That's good. If you're okay, then we don't have to go to a hospital. That will save us some time. I'm sorry."

"We're fine, Tommy. Both of us."

"We'll figure out another timetable, won't we?"

"I doubt we'll even have to worry about that."

"Good." Tommy sighed dramatically. "Well then, that's over." He opened the door and got out. Sam pushed the button on the remote clipped to the visor. The garage door swung up with a creaking song of coil springs, revealing a bright red Dodge truck and a double-wide horse trailer.

Sam remained in the El Camino with the engine running, considering how close to failure they actually were. He watched Tommy walk around the side of the house and up the step to the front door. The man-boy's shoulders were slumped but he was doing much better. He was *lost in thought*.

It was, after all, a nutty idea, from start to finish—the kind of idea a disappointed man might dream about, tossing and winding up sheets in the dark of the night. The kind of plan a grieving man might consider when his life seemed pointless and the hours dragged on, and then got lost—time that simply vanished in large chunks, day after day, irretrievable.

Tommy was not the only one who could go Dipsy-Down.

Sam took his foot off the brake, slipped the El Camino in gear, and slowly pulled forward to the right of the horse trailer. The garage door closed and he sat in the dim orange light of the opener's single low-watt bulb.

He could not shake the memory of the cone-shaped explosion of blood and the officer spinning to the side of the road.

People had paid a severe price. The gears were turning. This wasn't just about Sam and Tommy.

"They have to listen to God," Sam murmured as he opened the door to the house. "They have to forget their hate and listen."

Near the end of his other life, five years ago, Sam had first met Tommy. He had driven out to the house and knocked on the front door and announced that he wanted Tommy's help.

Tommy had been desperate for company. The time for confession, it seemed, had arrived. Tommy had wanted to explain himself and all that he had done and why.

Sam had accepted Tommy's offer of a tour of the winery. It could have been the biggest break of Sam's career. Tommy had been pitifully vulnerable, telling his story with hyperactive enthusiasm . . . and then, without warning, as they drank orange juice in the big kitchen, Tommy had crashed and burned.

Utterly terrified by what he had revealed to a stranger, Tommy had fled and hidden under a blanket in his smelly, crowded bedroom. Sam had followed the man-boy, had seen the walls covered with bookshelves, posters, and magazine pictures of Jennifer Lopez—J-Lo, the queen of Tommy's inner sanctum.

Around his twin bed, Tommy had piled stacks of texts and magazines, their edges bursting with color-coded Post-it notes.

Sam had watched the man-boy cower and a switch had turned on in his head. He had followed the path between the bedroom stacks and put his hand on Tommy's shoulder. "What a brave, brave man," he had soothed. "Do I *ever* understand. A brilliant guy like you. They all want a piece of you, don't they? Let's go back to the living room. Let's talk. I bet that together, you and I can work this out."

Tommy had pulled back the covers and peered out at Sam like some pink, wet-faced gargoyle. "Not really," he had said.

"Really," Sam had said.

Tommy had sat up. "You believe me?"

"What's not to believe?"

"You want to see more?" Tommy had asked, wiping away the slicks of moisture below his eyes and nose.

Sam had realized he had the power. Tommy was his. This was the find of a career—something that could change everything for him.

Or it was the find of a lifetime. Something that could change everything, for everybody.

"Show me as much as you like," Sam had said. "I'd like to see it all."

CHAPTER THIRTEEN
Quantico

"They're going down."

William hunched and rubbed his jaw to keep it from aching. There was little enough to see on the screen—blurry images from the two helmet cams, people sitting in the back of the bomb squad truck. And little enough to hear—bombnet had fallen mostly silent back in Eglin and Redstone and Washington, DC.

The students were transfixed. This is what some of them would end up doing unless they made some serious decisions right now. But William could tell. They were into it. They were as focused and intent as if they were on the actual scene, offering helpless murmurs of advice to their onscreen counterparts. They were already thinking like agents. William was scared as hell. That was his father in there, once again risking his life, unconcerned about family or friends—duty was all.

Duty came first every single goddamned time, no matter how much it might cost.

That had made William angry when he was a boy. Now, he didn't know which side to come down on. Because he was sure that his father was having another big damned adventure. Another day in the life of a hero. Jack Armstrong, all-seeing, all-knowing G-Man, Jimmy Stewart with a biker's build.

"I will stand," Fouad said, getting up. "You will sit."

"Thanks," William said. His legs were shaky. He replaced Fouad in the chair. Fouad stood beside him, arms crossed.

"I hate the suspense," Fouad said. "I am here for it, but I hate it."

"Thanks," William said again, but he wasn't paying much attention.

The pictures from the helmet cams had brightened and the experts at Eglin were talking again, speculating on the wires and posts outside the barn, the fryers, the long stretch of tape, and why Griff was still going after a little girl.

CHAPTER FOURTEEN
Washington State

Griff took a deep breath. He was starting to feel the old claustrophobia—unable to catch a deep breath, the sensation that first his nostrils and then his throat would close up and he would suffocate. Bomb suits always had that effect on him—the warmth, his stale breath bouncing back from the faceplate, the squeezing closeness of all the armor and the weight, more and more overbearing.

Andrews was suddenly in his ear. The volume seemed to have gone up. Griff was sensitive to all sounds. "I'm patching through George Schell from Eglin."

Schell had gone with Griff through EOD school at Redstone. He was a short whippet-wire guy with thinning hair and sharp gray eyes and a quick temper that miraculously vanished when he worked around ordnance.

"Griff, we've been discussing this in the room here," Schell said, "and we've come up with a crazy idea. Have you ever heard of Alfvén waves?"

"No," Griff said, annoyed. "I don't pay much attention to hairstyles."

"This is physics," Schell said. "Listen up. We're going through a major solar storm. They can trigger electrical currents in power grids. Alfvén waves. I don't see how a few acres of strung wire can pull in much of a current, but then, it might not take much, right? Do you see anything like a spark gap, something that could be a low-amp, high-voltage fuse?"

"No," Griff said. Then, to be polite—and because, frankly, the idea made his stomach churn—he added, "Not yet."

"I knew it," Watson said, under her breath. "Like Rose said. He was watching the skies."

"Hush," Griff said. "George, explain this dumb idea to me." *Clever people. Just shoot them all.*

"Let's say we get a big pulse from space," Schell said. "The wires on the posts could pick up a current and feed it into the barn. The current could be strong enough to set off a fuse or trigger something else."

Andrews added, "I'm standing outside the truck. It's completely dark and I can see the aurora, Griff. It's spectacular. There's a big pink and orange corona overhead. It's like staring up at God's eye. Maybe it's just me, but He looks unhappy."

"Fuck," Alice Watson said.

"Is this idea credible?" Griff asked.

"You told Andrews this was the Patriarch's piece de resistance," Schell said, using English not French pronunciation. "He's been making bombs for sixty years. You tell me what's credible."

"Amen," Watson said.

Griff gave her a critical squint. "Bombers don't play dice with timers or fuses," he said. "How would he know it wouldn't go off while his family was still here?"

"He might have flipped a switch as soon as you drove up," Schell said. "Put his fate in God's hands. And yours, too. Isn't that his style?"

"Pull out, Griff," Andrews said. His voice was steady but Griff could tell. "Let 'em drop a doodlebug."

"Divine whim," Watson said, dead-pan. "God is the timer. Very clever. You boys are scaring me." She was facing him from the other side of the trap door.

"That's nuts," Griff murmured. "God doesn't make lights in the sky. Magnetic fields and particles do that, right?"

"If you say so," Schell said. "What would the Patriarch think?"

Death to the Jews. Griff walked around the trap door. He was beginning to have real doubts about there being a little girl anywhere in the barn. But he had to make sure. She might have gone down into the basement to hide. The Patriarch would have certainly taught his children to be afraid of police, of government agents. There might not be enough time to get the big bot in here to move that hatch—certainly not time enough for them to reach minimum safe distance if the hatch was hot.

He wanted us to go deeper, see a little more of what he was up to. The trap door is not rigged.

Twenty years he had worked on the Patriarch's case. Twenty years of his life, off and on, hunting down an elusive mystery—how and why—until he thought he knew the man without ever having met him. The profiler's illusion, of course, is that his work is a science. Illusions are like thick layers of fat. They slow you down and eventually they kill you.

"The wire runs the length of the barn," he told Andrews and the boys and girls across the country, on bombnet. "It jumps to a board ramp and probably goes all the way down to the floor of the cellar."

"Could be double-stranded tape, live current and ground," Schell said. Bombnet had appointed him spokesperson. "Do you think it's attached to a charge?"

"I think it's a guide tape for some sort of mechanism," Watson said, and challenged Griff to contradict her. He did not. Instead, he said,

"I'll go down there and find the girl. We won't need two. Back out of here, Alice." He meant that literally. The bomb suits worked best facing a blast.

"You first," Alice said. "I'll hold your mitt."

"You really believe this stuff about elf-vane waves?" Griff called out, louder than necessary. "I'm looking at a trap door. I think the girl might be hiding down there."

Andrews spoke up again. "Bombnet wants you out of there. They think Schell's boys have come up with a credible theory. Some of the guys have pulled out their electrical textbooks and calculators, but their gut says it could be done. Redstone, Eglin, Washington—one and all, Griff. It's unanimous."

"The Patriarch wants to tell me something," Griff said. "He'll try to make me pay, but I think it's going to be interesting."

"What the fuck does that mean?" Schell said, his voice skipping in and out. Satellite communications were suffering—that's how big the solar storm was, way above them, up in God's cruel heaven. The aurora was just a sideshow.

The video feed from their helmet cams was probably suffering, as well.

"Law enforcement officers make irrational decisions if they've been through a bout of depression," Schell added. "Their priorities get all screwed up. They act out resentments . . . taking risks. Cap Benson tells me . . . from depression."

"Who the hell hasn't in this business?" Griff asked. Was it true? Was there a death-wish here? *I honestly don't think so. I'd like to see William graduate from the Academy. I'd like to see him prove his asshole father was wrong.* "Cap, stop telling tales out of court."

"Sorry, Griff. Just get out of there."

"There was something big going on down here. Don't you feel it? I'd like to know what it is, wouldn't you?"

"No," Andrews said.

"Screw it, Griff," Rebecca said. "I'm not seeing anything of interest. Get out. We'll do everything we can to grab evidence later."

"Griff, everyone here—" Schell was saying.

"Well, I'd like to find the girl and look around a bit, and then I'll get out, pronto." Silence on bombnet. Griff could imagine Schell stomping and cursing in that faraway room, or just standing there—shaking his head.

"We're on our own, Alice," Griff said. "You feeling depressed?"

"No, sir," Watson said. "I want to see what's down there."

"A basement beneath an old barn. I'm sure it's a wonderland."

Watson grinned. But then, she was always grinning. Her mishap had left her looking like death's girlfriend.

He reached the toe of his boot under the trap door and worked to push it aside. It scraped out a hollow groan as it moved. Watson aimed her light. The ramp was a long one. The basement was big.

Griff fought back against the sensation that the suit was clamping down on him. *Fear is the mind-killer,* he told himself, quoting from a novel he had read as a teenager. *Fear is the Little Death.*

But another voice was telling him, *Fuck that. The Big Sleep is a lot worse than the Little Death.*

"The brain's a bitch," Watson said, "you know that?"

Griff chuckled. That's why he had chosen Watson. When they worked these situations together, she always seemed to know just what he was thinking. The ramp board was wide and thick and felt sturdy. He figured it could hold him and the bomb suit, but not the both of them. "I'll go first," he said.

"By all means," Watson said, with a stuffed-sausage kind of curtsey. She steadied his arm as he got up on the board. From that point on it was an awkward little ballet, shuffling sideways, feeling the board bend, wondering if carpenter ants or termites had been busy down there.

Watson watched as the darkness swallowed him. His helmet light plunged off into the gloom like a smudge of white chalk. After an impossibly long time, hours it seemed, he reached a solid floor.

"All right, I'm down."

"Back off the board. I'm coming," Watson said.

He turned to his right. The stalls above were echoed by stalls below. He turned left. Just a few feet away, something moved—something he could not make out, that he saw but that his brain could not analyze. The plastic in the face-plate reduced and distorted visual cues. He lifted his head slightly to put the outer glow of helmet light on the object.

Watson seemed to descend in record time. Her light flared across his own.

"Jesus H. Christ. Hold off," he said, raising an arm.

"What is it?" she asked.

He began to take a step forward, then stopped. Attractive objects lured you through tripwires. You never reach the object or solve the puzzle. "I found our little girl."

A cardboard cutout of a child with a red wig on top had been mounted on a motorized toy offroad vehicle. The big toy was still faintly whirring and butting against a concrete wall. The vehicle had followed the taped path, carrying the bewigged shape out of an upper stall, through the barn, and down the ramp like a target in a shooting gallery. Simple enough and effective. A small music player had been duct-taped to the back of the toy. It was still making weak little sobbing sounds.

"What set it moving?" Watson asked. "A timer?"

"Our bot crossed the tape," Griff guessed. "A few seconds delay—then, bang, the fryers."

The stick supporting the cutout slipped to one side and the silhouette fell to the floor, setting loose the toy to whir into a corner like a frustrated bug. It dragged the flat image in a half-circle. Then its motor stopped. The music player stopped as well.

The cellar was quiet—except for another, more distant whirring sound.

"There's no little girl," Watson told the people outside.

"Copy that," Andrews said. He sounded exhausted.

Oddly, other than feeling hemmed in, confined in his own protective coffin, Griff was not doing too badly. He was no longer tired. This place was interesting. The trap door opened through the wood floor on the north end. Where he stood now, the floor directly above was probably four or five inches of reinforced concrete. North and south, the floor above was not concrete, but wood over frame—both ends of the barn.

He swiveled his light. In the beam the air looked foggy. He aimed the light higher. Back in the truck they would see the video. They would see almost everything he was seeing. (But what about the interference? He could not answer that, so he ignored it.) Glittery dark powder fell from a series of long wire racks suspended on ropes just below the concrete ceiling.

Somewhere, a small electric motor was humming with a ratchety rhythm.

"Do you hear that?" he asked Watson.

"I do," she said. Her light fell on gallon-sized steel cans and bulging sacks piled in one corner, not unlike the sacks of flour and sugar upstairs, but wrapped in clear plastic. A toppled can had spilled brownish chunky powder across the otherwise bare dark gray floor. Griff lifted a can. He scanned the label. A stylized swallow hovered over the brand name and description,

Crumbled Yeast
Product of France
EU Export License 2676901

"Yeast," Watson said. "You ever bake bread, Griff?"

"I've made beer," he murmured. "Was that what they were doing down here? Hey, Becky—should we call in the revenooers?"

No answer. He chuckled just to give himself an audience.

Twelve workbenches had been arranged in rows along the south side of the basement. They looked worn and splintery and dark. Watson's feet raised puffs. The floor was coated with the glittering powder, not yeast. Beyond the tables stood a long trough or sink and suspended beside the sink, a long wooden box topped with a sheet of transparent plastic. Holes cut through the sheet still held inverted black rubber gloves.

"That's a glove box," Rebecca said. "Look around that area."

"I don't see any expensive equipment," Griff said after a moment. "Maybe they took it with them."

Watson pinched a wrinkled blue and yellow piece of plastic off one of the benches. It unfolded into a protective hood with a transparent face-sheet. A corrugated plastic tube—made to be attached to an air supply—dangled from the back of the hood.

"Part of a biohazard suit," Rebecca said.

"What the hell were they making down here?" Watson asked.

"Not beer," Griff said. "Chambers didn't drink."

In the stall across the aisle, wooden boxes marked in Chinese had been stacked—supplies for fireworks, possibly. An ax leaning against the wall had been used to break some of the boxes into kindling. Molds covered a plastic shelving unit—bigger molds cut in half longitudinally from pieces of metal pipe, smaller ones carved from pieces of wood—for packing charges.

A regular clandestine whizbang factory.

Brewer, baker, candlestick maker . . .

In a stall to his right, he saw a pile of plastic parts, topped with what

looked like the workings from a computer printer—thin bars of steel forming a track within a carriage, a plastic ribbon striped with copper leads dangling to one side. Three ink capsule holders lay near the back of the bench,
wrapped in baggies.

"Closer in, please," Rebecca said.

"Some sort of computer printer," Griff said, and turned.

"Go back, Griff. Let me see the brand."

Griff obliged. "Epson, I think," he said. "Older model. What's it to
you?"

"How many?"

"Just this one, so far."

In the next stall, two box kites leaned worn and ragged in a corner,
frames snapped and tangled up with string.

For checking wind direction.

Griff shook his head, a useless gesture behind the helmet plate. A filthy
gray place. Junk everywhere, but with a pattern, a selectivity—not the normal accumulation of debris from farm life. If only he could figure out the
pattern.

His light stabbed down at something broad and white on the gray dirt
floor. He tried to focus on it.

"Can you guys see this?" he asked. There was no answer, only a digital
speckle of notes. He bent over, reached down as best he could—but his hand
could not reach the ground. He would have to kneel. Slowly, gingerly, he
got down on one knee and lifted the edge of a strip of paper. It was part of a
city map. It had been torn in thirds, the rips following the folds, and leaving
behind only part of the name of the city.

-esia, Ohio

"Can you see this?" he asked again, holding up the paper in his lamp.

"It's fuzzy," Schell said. "Not enough resolution, and besides, we're losing—"

More digital bird-notes.

Watson peered over his shoulder. Her gloved hand touched the partial
name of the city, brushing away gray dust and sparkles. "What are these?"
she asked, her thick mitt following red arrows and curved lines advancing
over the interrupted streets.

"Wind direction," Griff said. "Drift."

*The wire grid. The powder on the leaves. They could have been measuring
wind drift in the yard. But what were they packing in the charges?*

Yeast?

He got to his feet, trying to fold the map and put it in his pouch. He smelled something like ethanol and singed rubber.

Watson leaned back and again aimed her light high. The air was fogged by drifting curtains of sparkling dust. Griff saw it then. He saw it all. The frames hanging from the ceiling were being vibrated by an electric motor. A few yards in front of him, he saw and understood the device, the arrangement—a short rubber pulley, an off-center cam with a jiggling post, thin cords attached to all the frames. The dust was falling through fine holes punched in aluminum foil laid in the frame troughs.

The entire apparatus was like a gigantic flour sifter.

At the far end of the room, behind the workbenches, something sizzled. In the corner of his eye, Griff saw a tiny flash of light. In the suit, he had to move like the Stay-Puft marshmallow man. He faced the south wall with three ponderous steps. Two wires had been strapped vertically to the rough concrete wall, inches apart. They looked like copper centipedes.

"That is sure as hell a spark gap," Watson said. "Let's—" She was interrupted by another sizzle as a loop of electricity surged. It curled and snapped between the ends of the wires and then stopped.

Griff let out his breath.

The strip of map fell from his gloved hands.

Fine dark gray powder lay an eighth of an inch thick all over the floor. The sifters had been vibrating for at least thirty minutes—filling the air with a fog of tiny particles.

He moved toward one of the stalls. "Rip-and-zip," he told Watson. "Let's get out of here."

"It's partly aluminum powder," Watson said. She held up her gloved hand and brushed it with a thick finger. Her voice was childlike, filled with discovery. "Mixed with shellac or rubber, maybe. Jesus, Griff—isn't that what they use for solid rocket boosters?"

"Get behind a wall," he said, watching the spark gap.

"Screw this," Watson said, her voice going up a notch.

He could no longer see the back of the cellar. The fog was too thick. He could see the sparks, however, reaching out like greedy white fingers in the murk.

He began to pull at the releases. They might make it if they ran as fast as they could up the ramp and out of the barn. Dropping and flattening a few yards from the barn, they might survive—if they weren't hit by shrapnel or falling debris.

He could imagine the pathways of the force—echoing, compressing, like a monster pushing up with its shoulders, doubling in size each thousandth of a second. The blast would shove against the reinforced concrete, squeeze between the ceiling and the walls, escape through the wood floor at each end, then blow out the concrete floor and lift the entire barn like a cracker box.

Alice tore at her releases in the gray billowing pall.

The gleeful sparks leaped. He would not get out of the suit fast enough. It was so quiet in the basement—just his breath and the jiggle of the racks and a faint sizzle.

Andrews whispered in his ear. "The whole sky's on fire out here, Griff. You should see this."

Oh, he did.

It came down for him as an instant wall of flame and grabbed him by the neck and the crotch and the armpits, a huge swirling brightness that seared his eyes. His ears went quickly, so he heard nothing as he was tossed to the back of the stall at the speed of an angry thought.

Years later, when, miracle of miracles, he thought he might have gotten away, the pain struck.

CHAPTER FIFTEEN
Quantico

The study lounge was quiet for seconds after the screen went blank. No one could believe what they had just seen.

William could not breathe. His eyes had misted over and his hand had actually broken the chair arm.

The barn had blown apart at both ends. A split-second later, the middle had lifted and flown outward in pieces chased by hungry, ugly curls of red and orange flame. Agents had dropped to the ground behind black bomb shields lined up like tombstones. Rubble had rained. A large chunk of frame and siding had crushed the roof of the bomb truck, dropping the truck on its shocks like a stunned bullock.

William had seen one agent, unable to get behind a shield fast enough, fly backward with feet dangling like a doll's. Smoke and dust had immediately made viewing almost impossible. And then the entire screen had blanked.

A chair creaked. Fouad put his hand on William's shoulder. Then, shouts and everyone standing, talking. William jumped up from the soft cushions and slammed into the end of a couch. As someone reached out to steady him, he threw up his hands, glared, then ran up the steps for the phone bank. He didn't have change. Fouad was right behind him, and somehow, Fouad had his phone card out and quickly dialed in his access code.

To William this was all transparent. He hardly saw any of it. He had bitten his tongue again. He tasted the blood in his mouth and knew it was going to hurt. But a certain bitter irony lapped up like a salty sea around his broken thoughts and fear. Here he was, in one of the nerve centers of the law enforcement world, and he was calling his mother to find out what had happened, to see if she knew anything.

Fouad was not judging, he was just there, and then so was Jane Rowland. William, who towered over them both, saw Pete Farrow striding down the short hall toward them.

"Who're you calling, Griffin?" Farrow asked.

He had not finished dialing the number. He could not remember the last four digits. "My mother," he said. She had moved into an apartment recently, selling the big old house. The house where he had grown up.

"I think we should take care of that. We don't know what happened out there. Not yet."

William stared at the receiver in shock. "Okay," he said. Then, plaintively, "Did anybody see? Did Griff get out?"

"I don't know," Farrow said. He took the receiver out of William's hand, gently prying loose his fingers, and hung it up. Then he gripped William's elbow. "Let's go."

Fouad and Jane Rowland followed. Rowland's face was pale as a sheet. Behind them, members of their class stood in a cluster, staring.

Then they were walking back down the hallway past all the pretty prints. Past the chapel. The chapel was empty. For some reason that struck him. They climbed a flight of stairs. William wasn't sure where they were going. He could hardly see. He stumbled on the steps. He was crying. He felt ashamed for a moment then looked to one side and saw that Farrow had tears on his cheeks.

They all converged on Farrow's office. Rowland pulled up a chair. William sat. Someone handed him a cup of water. He sipped. Farrow gave him a handkerchief. William looked down and saw a little blood on his shirt, from his tongue. He wiped his lips and blood came away.

"Take a deep breath," Farrow said. William took it as an order and sucked in a scant mouthful of air.

"I need to know," he said and dabbed at his lips again.

"We'll all know soon," Farrow said.

"I want to fly out there. Can you get me on a plane?"

"We'll see," Farrow said.

"I'm sorry," William said. "I'm a mess."

Farrow bent over him. "You have to maintain, Agent Griffin," he whispered in William's ear. "This hell is just beginning."

An agent whom William did not know stepped into the office doorway and spoke in a low voice to Farrow. William caught part of the conversation. At least one dead, several injured. That was all they knew. The barn, what was left of it, was burning. He tried to stand but Jane Rowland was behind him, hands on his shoulders, and for some reason she was holding him down. He looked up at her, twisting his neck painfully. She stared straight ahead and dug in her fingers.

Somehow that calmed him. He stopped struggling.

Farrow knelt in front of him. "They haven't found your father. We've lost people outside the barn. One at least. A lot more are injured. It's an inferno. They're bringing in fire trucks. You saw what happened, William."

Graduation would have been the day after tomorrow. They would all drink beer in the boardroom. They could hang out with the instructors and the National Academy people, listen to their stories, smiling and nodding and being humble like the rookies they were. Rowland, Fouad, nearly all of the others, would get their credentials. They would be agents. Agents behaved in a certain way, the FBI way, different even from cops. Learning the FBI way—by osmosis, observation, cruel comment, or just plain being emotionally pounded on—was part of what Quantico was all about.

William stilled an urge to shiver. With Fouad in front of him and Jane Rowland holding on to his shoulders, he kept himself stiff as a ham.

Farrow was right.

This hell was just beginning.

CHAPTER SIXTEEN
Temecula, California

Tommy's mother and father had been in their late fifties. Ten years before, using money they had earned in the stock market boom, they had paid a premium for the sprawling Temecula property. They had then invested two thirds of their life savings to turn the old hillside estate into a boutique winery.

Their plan had come a cropper in the wine glut of the last years of the twentieth century, and then had ended with an insect invasion and Pierce's disease. Never very savvy about either business or the needs of their strange child, they had fallen to arguing, and then to planning for divorce.

Tommy was sensitive to noise.

The world had become too noisy.

In 2000, his parents had died from food poisoning. Sixteen-year-old Tommy had been spared. Everyone around Tommy in those awful days had considered him incapable of taking care of himself. Not quite an imbecile, but strange and inept both socially and financially, so the will had described him: a naïve incompetent.

He had spent most of his time working in a concrete room off the underground vaults where the estate's wine was stored in rows of oak barrels. "All he ever does is putter with chemistry sets and computers," the probate court had been told by one of his uncles, a rich fellow who had no interest in the property, the inheritance—or in Tommy.

Tommy had inherited everything, but the court had appointed a caretaker, his father's older sister, Aunt Tricia, to watch over his interests until his majority. A cheerful, outdoorsy, garrulous woman in her seventies, Aunt Tricia had refused to take no for an answer, much less sullen silence, and she had promptly packed a few bags into her old Jaguar coupe and taken Tommy traveling.

They had spent three months on the road, between August and October of 2001. They had visited Oklahoma and Illinois, then driven south to Florida and back up the coast to New Jersey and New York. Tommy had been miserable, terrified by so many strange places and strange people—and by what he had heard on the news.

They had then returned to Temecula. Resolute to the end, convinced that Tommy must finally grow up, the formidable Aunt Tricia had been planning a second trip when she died in November of that dreadful, noisy year.

After her death, Tommy had mustered up enough courage to approach several local attorneys before finding one desperate to earn some fees. The attorney had brought Tommy out from under the shadow of court protection. Tommy had then inherited the remainder of his parents' money, enough to pay taxes and keep him comfortable—if he could ever be comfortable.

Tommy had sought to hide away from a world he knew was trying to find him, a world going to war (he believed he was partly to blame for that), a world that made unexpected and unwanted phone calls and sent him suspicious junk email with impossible promises and lures, a world he knew wanted all of his money and cared nothing for him—an inhospitable world he *"thought"* was going completely mad.

He had stripped away the winery's signs and erected a barrier across the road to the vineyard.

Within a few years, the winery had been forgotten. The fields, hidden in rolling hills, had dropped off the tourist maps. Tommy had kept to himself, staying well away from the watchful eye of Homeland Security, even after federal edicts had required registry and yearly inspection of wineries, breweries, and other facilities capable of growing large quantities of microbes.

Aunt Tricia's jaunt across America had taught Tommy that he had wellsprings of unknown strength. Still, he preferred to leave the estate only at night, driving the El Camino or the red Dodge pickup. Rather than buy more equipment and attract unwanted attention, Tommy had burgled local high schools, junior colleges, even a university, to get what he needed, based on what he read in his large collection of textbooks and stacks of science magazines.

Tommy had proven himself much more than an idiot savant—he had become a wizard of improvisation and stealth. But for Tommy, stealth was not a goal in itself. His true delight lay, as always, in reading about nanotech and biotech, playing around in his lab, learning new techniques—and having people leave him be.

Until he needed to reach out and touch them.

As far as Sam could judge, Tommy had only done that two or three times—the first time with his parents, the second, in 2001, with the mailing of fifteen small envelopes.

The death of Tommy's aunt was an unknown. Tommy did not discuss it.

But Tommy had grown bored. He was discovering he could do many wonderful things in his small lab, things the experts said were impossible, and he could do them cheaply and efficiently. He had a gnawing wish to be important, to be recognized.

And so once again he had reached out, this time to offer his services to someone who might appreciate them . . .

Some acquaintances that Sam had acquired in a professional capacity—people deeply interested in ecological issues, or in animal rights—had told him about a strange young man who was offering up his odd skills; a creepy little runt with big hands and a large head and pig-eyes. Tommy had come to Sam's attention at an important moment in his own life, a time when he was being stalked by grief and finding his calling—all that he did, all that he thought he believed—less than convincing.

In a professional capacity, Sam had decided to check in on Tommy. In some respects, Sam and Tommy were alike. Sam had been doing some burgling of his own. He had collected surprises about which he had not informed his superiors. Sam and Tommy were both foraging through a world changing far too rapidly to even begin to realize where dangers might hide.

For Sam and Tommy, things had clicked into place like the tumblers in a door lock, and that door had opened onto a new life. Sam had applied all of his charm—bringing groceries, books, installing a new generator. Tommy had stopped retreating under the covers in the middle of every visit. He had blossomed under Sam's patient attention. The man-boy had even learned a number of rudimentary social skills. He could go out in the daytime, if necessary, and run errands. He could meet people without turning away and mumbling.

And since Sam's appearance, Tommy had not reached out to touch anybody. Sam had assured him they now had a higher purpose. Of course, putting Tommy to use again put a final nail in the coffin of Sam's former life, his career—everything he knew.

But those things had long ago stopped being important.

Meeting Tommy had stopped Sam from giving up and killing himself.

CHAPTER SEVENTEEN

At altitude, the big gray and green C5A flew smooth as silk, even filled with two tanks, five armored vehicles, tons of crated cargo and twenty passengers. Two military brats—a seven-year-old boy and his ten-year-old sister—were running up the aisles between the seats, trying to play basketball with a tied-up roll of plastic bags. The constant throbbing low-level growl of the gigantic turbo-fan engines had lulled most of the other passengers to sleep.

Farrow had driven William Griffin to Andrews to join the flight from Georgia on its way to Washington state. The FBI had quickly wrangled an Air Mobility Command ticket.

William slumped in his seat. His eyes were heavy-lidded and he was fighting to stay awake, but he had refused coffee as the cargo officer had worked her way aft with a steel pot and a stack of foam cups. He did not want to sharpen his jagged emotions.

The basketball brats were now goggling at the tie-downs and chains that imprisoned two Stryker armored vehicles. William had flown AMC twice as a young boy, on much smaller aircraft. They had spent some time in Thailand and then in the Philippines. His father had been gone for much of the time, leaving them to fend for themselves in spartan base housing at Subic that dated back at least to the 1950s. All he remembered now of those years was his mother hoisting him up into a garishly decorated Jeepney and his father cleaning volcanic ash off their Subaru station wagon.

The cargo officer walked back down the aisle again and asked William if he was FBI. "We have a satcom relay for William Griffin," she explained, and handed him a wireless headset. "SCA Keller."

"SAC Keller," William corrected with a thin smile. "Special Agent in Charge."

"Right," the officer said, and stood back with her arms folded.

"William Griffin here." He listened. Griff had been pulled out of the wreckage. Life Flight had transported him to Seattle. He was in critical condition, but he was alive.

"Does my mother know?" William asked. "They were divorced. She doesn't live with him . . . she's moved out of our old house, too."

"I've notified your mother," Keller said. "She says she's not well enough to travel. You'll have to represent the family."

"Thanks." William stared straight ahead again. Then he frowned. "How could he have survived? How is that even possible?"

"They haven't found your father's partner, Alice Watson," Keller said. "Two State Patrol bomb techs were crushed in their truck. One's dead. Another FBI agent, Rebecca Rose, was pulled from the back of the truck with minor injuries. She's at Harborview with Griff. Luck of the blast. I'm stuck here in Washington until tomorrow. You will check up on your father, attend a courtesy briefing from the investigation team, and then you will immediately report to your probationary assignment, wherever that may be. Your creds are being shipped to my office in Seattle. Watch over your dad for me until I get there, will you?"

"Yes, sir," William said.

He returned the headset to the officer.

The flight droned on.

The C5A was banking. The cargo officer told the kids to stop playing bag-ball and take their seats. "Strap in," she instructed as she walked along the short aisle. Behind and in front, the armored vehicles and cargo containers groaned under new stresses. It was like flying inside a long church, William thought. Strykers and boxes full of weapons filled almost all the pews.

But there were still the children.

For some reason, thinking of them brought tears to his eyes.

At the very end, William had aced Rough-and-Tough. In the simulated raid he had sent twelve bad guys to "God's courtroom," as Farrow had called it—twelve swift and positive kills. Farrow had marked him down for some sloppy moves but had still checked his box.

William had behaved the way he thought his father would have, and that night, he hadn't joined the others in the boardroom to drink a beer or two, and he hadn't slept a wink.

CHAPTER EIGHTEEN
Washington, DC

Fouad sat in the passenger seat of the hybrid Ford Preamble, watching the trees and fields and suburbs go by on 95. The gray man driving was mostly silent, intent on traffic. He wore a black suit and a narrow tie and though his face was unlined his hair was gray and he had a grayish pallor. But then to Fouad, many European-Americans appeared slightly gray. It was working indoors, perhaps.

Fouad had been instructed to ask no questions until he arrived. "Your driver isn't part of BuDark. And if you want to be, you'll play by the rules. Remember. We need folks like you. Folks with your expertise."

And that was . . . ? Fouad had not asked what expertise they were looking for. He presumed language. There had been plenty of rumors during his twenty weeks at Quantico about "sudden career abductions."

Now, the gray man turned the car onto an onramp and led them through an industrial park. Young maples lined the well-trimmed lawns bordering the newly blacktopped roadway. They were still in Virginia, and if the interview went badly, he might make it back to Quantico to join his fellow agents in the cafeteria for the Wednesday night dress-up dinner and next day's graduation.

Fouad wondered how William Griffin was doing. Such a thing, to watch one's father caught in such a disaster. It should not have happened. Fouad could not imagine seeing his father die in such a way.

The gray man parked the car in a nearly empty strip before a large, rectangular white building. "First glass door on the left," he told Fouad.

Fouad exited the car, said thank you, and stepped up to a blank gray door. A small black sphere mounted over the door hummed as he approached. A bar of red light swept over his face.

The door sighed, clicked, and popped open a crack.

"Come in," said a tinny voice through a plastic speaker grill.

A young trim blond man in blue jeans and a white business shirt stood on the opposite side, wearing a smile and a pistol in a shoulder holster. "Mr. Al-Husam, welcome to Building 6. My name is Swenson. I'll be your escort during your visit. Please stay close to me until we reach your destination."

"Thank you," Fouad said. "I am told I will be meeting with a Mister—"

"All a sham," Swenson said, gesturing for Fouad to follow. A long hall stretched past nine unmarked doorways. The lighting was bright and cold. There was no carpet on the floor. Fouad guessed, from the way their voices echoed, that the walls were concrete. "I'm taking you to a room where you'll fill out some forms. After that, Agent Dillinger will interview you."

Fouad could not help but smile. "Dillinger?" he inquired, over his shoulder. "That is a sham, as well."

Swenson's face turned serious. "That's his real name. Quentin T. Dillinger. Fine Virginia family." Then he winked, and Fouad had no idea what was true and what was not. Swenson took out a key and unlocked one of the doors. "I'll leave this open and stand right outside," he said.

There were many forms waiting on a heavy steel table in another featureless room. The forms repeated what he had already revealed about himself when applying to the FBI, and added some questions that had not been asked that first time: whether he supported the House of Saud in the current crisis, his opinions of American foreign policy in Iran and Iraq over the last fifty years, what he knew about Mossadegh and Shah Reza Pahlavi and John Foster Dulles and Allen Dulles. He knew a fair amount. And finally, whether he would truthfully translate the communications of any Muslims, without regard to their shared faith or their well-being or whether or not the details they were providing were in his opinion relevant or simply embarrassing.

That had been a nagging problem with Muslim translators—their loyalty to the *umma,* the community of Muslims.

Fouad wrote steadily for an hour, filling five pages with close, neat prose, then considered perhaps he was being too candid. The FBI did not appreciate show-offs, or shows-off. He still did not always know the correct form for such plurals. Courts-martial, for example.

The door to the small room opened.

"We're ready, Mr. Al-Husam," Swenson said.

"I do not need to finish?" Fouad asked, lifting his pencil.

"No, sir."

"Thank you," Fouad said.

Swenson stacked the papers and passed them through the door to an anonymous pair of female hands.

Twenty minutes later, Fouad was sipping from a bottle of Pure American Springs water. He pondered the ubiquity of flags on food packaging and drink containers, and the almost Semitic quest for purity Americans lavished on their indulgences. Swenson returned, rapped lightly on the door, and asked him to follow.

And now they came to the end of the hall and a double doorway, one side of which opened as they approached.

"Nothing of this meeting will be discussed with anyone outside, ever," Swenson said.

"So I agreed," Fouad said. The way Swenson eyed Fouad's features—with a critical, unabashed perceptiveness—made him uneasy.

"Don't mind me," Swenson said. "New people give me the willies. Dillinger is expecting you."

Special Agent Dillinger—he did not say in which bureau of federal law enforcement he served—sat behind a steel desk. He had thinning hair and a sleepy look and his tie was rumpled and loose. His lips were full and slightly slack. To Fouad, he resembled a used-car dealer at the end of a day without customers. A slim telepad and a small, disorganized stack of papers were the only things on his desk. The room's lighting was cold and ancient—two ranks of naked fluorescent tubes. Two chairs waited in front of the desk, turned toward each other at forty-five degrees. Fouad sat in the left-hand chair. Swenson closed the door on them.

"Talk to me," Dillinger instructed, blinking as if something was irritating his eyes. "Personal history first."

"I am an American citizen soon to finish twenty weeks of training at the FBI Academy," Fouad said.

"Tell me about your grandfather."

"Perhaps you know of him."

"Give me your perspective."

"He left Iran in 1949. He had been an operative in the American OSS during World War Two, but after the deposing of Mossadegh, he quit and returned to Beirut. He was killed there in 1953. My father was ten years old at the time."

"Did the CIA assassinate your grandfather?"

"I believe—I have been told they did."

"So he rusticated. He deserted."

Fouad shrugged. "I do not know details."

"But you are still willing to serve the United States."

"Yes. Of course. I am an American citizen."

"Naturalized, shortly after your birth."

"Yes. My father also worked for the CIA, in the nineteen seventies. He retired in 2003 and he and my stepmother now live in North Carolina, with a second home in Colorado."

"Tell me about your travels, as a boy."

"My father served in Lahore and in Riyadh. He was in Kuwait during the invasion, and that was where I was born. My mother nearly died giving me birth, because Iraqi troops had stripped the hospital of necessary equipment. My father shot three Iraqi soldiers who were looting and raping nurses. He hid us in the basement of a mansion belonging to a Kuwaiti businessman. He came back for us after the Americans pushed Saddam's forces out of Kuwait. My mother died when I was ten. My father remarried in 1998, to a Filipino Muslim servant. Thereafter, until his retirement, he worked in Cairo, Jordan, and in Gaza. I was with him in Cairo until I was sent to my aunts and uncles in California. He returned there after his retirement, missing one arm and one eye."

"That's quite a story."

Fouad tipped his head to one side. "It is mostly my father's story."

"I hear you have a gift for languages."

"I grew up speaking English and Cairo Arabic, and later I acquired Tagalog. I also picked up Pashtun, Farsi, and Aramaic from servants and teachers. Later, I studied international relations and languages at Georgetown University. I speak five Modern Southern Arab dialects."

"You don't happen to have a degree in accounting, do you?" Dillinger was grinning. The expression did not suit him.

"No. Military science. I had hoped for a time to join the army, Special Forces."

"Excellent. Do you know who requested this interview?"

"No," Fouad said.

"Your father's former boss. He was an officer as well, but he now works for us. He has immense respect for your father."

"My father would be very glad to hear that," Fouad said.

"Good. Do you know what BuDark hopes to accomplish?"

Fouad leaned forward. "Am I allowed to guess?"

"Be my guest."

"You wish to find common ground with the parties and groups now invading Saudi Arabia, out of Sudan, Yemen and Iraq. They are likely to be victorious. It is possible, though I do not know this, that the United States is supplying aid and arms to some of these factions, in order to maintain future supplies of oil. You wish to have those who speak the language infiltrate and relay information."

"Astute analysis," Agent Dillinger said. "That's not what we're up to."

Fouad leaned back. "No?"

Dillinger shook his head and drew his lips down at the corners. "We put out nasty little fires that show signs of spreading. All sorts of fires. We need special people in the Middle East, flexible people trained in law enforcement—military training is helpful, too—and of course with exceptional language skills. If there's a fire . . . you'll be in the thick of it. Have you ever been on Hajj?"

"You know I have not."

"Perhaps you'll get your chance," Dillinger said. "You will not graduate tomorrow. You will vanish and even your stepmother and brothers will not know where you have gone."

"I see," Fouad said. "And my father?"

Dillinger shook his head.

"The Academy?"

Dillinger smiled. "Be ready to pack your things and leave immediately. I have your creds."

"I am accepted?"

Dillinger nodded. "This will be your probationary assignment. Lucky boy." He removed a small folding vinyl case from the desk drawer and passed it to Fouad.

Fouad opened the case.

"Welcome to BuDark, Special Agent Al-Husam."

Fouad weighed the case in his hands. He looked up at Dillinger. "Am I other than FBI?"

"You're definitely Feeb-Eye. BuDark is interdepartmental. We all play ball for the time being." He stood. "You'll join a select team with a tight focus. Stay flexible. You'll get jerked around at first; prove your value and go with the flow. You'll likely travel to a few southwestern Asia hellholes in the company of some reasonably excellent folks. Me, I'm stuck here. I envy you." Dillinger waved his hand imperiously and the door opened. "Mr. Swenson will take you across the river. Good luck."

CHAPTER NINETEEN
Temecula, California

Sam stood in the large kitchen unwrapping a tray of frozen lasagna. He turned on the light over the sink. The rest of the kitchen was dark. Tommy's mood swings had been exaggerated by the extreme pace they had set. Sam had been anticipating problems, especially if something went wrong.

Lots of things had gone wrong. And Tommy had been taking them all with relative calm. The episode in the car had passed comparatively quickly.

Sam heard a whisper of sound behind him and froze for a moment, holding his breath.

This is it.

Tommy cleared his throat.

"I can recover a third more product now, maybe half. I might be able to work double for the next few weeks and get enough product made to do almost everything we planned. That's what I'm '*thinking*,' Sam."

"Tell me more, Tommy," Sam said.

The man-boy stepped to the center of the kitchen. Sam turned. Tommy's long fingers seemed to move on their own. They made wild shadows on the kitchen walls as they bent and stretched, as if trying to conduct part of the conversation in sign language. "I think we can do without the extra printers, if the ones we have don't break down. I have plenty of cartridges, enough to last. That's what I '*think*.'"

"Show me, Tommy."

"Not necessary," Tommy said, rocking from one foot to another. "It's under control. I'm just saying, we'll have enough product, but I don't know where we'll get it packed for, you know, delivery."

"We'll think of something," Sam said. "Want to grab a bite to eat?"

Tommy chuckled. He reached out and grabbed something from the air, then stuffed it into his mouth. "There," he said.

"Real food," Sam persisted.

"All right," Tommy said. "If you '*think*' I'm hungry."

"I think we're both hungry," Sam said. "Lasagna would be good."

"Lasagna is good," Tommy said. "I'll do some work, then we'll eat. You can wait here."

"Let's eat first," Sam said. "We'll think better."

"You're right. I've been following your diet plan. I've been pretty bright lately," Tommy said. "That's why I'm not so upset about the printers. I '*think*' I have a way to double the output." He marked more quotations in the air and grinned toothily.

"Great. This will take about twenty minutes. Why not set the table?"

"I will."

"Did you wash your hands?"

Tommy grinned and went to the sink. "Not a problem, Sam," he said reassuringly. "I've been very careful."

"Yeah, but you still pick your nose. I've seen you."

Tommy began laughing. His laughter turned into a bray. "Yeah, *right*. At least I don't *scratch my butt* when I get out of a car."

"I never do that," Sam said, indignant.

Tommy danced around the kitchen, plucking his pants bottom. "Wedgy, wedgy!"

CHAPTER TWENTY
Seattle, Washington

William looked through the window into the surgical unit. He could not see his father, not clearly—just a lump covered with blue and green sheets, here and there a spot of what looked like ground red meat showing through, where people in full-out surgical suits, with their own air tubes trailing after them, probed with shining, curved tools and murmured to each other. He could hear the whine and whir of drills and saws and pumps.

One of the surgeons looked up and gave a muffled laugh to someone's joke. The OR head nurse had told William they had been working for three hours.

William's knees turned shaky. He sat on the chair. Special Agent Dole from the Seattle Field Office, barely older than William, slender and blond and wearing a brown pants suit, handed him a bottle of water. He drank and watched. All night agents had come in and out, clapping William on the shoulder, saying little, watching the surgery for a few minutes and grimacing as if at some weird object lesson.

Someone named Cap Benson arrived and told Agent Dole she could take a break. He had bandages on his face and around the back of his neck. "I was with your dad, up until the last . . . the barn," he said, his words muffled by a swollen jaw. Benson sat on a plastic chair beside William. "He's going to make it."

William nodded. It did not look good. The OR nurse said surgery could go on for another three or four hours. They were pulling Griff's face forward and setting shims. The shattered bone was being debrided and they were picking out the chips, soaking them in saline and ReViv, and arranging the best of them back on strips of mesh like mosaics. As they set and repaired Griff's shattered legs, they were also borrowing pieces of bone from his hip and femur to transplant to his skull.

Jesus Christ, Dad.

The observation room had pale blue walls and scuffed linoleum tile and smelled warm and clean. Benson smelled rank, as if he had not showered in a few days. To tell the truth, he looked more than tired—he looked a little crazy.

"Griff's one tough son of a bitch," Benson said.

William nodded like a clockwork. All his life he had reacted to his father in one way or another—as authority, something to be rebelled against, something to be loved or feared or even despised. He could not remember ever thinking of Griff as a friend. That raw-meat lump in the OR had guided William's entire existence by example or counter-example, seldom by encouragement, most often by a scowl or gruff warning, several memorable times by the belt.

"Your dad's a hard man, isn't he?" Benson said.

"Yeah," William said.

"Tough as nails. And lucky, goddammit."

CHAPTER TWENTY-ONE
Maryland

"The whole world loves to beat up brown men," the prisoner said as he sat, with great care, on the old wooden chair. His face gave evidence of that: both eyes swollen almost shut, one cheek bruised and puffy, lip split and stitched in three places, neck marked by fading Taser jolts. No doubt he had similar burns around his genitals and rectum. Cingulated bruises and abrasions caused by hanging from handcuffs formed yellow and green half-moons on his inner wrists and needle marks crawled up his arms.

Fouad Al-Husam stood in a corner, out of the light. An agent who had been introduced to Fouad as John Q. Anger paced around the central table and the seated man. It was a scene as old as time; a small room, shadows, and a man whose life had value only so long as he could give useful answers.

He had been *rendered*. Shipped secretly from one country to another; in this case, from Egypt to the United States. As Fouad well knew, the reverse was usually true. Fouad was here as a trainee and an observer. Already, his stomach was being tested.

"We're not going to beat you," Anger told the seated man. "We don't do that here."

"I'm grateful," the man said. He had a broad face with a hawk nose and a good black head of hair and his face was squat and his neck was long. Hands and wrists stuck out of too-short orange sleeves. "Will you send me back?"

"Back to where?"

"I do not know where I was," the man admitted with a shrug. "I could not see where they took me. I was blinded by my own blood."

"Do you know a man named Al-Hitti?"

"I know a few men by that name. It is a common name in Egypt."

"The Iraqis tell us a man named Al-Hitti paid to have people killed. We found them in a house in Sadr City. They died painful deaths."

"I am unhappy to hear this," the man said. "If I knew such a man, I would tell you."

"You know him."

The man on the chair shook his head weakly.

Anger leaned over and with some gentleness pulled his head back by the hair. "Nobody here tolerates disrespect. You will respect me. It's part of our fucking culture. You will sit up straight."

"I am sitting straight."

Anger pressed the man's back with one hand. "Straighter. You have also met a white man named John Brown or John Bedford. He's either an American or a Brit. We don't believe he's Canadian, despite what some Iraqis have told us."

The man in the center of the room looked around through his bruised eyes and then stared down at the table. "Bedford," he said. "That is in Massachusetts."

Anger turned his back on the man in the chair and faced Fouad. "Talk to him."

Fouad took a step forward. He spoke in Arabic. "Has your treatment been better since you were brought here?"

"They let me sleep," the man replied. "I still can't eat. I think they ruined my stomach."

"They tell me you were born in Jordan."

"Yes."

Anger moved swiftly and grabbed the man's chin. "What do you know about anthrax?"

Fouad was startled by the intrusion. The captive took it as a matter of course. "A disease of cattle and people," he said. "Someone in America sent letters. That is all I know."

"Anthrax refers to the black lesions caused by the germ," Anger said. He waved his hand at Fouad as he paced. "Translate this for me. Like coal. Shiny and black and painful. These victims were kidnapped off the streets of Baghdad, taken to Sadr City, and there they were forced to inhale anthrax powder."

Fouad translated.

"You are telling me too much," the man protested to Fouad in Arabic. He pleaded with his eyes, one brown man to another. "I do not wish to know these things."

"Does this knowledge disturb you?" Anger asked. Fouad translated, feeling sick.

"It is having the knowledge that is dangerous," the man said, this time in English. "When you are done with me and give me back, and the Egyptians ask questions, they will see that I know some of which they are asking, and they will assume I know more. Do not tell me any more. It will kill me."

"Did you introduce Mr. Brown to Al-Hitti?"

The man in the chair bowed his head. "So many planes and trucks and rooms," he said.

"We're done," said Anger. "Send him back," he instructed the guards. "Let the Egyptians finish him."

"No, do not send me back. I do not know Al-Hitti. I have not met him!"

Anger took Fouad's elbow. They walked out of the room together. The door closed softly, muffling the captive's pleas for mercy. In the green hall outside, Anger kept pacing, finger to chin. "How does that make you feel?"

"Sick," Fouad said.

"Stock up on Pepto. You're going to see worse. But since the UN threatened to bring war crimes charges against us, we have strict limits on what we can do. You will not be called upon to actually interrogate someone. You may, however, witness such interrogations. Understand this. We would stop torture if we could, because the information we get from tortured detainees is so difficult to filter and reconstruct. But our Muslim allies, especially those at the General Directorate, they seem to believe agony is good for the soul. They keep handing us bullshit they've proudly extracted through the application of extreme duress."

Fouad was confused. "How am I supposed to act when I see such things being done?"

"We need fresh detainees. We need them unspoiled. If, in your opinion, a detainee might have information of use, you will work to get him—or her—rendered before torture begins. We will interrogate them ourselves. We use techniques that produce remarkable results without much pain. If you can't accomplish that, you will report in exact detail who is being tortured and by whom. So, your first assignment is unpleasant but very important. You will travel with a small team to Egypt and to Jordan, and to some camps in Kuwait, to observe rendition prospects and make reports. Are you up to it?"

"I will be saving them from torture?" Fouad asked.

"Only if they're useful. The rest, I'm afraid, will have to rely on Allah."

Fouad's face grew dark. "This American, Brown or Bedford, he is real?" Fouad asked.

"Sounds like hooey to me, but some people in Baghdad used anthrax on a few Shiite Muslims. Their leader might be a man called Al-Hitti." Anger fixed his stare on Fouad. "That's all we're cleared to know, for the time being."

"You will use your techniques on this man?"

"No," Anger said, shaking his head in disgust. "They filled him full of crude drugs in Egypt. He's a wreck. If we do what we do best, we'd kill him."

That afternoon, Fouad moved into a motel room near the Marine base and less than eight miles from the Academy. All the other rooms were filled with agents from Diplomatic Security, Homeland Security, the FBI, and the CIA, and all had been instructed not to talk to each other.

BuDark indeed.

He had yet to learn the real name.

CHAPTER TWENTY-TWO
Temecula

Sam—he had many names now, but to Tommy, he was just Sam—sat on the porch listening to the soughing of the mourning doves. Dawn was a hint of striated light in the east, like a flaw in his vision breaking up the perfect darkness. The land around Tommy's house was quiet but for the doves and a few songbirds tuning up for the morning battle of the bands.

Sam spread his bare toes on the splintery wood and sniffed the cool, sweet air. All he could see other than that blemish of dawn was a hard, rough road finally arriving, however long it might take, at failure. There were so many details to get perfect, so many pitfalls to avoid, and he felt sure that somebody would soon be on to him.

The disaster of the truck and the patrol car. And the glove. He could not remember what he had done with the glove after pulling it off with his teeth. He might have jammed it in his pants pocket. It might be near the burned-out cruiser, in which case it was in the hands of the police and probably the FBI. It might have fallen out on the long walk before he was picked up and given his ride. Good cops might work those miles of highway and find it. Either way, he had screwed up. Compounding that, his weakness: the woman in the green van, Charlene.

It was hard to remember what he had actually *told* her.

Sam wanted a cigarette and he hadn't smoked in fifteen years.

They would get skin cells out of the glove. They would have the skin cells and the DNA from the blood, and oddly, they would not precisely match, and that would tell them there had been two assailants at the scene. Brothers, perhaps.

That might slow them down.

Everything about him came in pairs, including his moods—back-to-back despair and supernal confidence with nothing in between but little warning flashes, anxious sparks of light he could almost see.

Morning was the hardest for Sam.

Walking through the kitchen and the back door and down a flagstone path between overgrown lawn and what now looked like pasture, Sam used Tommy's ring of keys to open the first warehouse. He passed between the stainless steel tanks rising from the concrete floor like the heads of giant tin-men with protruding steel mouths.

At the end of the warehouse a flight of plain wooden steps descended to the cellars—three concrete tunnels that stretched off for a hundred feet beyond the warehouse foundation. Sam switched on the ceiling lights. His soft-soled shoes padded silently down an aisle flanked by stacked casks of old French oak and cheaper young American oak. Here, sleeping in quiet darkness, the wine had been meant to age and acquire flavors from the wood—a hint of vanilla mostly—and soften its sharp edges in preparation for the bottling that had never come.

Tommy's parents had died before they could enjoy the results of their final vintage.

Last year Sam had used a glass funnel—a wine thief—to sample some of the casks through their rubber-stoppered bungholes. The wine had turned lifeless and flat and no wonder. The floor under the casks was stained purple, sticky and slick. The barrels had leaked.

The vaults echoed and the cool still air smelled of moldering oak and dead wine.

At the end of the longest tunnel, during the winery's construction phase, Tommy's father had left a room twenty feet square open for Tommy's use. The room had been plumbed with hot and cold water, two large steel sinks, and a floor drain. A small high window could be poled open for ventilation. There, he had trained his son in basic biology and wine lab techniques—yeast culture and fermentation.

Perhaps that had been only way they could connect emotionally. Sam tried to imagine the father's satisfaction at his son's native ability.

The rest Tommy had figured out for himself or researched on the Internet, a cornucopia of odd knowledge. According to Tommy both his mother and his father had been thrilled that Tommy was finally revealing his talents. Still they had never bothered to check up on what he was actually doing. Toward the end, they had had their own troubles. Tommy had been kept busy and out of their hair. Whatever scientific equipment he had asked for, in their guilt they had bought, despite the cost—and he had asked for some unusual things.

Sam opened the metal door and switched on the sun-white lights. The lab glowed. In pristine silence, he looked across tables crammed with a centrifuge and incubators, stirring platforms, small hot boxes—sealed Plexiglas cubes with glove holes, neat arrays of pipettes on white plastic cutting boards, a shelf covered with antiseptic spray cans and wipe dispensers, glass beakers and test tubes mounted on wall racks, small packets of French wine yeast.

Near the back stood a much larger box made of sheet steel and half-inch Lexan: eight feet tall, twelve feet wide, three feet deep. The seams had been caulked with thick beads of silicone putty and the whole was now mothballed—wrapped in multiple layers of translucent Visqueen and strips of duct tape and blue masking tape. This had been the first of Tommy's amateur production facilities. He had built it at the age of fifteen. At that time, he had been convinced his parents were out to kill him—the first of his major delusions. And so he had set about cultivating *Clostridium botulinum*—while contemplating the contents of a small vial he had been unfortunate enough to find at his high school.

That had been the turning point in Tommy's life: someone's simple if egregious oversight, a monumental mistake made for reasons no one would ever understand by a man unknown, perhaps dead.

Tommy had spent much of his free time in the high school's science storage room arranging supplies and cleaning glassware. He had found a wax-sealed vial wrapped in cotton in a taped-up cardboard box, pushed back on a high shelf behind jars of chemicals. He did not know how long the box and vial had been there: perhaps since 1984, just after the school had been built.

He had immediately recognized the name penciled on the vial's red and white paper label: *B. anthracis*.

Tommy had no idea where the vial had originally come from but Sam could hazard a guess. It might have been purloined by a teacher who had once worked in bio-weapons research. Perhaps he had smuggled it out of some lab as a souvenir or a trophy.

Perhaps he had dreamed of being allowed to teach a course on the glories of germ warfare.

Tommy had pocketed the vial and taken it home, where, he told Sam, he had spent many nights lying in bed staring at the beige powder, wondering what it all meant, whether it was even real.

So much *potential*.

So much power.

His parents were fighting every night, driving him under his bed pillows, weeping in terror. He had seen a cable TV program about prehistoric animals that depicted the plight of a pair of reptile parents two hundred million years ago. Harried by a small, swift dinosaur predator, they realized they would have to find another burrow—pull up roots. But they could not move their newly hatched offspring. To avoid wasting precious nutrients, they ate them.

Tommy had become convinced that this was what his parents were planning—not to eat him, but certainly to kill him and move on. In self-defense, he had laced an open can of mushrooms in the kitchen with just a drop of liquor from his toxic culture of *C. botulinum*. To Tommy, the logic had been obvious—but he did not watch television any more. He found movies and TV programs too disturbing. Even comedies gave him nightmares. The expressions on the faces terrified him.

Weeks after their deaths, in between court appearances and even in the presence of his first court-appointed guardian, Tommy had begun his second phase. His brilliance had almost immediately manifested itself. He had started by culturing pinches of anthrax in a broth whose recipe he had found on the Internet.

The basement lab had filled with the scent of stewing meat.

Since not every scrap of information he had needed could be found on the Internet, Tommy had improvised. He had devised several original techniques for preparing and refining his goal: weapons-grade aerosolized material.

Washing, re-drying and re-grinding had removed the dead cell debris, leaving a solution of almost pure spores. The resulting fine powder still had a tendency to clump, however, because of static when dry, and because of moisture when exposed to humidity. He had experimented with suspending the powder in various liquids, and finally arrived at his own ideal formula, using chemicals actually found in printer inks.

Some of those early products he had stored in jars, to avoid waste and as a record of his progress.

But Tommy had known from experience that simply drying and grinding would not prevent clumping. The problem had then become to re-deposit the anthrax in very fine grains, already separated and containing fewer than four or five spores per grain. His brilliant answer: common inkjet printers. He had replaced the ink in the disposable printer cartridges with his special solution of chemicals and, at first, brewer's yeast as a substitute for anthrax. (Once again, Tommy had suspected that using anthrax's close relation, BT or *Bacillus thuringiensis,* ordered from a garden supply store, might result in his being tracked. Yeast, however, he had in abundance—left over from the winery.)

First on heavy paper, then on eight-by-ten-inch glass plates, Tommy had printed out millions of dots of dry solution—tiny granules containing only one or two spores, far finer than he had believed possible. The solution, when expelled through the printer cartridge nozzles, produced a microscopic, silica-wrapped bead that sat high on the glass plate when dry, but strongly resisted mechanical dislodging. The plates could in theory be carried around with minimum precautions, separated only by waxed paper.

Tommy had worked through ten pairs of glove holes arranged in two levels, front and back. A rolling stepped platform once used to stack barrels had allowed him to reach the upper level.

His next act of genius had been to array the plates on a rack in a vacuum chamber at the right end of his large hot box and statically charge them using an apparatus he had borrowed from an old office Xerox machine. The microscopic granules had lifted free and flown to a grid of tiny wires where they had discharged, flocked up briefly, and then been drawn by gravity to a Teflon-lined chute and into small jars. He had kept a long brush in the box, just in case the spores stuck on the wires or in the chute.

He had then networked six printers, so modified, and had finally begun depositing the real thing: weapons-grade, aerosolized *Bacillus anthracis.* Throughout, he had kept everything sealed in his hot box factory, even the glass plates, which he recycled.

If there had been accidents he had not told Sam—but despite never having been vaccinated or taken antibiotics, both of which could also have been traced, Tommy was still among the living.

After filling two jars with superfine spores, he had capped them, sealed them with caulk, and soaked their exteriors in bleach to destroy any residue.

He had finished in early 2001, just as his aunt had moved into the house. This first lot—fifty grams—had taken Tommy six months of hard, steady labor.

For a complete amateur, working alone, he had done very well indeed.

A year after starting his project, in the company of Aunt Tricia, Tommy had traveled to visit relatives in New Jersey and Florida. Along the way, he had insisted on dropping by local post offices to buy commemorative stamps. Taking walks alone at dusk, he had visited public mail boxes, carrying his specially prepared envelopes in plastic bags within a larger bag. From these boxes Tommy had injected fifteen light, deadly packages into the bloodstream of the U.S. mail.

Five had eventually been discovered.

He had no idea where the other ten were.

Tommy was one of the most wanted people on Earth. In the summer and fall of 2001, his hobby had shut down the U.S. postal system and much of the American government. He had killed five people, sickened dozens, and terrorized tens of millions.

By fitting nobody's profile, he had eluded the greatest manhunt in domestic American history.

Tommy Juan Battista Juarez was the Amerithrax killer.

CHAPTER TWENTY-THREE
Seattle

William Griffin sat at the tiny table in the old coffee shop on Broadway and waited for his coffee to come up. He rubbed one eye with a knuckle and stared through the window at the rainy street. Last night had been rough and he had not been able to get to sleep until four a.m. Griff's heart had stopped for the ninth time. The doctors had expertly re-started it, then continued surgery.

Six days of surgical procedures. Maybe Griff's spirit was already downing drinks with the old boys up in Omega Precinct. Maybe they were laughing and laying bets on how long it would take Griff's body to realize the owner had gone AWOL.

William pursed his lips and felt his eyes go out of focus.

Hey, Griff, time to choose your heavenly name.

Heaven? Christ, boys, I assumed . . . I mean, the liquor in this bar is terrible.

Assume nothing. We make the booze ourselves. God likes cops, Griff.

Bullshit. God's a judge, not a cop.

Then what are angels? You come up here, join our precinct, pick up your flaming sword, and you go back down, invisible like, and kick some ass. Never have to Mirandize anybody. And the judge never denies a warrant.

"Americano, no sugar?" the waitress asked.

William accepted the cup. Taking his first sip, he saw a slender woman with a bandaged cheek, intense hazel eyes, and auburn hair peering through the window. She was wearing a gray pantsuit and a peach-colored blouse with a loose ruffled collar. Another bandage covered her right hand. She gave him a small wave, then opened the door, setting off a clang of cowbells.

"Mind if I join you?"

"Excuse me?" William asked. He was in no mood for conversation.

"My name is Rose. Rebecca Rose."

Now he placed the face and he certainly knew the name. "Sorry," William said, transferring his cup and holding out his hand. "I'm William Griffin."

"So I guessed," Rebecca said. "Pardon me if I shake southpaw. Sprockett told me you'd be here. I'm your driver."

William looked incredulous and pulled out a chair.

She sat. "I'm taking you with me to the farm."

"Thanks, but I'd like to stay here until they know something for sure."

"You're on FBI time. Keller thinks you need a break from the hospital, and so do I. They checked me out an hour ago. Then they let me see Griff. Your father's not going to recognize anyone for days, maybe weeks." Rebecca stretched out her long legs. She had a third bandage around her left ankle. "Hiram Newsome thinks Griff might have broken open an important case. Maybe two cases, one old, one new. He asked Keller for you to be temporarily assigned to the taskforce."

Newsome was another legend. William had met him once in a hallway at the Q, a big, bear-like man with a square face and large, sympathetic eyes. Despite his exhaustion, William's pulse quickened. He looked around the coffee shop. There were two other customers, both in a far corner, and the barista was busy grinding beans. "I'm listening," he said.

Rebecca leaned forward, drawing in one leg. "The hell you say." She tapped the table with a long fingernail, freshly polished. Some of the polish had smeared beyond the cuticles. She had applied the polish herself, William judged, with her bandaged hand. "You are about to pass Go and dance straight on over to Park Place. You'd better do a hell of a lot more than just *listen*."

William felt the coffee kicking in. "Is this for my sake, or for Griff's?"

Rebecca leaned her head to one side. "Right. Someone will tell Griff we're giving his son a free pass, a terrific case, outside of the rules, and that will give him the will to live. That will perk him right up." She raised her eyebrows.

"Sorry," William said.

"Farrow recommended you."

"He did?"

"That puts three aces up your sleeve." Rebecca shaped her hands into cups, then pretended to mold something in the air over the table. William watched her bright eyes. She had the tightest little dimples. "When Griff is himself again, we'll bring him back in—and you will brief him. Four aces. It doesn't get any better than that for a junior G-man."

Rebecca finished molding and tossed him an invisible ball.

He held up one hand and caught it.

"There you go," she said. "Simpatico."

CHAPTER TWENTY-FOUR
Temecula

Sam walked around the Visqueen-covered box. When Sam had first shown up on Tommy's doorstep, he had not used the old hot box for over a decade. To the best of Sam's knowledge, the last time Tommy had used it had been three years ago, to prepare the genetically modified anthrax samples delivered to Honduras and Iraq.

Tommy had found it easy to induce the anthrax to take up plasmids—small loops of DNA—containing bioluminescent genes. The modified bacilli had grown with unaltered enthusiasm and within two weeks Tommy had produced another twenty grams of purified anthrax spores, a trillion spores per gram.

Roughly four thousand spores, inhaled, would be enough to cause death in fifty per cent of individuals. This was called the LD_{50} number, LD short for Lethal Dose. As few as a hundred spores could cause death if inhaled by the elderly or the immune-compromised. Children seemed to be more resilient.

Sam studied the box. Some of the Visqueen had been pulled aside. The power was on. A small quiet blower fan was running, attached by flexible plastic tubing to a HEPA filter mounted in the room's high window. Bottles of bleach and tins of alcohol had been stacked in a vacant corner.

Sam gingerly pulled aside a long, horizontally ripped sheet of plastic. Four layers beneath had been taped shut but could easily be opened to allow access to the glove holes.

On a nearby table Tommy had mounted a small glass-fronted incubator loaded with Petri dishes. A jar filled with solidified agar sat next to the incubator. On a corner lab table, a single flask of pinkish liquid like strawberry milk was being rocked in a mechanical cradle. Tommy was working on something new.

He was using his lab again, and his special box, without telling Sam.

In the shed, Sam put on a SCBA—self-contained breathing apparatus—and then a loose green plastic Seal-Go suit and helmet with a carbon-filter industrial mask. The suits were warm and puffed out like balloons after a few minutes but Tommy insisted on them—and washed them by hand at the end of each week. He still had dozens of unused suits in boxes in the warehouse.

The trek to the rear barn took two minutes. Sam walked over gravel and broken asphalt. The barn had been built during the house's pre-winery days and was beautifully made of brick and wood. It covered three thousand square feet and in layout was much like the barn on the Patriarch's farm except that it had no basement.

Sam opened the small door at the side—the only entrance they used now. He stood in the computer room watching small monitors on six networked machines. The lights in the computer room were left on all the time but the lights in the barn itself were now reduced to a minimum.

Ramping up powder production had been Tommy's most brilliant accomplishment so far, and he had done it with simplicity and ingenuity. He had laid thick plastic sheeting over the barn's interior, including the ceiling, and had then hung an additional series of curtains using guidelines he had found on the Web for removing asbestos. There was no way Sam could know how thorough Tommy had been but Tommy was nothing if not obsessive. Sam had seen no trace of residue anywhere in the computer room or on the approach to the barn. If he had, he would have backed off immediately.

Tommy had worked his science down to a mind-numbing routine. The suits were surplus models from computer chip manufacture, designed to block volatiles and effective at filtering extremely fine particles. But Sam was not about to take any obvious risks.

The door into the main barn opened with a swish of rubber seals and a hiss of air—negative pressure maintained by a HEPA-filtered fan on the other side. When the factory was working, a fine spray of water played outside the air filter outlet, designed to catch dust and drain it through a large PVC conduit into a deep concrete catch basin where it would just settle and . . . sit.

Not even Tommy went near the catch basin.

Sam walked along the inner curtain. Through the last layer of plastic sheeting, in the dim glow of a few scattered fluorescent bulbs Sam saw twenty rows of inkjet printers now dormant while Tommy slept, twenty printers per row. The printers in the last four rows still had glass plates mounted under their rubber rollers ready to resume work later in the day.

For this final job, Tommy had specified one particular printer model, with finer dots-per-inch capability than the models he had used in 2000. Week after week, for ten months Tommy had filled four hundred ink cartridges with slurry, walking up and down the rows in his plastic suit, carrying the glass plates to the collection chamber . . . and the sealed bottles containing fine powder to a metal shed next to the barn, where they had been loaded into crates ready for transport. Still, it had not been enough.

Ambition had forced Sam to find a partner, to seek a testing area even more remote than the winery, and to plan for another factory.

If they had been able to deliver the printers to Washington state—

If the Patriarch's estate had not been raided—

Those plans had collapsed with two quick blows. Having tasted failure for the first time, Sam had no way of knowing all of Tommy's thoughts, his concerns. He had been dealing with the Boy from Another Planet for so long that he had almost let down his guard. But now he was certain that Tommy's plans had changed, and he needed to know why—and how.

The barn looked as it had for the last two years. Sam circled the sheeted areas, lightly stroking the rippling plastic with his gloved hand. Nothing new, nothing obvious. What was he missing?

A rear door to a storage closet attracted his attention. The door had been opened recently. Visqueen had been pulled back and taped up. Sam examined the deadbolt keypad latch. That was new. Tommy had never locked anything before. Sam couldn't just break open the lock. He poked at the keypad in frustration, without result, then turned to leave.

On the opposite side of the door he heard a scratching sound, weak whining, then a steady, rhythmic thump-tick.

He examined the keypad again. He tried Tommy's birthdate. No go. Then Sam punched in 09-enter-11-enter-01, the date Tommy believed had signaled the world's descent into noisy madness.

The day that Tommy had decided anything he could do to strike out, strike back, would be fully justified.

The door clicked. Sam pulled it open.

Inside was a brown dog, a beagle-terrier bitch with jutting ribs and staring brown eyes. In the half-dark, the dog fixed on Sam as she paced in a quick, tight circle. She could not stop circling despite her fear, her eagerness to escape.

In opposite corners lay two other dogs, eyes glassy and legs straight, black blood sludging from their noses and rectums. They were dead. Sickened, Sam closed the door and locked it.

He walked back to the entrance, pulled off his suit, and returned to the porch.

Tommy had been the means to an end and Sam had played his part well, convincing even himself sometimes. Over the years, so long as Tommy had been vulnerable, cooperative, and open, Sam had almost forgotten what Tommy actually was.

He walked over a packed dirt road through the vineyards to the metal shed north of the warehouse. Inside the shed twenty neat wooden crates lay stacked on pallets on a concrete floor. Each crate contained ten starburst shells assembled at the Patriarch's farm over the last year, shrink-wrapped and cushioned in shredded newspaper and sawdust

Sam took a handcart and hauled two crates at a time to the garage. It was almost eleven but Tommy was still asleep.

In the garage Sam loaded the crates into the back of the horse trailer, stacking them against a welded metal bulkhead that separated the rear storage area from the launcher.

Tommy's improved productivity no longer mattered. Time was short. They had enough for one test and two prime objectives. Rome would have to be given a pass. Sam had already picked out the test city. A town nobody would remember.

A town it might be good to forget.

When he had finished loading the trailer Sam looked in on Tommy's small bedroom. The boy-man lay on his stomach in the twin bed and made a faint "snuck" at the end of each whistling intake of breath. He sounded like an old dog. On a small nightstand Tommy had propped four ponderous veterinarian's texts on the diseases of cattle. Walls not obscured by bookcases were covered with posters and magazine photos of one woman: Jennifer Lopez. Tommy had first read about J-Lo in his mother's copies of *The National Enquirer*. Somehow many years ago she had become Tommy's ideal and to this day he remained faithful to her.

Tommy had caused so much grief.

But Tommy had not caused Sam's grief.

The sun shone through the branches of the old oaks east of the house.

"I'm awake now." Tommy walked through the French doors and stood on the porch beside Sam. He twisted slowly back and forth on his ankles. He was wearing boxer shorts and a tie-dyed t-shirt. He had something "on his mind."

"I guess if you have a lot of money, women will pay attention to you," Tommy said. "That's what I hear. Is it true?"

"I suppose it is. Some women."

"Have you *'given any thought,'*" Tommy marked out these words with crooked finger-quotes, "to maybe asking for money *not* to do the things we're doing?"

Sam paused before answering. It might or might not be a serious question. "No," he said. "I haven't."

"Well, we could bring in a lot of money, but I haven't figured out how, because the way I *'think it through,'* we'd probably get caught trying to spend it."

"Probably," Sam said.

"The whole world's fighting and we'll help them stop fighting. It'll be a lot quieter. That's worth something, isn't it? I've learned a lot from you, Sam."

"You're my main guy, Tommy."

"Yes. For now." Tommy sat on the wicker chair beside Sam. "But after we're done I'm afraid you'll just move on. I'd like to work with you on the next thing, whatever it is."

"I'd like to work with you too."

"Maybe it could be something about making money so I could have some sort of life. But whatever, Sam, you're not telling me what it is."

"I'm still thinking."

Tommy rushed to add his own air quotes as Sam said "thinking."

"But you'll be in on it," Sam said. "I want you to feel important."

"I *am* important." Tommy moved his large head back and forth, wispy long hair dancing around his eyes. "But I'm a grown man and I've never been to bed with . . . slept with . . . anybody, a woman. I suppose that isn't so important, but you seem to think it is."

"Do you want to sleep with a woman?"

Tommy snickered. "I'd like to do more than just *'sleep,'* Sam."

"Of course," Sam said.

Tommy's face went from puzzled to smooth. "Tell me how noisy it is out there, everybody arguing. We'll make it quiet again, won't we, Sam?"

"We'll sure try."

"So tell me again. Tell me the story."

Sam took a small breath, keeping his face neutral. "It's a deeply troubled time we're living in, filled with lies," Sam began. "Everybody's stuck in history."

"Like elephants in a tar pit," Tommy said, following the formula.

"Exactly. Nobody knows how to escape because lies and hatred are like tar. You understand that, Tommy."

"You hate and you lie and you get stuck."

"Right. And nobody knows how to pull themselves out. They're all stuck."

"They lie about God. God is like tar."

Sam nodded. "For these people, God is hatred. God used to be about love."

"Lizard Mommy and Daddy used to be about love," Tommy said, almost crooning. "Trouble made them hate and lie."

"So many people need doctors to cut out the hate. We're the doctors."

"We're performing surgery. We'll cut out the hate."

"Surgery is delicate and loving, even when you have to cut. Surgery preserves life."

Tommy's shoulders shook. "If you had come earlier, you could have saved Lizard Mommy and Daddy."

"You did what you had to do, Tommy. But together we're going to make a change."

Tommy wiped his eyes and the wicker chair on the porch creaked under his enthusiasm. Sam watched Tommy until the man-boy's motion had slowed and he perched on the edge of the wicker chair with eyes half-closed, sated by their ritual. "I like to hear about what we're doing," Tommy said. "We're doctors."

"Right, Tommy," Sam said. "You and me, we're going to cure the planet."

"I love you, Sam," Tommy said. "You saved me. I hope I can return the favor."

"You're the man, Tommy. You're the one we're all going to owe favors to someday."

Blissful Tommy.

Sam leaned back and folded his hands behind his neck.

Tommy did the same. "It feels right, doing it here in the winery, doesn't it?"

"Trampling out the vintage," Sam said. "Real grapes of wrath, Tommy."

PART TWO

Pillar of Fire

CHAPTER TWENTY-FIVE
The Patriarch's Farm
Snohomish County

The air over the farm was as still as a sucked-in breath.

The blast region was cluttered with ripped and dented plastic barrels, big gas cylinders, chunks of concrete, blown-out wooden walls, and debris of every size, including splinters fine as toothpicks. Trees behind the barn had been set on fire and a thin haze still lay over the farm.

The farmhouse nearest to the barn had been pushed from its foundation and leaned to one side, boards shivered from its walls, windows blown out. The farther house, shielded by the main house and some trees, had survived, but its windows, too, were gone. Someone had taped blue plastic over them.

William walked past stacked piles of debris to the big hole in the ground where the barn had once stood and stooped to peer down. The central pit—the middle of the barn's basement—was a maze of concrete-crusted rebar. Reflective tape had been laid over the barn's rectangular outline in a grid, staked on all sides, large coordinate numbers glued where the tape crossed.

Rebecca stayed a few steps back, giving William his space, his time.

William looked for, and found, the two red flags poking out of the rubble that marked where two agents had been found—one dead, one alive.

A man spoke with Rebecca. He was middle-aged and pale, with mousy brown hair combed back from a broad forehead. His suit was black and his tie was red. They walked to a marked-out square where the bomb truck had been. The man pointed to a blast shield still on the ground and marked by an evidence sticker. Rebecca pointed to William. They approached.

"Mr. Griffin, my name is Aram Trune. I'm FBI liaison to the National Counter-Proliferation Center. I hope your father is doing better."

"Liaison?" William asked, still stunned by the pulverized nature of the rubble.

"We're tasked with helping focus the Bureau's relationship with the new administration."

"Where was Griff found?" Rebecca asked Trune. "I was pretty much out of it after the blast."

"So I hear." Trune stepped up to the edge of the pit, marked by a sheared-off line of studs and a narrow, ragged overhang of concrete, and pointed. "He was pushed into the back of a concrete stall. The wall fell over him and deflected the main force. Most of his injuries were from crushing. Agent Watson—" He shook his head. "We've just removed the last of her."

"What sort of explosive was it?" William asked.

"Perchlorate and aluminum powder in a polybutadiene base," Trune said. "We call it a Thiokol special. Basically, it's what they use in solid rocket motors, like on the old space shuttle. The explosion was triggered by a spark mechanism." He pointed to the tangled remains of the poles and wires spread around the farmyard and the field. "Induced current from the upper atmosphere, flowing through a network of wires. The Patriarch wanted God to take the blame."

"Will He?" William asked.

"Beats me." Trune said.

Trune guided them through taped-off and gridded patches of land to the operations trailer, a double-wide thirty-footer with an incongruous porch and lots of gingerbread. Inside, agents and investigators had set up marker and bulletin boards, a big screen display, and folding tables on which they had laid out and were cataloging evidence. Two technicians were transferring bagged pieces of burned, melted plastic and metal and what might have been shrapnel to the central table. A third was preparing to photograph them.

William and Rebecca stood by the table. Rebecca bent over and examined thin blackened metal rods. "How many?" she asked a diminutive female technician.

"Fifteen or twenty units, plus cables," the technician said. "We found them in a heap beside some burn barrels, along with the remains of two computers."

Rebecca glanced at William. "Runners from inkjet printers," she told William. "Older models. Epsons. They don't sell them anymore. Did the Patriarch strike you as a computer geek?"

Trune maneuvered through the crowd. The room was quiet and efficient; those who were talking tended to move off to the kitchen or the back rooms. A woman started posting photo prints on the cork board: surveillance shots of members of the Patriarch's family.

William looked through the bay window off the "dining room" and saw another large trailer being moved up behind the house.

Trune slipped on green plastic gloves and lifted a section of steel tube about three feet long off the table. He held it up before Rebecca.

"Guess?"

"Pipe?" Rebecca ventured.

"Cannon is more like it." Trune replaced the tube within its marked outline on the graph paper that covered the table. He walked around the photographer and lifted a plastic bag. The bag contained a small amount of cream-colored powder. "We scraped this off the trees. There's a lot of it out there. Take a another guess."

"Anthrax?" William said.

Rebecca leaned forward to peer at the bag. "Yeast."

"Good guess," Trune said.

"We saw the bags in the barn."

"It's brewer's yeast," Trune said. "Baker's yeast, actually. All cultivars of the same species. Safe enough, I suppose. It's all over the rooftops, in the soil, on the leaves outside. Heavier concentration to the north. The wind in the valley blows from the south most days." He plucked three sets of gogs off a shelf and led them to the back of the trailer. "I've reserved a room and arranged for our local server to show the barn vids on demand."

"Glorious," Rebecca said as he showed them the unplumbed bathroom.

"The real potties are in another trailer. We have techs working the farm's septic system and all around the drainfield," Trune said. "Everyone on site is going to have blood drawn and receive a free CAT scan, until we're done processing the scene, and probably for a week thereafter."

William felt the sweat trickling down from his armpits.

"Okay, now tell me why they used yeast," Trune said, lowering his voice.

"Someone planning a biological attack could use yeast as a neutral test substance," Rebecca said.

"Are we talking weaponized anthrax here?"

"I don't know," Rebecca said. "But finely milled yeast disperses almost as well."

Trune whistled, then pulled back his coat arm, revealing a keypad. "Showtime, folks. I'll split the screen between Agent Griffin and Agent Watson. Anything catches your eye, let me know, and I'll zoom in."

*   *   *

"I'm dead," Rebecca said as they drove up the highway through the woods. "I've been cruising for forty-eight hours now on nothing but catnaps."

"No coffee?"

"Can't drink coffee," Rebecca said. "Makes me anxious. I start having dark thoughts. Isn't worth it."

"I can live on coffee," William said. "Caffeine is a vitamin."

"That's because you're fat," Rebecca said with a hint of a smile.

"I'm two ounces underweight for my height," William said. He was trying to untie the knot in his stomach. Talking—about anything—felt good.

"Just a roly-poly puppy. Where'd you start?"

"NYPD. I wanted to be in Emergency Services. Forget Jesus, ESU saves."

"Ha. Good luck."

"Right. So I worked vice for a year."

"Vice? What'd you do in vice?"

"I was a pretty boy."

"A pretty boy?"

William plumped up nonexistent breasts.

Rebecca pinched out her lips. "Put on some eye shadow. You would be kind of pretty."

"Skinny tranny with big boobs, blond wig, real fright city," William said. "I wasn't that good at improv, so they pushed me out and I transferred over to the big-ass headphone patrol . . . OCID, organized crime surveillance."

"Beats the cold New Yawk streets," Rebecca said.

"Sometimes I miss it. The ladies in their limos, smelling like fresh baked bread and Opium—the perfume. Their insides so warm. The limos, I mean."

Rebecca wizened her eyes. "Kid me not."

"I specialized in rich ladies."

"Rich ladies do not cruise the streets looking for trannies."

"Shows what you know."

"Tell me more."

"About organized crime?"

Rebecca reached over and lightly whapped his arm. "No, asshole. Rich ladies. What'd they like?"

"I only know what I offered."

Rebecca laughed. "All right, Pretty Boy. How much did you charge?"

"Five hundred an hour, global. We do the tropics, the poles, and then we do the equator. We get all *geo*-graphical."

Rebecca giggled—a genuine girlish giggle. William regarded her with surprise.

"Did you ever want blow off your bust, just lean in, close the door, and, like, follow through?" she asked slyly.

"No, ma'am. Most of them were in their sixties. Well-preserved, lots of tucks and no rolls, but still."

"Nothing wrong with ladies in their sixties. How old do you think I am?"

"Thirty."

"Bullshit."

"Thirty-nine, tops."

"Mm hmm. I knew an agent, she used to work vice in San Francisco. She's retired now. She once confessed that she thought about johns when she was with her husband."

"Now that's sick," William said.

"The young, handsome ones, anyway. She'd visit them in their cells. They'd be whimpering, she'd come in with her police baton, black leather, big silver and gold badge, high boots, tell them to act like the men they were. Then she'd imagine—this is all imagination, you understand—she'd imagine telling them to pull down their pants. Got her off every time."

William blushed. "Jesus," he said.

"It's all true," Rebecca said. "Cop gospel."

"Yeah."

"You don't believe me."

"When a guy's behind bars, he's the biggest loser on earth. For women, it's a complete turn-off. Most it does for them is bring out the motherly instinct, but not the . . ."

"The what?"

"I was going to say something crude, but I'm with a laaa-dyy."

"And don't you forget it," Rebecca said. She stopped to take a right into the town. They passed the white church and the grocery store and the service station, then the feed and tackle store, and that was about it until they came to the motel.

The parking lot of the twenty-room Meriwether Motel was packed with five-year-old American made sedans sporting antennae. The town was already filled to capacity and beyond—agents were staying in rented trailers on a used car lot.

A trooper from the Washington State Patrol met them at the main intersection. He was wearing a slicker against the drizzle. It was four in the afternoon. They showed him their creds and the trooper pulled up a sheet of paper in a plastic cover, wiped away rain drops, and told them to take a left on Boca Raton Drive.

"Rat Mouth drive," Rebecca said. "That is what we call setting the scene." She drove along the gravel road. "We got two females bunking together, and the rest are men, so do the puzzle—we're stuck with each other."

The last Mobile Agent Domicile, or MAD, had been crowded off the used car lot and into the back yard of a vacant wreck of a house next door. It was a fifth wheel trailer and had two beds, one in front, in the overhang, and one in back.

Rebecca took the one in back.

Around midnight, rain fell on the thin steel roof and woke William from a tossing sleep. The trailer had no power but was well insulated. He fluffed the hard pillow as best he could and sat up in the low space, feeling like a submariner in a hot bunk. He was sweaty and the rain wouldn't let up, wouldn't let him get back to sleep. Somehow time passed and he found himself struggling with a pile of forms on a desk that was too small, trying to puzzle through crooked bookkeeping that could reveal a pattern of long-term embezzlement, or was someone laundering money through a chap nine wrinkled greenhouse?

And what the hell was that? Something he definitely should know for the exam that morning.

Then the slammer swung down from the ceiling and aimed directly at his heart.

Wrong answer, Pete Farrow was saying.

Hotter than ever, William opened his eyes again and let out his breath. *You leave the Q, the Q don't leave you.* A line from the FBI Rap. He felt Rebecca walking around in the dining area, then heard her talking on her cell phone.

"You do what you have to do. I know . . . I would say that's a big maybe—best shot, not what I'd call it . . . Um. Then you just have to let it be. If that's what you're looking for." She had been speaking softly, gently, but now her tone took an edge. "High-class ladies don't go out for law enforcement. You knew that a year ago. It's not about what we bring home . . . Of course. Of course not . . . Well, I'm sorry to hear it. That's kind of fatal, don't you think?"

She uh-hummed without any spirit for another minute, then quickly said she had to go, goodbye. After long seconds of numb silence, she punched in a number.

"Hello, Frank. I know what time it is. And I know you're still working. Anything useful?"

William quietly pulled back the curtain and looked down the length of the trailer.

Rebecca paced the short narrow passage, clutching the phone to her ear and chewing on a thumbnail. She was wearing a flannel nightgown that revealed nothing but William was able to judge that she was in great shape. He looked below her raised elbows and realized he was trying to observe the impression of her breasts. He closed the curtain and flopped back in the upper bed, silently cursing himself for an idiot.

"Fantastic," Rebecca said. "What about the glove? . . . So what's the problem? Yeah, but what have we got here, some sort of marrow transplant, a leukemia patient? . . . Okay. I like good blood . . . Two guys, using the same glove? . . . Brothers. Come on. The morning is young, dear Franco. Call me when it makes sense."

William looked at his watch. It was two am.

"Are you awake, Peeping Tom?" Rebecca called out. "You vibrate the whole trailer up there, rolling around." She shoved back the curtain and shined a light in his face. "I got my four hours," she said. "You need more?"

"I'm good," William said, blinking.

"Get dressed. We're going back to the farm." She gave him a hard little grin and replaced the curtain.

William tugged on his pants and slid down the ladder. As he slipped his arms into his jacket sleeves, Rebecca emerged from the bathroom, toweling her face and hair. She handed him a squashed granola bar.

"This place sucks," she said. "Let's go."

CHAPTER TWENTY-SIX
Temecula

Sam pulled the truck from the garage and parked it on the drive. The moon hung cool and aloof between thin sheets of blue cloud, casting come-and-go shadows under the trees that fronted the house. He checked the tires and the oil, then did another inventory of the horse trailer's contents. They were well-packed but there was no margin for error. An accident in this truck would likely prove fatal to anyone within fifty yards.

He moved to the front and opened the trailer's side door to look at the launcher. It stood just over five feet high, including the plate-steel base.

Purity of heart is to will one thing. Kierkegaard.

Everything was set. Except for Tommy. He could not allow Tommy to reach out again. That would be an impurity.

He quietly closed the trailer door and latched it, then put on his own combination lock, a big one.

No sense letting anyone get at the pretty horses.

Sam gripped the vial in his left hand and slowly pushed open the door to Tommy's room. The small nightlight that Tommy always left on cast a dim but reassuring glow. All the J-Los watched Sam with seductive smiles. And in the east corner, surrounded by his celebrity angels, Tommy lay sleeping as he always slept—deeply and innocently, making his little dog noises.

Four or five times, Sam had stood here with this vial in his hand, trying to make up his mind. In his other life, facing someone who had done what Tommy had done and who had the potential to do so much more, Sam would not have hesitated to put a pistol to the man-boy's head and pull the trigger . . .

Now, the time had come for a gentler, slower farewell.

Sam had been too ambitious. He could live with cutting back on the number of targets. The point would be made.

Tommy's work was done.

He moved silently to the side of the bed, despite the plastic suit, avoiding the obstacles around the bed, the crumpled papers and candy wrappers, the cans that had once held chili, Tommy's favorite food when Sam was away. He could not smell the room now but he remembered the aroma well: like the monkey house at a zoo. Tommy's sheets had not been changed since Sam had done a load of wash five weeks ago.

Sam opened the screw cap on the vial, held the vial a foot above Tommy's head, tipped it, and let the powder drift. It fell in a small dense cloud, billowing almost like steam but fading at the edges, seeming to evaporate in its fineness, its purity. It fell with such a lightness that Tommy could not feel it and would not smell it, though he might notice it on his sheets and pillow in the morning. If Tommy turned and tossed, the powder would be smoothed into the fibers, where it would blend in and get lost, finer than any household dust.

Tommy breathed—*snuck, uck.* Sam watched as he vacuumed part of a billow into his nose. His cheeks puffed and a little cloud blew out between his lips like yellowish cigarette smoke. It rose up and reversed at a wave of Sam's hand, then drifted across Tommy's eyelids. Every motion made it lift from the smooth pale skin in tendrils that returned with caressing tenacity.

It wants to go home.

Tommy's masterpiece.

CHAPTER TWENTY-SEVEN
Snohomish County

Traveling on the shiny, empty highway, walls of silent, dripping trees on either side, William watched Rebecca at the steering wheel and tried to figure out who she was.

"I can drive," he offered.

"I always drive," she said.

Her face was thin and strong and attractive, good cheekbones supporting skin that showed no signs of laxity and had even firmed a little under stress—those tight dimples. She did not look as if she smiled often, neither did she have frown lines. Her tawny pupils were surrounded by a startle of whites, and when she looked at William he could not decide whether she might be a harsh mistress or a sympathetic schoolmarm, thank you ma'am, you're shore beautiful.

He cut off that line of thought—unproductive, unprofessional, and he wanted to keep his balls. "How long have you worked bioterror?"

"Twenty years, off and on, mostly off the last four years," Rebecca said.

"What's that about a glove?" he asked.

"Hatch Friskmaster," Rebecca said. "Left hand. I borrowed it from Arizona. It's being examined at Quantico."

"My father sent me a pair when I joined NYPD. Didn't wear them much."

"You never worked narcotics, did you?"

"No," William said.

"Frank Chao found skin cells mixed with fragments of silicone in the fingertips," Rebecca said. "Clear silicone caulk is one way to hide prints. It works—for a while."

"Tell me about your anthrax theory. I wish there was a file or something to read."

"I assume you're up on Amerithrax."

"September and October, 2001," William said. "Envelopes filled with anthrax spores sent through the U.S. Mail. Five dead. Never found the culprit but they—we—did make life hell for some oddballs with ties to weapons research. Until about six years ago. Then—nothing. Nothing I've heard, anyway."

Rebecca nodded. "The experts told us it was impossible to manufacture such high-grade material outside of a major defense lab. The thinking back then was it had to be some group or possibly a brilliant individual from Fort Detrick or Porton Down, maybe Rhodesia or South Africa—scientists with formal top-secret training and access to labs. Microbiologists working for us traced genetic signatures in the bacillus—anthrax is a kind of bacteria found in soil, amazingly similar to gardener's BT—"

"I know," William said.

"Traced them to the so-called Ames strain. Not actually from the University of Ames, Iowa, as it turned out, but isolated from a cow in Texas in 1981 and sent to a number of labs, including Porton Down, but not to Iraq or Russia. So we weren't dealing with another Sverdlovsk, 1979. That was good—Amerithrax wasn't mailing drug-resistant spores . . ."

Rebecca fell silent for a moment, then murmured, "After a while, I just learned to never touch my eyes, my nose. Always wash before going to the bathroom—and after. My hands got all dry, like a doctor's. I carried antibiotic skin cream wherever I went. Even affected my sex life. After a while, guys started to wonder about my little habits."

"Price to pay," William said.

"But I haven't had a cold or the flu in ten years." She smiled. "What's the cost-benefit ratio? There's an island near Scotland that's been off limits for forty years because of WW-2 research. The Brits spread anthrax over sheep in cages. Within three days, the sheep got sick and died."

"Gruinard," William said. "But that wasn't Ames, either."

Rebecca nodded appreciatively. "A scholar."

"I heard they finally decontaminated it in 1986."

"I doubt the real estate will ever be worth much. The spores can stay in the soil for centuries. Anthrax is a nasty little bug with a hardened spore and simple habits, all of them painful or deadly. One scientist I talked to called it 'the devil in the dirt.'"

"Aren't there vaccines?"

Rebecca nodded. "All sorts, plus antibiotics. Now, if someone's pretty far gone, they can also use something called Gamma Lysin. But nobody's ever convinced an entire country to get vaccinated. So we vaccinate first responders—doctors, nurses—and soldiers, off and on, who might be exposed. But the focus is off now. We haven't heard much about anthrax for years."

"You think It's going to happen again?"

"God only knows," Rebecca said. "But there is an alternate theory, about how it doesn't take Fort Detrick to mail an anthrax letter. Carl Macek, an agent and a good guy, he and I came up with it over drinks in a San Francisco bar one fine wet evening eight years ago. We had just attended a seminar on forensic nanotechnology—high-tech future, end of crime, all that crap. But I ran into a guy who told me they were using inkjet printers to lay down microcircuits and tiny plastic channels and things. And out of the blue, Carl asked him, 'Could you just deposit tiny little blobs? Less than five microns?'

"'No problem,' he told us. 'Could be a big thing in pharmaceuticals.' So Carl and I told News—Hiram Newsome. And News got it right away. We did some research, and we were both hot on it until the then-director started focusing on shit that nobody wanted to deal with. Pornography, of all things. And then political shit."

She took the turn once more onto the farm road. The car started jouncing but she did not slow.

"Where did it go after that?" William asked.

"Nowhere," Rebecca said. "It was a cold case. FBI had already taken a lot of heat for ruining the lives of a few innocent suspects. Well, innocent of spreading anthrax, anyway. Carl Macek died of a heart attack three years ago. And back then, News wasn't Ay-Dick . . . Assistant Director of Training Division."

She slowed the car. The scene was surrounded by mobile lights on tall poles. It looked like a tree farm on the night before Christmas. Analysts were still in the yard and clambering gingerly over the collapsed pit of the barn, doing their work through the early morning hours, even in the rain.

Rebecca parked beside an unmarked black panel truck festooned with antennas. She kicked down the emergency brake. "Our newly appointed director is busy trying to keep the bureau from being dismantled. News has more time in the bureau than he does, and a lot more contacts and probably more downright respect among field agents, and so for the moment nobody looks over his shoulder. And he tells me there's interest again, in high places. So, here I am. And you."

"You've got a glove, saliva, blood, and . . . ?"

"You *were* listening, you snoop. Some people killed a state patrol officer rather than let themselves be caught with a cargo of three hundred inkjet printers. Nobody knows where they were going—yet. Almost simultaneously, we find the remains of more inkjets on a farm in Washington state—a barn owned by a white supremacist. Why?"

"Maybe they were printing extra copies of *The Turner Diaries*."

Rebecca tightened her grip on the steering wheel. "I don't want to screw it up again."

William wasn't quite sure what to believe. He decided a neutral concession was best. "At Quantico, it's all just a game, until you think of the stakes."

"I hate games," Rebecca said.

"Anthrax," William said, and could not help shaking his head. "That kind of operation—it would take dozens of skilled, heavily protected workers and hundreds of thousands of dollars worth of equipment. We monitor all lab equipment and antibiotics sales."

"We didn't back then. Despite years of threats and false alarms, we didn't, God bless our pointy little heads."

William admitted that was true. "Have there been any recent cases in the U.S.?"

"One in Texas, last year. An illegal alien tried to eat part of a dead steer. Four others at a wedding party in Oklahoma. A family slaughtered and ate an infected sheep, medium rare." She gave him a wry glance. "Nobody knows what motivated Amerithrax. He sent out one envelope before 9-11, then 9-11 really set him off. His targets didn't make a lot of sense. Why lash out at *The National Enquirer*, for Christ's sake? No profile we could come up with panned out. Suppose Amerithrax was responsible for both the hoax letters and the real letters? For the different grades of anthrax mailed to different parties? Maximize the confusion and terror, conserve the best product—and wait for another opportunity."

"But no anthrax was sent out after 2001—or for that matter, after 10-4."

"And why not? Did he die, is he lying low, or is he just busy with something else? Suppose now it's the same guy, or a small group of guys—what if the process can be mechanized, privately financed, kept quiet for years?"

"That's a lot to suppose," William said.

"Carl and I did some calculations," Rebecca said. "If you had a fermentation tank of sufficient size and used a high-efficiency growth medium, and then you have, say, one hundred inkjet printers, you could, in theory, produce more than thirty kilos of perfectly weaponized anthrax spores in six months. Hijack a crop duster, and that's enough to spray every large city on the west coast. There isn't that much antibiotics in the entire world. Back in 2001, that's what we thought terrorists might have been planning—to use a crop duster to spray a city. The bastards couldn't get crop dusters so they took jetliners instead, a poor second by comparison. Now, suppose someone has stockpiled *tons* of the stuff, ready to go, right here?"

Rebecca got out. Over the car's roof she stared at him for a second, then said, "I want another chance, another look—without Agent Trune watching over our shoulders. Humor me."

The trailer was quiet. Only two police officers and two FBI agents remained inside, sitting before computers filing the pieces of information they had been handed earlier in the day and drinking black coffee from large cups.

Rebecca requested an access code to the server, then spun around a big monitor on its rolling stand. The monitor had been used to brief local chiefs and agents. She fast-forwarded through Griff's video until she came to the steel organ-pipe cluster—the hedgehog. Griff's voice hissed from the display's small speakers. "*They could use the tractor to haul that Calliope outside. I'm wondering why, though.*"

Rebecca paused. "You okay with seeing this again?" she asked William.

"So far," William said, and pulled up a chair. The other agents turned to watch. Rebecca resumed the video, then split the screen between the two helmet-mounted cameras.

Alice Watson spoke next. "*Fireworks,*" she said. "*Shit.*"

They had been looking right at each other, two thick monsters in olive-green suits.

Griff extended his thumb. "*I should have thought of that. Hey, listen up, guys. Alice just set off a little light bulb.*"

"*We heard,*" said someone off site, probably Andrews from HDS Redstone. "*Watch for devices triggered by bright ideas.*"

"*Well, why didn't we think of it earlier? Portable fireworks launcher. Atta girl. Why?*"

Rebecca ran the video back to the steel pipe assembly. "Looks like a hedgehog. What in hell is it for?" she asked in an undertone. "Can you actually use fireworks to spread a powder?"

Another man entered the room. "I heard you two were staying up late," he said.

They both turned and Rebecca shut off the monitor. She did not know him. He had tight black hair and broad cheeks and a turned-up nose. He was wearing a DS cap—Diplomatic Security. "You're Rebecca Rose, right?" he asked.

"Yes."

"And this is Griff's pup?" The DS agent held out his hand. "Sorry about your father. We're rooting for him."

Rebecca looked him over coolly. "What can we do for you?"

"David Grange. Special Agent Trune said I could take a look around, in the spirit of sharing."

"Do you suspect a threat to our esteemed State Department?"

Grange smiled. "The Patriarch has been on our list since before I was born. Congratulations. But more to the point, I'm curious as to why *you're* here."

"Fair enough," Rebecca said. "Have you looked at this apparatus?" She wheeled the display around to show him the hedgehog.

"Put it out for the smash and dent sale. It's mostly just little pieces."

"You've looked at it."

The DS agent squeezed his eyes together and looked as if divulging anything might be painful. "Griff should never have forced the issue," he said. "If he hadn't pushed the Patriarch, we could have gone in slow. We'd have more to look at now than just broken tubing."

William walked around behind Grange, leaving Rebecca in front of him. "I beg your pardon?" William asked.

"No disrespect," Grange said, twisting his head.

"FBI found the Patriarch, staked him out, alerted everyone to his presence," William said. "How is that a screw-up?"

"I didn't say it was."

"Same as."

"I beg your pardon."

Rebecca gave the DS agent a gesture with her hand and shoulder. "You've got cream on your lip, Mr. Cat. Willing to contribute something useful?"

Grange pulled up a folding chair and sat. "DS and FBI have a long history of friendly dealings. Though sometimes we do let you hog our credit." He pointed to the display. "The steel tubes are scorched inside and around the lips. Tests show traces of polybutadiene and sprinkles of aluminum—like the charge that blew the barn. Plus talcum powder and small glass beads driven down into the base. Do you know much about fireworks?"

"No," Rebecca said.

"You might want to learn. After all, the big question is, what'll they think of next? I hear you have some interesting theories, Agent Rose. Maybe we can compare notes. I'd like that. But not now. Too much doghouse stink in your agency."

"You're with BuDark, aren't you?" Rebecca asked.

David Grange stood and intoned, "You do not see me. I am not here." He walked through the rear door, waving his hand. "Give my best to Hiram Newsome."

Rebecca looked at the door. She wore a simple frown, like a puzzled little girl. "Pug-faced shithead," she murmured.

"Beg your pardon?" William asked.

"We live in an age of cooperation," Rebecca said. "But this case, this *bastard*, is mine." She looked back to the display.

"I know a little about fireworks," William said. "Griff taught me one summer at Lon Guyland. New York. If this is a launcher, it's weird. Custom job, small tubes. Rockets, not mortars. Backyard shows, not Disney World. My guess is, it would launch ten or fifteen simple starbursts in succession, not all at once—that much heat would warp the base—set to go off at between five hundred and two thousand feet. You'd load the tubes depending on where you wanted the starbursts to appear—left, right, center. Not a showstopper."

Rebecca smiled, impressed. "Why glass beads?"

"Insulation," William said. "Between layers. You can also use metal foil, paper wadding, sand, clay . . . sometimes, baby powder."

"Trune and Grange seems to think that this is the launcher that spread yeast all over the farm. What do you think?"

"I don't know," William said. "Gets pretty hot inside an exploding rocket. Should cook anything alive."

"That's what they said about *Columbia*," Rebecca said.

"The shuttle?"

"2003. Tumbled out of orbit, breaking up and burning. But big pieces came down."

"The astronauts all died," William said.

"Small things survived. An entire ant colony experiment was found intact, remember?"

He shook his head. "I was just getting out of college."

Rebecca ran the video back and then forward, several times. "That's what brought the deputy out here in the first place," she said. "Lots of starbursts over four or five nights. How much yeast in each charge? A few ounces? Half a pound?"

Then she advanced the video all the way to the bags of yeast stored in the basement stalls. "French. Good stuff, I guess."

William pointed. "They've been wrapped in double plastic. It's shiny. The inner bags aren't sealed. They've been closed up again with big staples."

"So they were," Rebecca said.

"But the bags look full. Maybe they had been opened and then—either they weren't used or they were refilled."

"Hm."

"But refilled with what—more yeast?"

"If the analysts had found anthrax, we wouldn't be here," Rebecca said. "Maybe the yeast was treated, mixed with glass beads. Maybe they used the empty bags to hold clay or baby powder." She ran the video ahead. Watson and Griff had pretty thoroughly recorded the barn's basement.

"Are those box kites?" Rebecca asked.

"Maybe," William said. "That could be a powder station," he added as Griff surveyed the benches. "Packing molds, shaping wedges."

"*Just fireworks?*" Watson asked on the video.

"Did the Patriarch do the packing?" Rebecca asked.

"His family, maybe. The kids. Griff and I put on a small show one August for some neighbors. Things going bang, what's not to like?"

On the video, Griff was watching sparks dance at the rear of the basement. They could barely see through the drifting haze of black dust. "*Screw this,*" Watson said.

Rebecca turned off the display. "The Patriarch wasn't doing it all by himself," she said. "And he wasn't the boss. This is not his style."

"What about his sons?"

"He'd never let his sons take the lead on a project. But that's not what I mean. He was working with somebody with new ideas. Somebody who convinced him it would be worth his while to stake his farm just to ride shotgun. Something huge."

The trailer let out a few creaks as the wind blew. The valley was sheltered and the air had been relatively still for weeks. Now, the weather was changing.

"Proof of concept," William said. "Box kites to check wind direction. And they could have launched a dummy load—yeast. Yeast wouldn't attract as much attention as large amounts of BT."

"But did they have time to finish?" Rebecca glanced at her watch. "I wonder if someone has caught up with the Patriarch's family. Maybe they're in protective custody. Maybe DS or Homeland Security has them."

"Wouldn't they let us know?"

"What do you think?" Rebecca asked. "We're second-class citizens, didn't you hear? We could ask and say pretty please."

"Another conference in ten minutes," one of the agents alerted them from the door.

"Five o'clock," Rebecca said, looking at her watch. "Gluttons for punishment?"

"Eight o'clock New York time," William said. "News cycle coming up, everyone wants to be on the same page."

CHAPTER TWENTY-EIGHT
Virginia

Fouad Al-Husam woke to the gentle pulse of jazz from the motel clock radio. He washed, laid out his rug, and performed morning prayers. After, he read the Quran for an hour, then repacked his kit.

The tortured man had looked like Fouad's uncle Salim, in his younger days, a handsome, smiling man fond of dispensing candy to his nieces and nephews at family gatherings. It was difficult to imagine Salim being tortured. Salim had been almost as much of a father to him as his own father.

The phone buzzed. Fouad zipped his kit and answered.

"Be ready to move out in ten minutes," a female voice said at the other end.

"Who is this?" Fouad asked.

"Lance Corporal Chandy Bergstrom. I'm your escort. There's been a change of plans. I'm to take all of you here at the Podunk Hilton to a military airport for rapid deployment. Will you be ready, Agent Al-Husam?"

"I will," Fouad said.

"Thank you. Big adventure."

"Yes, of course."

Fouad put down the receiver and looked around the room. He closed his Quran, slipped it into its leather travel bag, and returned the razor to his shaving kit.

CHAPTER TWENTY-NINE
Washington State

Rebecca had found them a decent motel just off the freeway in Everett. At two in the afternoon, William was asleep in his room but she sat on her bed—her hard, rented bed—with a glass of water balanced on the corner. She stared at the window. Daylight knifed through a crack in the drapes, then—a shadow. Someone with kids passed by on the walkway outside. A man and the kids laughed and tussled and a woman gently reined them in.

Real life. That woman did not have to sleep alone. That woman did not have an attitude that drove men away. Nearly everyone spent a life free from the immediate ravages of crime. They were the sane ones because they were isolated, deluded into feeling safe.

The insane ones broke their brains and bodies trying to protect them.

She removed her notebook and flipped through her shorthand record of the briefing at the Patriarch's farm. SAC John Keller had delivered the briefing to the governor and a group of top law enforcement officers. There were smears on the second page of her notebook. In the middle of the briefing, it had started sprinkling again.

Her slate chimed. It was Hiram Newsome at Quantico. "Rose here."

"Not much time, Rebecca. I hear Griff is breathing on his own. He's off the supercritical list. He could regain consciousness tonight or tomorrow."

"I'll tell William."

"BDI informs me they know the whereabouts of at least a few of the Patriarch's family, but that info is being kept in-house for the time being. Both Diplomatic Security and BDI have been behaving real peculiar lately. BDI may get whupped worse by the current administration than FBI, long-term. If DS is involved, that probably means BuDark. Alphabet soup gets cold fast, doesn't it?"

Rebecca could hardly keep the agencies straight any more. With each intelligence and security failure, successive administrations had multiplied the bureaucracies, perhaps in hopes of spreading future blame. She was least fond of BDI—the Bureau of Domestic Intelligence, which had been formed two years after—and despite the existence of—the FBI's National Security Service. It was rumored that BDI had been the source of much of the shit for which the FBI was now taking blame. "News, isn't it about time some of us got told what in hell BuDark is?"

"Well, they've taken one of our agents from the last class, Fouad Al-Husam, along with about twenty other Arab-speakers from FBI and CIA. BuDark has been raiding every agency in town *except* BDI and Secret Service, pulling out Middle East experts. I assume we'll be told in the next few weeks where they're putting our agents. If they feel the anxious need to be courteous."

"They're not CIA?"

"Presidential black ops would be my guess. I've had three meetings with the director in the last day and a half, and he's not going to fight a turf war unless we come up with something certain."

"Well, here's a certainty," Rebecca said, lifting a printout from her briefcase. "There is no anthrax in the ink cartridges from the printers found in the Patriarch's barn. But the cartridges didn't hold ink, either. They were filled with Canola oil. They may have been prepped but never used. And there were a lot more empty benches than there were printers."

"Something got interrupted."

"Two somethings," Rebecca said. "We took down the Patriarch, and the truck got stopped in Arizona."

"Maybe there's a third something," Newsome said. "I'm hearing rumors about anthrax being used against civilians in Iraq. Could that be connected?"

"I don't see how."

Newsome sighed. "Unless you find a connection, we're not going to get any help from DS. I can send you a couple of prime guys to help."

"Griffin's fine."

"Griffin's green."

"He doesn't irritate the hell out of me." Rebecca drew her brows together and looked at the sunny slit in the drawn curtains.

"You're a swell broad, Rebecca, you know that?"

"I'm a bitch, News. How are they treating you?"

"Don't ask. OIG is done with me but they're interviewing teaching staff tomorrow. The director and deputy director are going before Senate Judiciary on Wednesday. Senate reform bill is still in committee, but it's got firm Democratic support, so headquarters is activating contingency plans just to keep ahead of the curve."

"Screw the Dems."

"Mr. Hoover had a fine relationship with FDR."

"He was the last," Rebecca said. "They've been gunning for us ever since Louis Freeh ID'd Clinton's jism. Even before that. Good ol' Jimmy Carter got Clarence Kelley when his wife was dying—"

"Keep it to a simmer, Rebecca. I am."

"If BDI or some other agency has Patriarch family members in custody, I need to talk with them. My preference, give me one of the sons."

"I'll push. I should know by tomorrow."

"Be well, News."

She returned the phone to her pocket, then lay back on the bed—and rolled and grabbed the glass of water just as it started to spill. Fast as a cat. But sleep was never enough to keep her from feeling worn down.

Rebecca Rose was afraid of one thing—afraid that she wanted out. She had nine more years before she hit the GS-1811 wall, but still . . .

"This bastard is the last one," she promised herself, and closed her eyes.

It seemed seconds later, she choked and looked up to see a man with dirty blond hair leaning over the bed. He had one hand on her throat and in the other he held a Leatherman with the blade out and locked.

"My daddy's dead," he growled.

A ribbon of spit fell into her eye.

Thump.

William opened one eye and stared at the bed cover. He had not pulled it back—he was still dressed—and for a moment he wondered where he was and why.

He looked at the clock on the nightstand but that was no good—it had been off by four hours when he came in. It said ten o'clock. He guessed he had slept soundly for about two hours. So it was now about six. Time to think about finding some food and getting back to work. There was a Panda Express across the street from the motel. Something with noodles would taste good.

He washed his face in the bathroom.

Thump.

Rose was up and making noise. But it wasn't her style to make sounds loud enough to come through the walls. He glanced at the Lynx display. She was still on his team grid. Rebecca habitually kept her mike off but she had not switched to privacy mode, something older agents frequently forgot.

He lowered his arm with some embarrassment. Like looking in on a lady in her boudoir—he could get a sense of what she was doing by her vital signs.

He quickly wiped his face with a hand towel and pulled aside the curtain a few inches. A thin brown-haired girl in a pioneer dress—something in gingham, anyway, with blue checks and a kind of apron, real Little House on the Prairie—walked past. He heard the door to the right, Rebecca's door, open and close.

Rebecca had visitors.

He wondered why she hadn't told him.

"Shit," he said. Typical new agent, jumping at boo-squat.

But Rebecca was quiet as a cat. He did not remember ever hearing her move or even take a step. She wore rubber soles.

And the pioneer girl was completely out of fashion in this part of the state. Real Bo-Peep. This time, his curiosity about Rebecca's vital signs was purely professional. *If she's got Mary and her lamb coming up to the room, wouldn't I need to know that about a partner?*

He lifted his watch again and punched the display through her stats. Sure enough, her stress numbers were up . . . way beyond the levels of sexual stimulus. As well, her skin conductivity had altered and the sniffer in Rebecca's unit was picking up a distinct pong of stress and fear.

If she's a Lesbian, she doesn't want to be.

He unbolted the door, let the chain and latch down gently. On the grit-surfaced floor just outside Rebecca's door lay a piece of brass-plated chain. The end of the chain had been clipped with a bolt cutter.

William took a step. The next door beyond Rebecca's room was open. He looked left. At the end of the walkway stood a service cart hung with a laundry bag and stacked with fresh sheets and rolls of toilet paper, buckets filled with little bottles of soap and shampoo, and folded white towels.

He turned to face the rail looking out over the parking lot. In front of the motel, a plump woman in a brown maid's uniform ran across the street as fast as her stocky legs could carry her.

Getting the hell out.

Now was the time to jump to conclusions. Someone had taken the maid's pass key and deadbolt shim. They had brought their own bolt cutters for the chain.

This was real.

Gingham=pioneer spirit.

Christ, it's them. They found us.

William shut his door to a crack. Before his conscious mind could catch up, he had his slate in hand and had punched the button for agent assistance. Then he took his SIG from under the pillow. It vibrated in recognition of his keycode.

The automated Bureau phone voice came back; his location was pinpointed and local police or other agents would be there as soon as possible. "If you are able, leave your message."

"One agent hostage, one active, this location. Request any and all backup." He closed the unit and slung it on his belt. From here on, the slate would track his movements and relay whatever he was hearing to the Seattle first response center.

He put his ear to the wall. Through the plaster, just barely, he caught: *"Strip her. She's wired."*

Male, angry and not too old.

Then, *"How do you know she's a fed?"* A young woman or teenager. Paper crackled.

William's Lynx made a little wheep. Rebecca was now off his team grid.

"Check her purse."

"I don't see a purse."

"Then check her jacket!"

William opened the door again and flattened himself against the wall to the right. He knew better than to announce himself. They would cut or shoot her and then try to shoot him. If they had gone this far, they weren't too concerned about their own lives.

They had been followed from the farm, perhaps from the town. *Do they even know I'm here?*

From next door he heard a muffled grunt. Then the male's voice, louder: *"He went to get pizza, right? You kill my daddy and then you run off to eat pizza and fornicate, right?"*

The girl's voice: *"Keep it down, Jeremiah."*

"Get her badge! I want to make her eat it!"

They had opened the door to the wrong room first and found it empty. Then they had broken into Rebecca's room.

William sucked in a deep breath, letting it go with a quick and nearly silent *ohhmmmmmm.* He had learned that from a homicide detective.

"I'm going to slice you open like a squealing pig. We're going to watch while you bleed to death."

If he kicked at the door and went in now they'd kill her instantly. Backup would not arrive in time. He had just a few minutes, if that, while they toyed with her.

William looked at the maid's cart.

The young man with dirty blond hair and the finest little blue eyes—the girl had called him Jeremiah—tossed Rebecca's gun aside once he saw it would not fire for him. The girl kicked it under the television cabinet.

Rebecca sat hunched over on the side of the bed, her folded hands between her legs. They had ripped the buttons on her blouse and pulled it down from her shoulders, restricting her arm movements and pulling away her Lynx sensors. She had not been free to hit her panic button before it was on the floor. Her coat and creds were in the closet. She had removed her belt and packs before lying down and they were on the bathroom counter. The young man and the girl had not yet gone into the bathroom.

For the moment it was best not to talk. They wanted her alive long enough to have their fun and express themselves.

Jeremiah sat beside Rebecca, reaching around with his right hand and poking the tip of the gray blade against the right side of her throat. She could feel a drop of blood sliding like a warm slug to her clavicle.

The girl stepped closer, sideways, as if afraid, then leaned over. She gasped as Rebecca met her eyes, then reached out and slapped her. Rebecca turned her face to one side. Dressmaker's dummy. Let them think she was in shock. Not too far wrong. She must have been sleeping like a log. Her mouth tasted dry and sour. She could see the blood drop ooze its way down her breast. It spread out in the lace of her bra.

The girl reached into the folds of her dress and brought out a Smith & Wesson 9mm. She pointed it at Rebecca's head.

The young man shook his hair aside and moved the knife down. His left hand held her left arm at the elbow. His head was about six inches behind and to her left. He leaned awkwardly on the bed. He would go off balance with less than a nudge. If he fell, the knife would slice her throat but probably not cut anything vital.

Still, she hated being cut—any kind of cut.

And then the girl would put a slug in her brain.

"You raided private property," Jeremiah said. "You shot our daddy. You sent in the whole damned army and just shot him like a dog. Gutless cowards. You have no idea what we were getting ready for, what we had all planned out, *no idea,* do you?"

"I'm listening," Rebecca said. "Tell me."

"Tell you *what,* bitch?"

"Tell me what happened. I wasn't there."

"You're a damned liar!"

Spit flew again. She wanted to wipe her eye but didn't dare. The young man's spit from a minute ago was sitting on the corner of her lid, still damp. "What's your sister's name?" Rebecca asked. She could barely talk. The knife made a shallow slice as her throat moved. She grimaced. "Ow."

The boy backed the knife off half an inch. Good sign, for now.

"She's not my sister. She's my stepmother. Daddy had four wives."

"Oh."

Rebecca smelled oranges. Thousands of oranges.

"We're getting out of here. We have money, safe houses, they'll never find us. You'll never tell. You don't know it yet but you're *already* dead."

Jeremiah had rebalanced himself, a young man's natural caution, had pulled the knife back another inch and scooched himself forward on the bed. Not a well-trained move.

Also good.

"Right," Rebecca said.

"Where'd the other one go?" the girl asked. "We saw two of you check in."

"He left," Rebecca said. "He went back."

"Back where?"

"To Seattle. I'm off-duty."

The girl awkwardly gripped the 9mm in both hands. She didn't seem to know how to use it. Her eyes were dark brown and with her thin face and sallow skin she wasn't very pretty. Rebecca saw, through the long dress, that the girl was at least six months pregnant. She looked more worried than angry but the slap had stung. And her finger was making little jerks on the trigger.

"How long before you're due?" Rebecca asked, and then cringed inwardly. No need to remind her of her condition or her lost husband.

"You *slut,*" the girl said. "We were all doing God's work."

"Shut up," Jeremiah said. "Let's just cut her and get the hell out of here. We'll wait in the other room."

Again the knife touched Rebecca's throat and drew blood. She could feel the young man's arm tighten. She looked up at the window. Bright flickering yellow warmed the rectangle of inner curtains.

"Something's on fire," she said.

William heaped four rolls of toilet paper on the railing with tails dragging on the deck. He then squirted them all with streamers of orange-smelling fluid from the bottle of Goo-Gone he had found in the cleaning tray on the cart. Unwinding more toilet paper around the bottom of the railing, he made sure to leave a space in front of the door. He did not want them to shrink back into the room. He wanted them to open the door, look at the fire, and then try to escape—without hurting Rebecca.

"What the hell are you up to?" a man called from the parking lot. William took a book of motel matches—some people still rented smoking rooms, thank God—and lit the soaked, citrus-scented bundles. The result was immediate—a wall of brilliant flame right in front of the window to Rebecca's room.

He reached around and pounded on the door. "Fire!" he shouted. "Everyone out NOW!"

For an agonizing few seconds, he hung back flat to the wall. He shot a glance out to the street through the flames and then to the left, at people milling in the parking lot. They were staring up, mouths gaping. He did not dare shout for them to leave. No sign of patrol cars or fire trucks or any other assistance. The smoke billowed black under the roof. What a stupid ass thing to do. What if the whole place burned down?

How long until the manager or someone came running with an extinguisher and stood in his line of fire?

He heard shrill, childish cries and a hoarse shout inside the room and then the door opened. William stayed flat against the wall. A hand clutching a steel blade poked out and then withdrew. He heard scuffling then a metallic pop—not a gunshot—and a mist of water puffed through the door. The room's sprinkler system had gone off.

"Fire!" William shouted. "The roof's collapsing! Get out now!"

A young man with blond hair lurched out, wiping water from his eyes, waving the knife as if fanning away the flames. William swung a quarter turn with gun in both hands, crouched, barrel pointing right at the center of the blond man's torso.

"FBI, drop the knife and get your hands up!" William shouted. "Do it now!" The flame ebbed but thick smoke blew onto both of them.

"Jesus!" the boy shouted. He did not drop the knife. He couldn't see William or his gun. The smoke had finished the job the water had started. William began a pull, let it off. The boy stumbled blindly away from the door, blade wavering, pointing straight out, then down.

"Drop the knife NOW!"

The young man shuddered and opened his hand. The knife handle hit the deck and bounced. Inside the room William heard a girl scream then a gunshot. The window blew out over the young man and he collapsed to his knees, covered with shards of glass. "Jesus, Jesus," he mewed.

Rebecca lurched out with a twist of blond hair in her fist. Her blouse had been ripped and pulled down around her shoulders. She tugged the girl in the gingham dress out onto the deck and flung her at the iron rail and the burning stacks of toilet paper. The girl bounced off, knocking flaming, smoking rolls down to the cars and asphalt. Rebecca and the girl were now between William and the crouching young man. Rebecca saw this through strings of wet hair and swung about with a dancer's precision, pushing the girl at William. William caught her, twisted one of her arms around, and had her face-down on the deck. He kneeled on top of her. Both of the girl's hands were empty but clutching, scratching at his pants. He pressed a knee in her back hard enough to make the vertebrae pop. The girl oofed and got quiet.

"Where's the gun?" William shouted.

Smoke rolled away.

The boy looked sideways, eyes wide and red. He reached out. Rebecca kicked the knife under the rail and over the parking lot. Then she kicked the young man in the side, hard, which put him once more on his back, and stomped him right in the groin with a bare bleeding foot. He curled up like a pillbug, alternately moaning and screaming. She flipped him over in the glass and pulled back both of his arms.

The manager came up from the other side, spraying foam over everything. "Fuck this!" he was shouting. "You trying to burn me out?"

"FBI," William said, wiping his eyes.

"I've called the cops, you fuckwad, I've called the fire department—"

"Got your cuffs?" Rebecca called out. The young man jerked and struggled and she smacked him hard across the back of the head, then forced his face into the glass. William tossed her the cuffs from his belt. She caught them through a swinging arc of foam.

Rebecca's broad, well-defined shoulders, smudged with soot, glistened as she bound the young man. With dripping hair askew, black brassiere revealed, slacks halfway down her hips—showing the top stretch of pink panties—she looked absolutely amazing. The young man gasped as she lifted her knee off his lower spine. The manager's foam finally ran out and he flung the tank against the stucco. It bounced and rolled. They were all covered with hissing, dripping retardant.

"Careful with the girl, she's pregnant," Rebecca warned William.

She *had* humped up strangely. He eased her over on her side. The girl moaned between quick bursts of prayer.

Gun. He leaned far enough to see a pistol on the floor of Rebecca's room, far out of anyone's reach.

"Room's clear," Rebecca said.

Below, tenants were backing out their cars and leaving. The manager shouted over the railing: they hadn't paid their bills.

Chest heaving, Rebecca toed a blackened, sodden roll of toilet paper. "What the hell was that?" she asked William.

"Advanced tactics," William said.

She sucked in her breath, pulled up the shoulders of her blouse, and gave him the sweetest smile. "You bastard," she said.

CHAPTER THIRTY
Turkey/Iraq

The Superhawk hit a wall of air over the endless wrinkled blanket of the Zagros mountains. It shuddered like a stunned ox and fell for a few hundred feet until the blades growled, bit air again, and whanga-whanged like a Jamaican steel band. Fouad had never heard a sound like that and it made him go pale. He clutched at the belt over his slung seat.

Across from him, Special Agent Orrin Fergus signed a thumbs up and then tapped his nose. Fergus shouted, "The shit is mostly over. We're coming into Diyala. That's an Iraqi *muhafazah*. Province or whatever."

"Governorate," said the master sergeant on Fouad's left. He was a compact, well-muscled man about Fouad's age, fully tricked out in flak plate and desert camouflage, helmet overlaid with headphone and gogs and a rucksack full of folded plastic maps. His dedicated satlink kept him fully informed about activity in the area—what little activity there was. He was a connected kind of guy and looked like a robot samurai.

The crew chief moved to the rear. "Down in thirty. Use the green bucket if you are so moved. Captain Jeffries does not like a slippery deck." He looked hard at Fouad. "First time?"

Fouad nodded.

The crew chief used his boot to shift the bucket next to Fouad.

"I will be fine," Fouad said, looking up with wide black eyes.

The crew chief grinned and walked back to his position on fire control.

"They call Kifri UXO Central," Master Sergeant said. "Decades of back and forth between the Kurds and the Sunnis. The national animal is the Gambian rat. They use 'em to sniff out mines and ordnance. Happy little beasts, work like sonsabitches. Last time we were through here an Iraqi film company was making an epic about Arabs stomping Persians fourteen hundred years ago. Pretty big deal. Then the director stepped on a Coalition bomblet and blew off his leg. Took out a cameraman, too. Shit. They were feeling pretty low that day."

"Do they mind that we are here?" Fouad asked.

"The folks in Baghdad mostly don't give a fuck," Master Sergeant said with a grin. "They're supposed to be our allies, so we turn a blind eye when they kick Kurdish butt."

Orrin Fergus moved over to Fouad's side and shouted into his ear. "We're going to meet up with Tim Harris's team in Kifri. You'll conduct the interrogation for us. Harris's accent just makes 'em blink. How's your skill at the local dialect?"

"I don't know," Fouad said, feeling unsure of himself, and for reasons other than his stomach. "Here they may speak Arabic, but also Kurdish, Turkish, or even Aramaic or Assyrian. If they are Yazidis—"

"This year, they mostly speak Arabic," said Master Sergeant. "At least that's what we've been told. I love surprises, don't you? We'll find out when we get there."

"If we find bodies, I'll be busy," Fergus said. "So keep your eyes and ears open. Talk to the locals, if any, but keep your cards close. I hear there's a fellow named Tabrizi or something like that waiting in town. They don't need to know anything from us. Since we haven't been issued MOPP gear, just filter masks and BAMs, anything requiring major decon will delay our start by ten minutes while the crew seals the cabin. We'll have to wait for decon until we get back to Incirlik. And if we're dirty or acting weird— well, I hear Kifri is outstanding this time of year."

Fergus specialized in bioweapons and had been qualified as a medical examiner before joining the FBI. Fouad muttered the acronyms under his breath: MOPP was Mission Oriented Protective Posture, BAM was Biological Agent Monitor.

The Superhawk circled the town.

"Drop in five," the captain announced. "Master Sergeant is your god. We drop and then we go park and we will pickup, and you will be there on his command."

Fouad nodded compliance, though the pilot could not see him.

Most of Kifri looked like a collection of shoeboxes kicked open by unruly children. Shattered brown domes and hollowed-out two-story houses clustered around the skeleton of a bazaar. Only a few of the houses and buildings were still standing. Six years of civil war and Kurdish cleansing and decades of tyranny before that—including phosphorus bombs from Saddam—had sucked most of the life out of the town. The Superhawk flew south over a ruined military installation, an antique, war-stamped moonscape.

These were the leftovers from when Americans had briefly dreamed they could save the world from terrorism, one miserable tyranny at a time. Now, a few Yanks still flew in, around, and about, and the Iraqis did very little if anything to stop them—everybody knew they were just buzzing, like flies.

Kifri was a poster child for the cancer of history and hatred and nation-building. Nations don't get built—they grow like mold. Iraq was a whimpering mess, abandoned on the sidelines of a new war. Iran was the center of action now. Defiantly nuclear, it was being taken on—diplomatically, so far, but with many threats covert and otherwise—by the UN, Europe, Russia, and even China. The Americans had opted in as junior partners, allowing that its allies had a bigger stake because they were within range of Iran's missiles.

Americans no longer had much heart for direct fighting in Iraq, so they flew support and reconnaissance and pounded the ground in a few areas, hunting up intelligence.

Fouad tried to keep from shivering. Fergus and Master Sergeant shared a smoke. The sun through the windows swept brilliant squares over their chests as the Superhawk circled, and then they slowed and dropped. Master Sergeant unstrapped, found his balance, and motioned for the crew chief to throw open the door. The mid-morning glare blinded Fouad. Then he saw pale brown houses, broad unpaved streets, dry potholes, craters, broken windows under shattered wooden awnings, a two-story government building, Iraqi guards sitting and standing around the brick steps, smoking cigarettes and watching—and a Humvee flying a blue and yellow flag from its high antenna.

Fergus grabbed Fouad's arm. "Let's go."

They jumped to the dirt street and ran from under the shadowy wind of the blades. A man in a khaki shirt and pale green cargo pants with lots of pockets, a camera around his neck, a big red head of hair and no hat matched speed and pumped Fouad's hand and then swung about and waved to the Superhawk pilots. Fergus introduced him. This was Special Agent Tim Harris, Diplomatic Security, liaison in Iraq between the FBI and the CIA and definitely part of BuDark.

The pilot lifted the chopper away. Fouad looked over his shoulder.

"Welcome to Kifri, home of the stupid and the brave," Harris said. "The weather today is dry and slightly uncool, sporadic pissing contests with the police guard, but no sign of a storm. We now proudly fly the blue and yellow flag of official Baghdad approval because they want to know who's using anthrax to kill Kurdish Jews in a town where there should not any longer be Kurds, much less Jews."

The Master Sergeant opened the Humvee's door and sat shotgun. He carried a machine pistol with an assault clip like a flattened ram's horn. Harris had two Glocks, one in a shoulder holster, the second under his left cuff, above his boot. The Humvee had a ROAG—Remotely Operated Auto-targeting Gun—a rapid-fire twenty millimeter mounted over the roof like a small steel sewage pipe.

Inside, with the engine running, the Humvee cooled quickly. They were surrounded by two inches of punch-suck armor, just barely enough to stop an old RPG, not enough to worry the nose-heavy, slag-splat anti-tank shell currently in fashion in these parts. Three UAVs—automated aerial drones—relayed data from hundreds of meters in the sky. Screens in the dashboard popped up as Harris spun the vehicle about. Sensors started pinging like sonar in a submarine, scoping out potential targets. Echoes from around corners attracted particular attention. Sound trackers on the roof could zero in on weapons action and coordinate return fire through UAVs and their only other air support, the Superhawk.

The vehicle had a Combat Guidance unit—it could drive itself to a rendezvous if its drive train and wheels were intact but humans inside were incapacitated. Fouad could not help but believe that it had eyes and ears and a will of its own. Machines had evolved faster than men in the fog of war.

The large white house on the outskirts of Kifri might once have been comfortable: a cement-walled single-story square surrounded a courtyard, the square itself fenced in by battered black iron and what might have once been a cactus garden. For blocks around, all the other houses were rubble.

The Humvee rumbled over a toppled gate and stopped. An older man in a worn dirty business suit with a white kerchief wrapped round his head stood up from the porch and lifted his arm. Fergus stepped out first. Master Sergeant was more cautious. He moved slowly, surveying everything with critical eyes.

"Superhawk is parking, gents," he announced, tapping his headphones. "We have forty-five minutes and you know I will pull y'all out before that."

Harris opened his door last, throat bobbing.

Fouad followed Fergus and they stood by the Humvee.

The older man in the white kerchief approached Fouad with a suspicious glance at the others and cautiously extended his right hand. *"As-salaamu aleikum,"* he greeted. Then he hugged Fouad and sniffed his cheeks. "I am glad you are here. It is not proper, what happened. We must be careful. This still is a house of death."

All heads turned. An engine roared far off down a deserted street. A small rust-pocked Subaru Forester drove up to the gate in a cloud of dust. A tanned hairy arm stuck out and waved. Master Sergeant tapped his headphones as if to knock out what he was hearing. His lip curled.

"Gents, home office says we have a mandatory guest."

"Hell, Kifri is the last place I'd expect to find Saddam's hidden stockpiles," the large, barrel-chested man said as he approached the group through the gate. "My name is Edmond Beatty. Friends call me Beatty. To whom am I addressing my concerns?" He held out his hand and raised a bushy eyebrow.

Master Sergeant introduced the group but the older Iraqi held back in the shadows, glaring resentfully.

Harris said, "Beatty and I know each other already."

"Pleasure's mutual," Beatty said.

Fouad shook hands but felt he was missing something crucial—history. "And why are you here, Mr. Beatty?" he asked. Boldness seemed called for—Harris did not like the man and neither did Fergus. Master Sergeant seemed irritated but also amused.

"I'm a retired colonel," Beatty said. "I served in Iraq in GW 2. Don't ever call it the Coalition War to my face. Right, friends?"

"Colonel Beatty is something more than local color," Fergus said. "He was given a State Department assignment, at the behest of six senators, to continue the search for Saddam's chemical and biological weapons. That assignment has not been revoked, unfortunately."

"I heard about your plague house on the weed vine," Beatty said. "I wish you gentleman had called me. I could have scurried up here and gotten the facts and that would have saved the U.S. taxpayers some real money. Superhawks are expensive pieces of machinery. Bright and shiny. I am well acquainted with Dr. Mirza Al-Tabrizi. He represents the Shiites in Kifri, kind of a pooh-bah for the oppressed majority. The Kurds seem to like him, too. That does not make him an objective source, in my book."

Al-Tabrizi folded his arms and leaned against the closed door.

"We'd appreciate your standing second fiddle on this one, sir," Master Sergeant advised in a low tone.

"That's *play* second fiddle, not stand. I've been here, continuously, longer than any other American soldier," Beatty said. "A true gentleman never gives up on a good cause." He turned to Fouad. "Sir, like Fergus, you are Special Agent, FBI, am I correct? And connected somehow with this Bureau of Ultimate Darkness, or whatever the hell it's called now?"

Fouad was about to speak when Beatty moved in, towering over him. "They drag you in here to interpret?"

"His identity is not important to you, Beatty," Harris growled. "Bad enough you know who we are."

Beatty swung around and looked them all in the face in sequence. "I speak Kurdish, Turkish, Farsi, Urdu, Pashto, and Arabic," he said. "Six or seven dialects."

"All with a Tennessee accent," Harris added.

"True, but I am understood wherever I go in this country. And who are we interviewing? Any live people, this time?"

"Sir," Master Sergeant said, more forcefully. "You are subordinate to our mission. Whatever help you can render will be appreciated but you are not in charge here."

"Well, who in hell *is* in charge? On the ground, I mean."

"That would be me," said Harris.

"Lead on," Beatty exclaimed with a broad smile. He clapped Harris on the back. "I will call you sir, and mean it. Just explain to me what in hell anthrax is doing this far north."

Inside the house the stench of death was strong, but carried on wafts of cool moist air, the smell seemed somehow unnatural and frustrated. Fouad watched the men move through the empty trash-filled rooms with detachment. He did not like this strange sense of calm. There was a perversity in him that his mother would not have appreciated but that his father might have understood too well, and it had been exaggerated by his training at Quantico. *To see the awful things is to see life as it really is. It makes you sharper, stronger, superior. You can stand it when others cannot.*

That is why young men go off to war.

The house had looked better from the outside. Most of the rooms were open to the air, with gaping shell holes in the roof. The courtyard was filled with broken and burned sticks of furniture. Someone had tried to stay warm in the winter.

Al-Tabrizi took Fouad by the shoulder. "Be at ease with me," he said in Arabic. "I take solace that Muslims at least sometimes speak with these men and temper them. The bull, Beatty, is not respected around here. He has made too many deals, spoken from both sides of his mouth to gain information."

"I heard that, you old bastard," Beatty called out.

Al-Tabrizi ignored him.

"Then tell me, what brings you here?" Fouad asked the old man.

"A pious man spoke out of turn for the sake of his closeness to God. Some of my people went at his behest to this house and found the Kurds, these Jews, dead. Ice was brought by police. Had they been Muslims we would have buried them . . ." He shrugged. "It is possible the Sunnis have been doing experiments with our poor Jews. I do not know. They have no respect for life."

"Amen," Beatty said.

Walking around the courtyard, they approached the back of the house—the kitchen. A pump handle stood in one corner before a small stone and mortar cistern.

Fergus slipped on rubber gloves. He removed from his rucksack more gloves and fine-filter masks with little rubber bellows and a jar of nose cream and handed them around. "Slip these on and fasten them tight."

"Nobody else has fallen ill," Al-Tabrizi said, this time in English.

Past the kitchen, stepping over broken glass and empty cans, they came to what might have once been a workshop or a storage room. In the center of the room, blocks of ice had been arranged in a flat igloo and shaved ice had been sprinkled over a tarp that partially covered the blocks. Naked feet stuck out from under the tarp, heels soaking in puddles of filthy water.

Master Sergeant put his gloved hand over his mask. Harris stood with hands on his hips staring critically at the wrinkled and discolored feet.

Al-Tabrizi handed Fouad an old and battered compact flash memory card. "We took many pictures before the ice arrived, donated by a hotel and a hospital. The people who did this left Kifri two days ago in a truck. We have pictures of them as well. If we have disturbed the truth of what is here, I apologize, but you understand . . . There was urgency."

"All right," Fergus said. "Gentlemen, lend a hand. Let's pull one of them out."

"Then they haven't been here more than a few days," Beatty said. His voice had dropped by half in the smelly chill of the back workshop.

Fouad moved to help Harris and Fergus tug a corpse from beneath the nearest igloo of ice. It was an older woman, naked but for a single undergarment. Her face was a mask. Her mouth fell open in a dead scream. Her tongue was swollen and black.

"They are not from Kifri," Al-Tabrizi said. "They were brought here from farther north by men in trucks. Workers who were paid to clean this room and prepare have told me the men who delivered these poor souls were bragging they had something that would kill only Jews, and that the planet would soon be cleansed."

"Jesus," Beatty said.

Fergus checked the woman's skin. Her legs, torso, and one arm were covered with wide black scabs. He removed a microlume, a small plastic plate, from his belt pack, pulled out a red tab, turned her head, and rubbed the tip over her tongue, then examined the read-out. He did the same on an eschar—one of the flaking black lesions on her chest.

"It's anthrax, both pulmonary and cutaneous," he said. He pointed to black marks and splotches on her stomach and around her ribs. "GI as well. They must have made her eat some of it." He examined the card's display from a few inches, scowling. "I see protective antigen, edema factor, and lethal factor—PA, EF, LF—but I'm also getting something unfamiliar. Could be a new plasmid." He looked up at Al-Tabrizi. "I have to take internal samples. It would be better if you left the room. I will do my best to be respectful."

"I will stay," Al-Tabrizi said. "It is my duty, and the necessity is clear."

"Sir, we're talking about the likely release of bacilli made even more virulent by vegetative mutation inside a victim," Fergus said. "Please leave."

Al-Tabrizi glanced at Fouad. "He is a good doctor," Fouad told the Shiite.

They stood outside and made sure their masks were tight.

"Is that even possible?" Beatty asked. "Can they target something like this to Jews? And how in hell would Saddam hide something this big for so long?"

"We're pretty sure it wasn't Saddam," Harris said.

"He made tons and tons of the shit. If not him, who the hell is it? Goddammit, boys, this could be what we've all been looking for. My senators—"

"Sir, you are not to speak of this to anybody," Master Sergeant cautioned. "Not even your senators."

"Well, how in hell—I'm not in your line of command, son."

Master Sergeant lifted his H&K. "Sir, I have been instructed to tolerate your presence, so as to access whatever information you may provide, and so as not to create another partisan mess in Washington. But I am authorized by the Commander in Chief to prevent this information from being leaked by anyone, including you. Do I have your word as a patriot and a military officer that you will keep absolutely silent about everything you see and hear today?"

Beatty's face stiffened. He raised his gloved hand, keeping it well away from his face and body. "When you put it that way," he said, "on my mother's grave, I so swear."

Al-Tabrizi stood in an outer doorway, gasping and trying not to be sick. As Fergus came out of the death room, Fouad approached him and quietly asked, "Can these people now be properly buried?"

"They should be burned," Fergus said.

"That is not the custom," Al-Tabrizi protested.

"If dogs get 'em it could spread all over town."

Master Sergeant intervened. "Sir, we won't be able to return for the next day or so and we certainly can't take them with us. We do not want to violate local customs. That might attract even more attention."

Harris nodded to Al-Tabrizi. "Tell the burial detail to wear masks and hospital gloves and to bury them deep, where no dogs will find them," he suggested. He removed a glove, reached into his jacket, took out a thousand-dollar bill, and gave it to Al-Tabrizi. "For expenses, headstones, whatever."

Al-Tabrizi took the money but refused to look at anybody now. He had tears on his cheeks, tears of anger and shame.

Beatty returned to his vehicle, walking beside Fouad, Harris, and Fergus for a few yards. "Doesn't matter what we do now, what we give or what we try," Beatty said. "They needed twenty years to learn democracy. We gave them five. When the Baathists rose up again and the Shiites allied with Iran, we supported the Sunnis with money and weapons, bless our pointy little heads. That cranked up the old death machine all over again. When we pulled out, we left the whole country twisting on a short rope. God have mercy on us all."

Master Sergeant followed them, walking backward, face to the battered white house. Beatty gave them a brief wave, climbed into his Subaru, and put it in gear, spinning up a rooster tail of dirt.

The Superhawk roared overhead and made its dusty landing.

"I hate dust," Fergus said. "Could be spores everywhere." He pulled a canvas-wrapped plastic box from the wall of the helicopter and showed them syringes pre-loaded with Gamma Lysin. "We'll all carry these, just in case."

CHAPTER THIRTY-ONE
Seattle, Harborview Medical Center

SAC John Keller joined William in Griff's hospital room late in the evening. Keller turned a metal hospital chair around and sat on it with his long legs jutting out like a crane fly's. In his late fifties, thin, with sculpted Appalachian features and large gray eyes, he looked like a particularly conservative accountant or an undertaker and more likely to be William Griffin's father than the man in the hospital bed, behind the plastic curtains, even in his better days.

They said very little for the first few minutes of Keller's visit. Griff hadn't moved except for the rise and jerky fall of his chest. "They're going to transfer him to Swedish in a week, I hear," Keller said.

"That's what they tell me, sir."

"He's going to make it. He's tough. I've worked with a lot of fine agents and I have never known anyone tougher. We cannot afford to lose agents like Erwin Griffin."

Keller was thinking out loud. Agents had come in and out, observing Griff in his bed and all of them without exception had begun to think out loud as if at confession.

Keller glanced over his shoulder at William. "I hear you spend an hour here each day."

"I'm waiting for OPR to return me to duty," William said.

"Right." Keller smiled. "Rose gave you one hell of a spirited defense. Told me she'd be dead if you hadn't turned arsonist."

"I'm not allowed to speak about the matter, sir."

"It was certainly unorthodox."

"Yes, sir."

Keller pushed to his feet and brushed off his midnight-blue pants. William stepped aside in the small space as Keller strode for the door. Keller paused, turned, and held out his hand. "Thanks."

"Sir?" William shook with him.

"We need fine agents. Hate to lose any." Reaching into his jacket, smiling like a bandit, Keller pulled out a length of white toilet paper, about a yard's worth, hung it around William's neck, and made a quick sign of the cross. "May this wipe away your sins."

Pleased with himself, Keller closed the door behind him.

William sat in the metal hospital chair the same way Keller had and leaned his chin on the back like a puppy.

Griff's face, in the shadow of a steel cage studded with screws, was a map of sutures held together by shining glue and plastic strips. His nose and cheek bones had been pulled back into place from where the bomb suit's face-plate had squashed them. Shims of sterile cartilage interlaced with stem cells from his own marrow had been inserted between the bones. They made little bumps under the sutures. Nose cartilage had been removed so Griff's face was still flat, and he would need more reconstructive surgery later. His mouth was full of so much plastic tubing that he couldn't speak even had he been conscious.

"Come on, Griff," William said. "I need some advice right about now."

Griff opened his eyes. The eyes surveyed the ceiling, but did not turn either left or right. They closed.

Still no Griff. Just the body fighting along as best it could, waiting for its owner to return. Waiting for the commanding presence it had been used to for so many years.

Like William himself.

An hour later Rebecca arrived with two coffees in a cardboard carry box. William jerked out of a stiff slumber on the metal chair.

"It's four a.m.," she said, staring through the plastic at Griff. Her eyes glinted like onyx in the penumbra of the room's small night light. "They're holding the wife and son at Seatac. Since we bagged them, News has arranged for us to interrogate them before anyone else. But we have to get in and out before eight. Drink this, then come with me," she said.

"I'm on probation," William said.

"Did Keller avoid you like a pile of dogshit?" Rebecca asked.

"No." William pulled the toilet paper from his pocket and let it unfold. "He put this around my neck."

Rebecca's smile transformed her. Again those dimples that could only be improved with cat's whiskers. She pressed the quilted paper between her fingers, lifted it for a sniff, and stroked it as if it were velvet. "Order of the lilac garter. Welcome back to duty."

CHAPTER THIRTY-TWO
Middle America

The only place Sam could now be at shallow peace with himself, with his plans, was the open road—driving the old Dodge, dragging the horse trailer over long, flat miles between scattered rocky plateaus, past odd grassy humps rising from gravel-bedded alkali flats, desert towns whose gutters flowed with olive-colored water after a heavy rain—all of them cut through by endless ribbons of cracked and eroding asphalt—and at the end of each day, each great segment stricken from his map, spartan rooms with worn carpets in little strip motels.

He tried not to think about the past—everything his father and grandfather had worked to build being squandered, a country turning inward, distracted by fear and greed. He could not help but see these rough untended roads as the truest, deepest sign of an America once too fat and happy to stand up to the plate and bat a really smart game, and then, after 9-11, too lost in its own paranoia and bitterness to realize that it was being taken for a nasty ride.

It was not so odd that around that same time, in the forests and towns of the northwest, land of both outlandish, Godless liberals and the most rough-hewn pseudo-Christian bigots, he had picked up both the skills and the psychology necessary to play the quintessential anti-Semite.

At first, it had been a performance . . . Going to the world's hardest places, learning the languages, putting on the garb and assuming the customs—mortifying his white man's flesh—a spectacular series of patriot tricks, with himself the ultimate magician. But after 9-11, grimmer and emptier, having burrowed deep into America's spiritual rectum, having trusted his leaders and committed so many crimes—and having signed on for a mission that even he could not carry out—the smell had finally tainted him.

And then had come 10-4.

And the madness.

* * *

On the third day of his journey, Sam turned on the truck's radio. Keeping an eye on the long straight road, he set the scan button and popped through the spectrum of on-air broadcast stations. Lately, satellite radio had been eating their lunch, but there was still a high-power, hearty breed of broadcaster hiding in small brick buildings beyond the endless cornfields, relaying the ruminations and rants that still drew, last time Sam had checked, over twenty million listeners in the U.S. of A.

Sam finally found the station he was looking for—pay for pray radio.

A preacher was speaking in a steady bass drone. "It is now once again a crime to slaughter an innocent and unborn child, but how much greater a crime to mislead a soul into damnation? How much greater a crime to put the ring of sin through a man's nose and pull him onto the pathway of deception and misery that runs straight to eternal hell, to pain beyond imagination and fire that never ceases to burn? How much greater a crime and a sin to lead to damnation that which is immortal, a man's soul, by sharing sinful thoughts, by spreading the awful secular hatred of those educated at big city northern universities, or those who speak day in and day out on television and on the Web, in books and movies, passing along their evil delusions? How much greater a crime is that, and why is it not illegal, I say, and punishable by death? We have the power still! We have the center and the heartland! Yea shall these bellwethers, these evil curly-horned and slit-eyed rams of the devil that so mislead our flocks, shall they all be—must they be!—judged by more than the soft hand of Jesus, but by the hard stern hands of God's sworn and devoted servants, and put to the sword of holy truth . . ."

Sam wiped his eyes. The heat was enormous. So much searing pain, memory, grief, stoked and banked coals fired by those who spoke for God but refused to listen to Him. Murderers and sinners all.

Sam knew how to deliver vengeance and medicine all at once.

Sam had recharged.

CHAPTER THIRTY-THREE
Iraq

Fouad could not get the dead woman's expression of slack horror out of his thoughts. How she had suffered. Muslims killing innocents again. At least it was to be assumed the guilty ones were Muslims. He leaned his head back against the bulkhead of the Superhawk's cabin. The soft roar of the engines and the wind had permeated his entire body.

Outside, day had faded to night. The cockpit was lit with red, green, and white, and the pilots' helmeted heads made little bobbing motions. Beside him Fergus was asleep. Riding with them back to Incirlik, Harris stared fixedly at the port in the emergency access hatch across from him as if sighting on a distant star. Master Sergeant carried his rifle like a baby in the crook of his arm. The crew was forward, leaning over their gear or lost behind thick helmets and goggles, surveying the terrain.

Fouad shut his eyes. He opened them to see a radiance in the cabin. The sun was rising in the southeast. Had he slept so long? No, the light had a brilliant pearl gray cast—spooky, all wrong. Not the sun.

"What the fuck?" Master Sergeant said. He shouted forward, "We got flares?"

The glow lingered, pulsing, then slowly died through a spectrum of greens, oranges, reds, and finally dull brown.

"That was no flare," the crew chief shouted.

"What was it? Where?" Master Sergeant unbuckled and stepped forward to the cockpit door, tapping his headphones with a scowl. "Satlinks are out. I'm not getting anything."

"We're going to set down for a spell," the co-pilot announced.

"Why?" Harris shouted forward.

"That was a nuke," the captain said. "A couple hundred klicks away, but definitely a nuke. This chopper is hardened but ITAR rules say we land after any strike. There's overcast ahead at angels three, so I'm taking her down now." ITAR referred to the Iranian Tactical Area of Responsibility.

"We're still over the mountains," Master Sergeant said. "Extreme washboard down there."

Fergus looked at Fouad, then at Harris. "Best guess?" he asked.

"Someone took out Shahabad Kord," Harris said.

"Northern Zone, Iran," Fouad murmured. He had been studying the maps earlier. His father had taught him to always know where you were going and what you might find there.

"That's nuts," Master Sergeant said. "Who would do that? Israel?"

"Shahabad Kord has—or had—some intermediate birds on standby," Fergus said. "Shahab 7s."

Shahab. Shooting star.

"Iran's been using them as a last-ditch bargaining chip. Could be Israel, could be NATO." Harris looked both shaken and disgusted. "Only a matter of time. Lucky us. We just saw history being made."

The Superhawk descended at a steep angle. Again, the rotor blades were making that growling steel-drum sound. Fouad could hardly believe what was happening, what he was being told.

Muslims are roasting in nuclear fire.

He felt his stomach leap and pressed his lips together. He could taste the sour acid in his mouth. It made the backs of his teeth feel rough.

"Hang on," the pilot called back. "Anyone have a Michelin guide? How about finding us a nice hotel with a big parking lot, some shish-kabob and cold beer?"

Fouad closed his eyes and inclined his head to pray.

CHAPTER THIRTY-FOUR
Washington State

Rebecca Rose again insisted on driving. William Griffin sat quietly, trying to appear relaxed with hands gripping one knee. Early morning traffic was light as they headed south.

The Federal Detention Center rose dusky gold in the early morning light, a wedge of two pale angled monoliths atop split arcs of brown concrete brick. To William the facility looked like a huge piece of chocolate cake topped by twin Lego slabs. "Kind of pretty, don't you think?" he asked as they passed under an ornate radius wall, into the shadow of the imposing wedge.

"I've never seen a pretty prison," Rebecca said.

They passed their credentials through narrow openings in thick security glass and were shown into twenty feet of curving arches mounted with sensors and interrupted by sampling stations. They were subjected to sniffers, iris-scanned, fingerprinted, gave a little blood, and then opened their mouths for a buccal cell swab. These details were tested, logged, and checked against an unspecified number of federal criminal and citizen databases.

Ten years before, most federal prisons had become super-sensitive about the political, viral, and bacterial loads of their inmates. All visitors—even sworn peace officers—had to undergo biota exams along with the security checks. Some prison wardens saw their facilities as ecological preserves—pathogen restriction was as important to them as any other form of safekeeping.

"You both test negative for HIV, HCV, HPV, PhD., and DDT," the chief of security told them. "But you should have taken care of that parking ticket," he said to William.

"I was sixteen," William said.

"Hey, we're on your side," Rebecca snapped.

"Sure. Agent Griffin, you appear to have an open case before the OPR.

We have some concern that you are truly an active duty agent, as specified in your signed affidavit."

"I'll vouch for him. And I'll take back my slate, if you'd like me to make a few calls . . ."

"We're just being extra careful. Our farm kids are attracting a lot of attention. You're lucky to even see them."

"We live in an age of cooperation, right?" Rebecca asked. She took William's shoulder and pulled him through the metal swing gates and then left into the waiting room. Their visitor escort arrived ten minutes later, a beefy Latina with large somber eyes and little to say or be cheerful about. She also was not impressed that they were FBI. The Latina took them deep, through two more glass-and-steel checkpoints, and introduced them to a young guard with spiky white hair and tattoos on his hands.

"Warden Deiterly extends his greetings," the tattooed guard said, reading from a digital slate and then cross-referencing with a clipboard. "We can access you to only one prisoner, Jeremiah Jedediah Chambers. Your requested pregnant female, Hagar Rachel Chambers, has been transferred to a medical facility for treatment. You have until eight a.m. U.S. Marshals will pick up Chambers at nine. He will then no longer be a guest of SeaTac FDC."

"Who's taking custody? And where are they taking him?" Rebecca asked.

"ATF, I believe," the white-blond answered. "Maybe BDI. We can't reveal destinations. You probably know that."

"No claim by the FBI?"

"Not that I can see," the white-blond said, referring to his clipboard.

"Has he asked for an attorney?"

"Not yet. He's a bumpkin. But we like to extend all due civil rights to our prisoners, even the idiots, so he's been assigned a VC—virtual counsel. We call our VC Max Detention. You don't have to pay him much mind."

He opened the door to the interview room.

"We'd better give this our best shot," Rebecca murmured as the door closed and locked behind them. "I don't think News expected to lose them so soon."

"Lose them?"

"If you haven't noticed," Rebecca said, "we're in the thick of a free-for-all turf war." They sat at the rectangular table.

Jeremiah Chambers stood at the inmate door and was buzzed in. Two guards accompanied him. One of the guards touched a remote control and an old faded plasma display swung down from the ceiling to the right of the table. Chambers was shackled to the single chair across the table. His hair had been cut to a thin shag and he was dressed in brilliant orange jail togs. He wore slippers but no shoes. There were cuts on his face—from their encounter, William assumed. Chambers immediately lay his head on the table and closed his eyes. One guard gripped his shoulder and squeezed, hard. Chambers flinched but did not sit straight.

The screen switched on. They saw a backdrop of a bookcase filled with law books. A dark-suited figure faded in over the bookcase.

"Is this the virtual counsel?" Rebecca asked.

"Yes, ma'am. You have two-way with the VC," the white-blond said. "I'll be sitting in on this session."

"No objection," Rebecca said.

At his nod, the escorts departed. The guard patted the screen with mock affection. "Max is better than some of the live ones."

The virtual counsel appeared to be about forty-five years old and prosperous. His eyes had a discerning expression and he exuded reassurance and confidence. "My provisional client is facing charges relating to an assault on two FBI agents. He has been denied bail as a material witness before the Federal Internal Security Court."

"I did not know that," Rebecca said. "Thank you." To William, she said, "BDI again, and probably Secret Service."

The VA continued. "A protest against his transfer into secret federal custody has automatically been placed before the state intermediary security court in Olympia. Other charges, open and secret, may be pending. I advise my provisional client to answer no questions relating to these matters until a human attorney is present and the pending charges to which I am not privy have been made clear to that attorney." The VC sat back with a look of deep concern.

"He's done," the guard explained. "He doesn't usually say much after the first outburst."

William was appalled by this expedient but kept his face blank.

Jeremiah let loose with a sad jailhouse laugh. "He's a ghost. I have no rights."

"If you don't remember us, you should," Rebecca said. "You and your step-mom tried to kill us. This is William Griffin. His father is the agent who shot your father."

Rebecca now had Jeremiah's complete attention. He sat up and placed his shackled hands on the table. His eyes bore into William's.

"William's father was killed in the bomb blast," Rebecca added, with a sidelong glance, King's X. "So you two have a lot in common."

Jeremiah shuffled his hands together. "Like picking weeds and killing bugs. I make myself a big pile of bugs," he pinched and dropped one on an imaginary pile, "and I don't care which ear of corn they chewed on. They're all dead."

"Well, we're not dead, Jeremiah. You may have tried to be a stone cold killer, but I think all you really wanted was to talk, not to commit murder. You wanted to tell your side of the story. That's why I'm here this morning. William is here because you screwed up and busted into the wrong room."

Jeremiah knit his brows. "You don't know anything about me."

"But some of the things you said in that motel room——"

"All conversations in this room are being recorded," the virtual counsel said. "If we are referring to the scene of an alleged altercation, my provisional client should remain silent."

"We're not in court, Jeremiah," Rebecca said. "This is off the record, for now."

"I advise my client that nothing said in this room is off the record," the VC commented.

"They put drugs in the food," Jeremiah said. "All the cells are bugged. They strung wires through the cement when they laid the walls and floors. Microphones and cameras everywhere. That's what I've been told."

The VC flickered but added nothing.

"I was just curious——" Rebecca said.

"How does it feel?" Jeremiah interrupted. He had not taken his eyes off William. "My daddy was my whole world. He left behind sons and daughters and grandchildren—he had four wives, you know—his flock . . . He was our Abraham. You can't know what our life was like, how good it was. We lived in the presence of a true man of God. Some said my father *was* God."

"My father was a hardnose," William said. "Sometimes he made my life hell."

A film fell over Jeremiah's gaze and he glanced to one side. "We just want to be left alone."

"My father beat me when I didn't meet his standards," William said. That was mostly not true, but he was following Rebecca's lead.

"I advise my assignee not to discuss any alleged beatings," the VC said.

Jeremiah lifted his eyes. "Your father's dead, that's fine. One more bug." He looked at William with slit-eyed curiosity. "Don't you want to put your hands around my neck and chicken-choke me? What kind of family——"

"Why did Chambers make you leave? Why didn't he let you stay on the farm?" Rebecca asked.

"My father never really trusted me with anything important," William said.

Rebecca folded her hands, interested in the developing tension.

"Well, that's sad," Jeremiah said, with a remarkably believable tone of wisdom and pity. "My father was a fair man. His rules was hard but we got praise when we did good."

"Who came to see your father at the farm?"

"Sheep seeking fodder," Jeremiah said. "Pilgrims."

Rebecca opened her small folder and pulled out a picture of an inkjet printer. "Who brought these to the farm?"

Jeremiah looked at the picture. His eyes cleared and his lips thinned.

"Someone came to the farm and gave some of these to your father," Rebecca prodded.

"We was printing up flyers. I was learning to set up a print shop."

"Good job skills, great for getting work in the outside world," Rebecca said. "But you don't care about the outside. How often did these people visit?"

Jeremiah chuckled. "They stood in line. We shooed them like flies. You don't know nothing."

"There was only one," Rebecca said.

Jeremiah stared into a corner.

"He brought bags of yeast," Rebecca said. "And the stuff to make fireworks."

"We packed fireworks. We sold them like Indians."

"Why put yeast in the fireworks?" Rebecca asked.

Jeremiah cocked his head and winked at William. "She's doing all the talking."

William folded his arms. "She does the hard work. I listen."

Rebecca passed William a quick smirk. "Jeremiah, why did you spread yeast all over the farm?"

"Alleged yeast," the virtual counsel said.

"We did a lot of baking," Jeremiah said.

"Did you bake with the yeast that the visitor brought?"

Jeremiah shook his head and leaned forward, shackles singing against the table. "I'm glad your daddy's dead. I hope your brothers and sisters are all sobbin' their guts out."

"I'm an only child. Your father didn't trust you, did he?" William shot back. "He didn't trust you to defend the farm, so he sent you away. Why was that?"

"He loved us. He loved his children. God told him he had been discovered, and that soon all the minions of Federales Satanus would be on us. We didn't want to leave, but we obeyed his plan."

"Well, it's over now and I thought you should know," Rebecca said. "Your visitor—the man who brought the printers—was an undercover FBI agent. We sent him to the farm and he sold your father a bill of goods. You are such rubes. The FBI convinced you to do useless work and then got you on a terrorism rap. Sweet." Rebecca leaned forward. "Do you know what a sting is, Jeremiah? Your father fell for it. And now, all of you are heading deep into the Federal Internal Security System—and none of us are ever going to hear about you again. No headlines, no trials, no appeals. You're goddamned for sure."

For a second, naked fear played over Jeremiah's face. William almost felt sorry for him. "The yeast was just a test," Jeremiah said, struggling to keep control. "We did not pack *yeast*. The sheep died, didn't they?"

"Would you like me to bring our agent into this room? I can make a phone call and have him here tomorrow. Right now, he's in Florida, on a well-deserved vacation. Would you even recognize him? I don't believe you ever met him."

"I won't be here," Jeremiah said, eyes going to the barred door.

"Did your father let you in on those discussions?" William piled on. "Did he trust you?"

"We all was there, for different meetings," Jeremiah insisted.

"Convince me. Tell us what he looked like. Maybe then we'll believe you," William said. Rebecca pinched his knee, hard: he had gone too far, too fast. But it worked.

"He was a tall guy. Taller than you." He pointed at William.

"A *tall* guy, Jeremiah? That's it?" Rebecca asked, contemptuous.

"Blond hair. Dirty blond, sun streaks, not like this *freak*." He rattled his shackles at the guard. "He wore jeans and boots. I . . . I don't remember any more, but I *was* there!"

"Tell us if there was something distinctive about him, Jeremiah," Rebecca ventured. "If you can't tell us what he looked like, we know your daddy didn't trust you."

The young man's face worked into a frown of concentration, then anguish, as if a fish were about to slip from his hands. "One eye blue, one eye green," he cried out. "I was *there*."

Rebecca did not let up. She hammered. "What did you think you could accomplish—something big, something that would change the world? What in hell kind of story is that? You're just a bunch of rubes, raised like farm animals—how in hell could you hope to *hurt* us?"

"We was being trained! I was learning networks, to set up the printers when they came, and some of us was learning how to pack explosives and make fireworks. We packed boxes and boxes of them. We been packing them for a year now. Enough bugs to kill all the Jews in a big city. Where are all those boxes now, huh? You tell me that!"

"Packing them with *anthrax*, Jeremiah?" Rebecca asked, eyes wide, mouth open in disbelief.

Jeremiah sat back smiling.

"Is that what you were told?" Rebecca asked.

He put on a nasty, sly look. "The sheep died. You'll learn."

"Jeremiah, if you used real anthrax, why aren't *you* dead?"

William felt his stomach tighten.

"You don't know nothing," Jeremiah said. "We wore masks."

Rebecca pushed back her chair. "What kind of masks, Jeremiah? Red bandannas? What about your skin? Were you all vaccinated?"

"We don't believe in that," Jeremiah said. "God protects those who do his work."

"Oh, really? If you had actually been packing anthrax, you'd *all* be dead by now."

Jeremiah shook his head violently. "We cleaned it up. We burned it. You'll never find anything."

"We haven't found a trace of anthrax. You're the one who's ignorant."

Rebecca touched William's arm: tag team. He moved in, though he felt lost in the story by now. What was fiction, what was horrible fact?

"We set you up, Jeremiah, all of you. There was never any anthrax. What other whoppers did your father swallow?" William asked.

"You just wait and see," Jeremiah said. "I ain't talking any more." His face twisted in doubt and confusion. "I don't believe anything you say." Then he started to wail, "I'm telling you, some of it I just don't remember! They're putting stuff in my food. This place is making me crazy. Maybe I *am* sick. Would they get me help if I was sick? I think I need a doctor. I need a lawyer."

"We're done here," the virtual counsel said. The background on the screen began flashing red. "Questioning of my assignee must stop, and human counsel must be physically present for any further interviews."

The guard had put some distance, as much as he could, between himself and the table.

Rebecca stood. "Get our boy a doctor, then a lawyer," she suggested. Then, acid, "Check him for *anthrax*."

Rebecca was on her phone as soon as they had left the detention center. In the parking lot she made three calls: one to Hiram Newsome in Virginia, one to John Keller, and one to a doctor name Bobby Keel. She slipped the slate into her pocket and took out a handkerchief to wipe her face.

"Are you all right?" William asked.

"Right as rain. This is nuts," she said. "Pack anthrax for a year in a dusty old barn and live? I don't believe a word of it."

"Can we afford not to believe?"

"I *know* anthrax, William. The anthrax we dealt with back in 2001 graded out at one trillion spores per gram, so fine it acted like a gas. It went *everywhere*."

"Maybe he's smarter than he looks. He was having us on, playing back our story and upping the ante."

Rebecca shook her head. "They might have been creating a diversion. The farm might have just been a testing station."

"Who's Bobby Keel?"

"A veterinary epidemiologist," she said. "We need to know if any sheep near the farm have come down with anthrax." She unlocked the driver's side door. "A tall blond man with one blue eye and one green eye. How about some breakfast?" Her hands worked like an ex-smoker searching for cigarettes, the cop's second drug of choice. Then she turned the key in the ignition and switched on the radio. They caught the tail end of the news:

"*. . . no confirmation from the White House that the seismic tremors detected around the world came from a thermonuclear explosion in northern Iran. A State Department spokesperson is quoted as saying that the demolition of large ammunition stores can create a similar signature, but weapons experts disagree.*"

Rebecca gripped the steering wheel.

"Kind of puts what we're doing in perspective, doesn't it? Anthrax killed five people in the U.S. I wonder how many are dying out there, in Iran or *wherever the Christ it is?*" She pounded the wheel to each shouted word. Then, quieter, "This will suck up every resource, distract everyone. We're sunk." She bowed her head over the wheel. "Shit."

After a moment, William said, "I can drive."

"Then drive, *Goddammit.*"

She turned the car off in the middle of the parking aisle and they exchanged seats. William watched her from the corner of his eye. She was trying not to bite her fingernails. Beneath the chipped polish, they were already down to the quick.

CHAPTER THIRTY-FIVE
Silesia, Ohio

He was about to put decent Americans in peril, make them unknowing sheep before a new American Trinity: and so he came to an inland shipwreck of a town washed up on the midwestern shores of that endless tidal sea of red ink—the young out of work and moved away, the old begging along the highways.

The town he had chosen had once boasted a population of fifteen thousand, too many even for Sam's angry, fanatic heart.

Now, at five thousand, it was just about right.

At seven-thirty, the tavern parking lot was nearly empty. Sam parked the truck and trailer, taking up two spaces, then got out and stretched. The moon was up, a crescent hanging one handspan above the low skyline. The dingy neighborhood on the outskirts of town was quiet. The single-story brick-walled tavern made a small pool of friendly light—orange and red neon from beer signs, a golden glow through the small windows—in the general grayness of warehouses and grain elevators.

Sam was hungry but he did not much care if the tavern served food. He had been shoring up against a heavy wave of black doubt. He needed something to distract him. Something to temporarily replace all he had lost—the warm press of willing flesh, a moment of oblivion.

He entered and stood by the door. Four women sat at the bar. They had long ago stopped looking for Mister Right. All they wanted now was what Sam wanted—a night when they weren't too lonely.

Young or middle-aged, it did not really matter. Just as long as he could stop the little machine in his brain and get a good night's sleep.

Tomorrow would be a busy day.

CHAPTER THIRTY-SIX
Seattle

Griff had his eyes open and his lips—what could be seen of them—were trying to move but speech wasn't on the menu and would not be for days or weeks to come. He could, however, move his arm and hand, and one of the agents standing vigil had set out a legal pad on the bed and taped a large marker to Griff's hand. The markings recovered thus far were taped to the wall beside the medical monitors, showing substantial progress as jibs and jabs settled into single large letters.

Now Griff seemed to have returned in force. He was aware that William was in the room, and he made soft but determined grunting sounds. William held up the pad so that Griff could see it and Griff wrote in large block letters, with so much effort at control that sweat beaded up on his cheeks,

WATSON?

William looked his father in the left eye—the only eye that showed signs of life—and said, "She's dead, Father."

Griff looked at the ceiling and blinked. William knew that even had his father's face been capable of showing emotion, Griff would have tried to suppress it, to let it out in private later when no one could see him.

Griff again looked at his son. William flipped to a new page. Griff wrote two words with no space between:

WHATFIND

"Fireworks makings, bags of yeast, inkjet printers," William said.

Then,

VID?

"We got video, and we've all seen it, if that's what you mean," William said.

WHYYUO

"Does that mean, why am I here?"

Griff nodded, then winced.

"Special Agent Rose has taken me under her wing," William said. "Out of pity for you." He smiled.

REB

"Right, Rebecca Rose."

PRNTRS MPORTNT

"We know, Father," William said.

NEWS

"Hiram Newsome? He's supervising," William said.

Griff shook his head, wrote N, then

NWS ABUT JEW

William thought this over for a moment, then said, "We're investigating what someone told the Patriarch, about killing Jews. We're not working on this alone."

Griff closed his good eye, squeezed it. The other remained open. Then he looked at William and scrawled, with quick, sharp strokes,

D JEWS A-BMB?

"You heard agents talking about Iran?"

Griff nodded.

"So you're asking, did Israelis drop a bomb on Iran? We can't get a straight answer from anybody," William said.

MAD, Griff wrote.

"True enough," William said.

Y YEAS

"I don't understand that one."

Griff stroked in a rapid W and then a T: WY YEAST.

"Maybe to study dispersal of a biological agent."

NTHRX

"It's a possibility."

FND NTHRAX

"No. No traces yet of anthrax in the barn, or anywhere else, for that matter." They were almost out of paper. "You should rest now, Father."

Griff shook his head and glared.

"Now you're scaring me, Griff," William said. "You're going to turn into Donovan's Brain or something if you keep it up."

Griff continued to glare.

William shrugged, turned the pad around, ripped off the cardboard, and placed it on the opposite side, giving Griff more relatively blank paper—minus marker bleed-through.

CREDS

"Yes, Father. I did get my credentials."

ASSGN OFFC?

"Not for the moment. They sent me out here to watch over you, and, like I said, Agent Rose has me working with her. I . . . had a moment with some flaming toilet paper, to distract . . ." He wondered how much of this story Griff could stand. "It worked, but I'm being investigated by—"

Griff shook his head and continued to glare.

"Right. Not important." William drew close to the plastic curtain around his father's face.

ESIA

"What's that mean, Father?"

ESIA, again. Griff was trying to make sounds and the effort cost him.

OHI

The last letter started off as a U. He capped it with a slash. It looked like an upside-down hat.

"Is that Ohio?" William asked.

Again, the short nod, followed by a tic—the only grimace he could make now.

SV LIVES

Griff pushed the marker against William's hand, leaving a black streak, and tried to grab his fingers. Then the good eye closed. His father's hand spasmed, then relaxed.

William sat with tears dripping down his cheeks, he could not help himself, he felt so much, all of it contradictory, for this broken man with the unbroken spirit.

SAC Keller and Rebecca entered the hospital room. "We're attending an inter-agency pow-wow tomorrow morning," Keller said. He handed William a vinyl folder. "You'll team with Rebecca."

"You're completely off the hook," Rebecca said. "Someone in OPR apparently likes the way you think."

"Not even weird enough to become the stuff of legend," Keller said dryly. "Has our Michelin man decided to say something?" He waved at the scrawls pinned to the wall.

"He's curious," William said, and showed them the pad.

Keller flipped through the sheets, both sides. "We won't put these on display, I think," he said, and took the pad from William, slipping it into his briefcase. "Until we figure out what's happening, we stay real cozy. Anybody not vetted by headquarters, even fellow agents, are to remain in the dark. And that includes Griff. What in hell is this?" Keller pointed to the two sheets marked ESIA and the awkwardly slashed OHIO.

"I don't know," William said. "He fell asleep."

"Could be 'Asia,'" Keller said.

Nurses and doctors entered and told them they should leave. Griff was being taken away for more scans.

CHAPTER THIRTY-SEVEN
Northern Iraq, near the Turkish Border

Fouad had walked around the Superhawk twenty or thirty times, he had lost count. Each time, he had surveyed the broken clods of dirt in the abandoned farm field, the yellow stalks of old hay mixed in with the clumped, clayey soil, the surrounding mountains—extreme washboard, Master Sergeant had called them. He did not know the names of any of the surrounding peaks, or even if they had names. Despite studying the maps, he knew so little about this part of the world. He was just another ignorant American. He could speak many of the languages but not like a native—he did not know the local phrases, the local traditions—he did not even know whether this field had lain abandoned for years or decades, a poor effort in a high and rugged land. And now hard, icy snow was stinging his cheeks. They had not dressed for such cold. The air was cooling rapidly as the sun dropped closer to the horizon.

What if it has finally come. The fanatics have won, and it is Islam against the West, and the West . . . that is me, my people now, must bathe the Middle East in a sea of flame. Like a lion stung too many times, ripping up a nest, killing all the silly, stupid hornets.

Where will I stand? Unbelievers all around. Who am I to stand alone among them, when the umma *is dying?*

Fergus plodded out to where he was standing. They said nothing for a while, just wincing at the hard snow and watching the sun dim behind yellow streaks of clouds blowing away from the nearest peaks like feathery wings.

Fergus said, "Master Sergeant tells me the bird's back up."

"Bird?" Fouad asked.

"Satellite links. We're getting our instructions. We'll be going soon." He looked around the clodded furrows. "I can't believe someone wasted a plow. Wonder what they used to pull it? Sherpas?"

Harris joined them. "Small talk, gentlemen?"

"I was just asking Fred here how long he's been in the FBI."

"Not long," Fouad said. "This is my first assignment."

"Wow," Harris said. "That's not typical FBI procedure, is it? Diplomatic Service, now, they take their newbies and dump them straight into the worst hellholes. Trial by fire."

Fergus grinned. "Luck of the bid lists, right?"

"Right. You ask for Paris, you get the stans."

Fouad looked between them. "The stans?"

"Uzbekistan, Kazakhstan, Turkmenistan, Pakistan," Harris said. "My wife absolutely *adored* Pakistan. Our first child was born there. We got divorced six months later, after I bid on Frankfurt and got Tajikistan."

"Ah, divorce," Fergus said. "The patriot's annulment."

"I want to get home and crawl under my blanket and not look out," Harris said. "Being scared for nine hours straight *hurts*. My head is pounding, my back and neck are tight as springs, and I have to take a shit but my sphincter is clamped tight as a vice. I keep wondering when the next nuke is going to go off and where, and I don't want to be caught taking a squat, mid-grunt."

Fergus laughed and beat his arms together.

"Screw anthrax," Harris said, the wind almost blowing his words away. "That's small-time shit."

"I wonder when Beatty's going to finally leave Iraq?" Fergus said. "Dedication is admirable in a man."

"He's an asshole," Harris said. "I learned to hate him when I was working here eight years ago."

"He seemed to have some humanity," Fouad said. "He seemed to care."

"Did you ever watch *Apocalypse Now*?" Harris asked. They both had, Fergus five or six times. "Remember Robert Duvall—what the fuck was his name—going up to the wounded gook begging for water, telling Martin Sheen that any soldier holding in his guts with his bare hands was a hero. Anyway, he gives the gook his own canteen—spills water on him—and then a young jock tells him about some righteous waves. Duvall jerks the canteen away before the gook can take a sip. Right on. That's America—a boatload of righteous sentiment, then we lose interest and pull out. We fucking go home and leave them to bleed to death."

"Beatty did not leave," Fouad pointed out.

"He's sticking around to prove a stupid point," Harris said. "Same difference. Screw that."

"Where do you want to go, right now?" Fergus asked, with a wry smile.

"Home," Harris said.

"Me, too. Fred?"

"I will bravely vote with the majority," Fouad said. Somehow, his turmoil and fear had transformed into light-headedness, even levity. He did not have a clue what would be happening to them in the next few hours. "I am a young agent, lacking all experience, and yet, because I speak a strange language, here I am," he said. "With you two strapping Yankees, and we are all feeling very mortal. We will have a beer many years from now, in a bar, and laugh. We will be great friends."

Harris gave Fergus a look. "You drink beer, Fred?"

"I have been known to, to my shame," Fouad said. "But not at the Academy. My father would hear of it."

"Harsh man, your pappy?"

"Not particularly," Fouad said. "But not a drinker."

"So if the anthrax isn't from around here, where is it from?" Harris asked Fergus.

"Anthrax is everywhere," Fergus said. "But this particular stuff is special. Current thinking is, it's our own domestic blend. One secret we've kept from John and Jane Q Public for a long time, is how many places in the U.S. used to work with anthrax. Agricultural schools, weapons research during World War 2—hell, back then every pharmaceutical company and university with a war contract worked with anthrax. Just inside the United States, we've traced leftovers to abandoned warehouses, old college labs, scientific supply houses. Nothing shocks me any more."

"Who in America still wants to kill Jews?" Fouad asked. "Are we after Nazis or American Fascists?"

Harris and Fergus immediately sobered.

"I am asking, who in America would make an anthrax that kills only Jews?"

The two men looked down and scuffed their feet but still said nothing.

"Someone thinks it is American Muslims?" Fouad ventured.

Master Sergeant called from the Superhawk's cabin. The wind shredded his voice. "We're leaving, gentlemen. All aboard!"

"Whoever the fuck it is, it can't be done," Fergus said to Fouad as they walked back across the rugged field. "There's no genetic marker or receptor that singles out Jews. You just can't breed that kind of germ. It's a scientific impossibility."

"So what is it they are trying to accomplish?" Fouad asked.

"Someone's lying," Fergus said. "Someone is delivering samples to radical Islamists and telling them a nasty fib. We need to know who, and we'd certainly like to know why." Fergus clutched his hat under the wash from the blades. Harris helped Fouad, and Fouad pulled up Fergus.

"Hell, you know what the fanatics around here would likely do," Fergus said. "They'd round up six Jews, any old Jews, and dose them—but why do a double-blind and test it on the faithful? That would be an abomination."

Fouad looked between them. They both returned his look, as if trying to figure out his disposition, his race, the psychology of all Islam, through his dark young eyes.

"Six Kurdish Jews," Harris muttered. "And a year ago, seven Shiites dead in Baghdad."

"Sunnis wouldn't mind killing both Jews and Shiites," Fergus said.

"And now you probably know as much as we do," Harris said to Fouad. "The more you know, the less it makes sense."

Master Sergeant welcomed them aboard, grinning with relief. "The hell with this, let's *motor*," he said. They resumed their seats and strapped in.

"If it is not modified to kill Jews, could it be modified to mislead fanatical Muslims? Simple souls that they are?" Fouad smiled his most ingenuous smile.

Fergus snorted. Harris looked around the helicopter. "Fred, are you impugning the intelligence of our enemies?" he asked.

"Perhaps to convince these simple souls that there is a way to win an old war," Fouad said. "And make them pay great sums of money to get it."

"An expensive fake-out," Fergus said with wry appreciation.

Master Sergeant listened intently but his heart wasn't in the discussion. "The whole world's got to change," he said.

"If Fred's correct, selling fake anthrax wouldn't be a major crisis, would it?" Harris asked. "It would be like selling red mercury to the Serbs. That cost Slobodan Milosevic six million dollars for squat—a high-yield explosive that doesn't even exist."

"But these American suppliers are not stupid people, if they can obtain or modify such anthrax. From who else would they extort money? From fanatics with equal hatred," Fouad suggested.

"Who would that be?" Harris asked.

"I am thinking out loud," Fouad said.

"Fred here believes we may not have the complete picture yet," Fergus said. "Maybe we're all thinking simplistically."

"Amen to that," Harris said. "That's always been our problem in this part of the world."

Master Sergeant closed the hatch. The helicopter rose from the old farm field, turned into the snowy wind, and immediately headed west, making a beeline for Turkey.

Once again Fouad had closed his eyes. He was in the middle of a vivid dream of sick and dying cattle. They had the most sympathetic and pain-filled eyes. The cattle began kicking over huge oil drums. He heard rapid sounds of banging metal. As he jerked awake, he saw Fergus slump forward. Harris had crossed the aisle and was fumbling with his hands to cover a fountain of blood from Fergus's chest. Master Sergeant calmly threw flak jackets at them. "Up front," he ordered. "Thicker armor."

Fouad worked his arms to get into a jacket. He helped Harris drag Fergus forward. Master Sergeant popped open a first aid kit and flung compresses and tourniquets in plastic bags at them. "Open 'em, tie him off, press 'em wherever there's blood," he instructed.

"Hell with that," Harris shouted back. "He's dying!"

Fergus was bleeding out in great gushes on the deck. His hands, held up in supplication, shook uncontrollably and his lips were blue in a chalk-white face. Despite the futility, Fouad went to work, helping Harris. They were covered in blood.

The Superhawk roared and veered and careened. "We're being painted!" the co-pilot shouted. Countermeasures screamed away from the chopper on both sides—flares and chaff. "Tango Victor Charlie, we got red eyes. Scorpios up our crack and we cannot shake 'em."

"Shit on a stick," Master Sergeant said, and doubled over.

The cabin hissed like a huge snake and filled with smoke and flame.

CHAPTER THIRTY-EIGHT
Silesia, Ohio

Sam parked the trailer by the curb at the north end of a pretty little park on the southwestern side of the town, about four miles from the warehouse district and the little bar where he had picked up Darly Fields, forty-two, divorced mother of two, currently working as a network maintenance supervisor for a feed supply company.

Next, he walked around the park with a little flag on a stick checking the wind direction and making notes on his city map of Silesia. On the south side of the park he had already counted three churches, all of medium size.

The wind was slow and relatively warm and dry for this time of year. All good. There was a big Town Talk bakery within a mile of the park, directly downwind. Silesia had three bakeries within range that shipped bread all over the state. There were twelve feed stores, and of course the silos and warehouses.

The Patriarch had told him over and over again, in the presence of his wives and his sons, of his plans for the Endtimes, should the Federales Satanus flood down upon them. "God and me, we've dreamed up a real surprise," he had said.

And so they had. But it didn't matter now. Shifting obstacles could be outmaneuvered, fixed obstacles could be worked around. Ambitious plans for five or six targets could be reduced to the two most important—and of course, Silesia. In the beginning Sam had hoped to have everything ready by the Fourth of July, but two Julys had passed with essential equipment and deals and personnel not yet in place.

Now it had to be a one-two-three punch. First the demo, followed within two months by the first city, and then—in the proper season—the most difficult and inaccessible target of all.

Past maximum heating, this was no time to let loose the first operational Pillar of Fire. He would wait until morning. And if the next morning was not good enough, if the wind had reversed and was blowing away from town, he would wait for the morning after that. But he could not wait forever. Like the Patriarch, Sam would have to put some reliance on God.

Sam pushed back his hair with one hand and kept a straight face as he walked over the short brown lawns and under the scattered shade of old oak trees. Of late, his features inclined to a fixed scowl of concentration. He was gaining lines in the wrong places. Soon nobody would trust him. Not that it mattered. Perhaps in the end he would become a true eagle-eyed John Brown with flames floating above his head, convinced that what he was doing was surely righteous—a true believer, like so many of the pious, hypocritical sons of bitches downwind from this new American Trinity.

God would not protect them. They weren't listening any more. Perhaps they never had.

If his instincts were correct, tomorrow was going to begin with a fine calm morning, a breeze blowing ever so lightly from the northwest.

CHAPTER THIRTY-NINE
Seattle

Rebecca knocked on the door to William's room just as he finished shaving. "Showtime," she called out.

They had moved into a suites motel downtown. The rooms were smaller than the rooms in Everett, and William preferred it that way now. Less to keep in his field of vision. But the rooms were also dirtier.

"Be right there," he called.

William put on his tie, adjusted his holstered SIG, made sure the recognizer was keyed, and slipped his arms into his coat. He checked his Lynx button display, which flashed a bright 1-1-2, fully operational, then swung the deadbolt and opened the door.

Rebecca was carrying a folder in one hand and her slate in the other. "Ammunition," she said. "To justify our existence. As I suspected, we have irritated ATF, BDI, and apparently Homeland Security. The triumvirate. Fortunately, the heat is pretty much off—nobody much cares about the Patriarch or anthrax at the moment."

"You've been here before," William said as he followed her down the hotel corridor, through the glass door, and out to the agency van parked by the curb.

"Yeah," Rebecca said. "I have."

SAC Keller sat at the head of the table in the tenth-floor office of the U.S. Attorney for the Western District of Washington. The view of downtown Seattle and two stadiums from the new Internal Security building was obscured by a layer of wet fog.

Keller stood and rapped his knuckles on the table to get their attention. "The U.S. Attorney has kindly lent his office for this meeting," he said. "He's in Washington, DC right now, fighting for his job, but he personally tells me that he hopes we will maintain the very most cordial interdepartmental relations in this time of world turmoil."

Several chuckles around the long wooden table.

"Times change, but crime is crime," Keller continued. "And we're here to share what we know, to clear up some details about what was, until yesterday, a front-page case."

Shuffling. Most of these people clearly had places to go and things to get done. To Rebecca, they resembled boys waiting in the principal's office. She pushed her folder back and forth on the polished table and glanced at William, sitting quiet and still beside her.

"Why are you always so calm?" Rebecca whispered to him as Keller passed around a pot of coffee and paper cups.

"Because you're going to pull a rabbit out of a hat," William whispered, with a look at her folder. "I'm just waiting to see what kind of rabbit."

"Maybe I have no rabbits," Rebecca said. "Maybe I'm fresh out of all my little coneys."

Keller introduced the agents and department representatives. Rebecca recognized Diplomatic Security agent David Grange, the pug-faced man who had irritated her on the Patriarch's farm. She had not yet met the ATF's new Deputy Assistant Director, Western Division, Samuel Conklin, a jowly man with nervous eyes, well past middle age. And she was surprised to find, arriving a little late and taking a seat next to her, the only other female in the room, a junior representative from CPSC—the Consumer Product Safety Commission. She smiled and handed Rebecca her card. Her name was Sarah North. With black hair cut in a page boy, North was plump, red-faced, and intense-looking, as if she had just scrubbed off Goth makeup and put on a tight brown suit.

Her presence did not encourage Rebecca.

"The Secret Service has declined to join our meeting today," Keller said dryly. "There are matters of international importance demanding their immediate attention."

"And ours," Grange said.

Keller produced one of his enigmatic smiles. "I thought that Deputy Assistant Director Samuel Conklin could begin."

Conklin arranged a packet of printouts in front of him, then fumbled with his slate and made a face. He drew himself up and rested his arms on the table. "First of all, I'd like to congratulate FBI for apprehending the Patriarch. That closes a major case. My deep regrets as to the injury and loss of your agents. When informed about the surveillance, and then the tragedy, ATF and DS offered our services in a difficult time for the FBI. Who says cooperation is dead? We all did a fine job, working through the evidence and the ruins. Very educational. A new type of fuse to add to ATF's long list. Because of the added possibility that the Patriarch case might provide clues about another old case, American Anthrax 2001, ATF was given the lead by the Attorney General to move to the front in a number of investigations, following the patterns we discerned in ADIC Newsome's activities. We regret not informing Newsome or his agents about our involvement, or the reshuffling of command—we did not mean to undercut anyone—but the Attorney General and the President do not have much confidence in the FBI. This is common knowledge."

Grange made a little rictus and looked out the window at the fog.

"You smelled a flower in all the old manure, and you decided to pluck it," Rebecca said.

"Well, yes, ma'am, we smelled a Rose," Conklin said, "and the FBI certainly has its pile to shovel."

Keller lifted his hand. His face had reddened, but his gesture was enough to make Conklin nod and make placating motions. "I was not in Washington, and I did not make the requests or issue the orders. I'm just explaining what happened. Carrying the message."

"Let's hear it, then," Keller said.

"We've had to sail into a stiff wind every inch of the way. I've personally reported to the Attorney General that SAC Erwin Griffin's entry into the Patriarch's barn was premature and ultimately destructive of what could have been crucial evidence."

"He had his reasons," William said. His face, too, was pinking.

"I'm sure," Conklin said. "Furthermore, the Patriarch was forewarned and managed to order his family scattered to the winds before FBI or local law enforcement could set up an effective cordon. Whatever his reasons, Erwin Griffin did not foresee this, nor did he plan for it. Since ATF and Homeland Security became involved, with the help of U.S. Marshals we have rounded up nine of twenty-two fugitive family members, in three states. Two were apprehended by Agents Rose and Griffin Junior here in Washington, after an unnecessarily dangerous scuffle."

"You didn't find them," Grange observed. "They found you."

Rebecca fixed her eyes on Grange's lips and nose.

"Adding comedy to farce, because of a prior bungled interrogation, we had to question one of the Patriarch's sons, Jeremiah Jedediah Chambers, in the presence of a poorly paid and seriously inept public defender. FBI bungled that one for us, as well. But my agents did follow up on what little we learned. And along the way, we found that Agent Rose had involved herself in another case, the murder of a Highway Patrol officer in Arizona. ATF and Homeland Security requested prior copies of lab results for that case and received them this morning."

"Have we received those results yet, Agent Rose?" Keller asked.

"No, sir," Rebecca said. She pulled a fist off the table to hide it, but the knuckles on her other hand were white. "I'm curious as to what they might be."

Despite his sharp tongue Conklin was not enjoying himself. He was old school and did not like making fellow agents squirm. Still, he was not about to blunt the edge of his story. "Local authorities in Arizona were happy to assist ATF because the FBI apparently behaved with its usual courtesy and professional respect. As well, we learned today that Agent Rose pocketed two key pieces of evidence and had them analyzed in Virginia. So we requested those results, as well, with the Attorney General's permission, and have used them to draw our own conclusions."

Keller glanced at Rebecca. She sat very still, her face frozen. Game, set, match.

William could not feel much of anything except an almost childlike bewilderment. Just a short time ago he had been at Quantico, trying desperately not to screw up and keep ahead of an ever-expanding curve. Now, it looked as if he was going to sink out of sight in the company of some of the finest agents in the Bureau.

"In ordinary times, all this might have passed with little notice," Conklin continued. "Agencies could have gone through their usual pissing up the side of the barn door—pardon me, ladies—and settled things behind the scenes. But these are not ordinary times."

"Samuel, if you're the messenger," Keller said, "let's just have the message."

"The message is, we've grabbed an empty Zippo. No flint, no fluid, no flame. We have nothing," Conklin said. "Oh, there are some interesting results—we have eliminated a major international criminal. But that has nothing to do with anthrax. It certainly does not merit further investigation, beyond the general cleaning up and writing of reports."

"What were the findings?" Rebecca asked.

"There isn't a trace of anthrax anywhere on the Patriarch's farm. Not in the barn, not in the woods, and yes, Agent Rose, we have sent out cadaver dogs and are digging up any suspicious sites around the farm. Despite Jeremiah's story, we have found no dead sheep. We do not anticipate finding any. To say that Jeremiah Chambers and Hagar Chambers are useless as witnesses is an understatement. They can hardly remember their own names. They are low-grade morons, whether from inbreeding or the Patriarch's beatings and indoctrination, who can say? They don't even know when they're lying. Furthermore, though Hagar Chambers is pregnant, the Patriarch is not the infant's father. We have yet to make a match, but we suspect the sire comes from completely outside the family—so at least it's not an incest baby."

"And in Arizona?" Keller asked.

"At our request, they sequestered and scoured the three hundred printers in that trailer. They found no signs of anthrax on the printers or in the recycled ink cartridges shipped along with them."

Rebecca coughed. She felt as if she had no more air in her lungs.

"At any rate," Conklin said, "no anthrax anywhere, and hence no additional evidence of interest to any of us. Thank you, John. That's my bit."

"Someone could have used the Patriarch's family to get ready for an anthrax attack," William said. "They could have used the yeast—"

"BT is commonly available. It's almost exactly like anthrax, easy to grow, and perfectly legal. If I were going to spread anthrax, I'd use BT for any rehearsal. Yeast just doesn't cut it, in terms of conspiracies," Conklin said, and looked sadly at his knuckles. "There's nothing here."

Rebecca slowly opened her folder. "They knew that we track BT," she said. "One of our master analysts, Frank Chao, decided to connect some of our apparently unconnected results. He compared the DNA from the blood sample in Arizona to the DNA of Hagar Chambers' unborn child. They match. I have the proof of paternity right here. Whoever shot our Arizona patrolman was in Washington state, where he impregnated a seventeen-year-old girl right under her elderly husband's nose, and he was very likely stopped in the act of returning to the Patriarch's farm to deliver a load of inkjet printers."

Conklin was momentarily conciliatory. "That's interesting. We will certainly let Arizona know about the match." He threw a warm smile in Rebecca's direction, below very cold eyes.

She nodded.

Conklin continued. "It may be they were getting hot from holding weekly orgies out there in the woods. It may be they were complete fanatics, planning to print and distribute millions of Nazi propaganda tracts. And maybe they were messing with yeast and spreading it around to develop their own special sourdough starter."

"That's bacteria, actually," Sarah North said.

Conklin shifted his gaze above the table, as if talking to the back wall. "Nobody knows what they were really up to, but there's still nothing compelling, Agent Rose. Not in this time of international emergency, when we need to focus all our resources."

Grange wanted to be heard, but Keller held up his hand. "I've received my orders from the Attorney General, by way of the Director," Keller said. "Hiram Newsome has been reprimanded for using bureau resources without obtaining official approval. We're reassigning Special Agent Rebecca Rose to Baltimore and instituting an investigation through OPR, to see if anything could have been done differently. Special Agent William Griffin will report to his original probationary assignment in . . . ah . . . New Jersey. I have been ordered to apologize to our fellow agencies, on behalf of the director of the FBI. There will be follow-up communications at a higher level."

"I'd like to say something," Rebecca said.

"I'd prefer that you didn't," Keller said. "Ms. North, while other charges are being prepared against the Patriarch's family, I've been instructed to hand over our evidence to you, as a representative of the Consumer Products Safety Commission, with an eye to prosecution for the production of illegal fireworks."

Sarah North stood with trembling hands. "Yes, sir," she said.

Outside the office, Rebecca followed Keller. William tagged behind at a discreet distance and caught the whispered conversation in mid-sentence.

"Iran has overshadowed everything, Rebecca," Keller was saying. "Fortunately, because of that, this fox-up won't matter much in the IG proceedings at Headquarters. We may all be able to stay on our feet in the middle of the bigger storm. But Hiram's still out on a limb. Talk to him—and I mean seriously—before you think about wasting any more effort."

"I will," Rebecca said. "Why did we attract so much attention? I mean, if we're such screw-ups . . ."

"Best guess? As far as Grange is concerned, BuDark was created to follow a peculiar trail, and your investigation looked like an interesting side path. Oh, one other thing. Apparently they sent a helicopter into Iraq to investigate something of interest to BuDark. It came within a hundred klicks of the explosion at Shahabad Kord and made a safe tactical landing in the Zagros Mountains—but was subsequently shot down by Iranians or Iraqis before it could make it back to Turkey. We had two agents on board. One of them was an interpreter, I think you know him, William. His name was Fouad Al-Husam."

"What were they doing in Iraq?" William asked.

Keller shrugged. "Headquarters is accusing DS of requisitioning our agents and then sending them on a deadly wild goose chase. There's a lot of bad blood. I doubt there will be any enthusiasm for anthrax for years to come."

Keller turned and put his hand on William's shoulder. "We'll take care of Griff. Keep your heads down and look to your careers, both of you," he advised.

CHAPTER FORTY
Northern Iraq

Fouad came down out of the hills with a backpack and a sack of provisions, followed by Harris, who was clutching a pistol in one hand. The brown plain ahead was dotted with yellow dust devils. Blue-gray clouds to the east and north threw long shadows over the red-painted mountains. It was empty and beautiful. There was no place to hide out there. It would be better to stay in the rocks.

They had fled the Superhawk's wreckage as soon as they could, as soon as they had made sure there were no other survivors, to avoid being found and killed by whoever had shot them down.

The small aluminum case filled with the Kifri tissue samples hung from Fouad's hip clip. He touched the radio attached at chest level to his flak vest, then turned back to watch Harris. Their analog voice signals were being jammed. The digital signals were not getting through, either, which was pretty surprising, considering they were transmitting directly to at least ten possible satellites. Someone was using chaff, aerostats, pop-ups, or possibly even other satellites to actively jam basic communications over the entire area—probably the Russians but perhaps the Turks as well. Having a nuke go off in your backyard tended to do that to people.

Or the radio was simply busted. The M2GPS on his belt was haywire, working only about half the time.

Their last hope was the C-SARB that relayed their position and aircraft ID in microbursts at irregular intervals. To enemy trackers, it would sound like cosmic hash—or nothing at all.

When Harris caught up, Fouad handed him a bottle of water from the pack. Harris was trying to look in all directions at once. His broken arm, slung close to his chest, was obviously hurting but now was no time for painkillers. They had about a week's worth of food. The water would last at most two or three days.

Harris took a drink from the bottle. "They'll find us," he said. "To them, it's like a day in the country picking flowers. They'll track us from the wreckage. They'll kill us and take pictures and spread our headless corpses out on the desert to dry. That's how screwed we are."

Fouad did not feel much more sanguine about their chances.

They had pulled Fergus and as much equipment as they could from the smoking ruins of the Superhawk. Master Sergeant, the Captain, the co-pilot and crew chief, and two other crew members, whose names Fouad had never learned, had been inaccessible, along with the more powerful weapons and most of the survival gear.

The forward bulkhead and the floor beneath Fergus, Harris, and Fouad had been ripped up and slammed to the back of the cabin by the initial impact and that had saved them when the helicopter had finally bounced off one boulder and ploughed into another. Fouad was not clear on all this. Some of the memories were returning, but right now, they were simply not relevant.

Fergus had died while they were still in the air. They had dug a quick grave and covered him with a hatch, the most they could do under the circumstances.

"Well, pilgrim," Harris said, trying to stand straight. "What's say we hide like furry little rodents."

Fouad checked his compass and the chart from the map pack. He had looked at the stars the night before, after arranging the sling for Harris's arm. They had not traveled far from the high barren field before being shot down. Or had they? He had been napping. Still, he thought he knew where they might be within twenty or thirty klicks. He hoped he knew.

Any crumb in a famine.

"You take the blanket," Fouad instructed Harris, who was already shivering. "Sleep. I will stand watch."

"I'm not going to argue," Harris said. He found a crusty, sandy place next to a large boulder, lay down gingerly, and pulled the silvery thermal blanket over himself. The sun was past zenith and the air was already chilly and dry. Fouad's throat hurt and his legs ached and his bruised chest felt tight. Breathing deeply hurt, as did pressing on his right side. Very likely ribs were broken. Finally, he was grateful for the extreme fitness regimen at Quantico. Victory over pain, Pete Farrow had called it.

"Any guess?" Harris called from the side of the boulder.

"Still in Iraq," Fouad said. "Near no place we would know the name of." He walked over, held the chart out to Harris, and pointed to a square several centimeters across. "Somewhere in here."

"Very good," Harris said. "Awesome. That's totally reassuring."

"Now sleep."

Harris saluted and lay back with a groan.

A few minutes later, Fouad heard him shout "Shit, shit, shit." Harris shuffled past him, brushing his pants with his good arm.

"Scorpion," he said. "Got my trousers but missed my leg. Fuck this. Fuck this to almighty hell. Did you know scorpions out here produce cyto-toxic venom? Like a recluse spider. Haemolysis, necrosis, ankylosis, kidney failure, you can even go off your head—even. Very nasty shit." His eyes were red-rimmed and his face looked hot from fever. He danced from foot to foot for a few seconds, then let out his breath with a whoosh and barely controlled his fall to one knee.

"Again, you are lucky," Fouad said.

"Yeah, lucky," Harris said. "Do you think anybody cares what's in this box?" He reached up to tap the aluminum case.

"For the sake of Fergus and Master Sergeant and the others, yes," Fouad said.

"Did you ever learn Master Sergeant's name?" Harris asked.

"No."

"Wait. I've got it here." Harris pulled out the duplicate tags that had been slung by the rear hatch, fanned through them with one hand, and read the stamped label above the ID chip. "Jerry Walton. Jesus. We're as dead as Jerry Walton."

"Sit and be still," Fouad suggested, patting the ground beside him. "They could have infrared."

"I don't want to take a pain pill," Harris said. "I want to be clear-headed when they kill us."

"Shh," Fouad said.

"Fuck, it hurts." Harris squatted beside him and they watched the skies over the plain. Soon, Harris was on his back again, asleep but restless. The last of the dust devils had cleared. The sun was within minutes of setting. Soon it would be dusk, then night.

Fouad used his compass and quickly oriented himself, then laid down the flap edge of the sack and knelt on it to pray. He had to begin before sunset. Eventually he would have to catch up on the missed prayers. To pray was more than relief, far more than duty; it was a marvel of renewed strength.

He performed four *raka'at*.

A few minutes later, Fouad heard Harris cursing softly in his sleep. This was a profanation, but what could be done? His companion was in pain. He finished his prayers, then added a *Ya Latif*. As the evening deepened and the plain was covered in a veil of grey, Fouad spoke in a soft voice,

"You who is gentle with children still in the wombs of their mothers, exhibit thy gentleness and grace towards us, a grace that befits Your Generosity and Your Mercy, O You who is the Most Merciful . . ."

He did not often pray for relief from his distress. It was his thought that God, even in his deep and abiding love, had many concerns and should not be bothered for petty ills and sorrows. This his father had taught him, though his mother had also said that God never tired of listening. But now was definitely the time for extraordinary help and guidance.

When night fell, they could not risk using any light, and so they would not see the scorpions.

"I am no longer your boss," Rebecca said. "You're buying the first round."

"You're still senior," William said. This brought a look from her that seemed at once angry and vulnerable. She turned back to the bar menu.

"For someone of my age and seniority, I *am* hungry," she said with forced cheer.

"Not what I meant, of course," William said. He smiled at their figures in the mirror behind the ranked collection of bottles filled with amber, green, blue, and pale fluids. "We could buy all of those and forget for an entire evening. That's what blue people often do."

"Tell me more about people who are blue."

"All right," William said. "We are few. We are blue. We protect him and her and *you*. I had a partner when I was working OCID—"

"Organized Crime Investigations Division," Rebecca said. "Right after getting kicked out of vice. That's how you got into FBI. The joint task-force."

"That's part of it. My father's reputation preceded me like Cyrano's nose."

"Cyrano? Was he a goombah?"

"Cyrano de Bergerac. He had a huge nose and flew to the moon. You know Cyrano. He wrote letters for a guy who was in love with Roxanne. But he was in love with Roxanne, too, so it was tragic."

Rebecca gave him a you-are-shitting-me stare.

"Steve Martin, Darryl Hannah," he said.

"Right." Rebecca lifted her martini. "Here's to romantic poetry and big noses. Tell me more about your partner. What was he like?"

"She, actually. We used hang out after work, plotting how to improve our record in the department. We were both pretty marginal."

"No hotshots?"

"Our instincts were hinky," William said. "We just naturally liked peo-ple."

"Bad juju," Rebecca said. She tapped the bar and asked for another. "This one is on me."

"Thanks," William said. "Anyway, it was good, and it was bad. We were great at interrogations. Together, we could get under the skin of a perp so soft and easy he didn't even know we were injecting verbal truth serum. My partner was great at psychology. Big brown eyes, plump, sort of a Mediterranean mama. The goombahs, as you say—and the Russians, but not so much the Cambodians or Vietnamese—just wanted to open up and spill their guts. There, there, she'd say, and pat their wrists as they signed off on their confessions. But we weren't all that good at pegging them, not right away."

"Bad for a cop," Rebecca said. "But good for the soul."

"Her name was Karen Truslow. Upstate New York money, but to her folks' dismay, she turned blue. We spent a lot of time in the backs of vans listening to taps, and when things were slow we made up a dictionary of slurs. We could use them, blue people, but nobody else. 'Cop' is mostly okay, but 'Copper' or 'Flatfoot' or 'Screw' or anything a Dick Tracy villain would say is a mortal insult."

"You liked her," Rebecca said. "But she died a tragic death and now you cherish her memory and feel guilty."

"No, she's still in OCID. She recommended I go FBI. 'They're not so blue. They pass.'"

"That's a lie," Rebecca said. "I'm deep midnight. But wait. I'm senior, so I'm wrinkled and faded, like old denim."

"You're fishing," William said.

"That means you think I'm hitting on you," Rebecca said, turning on her stool. "That I need to hook a compliment out of that manly, tall, broad chest . . . Whatever. Christ, I'm a cheap drunk. But tell me, young William Griffin. You saw me in my nightie. Is it all over for me?"

"You're tired."

Her expression drooped. "I'm gone. I'm dead. I'll crawl back to my desk and shuffle papers for the rest of my career. I'll retire with blue hair, my stomach hanging below my knees, and dream of filing cabinets. I'll be a faded blue bag hag."

William shook his head. "Let's pay."

"You don't like my company."

"I don't like my liquor talking with an anger chaser."

"What?"

William's serious face broke. "I'm tired, too."

"You're translucent. Milky blue. I can hardly see you." Rebecca waved her hand in front of his face. "Agent Griffin, is that you?"

"Anything else?" asked the bartender, a slender brunette with huge eyes.

"Some food," Rebecca said. "We'll take the buffalo wings."

"We call them angel wings," the bartender said. "Hot, mild, or boring?"

"Hot," Rebecca said. "Olives in parmesan. Goat cheese plate. Anything that tastes good to hungry people who are blue."

"Blue cheese dip for the wings," the bartender suggested.

"Right."

The bartender asked if they wanted more drinks. Rebecca asked for club soda, William, tomato juice.

"This will not be a problem, not for you," Rebecca told him. "This will be a void, a blank space in your record. You'll go to New Jersey and act as if nothing happened."

"Flaming TP," William said.

"No, seriously," Rebecca said. "Start over again."

"It's real, though, isn't it?" William asked. "Something's going on. Something bad."

"Of course it's real. Would Hiram Newsome lead you astray?"

"I know *you* wouldn't."

"Ah, well. That's a pity." She took the club soda and downed it. "I seldom drink this much," she said. "White wine with dinner. I have a delicate metabolism." She set down the glass with a thunk, blowing an ice cube onto the bar. "We've known about biohackers since at least 2000, but in the last ten years, they've grown unimaginably more common and powerful. They have journals, websites, they exchange little tricks of the trade. Right now, you can buy a gene sequencer on eBay for five grand. Using online recipes you can make your own RNA, your own DNA, which means you can make viruses—real ones, not computer viruses—including smallpox or Ebola. You can create plasmids that turn ordinary bacteria into killers. Amerithrax was probably one of the first killer hackers. We were too blind to see it. Now, it's international. People will die, and there is nothing we can do. We're focused on a single nuclear explosion—still chasing old nightmares. But some screwball S.O.B. who doesn't give a damn about atom bombs is up to something that could kill hundreds of millions, and six months from now, a year from now, if any of us are still alive, OPR will have us on the carpet, testifying about how the FBI missed another sterling opportunity. Congress critters will dine off our carcasses—if any of *them* are still alive. Maybe by then I'll have slipped into early retirement. I'll drown while fishing in a lake in Minnesota. But that won't help you, dear boy."

"Crap," William said.

"You dare disagree with the drunken blue lady?" Rebecca asked, eyes intense.

"It's not a tasty future. How do you hunt down a thousand killer nerds?"

"All I want to do is find one—just one—and make an example out of him." Her slate chimed. She put on reading glasses—the first time William had seen her do this—and examined the small screen at arm's length. "My God," she said.

"What?"

"Hiram Newsome has been dismissed. The director's purging the Ay-Dicks." She scrolled through the message and her face turned gray. "I need to go to the little girl's room."

Rebecca left him at the bar. The food arrived but William was no longer hungry. Still, he picked at a chicken wing and, despising blue cheese, dipped it in his tomato juice, hoping it would dilute the spiciness. It did not. But globs of chicken grease made the juice undrinkable.

Rebecca returned ten minutes later. "I made myself throw up," she informed him. "An old trick from my bingeing days in college. You should go do the same."

William shook his head. He had never seen Rebecca Rose look so vulnerable, even when she had had her blouse ripped in half, soaked in sprinkler water and tussling with a man twenty-five years younger. It made him sick inside.

Rebecca called to the bartender. "Got a pot of coffee?"

"Always," the bartender answered from the end of the bar.

"We are going to make phone calls," Rebecca said to William. "You will talk to New Jersey and tell them you're on your way. Don't make waves. And don't mention News or me in your résumé."

"Is it official?"

"Reuters and AP. Keller must have seen this coming."

The bartender brought two mugs and a stainless pot. "Anything for blue people," she said, and winked at William.

CHAPTER FORTY-TWO
Silesia, Ohio

Sam walked around the park at dawn, making one last check of the wind. Clear skies, a grassy zephyr blowing from the northwest, three to five knots: gentle and perfect. The dispersion plume would be beautiful, a slow, graceful fan descending over at least five square miles of Silesia. Having the Town Talk bakery right in the center of the plume was a plus, he decided.

To send this kind of message—his kind of message—one had to alter large volumes of flesh. Rotten flesh, killing flesh.

Meat makes more meat. Meat learns its cruelty from bad meat. In the end, they were all made meat.

By comparison, this is a kindness.

He arrived back at the truck in a foul, uncertain mood, his head zinging with sharp spasms of doubt. From the truck's glove box he took a foil pack of gingko biloba and swallowed three of the supplements, washing them down with bottled water. Pure superstition, he suspected—he could not even be sure he was affected—but what if he was? Then motivation, conviction, even a psychological edge could push him over the finish line, and all he needed was a few more weeks to spare before the blessed curtain fell and he could surrender to the fate he would be wishing on—inflicting upon—so many others.

He rechecked his plane tickets and the plastic packet of passports. From Cleveland to New York, from New York to Jordan, and from Jordan by way of chartered flight to Jeddah. RFIDs—Radio Frequency Identity tags—with medical and personal info and even DNA markers had been reprogrammed in all the passports. To Homeland Security, and to any foreign government keeping track, he would be a different man, on nobody's list.

For most of his adult life, he had kept in reserve his most personal and hidden trait, his mother's most wonderful genetic accident, as a kind of contingency, a backup plan for a difficult world in which most people had few secrets from the grimly curious authorities.

There was still a risk, of course—but much reduced.

One blue eye, one green. Who would know?

He rolled back and tied the tarp on the trailer, then climbed up and inspected the hedgehog through the wide opening in the roof. Each of the launching tubes had been capped with a plastic cup secured by tape. Opening the rear door, he sidled in beside the launcher and removed each cap, careful not to bump the tubes. The late summer air was dry but not too dry. Static was not likely to be a problem, but one never knew.

Then he removed the firing board from its box and hooked it up to the base of the hedgehog. On the board he flipped a toggle and ran the wand over the twenty live contact points. At the base of each tube, red diodes lit up, flickered, then faded.

All it would take was a quick swipe down the contacts, with the toggle reversed.

Sam unhooked the patch cord, coiled it, strapped it to the bottom of the firing board with Velcro, then placed it in the seat of the truck. Legs stiff, hands shaking, he unhitched the trailer and placed the calibrated brace under the tongue, angling the trailer back a few centimeters to the proper angle. At the last minute, he could rotate the trailer, angle it up or down a few degrees, based on wind direction and speed, within parameters he had calculated months before.

The park was almost deserted. On the far side he spotted an elderly man out for a stroll with his white Scotty. There would be a few shrieks and loud bangs. Then a pattern of simultaneous starbursts. Glass beads and chunks of clay and talcum would fall rather more quickly than the payload, rattling lightly on some rooftops, rolling down the rain gutters.

He was in the truck when he noticed the branches of the trees swaying along this side of the street, whipping around far more energetically than he liked. He frowned through the windshield, opened the door, and lifted his finger to the freshened breeze. The wind had shifted. It was blowing from the south at about ten or fifteen knots. If he fired now, even with the trailer properly angled, and if the wind reversed again, the plume would go out over the cornfields and empty lots north of town.

He returned to the truck and waited for an hour. At the end of that hour the wind was still back and forth, all wrong. He switched on the radio. The local weather station was forecasting turbulence for the next day or so—possibly signaling a front moving through and showers late in the evening.

Sam closed his eyes. He lowered the antenna on the firing box. Then he got out and hitched the trailer back onto the truck, stowing the calibrated brace.

God did not want it. Not now, not this morning.

After all this time, I have to listen. I have to be patient.

CHAPTER FORTY-THREE
Seattle

They say that
 They say that when the front side of your brain is squashed against the backside
 (They don't say that; who's talking here, anyway?)
 They say that when that happens, your consciousness retreats down your brainstem into your spinal cord and ends up in your asshole. I can't smell a thing but for this constant stink of sour blood and shit. All things would be equal, really, if I could smell something else, but then, I don't really have a nose any longer, do I? so it's what they call a phantom limb or organ or whatever. And maybe my brain is the same way. Now that it's squashed it's a phantom brain and can hurt or twinge or think nightmares are real or do whatever it damn well pleases.
 What a mess.

"Hello, Agent Griffin."
 This was somebody he probably did not know, standing in front of the bed, blocking out the most interesting part of the room, the part with the television. When the television was turned off and it wasn't blocked, he could play back anything he wanted on that ancient blank screen. He usually just played back scenes of dating, going through high school, getting drunk after graduating, getting in that car wreck that almost killed his future wife. Them parading around outside the car in the ditch, laughing and crying, then burying the beer bottles and the half-full pint of Wild Turkey before the sheriff arrived. That was back in Praise-be-to-God Silesia, Ohio.
 No, it wasn't. You drove through Silesia once, but that was not where the accident happened. Someone is standing in front of the television screen and I can't see it clearly now, where we had that accident, Georgina and myself, our

younger selves. William was never that stupid or that wild. He never told me about it anyway.

It wasn't Silesia, Ohio, it was . . .

"Hello, Griff, it's Kerry Markham. Deputy Markham. I'm here to say . . ."

They come through every hour on the hour, keeping tabs on me. I am their awful fate. I am diving into the deep ocean with an anchor chained to my foot.

What the hell happened in Silesia? It was the fourth of July and they were shooting off fireworks. No. I never saw that.

Kerry Markham. I still have a memory of recent events. Let's use it. I can see the TV now. There's Georgina and me on the outskirts of Duluth. I was right. It wasn't Ohio.

Kerry Markham was still talking. Griff decided to listen for once. "I'm sorry. Christ, I'm sorry it had to be you and all the other guys. I wish he had taken me down right at the start, me instead of you—and the bomb and all. It's been preying on me. Driving me a little bonkers, if you know what I mean, I get distracted so easily. I thought if I could just make it square—I'd get it all back again. My mojo."

So what in hell is it with Silesia? All I remember is that it had a lot of churches. Driving through the town, Georgina looked it up in the triple-A and told me Guinness had certified it had more churches per capita than any other town in the country. Surprising, because you'd think that should be down south somewhere. I should write that down.

Griff took the marker in his hand and scrawled on the legal pad, ESIA SILESIA OHIO.

Someone—Kerry Markham, a Snohomish County sheriff's deputy, judging by the color of his uniform—picked it up and looked it over. "I've been making notes myself, just to keep on the ball," Markham said. "I've gotten so distracted lately." He rubbed his neck and chuckled. "I shouldn't be losing my mind this early, this young, should I? My mind, my memory."

The marker fell to the floor and Griff went back to watching the blank TV until a nurse came in, saw his focus, and turned it on.

By that time, the deputy was gone.

His thoughts faded to gray. His hand made random motions over the pad. The nurse put the marker and the pad on the table.

"That's enough of that," she said.

William sat on the hospital chair and looked over the recent stack of scratches and broken words. Rebecca was in the hallway; she had been on her slate for the last two hours. They were checked out, bags packed, ambulatory—as Griff had once called being ready for action.

Griff lay with the plastic sheet pinned up and his mouth finally free of tubes. Fresh patches of pale green Gro-Guide had been spread over his cheeks and nose. The fingers on his elevated arm twitched, which the doctor said was a good sign, but his free arm lay with hand fisted like a dead bug.

William touched the fist.

"Silesia, Ohio. What does that mean, Griff?"

Griff turned his eyes in William's direction. "Churches," he said, and moved his eyes back to the television screen mounted near the ceiling. The TV was on but with the sound turned down. Griff's lips moved. William placed his face between Griff and the TV screen. "Hello, Griff?"

"Off," Griff said in less than a whisper.

"The TV? Sure." William used the bedside clicker to switch off the television. Griff continued to stare at the blank screen. William thought that had his father's face been capable of expression, he might have been frowning in concentration. His eyes showed that much.

"Torn," Griff whispered. His hand relaxed and started to move. His eyes switched left to look at his hand, then, for the first time, Griff looked at William. "Map."

"Torn map," William said.

"In barn. Silesia."

"Map of Silesia . . . in the barn."

"Churches," Griff said. He was staring at the TV screen again.

"Would you like the TV turned on?"

"No."

"Would you like to sleep?"

Rebecca came into the room and stood beside William. Her presence did not seem to register. Griff relaxed his fist and wriggled his fingers. "Write."

William put the marker in his hand and replaced the legal pad. Griff scrawled. "It still hurts to talk," William said.

"I wonder what doesn't hurt," Rebecca said.

Griff wrote: JWS IN SILESIA 0

"Jews," William said.

Griff drew a definitive slash through the 0, emphasizing that he meant zero. Zero Jews in Silesia.

"So?"

XTIAN

Then, JWS, again.

"Christians and Jews."

X THEM ALL.

"I don't think you mean kiss them all, do you?" Rebecca moved closer. "Griff, let me tell you what we think we know, and you just make a slash if you agree, or a circle if you don't. Right?"

Griff made a slash.

"You think the Patriarch wanted to kill Jews, period. Wherever."

Slash, then XTIANS 2

"Lions, nothing," William said.

Slash. Then, 0. Griff's entire arm trembled now. The writing became even harder to read.

JWS XTIANS

"All right," Rebecca said, staring at the pad with a concentrated frown.

ALL

Griff was writing on the blanket now. William paused his hand and replaced the legal pad with one from a box beneath the bed.

JWS XTIANS

"That about sums them up, Griff," William said. "So, where does Silesia figure?"

DESCNT FM JWS

Then, ALL CHLDRN JWS

"All right."

And then,

SILESIA

MOST CHURCHES

Griff's forehead, just below his hairline—the only part of his face, besides eyes and lips, not layered with Gro-Guide—was beaded with sweat.

"Right, Silesia," William said. "Most—greatest number of churches."

In rapid strokes, firm now, and covering half the page, Griff wrote:

CLOSE #1

"Close, but no cigar," William said. "The Patriarch hated Jews and Christians. All right. I'll believe that—lots of hate to spread around. What about it, Griff?"

The hand wrote:

Y MAP

"Good question," William said. "We can't see it on the video—but then, the signal was cutting in and out."

The marker was still going, but just making squiggles.

"Griff?" Rebecca said.

He could not keep his eyes open to look at the TV. Perhaps that was best. The blank TV was sucking away his memory. He did not know whether his son and the woman were still there or not. The woman looked familiar. He wondered if she might be his wife, but probably she wasn't. Too young.

The funny thing was, his memories were falling out in broad patches, he could actually feel them sloughing away. The whole process was almost pleasant—bad departing along with the good, fleas with the fur, older memories fading the fastest.

"He's asleep."

Rebecca shook hands with William. In the gray light outside the hospital, she looked ten years older than she had the day before, "Oh," she said. "Give me your receipts."

He reached into his pocket and handed her his envelope.

"FBI always wants paper, itemized. Guys usually forget these," she said. "I'll take care of them."

"If it's going to cause any more trouble—"

"No. You just got sucked along. Thanks for playing a good game. I'm glad your father is improving. It's pretty amazing, actually."

"What do you think he was talking about—writing about, I mean?" William asked.

"Loose memories," Rebecca said.

"What if it has something to do with the anthrax?"

"You heard the man. There is no anthrax. Save yourself some grief and get on with your career."

"You said it was real. How can you just give it up, no matter what they say at Headquarters?"

Rebecca reached out to grip his shoulder, "Don't ever grow up," she said.

William shook his head. "I suppose there's not much chance of that."

She climbed into the cab and he closed the door for her. The cab drove down the street and Rebecca did not look back.

That's it, he thought.

What a whirlwind.

CHAPTER FORTY-FOUR
Northern Iraq

Fouad's mother had had a confused notion about the Twelfth Imam, a concoction of fairy tales told by her grandmother or gathered from the stories in the many books and pamphlets that she had read in both Farsi and Arabic. "So we tell tales of exile and waiting," she had once said. "Who can it hurt?"

Her stories had grown more elaborate as the years had dragged on in London and the United States. She had invariably begun her stories with a formula: "So for now, this beautiful little boy—blessings and peace be upon him!—lives in a house made of ivory and precious stones, high atop a mountain, and day after day—and in appearance he is only five years old, this is a miracle! But it has been many centuries since and the doves and the Jinn who are Muslim protect him and carry messages to the towns and cities and prayers back—and day after day, he walks around the perimeter of this compound, which no satellite can ever see nor any pilot, nor any passenger in an airplane, and no eye that passes near can behold. And the air atop that mountain is so rarefied that no man who climbs to that altitude will remember what happened when he returns, it will all go blank in his thoughts, but for a beautiful impression of a child full of wisdom, waiting to rule under the banner of al-Mahdi, peace be upon him and his progeny. And that has been reported by some whom I believe. But of course your father does not."

She had told Fouad other tales as well, about Jesus—who had not died on the cross but whose essence awaited in another protected place—"Some say it is like this Twilight Zone, only friendly and beautiful"—and how Jesus (peace be upon him) would visit the boy, and they would eat almond cakes and drink coffee and sweet tea and listen to the soughing of the doves and the screeching of the falcons and eagles who constantly circled over the compound. And then she had added that all the great prophets and men of history who were waiting to return would also visit the boy, the greatest among them but for the Prophet, blessings and peace be upon him and his progeny.

A grand and never-ending garden party attended by the Buddha, by Zoroaster, and so on, peace be upon them all.

Near the end, the Alzheimer's took away her stories and she did not remember either Fouad or his father, and a nurse had attended to her. Months before the end she had spent hours talking on a telephone that was not hooked up, speaking with relatives he had never met—dead relatives.

Fouad had been ten years old when she had died. With his mother's memory had passed Fouad's already shaky belief in her stories. He had kept only the core—God and prayer. No fairy tales.

He pushed back against Harris under the thermal blanket. Harris moaned again, not very loudly. When awake, Harris was almost out of his mind with the dull throbbing pain of his arm and his ribs. The pills did not seem to do be doing much good.

Fouad saw the morning and stood beside the boulder, leaning against it. There were now distant figures on the plain, wandering between the whirlwinds like ants between huge silken scarves.

In the cold their water was holding up and they had plenty of food but that would not matter if the figures on the plain found them. In the moonlight two men had passed by just fifty or sixty meters away, no doubt following a trail from the wreckage of the Superhawk. There had been the shuffling of lightly shod feet and muttered conversations in Farsi.

So now Fouad did not dare stand up and pray. Under his breath, he said, "*Allahu Akbar. Allahu Akbar.*" But prayer was incomplete without the motions so he stopped and silently promised that these prayers would be made up for, all of them, when there was a place and a time. God was understanding and all-forgiving.

Fouad's father had been a severe and serious man and no doubt he had participated in many treacheries, and perhaps even now was involved in such. But his father had called prayer a blessing in life beyond measure, the moment when all else faded and the mind was quiet and in touch with the One that is One. In their years in Washington, DC, they had gone to mosque and prayed together daily until Fouad was sent away to school in Maryland.

There had been a few months in his late adolescence when Fouad had stopped praying, but he had soon found he missed the blessing of opening his heart.

Had they informed his father he was missing?

Harris lay quietly. Fouad gently lifted the blanket to avoid pulling it off his companion as he rolled over, and then realized that Harris was alert. His face was pink with fever.

"Do you hear that?" Harris whispered. At first Fouad heard just the wind. Then a distant roaring.

"Activate the C-SARB," Harris said.

Fouad looked around to make sure they were not about to be set upon by trackers. The figures on the plain were heading for another outcrop a few kilometers west. He switched on the beacon.

"Look for it," Harris said. "It's going to be a big one. They'll be doing, I don't know, atmosphere recon, taking samples to track fallout. A big chopper or an airplane, accompanied by Warthogs, maybe F-18s, F-22s. I don't think they'll come out here just for us."

"Shh," Fouad said. "Of course they will extract us. You are valuable. And the specimens."

"Who the fuck cares about some dead Kurds?" Harris said. "They'll come to track the radiation out of Iran."

Fouad turned, looked up, and saw the aircraft and it was as Harris had suggested—a very big helicopter and heavily armed. It was coming from the west and dipped briefly and arrogantly over the few figures on the plain but did not fire upon them. Then it sped toward the hills. He could not see or hear other aircraft. He crept to the edge of their rocky promontory, leaving Harris in the shade of the large boulder. This was the most dangerous time of all, Fouad knew. He left the C-SARB on but crept low in case pickets had been stationed nearby waiting for them to be rescued.

Watching the helicopter, still kilometers off, Fouad remembered more of his mother's story.

"For the great King of the Abbasids had worries of this boy, and his powers, and sent soldiers to search for him high and low, and found him neither in the Earth nor in the cities nor in the mountains. The doves hid him from sight, the Jinn made him invisible, and sometimes even his father the eleventh Imam, peace be upon him and his progeny, could not find him when he was at play . . ."

The C-SARB would guide the helicopter. Up until the last minute, he would try to make himself as invisible as that fairy-tale boy.

Then he heard a sound like a small animal being stepped on. Fouad glanced over his shoulder, expecting to see a bird of prey with something in its talons—an irrational hope. A piece of light fabric bobbed above the thrusting spine of rock that defined their promontory, within a few meters of the large boulder. Fouad crept along the gravel between the rocks, pistol in hand. He had studied the area that morning, looking for a place to pray, and remembered ways where he could stay hidden. He could not use the pistol unless he absolutely had to, it would attract attention. So he drew the knife from its sheath around his calf.

A tall, bony, bearded man in ragged desert camouflage stood up from a crouch. He had wrapped a dirty length of cloth around his head and it trailed down the back of his neck. His expression was of horrid satisfaction like a butcher who enjoys his work. He lifted Harris's severed head and began to bob up and down, a little dance of triumph and pride. He sang a quiet song in Farsi, too low for Fouad to understand.

His back was to Fouad.

Fouad ran from his cover and grabbed the man's knife hand from the lower wrist and twisted his hand and arm around and quickly had him back and down as he had been taught. The man's long serrated blade flew off to one side. So surprised, the man made not even the sound that Harris had made. He saw Fouad's face and seemed to think that this was a joking friend, wrestling with a fellow insurgent. And indeed Fouad was smiling reassurance. He covered the man's mouth with one hand and with the other pushed his blade just behind the man's prominent Adam's apple, twisted it sideways, and pulled up, then twisted again. The man quivered like a lamb, staring up in silent dismay. His blood flowed in a controlled stream, copious but not spraying or spurting.

Slowly the dying man's face grew sleepy and calm. His quivering subsided to slack twitches.

Fouad felt nothing except a formless loathing at something so stupid, so vicious, like an idiot who tortures kittens or birds. His father had cared little for the jihadists or those in the *umma* who supported them. "They will get us all killed," his father had growled over the dinner table after 9-11. "They care nothing for Islam, nothing for Allah. They are like jackals chewing on the foot of a tiger."

Now Fouad understood. He withdrew his knife. The man who had grinned and danced in joy at his work now appeared sated, with the expression that comes of having no blood in one's brain. His eyes sank back. Harris's head had rolled a couple of meters and lay face down, awful.

A few minutes later, as the helicopter fanned a great wind, Fouad let go of his kill and stumbled across the rocks to rearrange Harris. He waved his hands and began to weep.

There was nothing. Even as the huge machine set down, he was utterly and forever alone. He could not visualize his mother's face. God was not with him, and would never be again.

CHAPTER FORTY-FIVE
Silesia, Ohio

Sam slid the wand over the electrical contacts.

The pillar of fire rose in the early morning, brief and smoky. Twenty starbursts bloomed over the small park at an altitude of just over two thousand feet. They formed a curve with the highest end in the east and the lowest pointing north.

Somehow, given the silence and the stillness after the loud pops, Sam did not think there would be much fuss. And certainly nothing to attract attention to him. Doubtless only a few people saw the flashes of light before the dawn and wondered. Police might be contacted. There might be a report filed. A cruiser might be dispatched to search for anything suspicious.

Sam closed the lid on the trailer, put on his filter mask, cinched it tight, and got behind the wheel of the Dodge. He drove into the wind for a few minutes, then circled around, caught the freeway, and headed east.

He clamped his jaw and imagined the descending ragged plume of invisible dust, so fine, drifting and falling, rising again, spreading and dropping for miles; a few would hear the rattle of small glass beads on their roofs.

For all the angry people, for the righteous, for the zealots and the monsters: a small gift. A gift of the small.

So simple.

It had worked.

PART THREE

MEMORY

CHAPTER FORTY-SIX
Trenton, NJ
October

William Griffin stood in the parking garage at the center of six growing piles of sorted trash and wiped his forehead with his sleeve. He could not reach under his mask to wipe his nose, which was running continuously. No mask and no amount of cream could cover up the stench. The twelve-story building overhead contained three restaurants and fifty-two businesses that produced at least four tons of trash each day, sent down three chutes to dumpsters rotated out and stored behind a chain link enclosure to be picked up once every two days. This was the end of the second day and the dumpsters had all been full. And somewhere in the piles, they might find a paper coffee cup, chewed chicken bones, a receipt, a photo, a stack of paper inadvertently left unshredded, in close archaeological association with each other, with just the right set of DNA or fingerprints to connect four Thai scumbags currently in the custody of Border Security to trafficking in underage prostitutes.

Ten-year-olds.

Nine-year-olds.

Five-year-olds.

After only two months in New Jersey, the excitement was gone. This was awful work, sausage work. You never wanted to know these details about how life was made and what it was made of unless you were blue through and through, and even then you regretted it. Whatever its slim rewards—seeing children deported back to the situations their parents had found intolerable in the first place—it had to be done, to maintain his standing with his fellow agents.

The number of crimes you suspected were going on would never match your successes in capture and prosecution. But you did not turn back, once you knew such things intimately, face to face. The door would never be closed. As in a war, the spirit of the squad was everything.

Especially in the last stages of the political siege.

He had seen the headline on the online streamer of the *NYT*:

SENATE, HOUSE VERDICT FOR FBI: DEATH

William used a long stick to poke through the office paper debris sorted to his left. The cold fluorescent lighting in the parking garage made everyone look sickly, above their masks. Some of the agents wore sealed ski goggles, Tyvek suits, and full filtration gear as they waded through the trash contaminated—illegally, as it turned out—by unsorted restaurant food waste. Animal food waste was supposed to go down a particular chute and be hauled off to a rendering plant, from whence it would return as tiny little bars of hotel soap. It had not. Vegetable food waste and even old oil had been mixed and then the lot had been dumped in with the office and apartment waste. William had long since learned a basic cop truth: some people, in fact a lot of people lived life with little more sense of responsibility and guilt than a bug, intent only on reducing their random walks to a minimum of distance and effort just to get by, to get home and sit in front of their satellite TV or earn discounts on merchandise by signing up for sleep ads.

Five years in NYPD had given William a dark view of life, but it had been a concentrated one. Now, at the bottom end of Newark's thin blue FBI line, he was getting a more smeared-out, multifaceted view. The view of a squashed fly. So be it. The best jobs were the hardest. That's what he tried to tell himself when the going was so disgusting. Why would anyone want to be here, doing this? Better almost to be in the ME's office opening rotting corpses.

"Hey, Tracer, I just had a sentimental moment," he called across the pile to Tracy Warnow, who shared his general build and age. They had been called the Blues Brothers a few weeks ago but the name had not caught on—neither of them looked like Jim Belushi.

To nearly everyone, William was known as TP. Warnow was known as the Tracer.

"Do share," Warnow said. "If it brings tears to my eyes, it can't be any worse than this shit."

"Which would you rather attend, autopsies or garbage detail?"

"Autopsies. Hands down. Now tell me whether this is animal, vegetable, or mineral."

William walked around the paper pile and joined Warnow in peering over the steel rim of a dumpster. A greasy gray something lay in the bottom, refusing to be pried loose.

"Fungus, I think," William decided. "It likes it down there. It looks happy."

"If it gave up its secrets, would it make our lives any easier?" Warnow asked.

"Bag a couple of cc's, just in case," William advised. "If it's human, we can pass it on to Trenton P.D."

"I worked New Orleans for three years," said Davis Gorton, a forty-something, pasty-faced forensic bookkeeper on loan from Pennsylvania. "After two summer days, everything was like that. You couldn't tell a hooker from a dead pig."

"You guys looking for blank DVDs?" called a Trenton detective. "There's a pile over here. Looks like they were tossed down the chute the Thais used."

"Bag them all," Gorton said. "I love spinning discs all day."

William lifted his arm to retract his sleeve and look at the time. It was one in the morning. They would be down here past sunrise. Coffee did not help. Some of the agents used Zak-Hepsin, a legal variation on Tart, but William did not like the side-effects, which included—for him, at least—a couple of days of limp pecker. Not that he had had many opportunities to so fail in recent weeks.

"Coffee break, TP."

William had not seen Trenton ASAC Gavin North descend the ramp into the garage. He waved his arm at the piles. "Don't prolong the agony, sir. Give us a couple of hours. We'll have it sorted by five."

"You're dead on your feet. So's everyone else. We've set up a break room in an empty restaurant on the first floor. There's coffee and a few cots in case anyone wants to catch a nap." North waved his hand and whistled loudly. "That goes for everybody! Half an hour."

The first-floor vacancy was indeed bleak but a quiet, clean-smelling paradise compared to the parking garage. Counters and dividers and all but one of the tables had been removed and cooking and plumbing attachments stuck out from a grease-stained back wall. Linoleum patchwork marked the boundaries of the restaurant that had once been there. There was a bathroom at the back but the lights had burned out and William had to take a whiz in the dark.

He lay back on three plastic chairs with his eyes closed but he could not rest, not really. He had just signed papers to move his father into a rest home, on disability, and not just for recuperation. Griff was no longer his father; he was an empty shell living from hour to hour, recovering well enough physically—but memories of anything before the last few months were gone, or liable to pop up sporadically, peppered into brief conversations that within a moment or two seemed puzzling, inexplicable.

Yet Griff was happier than William had ever known him to be. "It hurts all the time," he had told his son last week, "but the hurt is on the outside. I can take that kind of hurt."

Tracer Warnow flapped out a newspaper and said, "Listen to this. Senator Josephson kicks a dead horse."

"We're not dead yet," William said in his best Monty Python accent.

"Just listen. This is better than coffee."

"I don't want to hear it," Gorton said.

"Gets your blood moving."

"Hand it here," William said wearily.

"You've got your slate. Look it up. I prefer newspapers. They belong to an earlier, civilized age."

William pulled his slate from his pocket and scanned the headlines from AP and Reuters. Nothing on Josephson: they were full of news from the invasion of Saudi Arabia. "Here's something to warm your cockles," he said. "ANTI-SAUDI FORCES ADVANCE ON RIYADH: THOUSANDS FLEE."

"Bastards are reaping the whirlwind," Groton said. "Mecca's next. Stay out of it, I say," he added. "I don't want my son dying to defend King Abdullah."

William moved past two more headlines: OHIO PUBLIC HEALTH: MEMORY CASES APPARENT FLUKE, and 10,000 ACRES BURN IN EASTERN SAN DIEGO COUNTY: *Blazes not yet contained, rain and floods may follow.*

"The whole world is going to hell," Gorton went on, his voice a low rumble. He had pulled out the last remaining picnic-style table and sprawled across it.

William frowned and tapped on the Ohio headline. The dateline read yesterday, Cleveland.

. . . hundreds of residents in Silesia, Ohio, and in at least five neighboring communities cannot seem to clearly remember events that happened years or even months ago. A few exhibit all the symptoms of advanced dementia. Doctors are puzzled by the diversity of cases, but all symptoms, according to Doctor

Jackie Soames of the National Institute of Allergies and Infectious Diseases, appear to tie into defects in how memories are processed. "Short term memories seem to be unaffected. Our patients can function on a day-to-day basis, and can even perform jobs that do not require deep memory. Most of them, however, remember little about their history of the past few years, or even why they live where they live, or how they acquired families."

Theories range from a new and unknown viral infection to BSE, or Bovine Spongiform Encephalopathy, commonly known as Mad Cow Disease . . .

William felt an urge to call Rebecca, but what was there to act on? A coincidence? Loss of memory had nothing to do with anthrax, of that he was certain.

He pinched his nostrils to stifle a sneeze, then read on about the fires in San Diego County.

"Hey, Agent Griffin! TP!"

He raised his head and saw the Newark SAC, Tom Hartland, standing in the open glass door of the empty restaurant. "Warden's giving you a re-prieve. You've got a ticket to Quantico."

William looked at Gorton, who smirked and shook his head in envy. Hartland escorted William to the street and a staff Lincoln Town Car idling at the yellow-marked curb.

"Get in." Hartland unlocked the car and climbed into the driver's side door. "Tell me, Griffin—what do you know about solid rocket fuel?"

CHAPTER FORTY-SEVEN
Bethesda, Maryland

Rebecca Rose stood on the brick porch, adjusted her long cashmere muffler—a luxury she had purchased for herself on the first crisp day of fall—and pushed the ivory-colored doorbell button. Behind the paneled door, chimes rang and a dog immediately began barking. She lifted her white paper bag with its box of See's chocolates. Alph tended to bounce when visitors arrived.

Nancy Newsome opened the front door, restraining a mid-sized Springer spaniel. Silver-blonde, wide-faced, with a sharp nose and pale blue eyes, pleasantly plump and wearing a tailored pink suit even at this hour of the evening, Mrs. Newsome immediately broke into a smile. "So good to see you, Rebecca! Hiram has been so looking forward. He's in his study."

Alph was beside himself with welcome. Rebecca patted him, gave Nancy a hug, and held out the bag. "To be rationed," she suggested.

"How awful of you," Nancy said conspiratorially. "I will hold these over his head whenever he irritates me. He will be so grateful. Hiram, I mean, not Alph." Another glorious smile, and then she ushered Rebecca through the classically Colonial hall and across elegant rugs of Persian design—but American manufacture—to the study. "He'll only come out if I tell him it's you," Nancy said, lips judgmental. "He's been on the computer and then on the phone since three. I'll give you both ten minutes, and then I'm serving dinner. Pot roast. Plain fare for just plain folks."

"Wouldn't miss it," Rebecca said. Alph tagged dutifully at her heels, past his initial glee but more than willing to be company.

Hiram sat half in shadow, his face moon-colored in the glow from an old CRT. One hand was holding a phone receiver to his ear and the other was moving a wired mouse on a foam pad so old its edges curled. The desk was covered with piles of printouts loosely arranged by topic—news stories, emails, copies from texts. The rest of the room—dark wood wainscoting, matching maple furniture, white walls, crystal cove lights pendant from brass fixtures—was immaculate. The walls were covered with plaques, framed photos, testimonials.

Alph nosed his master's leg and Hiram looked up. His face was unhappy in a Jovian way, an expression he had probably maintained all afternoon. "I'm on hold. Ah, forget it." He slammed down the receiver. "Did you hear Josephson's rant?"

"Good evening to you, News," Rebecca said, and pulled up a second chair to sit. "I've been trying to avoid it."

Hiram rotated in his desk chair, glowering. "Son of a bitch," he said. "Son of a loose-titted, sow-bellied, egg-sucking bitch."

"Yes, sir," Rebecca said, grinning her appreciation.

Hiram flung out his arm and lifted a page from the desk. "Read it. It's our death warrant."

She held the printout under a light.

"We are at the end of a long and awful period of the repeal and repression of civil liberties. Secret courts, secret files—all tied to a binge of muddled thinking that has done nothing to protect America, which became abundantly clear on 10-4. The FBI, as the most important law enforcement agency in our nation, has been complicit in many of these transgressions, and I think a break-up is long overdue. I say we remove the FBI from its homeland of radical indoctrination, and reconstitute its most talented and least culpable agents in a new agency, based on the West Coast, that deserves and rewards their best efforts, and does not lead them always down the paths of uncivil retribution for political ideas with which senior executives happen to disagree."

"Gasbag," Hiram said as she lowered the page. "What in hell would the bureau do in San Francisco?"

"Our offices would look pretty," Rebecca said.

Hiram snorted. He took the page and sadly finished Josephson's speech. "'A small hiatus in FBI activities is to be expected.' Oh, the mice will play, Rebecca. Let me put it politely, before Nancy comes in here with a bar of soap and a spittoon. As a nation, we're up shit creek."

"Some of it's true," Rebecca said.

"Makes it worse," he shot back. "The lick of Papa's strap is all the keener if you actually stole the cookie."

Alph put his paws up on Hiram's knee and stared soulfully into his master's face, muttering doggy sympathy. "Josephson's just a rooster crowing on the tomb. The President is the hangman. She called the director today and gave him his walking papers. Jesus wept. 'No confidence.' So who's next?"

Rebecca had been at headquarters all afternoon. "I brought some material for you to look over," Rebecca said. "Fair warning from some old friends." She handed him a clipped folder.

He lifted an eyebrow. The folder hung in Rebecca's hand. Then he grabbed it, pulled the clip, and muttered, "Too much goddamn paper."

Nancy appeared at the door. "Is Senator Josephson joining us?" she inquired archly. "Because I hear his name so often, I'm wondering what he likes to drink with his pot roast—beer or wine."

"Irish whiskey," Hiram said, lost in the pages. "Just a minute, Nancy."

"Table's set, Hiram."

"Don't get cross with me. The whole world is cross with me."

"Poor baby," Nancy said. She withdrew after exchanging a womanly glance with Rebecca.

"These are OPM internal vetting documents, Rebecca. How'd you get them?"

Rebecca said nothing, just looked sweet and simple.

Hiram riffled through the papers, eyes wide. "Sam Adams, they've got dirt on half the people I work with."

Rebecca leaned forward. "They're looking for somebody whose hands aren't covered with mud. Someone who can finish what he starts and knock heads—but the right heads, and with practiced charm."

Hiram's face went pale.

"I heard something on the weed vine," she continued. "Nobody knows if the rumors are true."

The phone rang. Hiram jerked, then sat up, looking as if he were about to be shot.

"Scrub your hands, sir," Rebecca advised.

A second ring. His lips twitched. "I won't do it," he said emphatically. A third. "I won't preside over a funeral. I'm not a damned undertaker." The phone rang for the fourth time. Hiram looked as if he were contemplating the easy out of just dropping dead. "Crap," he said.

"Answer the phone, Hiram," Nancy called from the dining room.

Hiram wrapped his forehead in one thick-fingered hand and rolled back to the desk. He picked up the phone and listened for a moment, then said, "Yes, Madam President."

Rebecca took the folder from his hand, pulled back the brass screen, and tossed the papers into the light and heat of the office's small fireplace. She walked into the dining room, where Nancy had just laid out on the damask tablecloth a large pot roast smothered with potatoes, carrots, and onions.

Nancy pushed through the kitchen door, balancing a tray of drinks in crystal glasses. "Elderberry wine?" she asked archly, and handed Rebecca a tumbler of Scotch. "Pardon me for my big ears. I do not countenance profanity, my dear, you know that. But what in *hell* are they about do to my husband? I've actually enjoyed having him around, the last few months."

Rebecca could not provide a comforting answer.

"If they take him back and move him up the ladder, will I ever see him?" Nancy sat with a flump on the nearest chair. "I remember Alice Sessions, way back when. I remember what they did to her husband. If the President has chosen Hiram without consulting the other senior executives, OPM will bring out the long knives. Hiram's a healthy man, but this could give anyone a heart attack." She stretched out her hand, tears in her eyes. "Give me that, damn it."

Rebecca returned the glass of Scotch. Nancy slugged it back neat.

The dinner was brief, the pot roast having been re-heated twice. They ate quickly and with hardly a word, and immediately after, Hiram retired to the study to make more calls.

Nancy insisted Rebecca stay for a glass of port. Sitting in the living room, she realized she was still wired—still on the grid, if anyone was tracking. She deactivated her Lynx and then looked at her slate: five calls from one number. She looked up the number. It was in Israel.

Nancy returned and caught her with her slate out. "Never mind me, dear," she said, a little tipsy, and set down a glass of Ficklin on the table beside Rebecca. "I know that look. Something demands your immediate attention."

Rebecca took a sip of port. "What an evening, huh?"

"I'm sure," Nancy said. "Use the guest bedroom, past the entrance and on the immediate right. It's quiet. I sweep the bugs out every day."

"Thanks."

The Jerusalem number belonged to a former Quantico student named Ehud Halevy, an international trainee now an officer in the Israeli Police—a brigadier general. The Israeli police used the whole range of military ranks. Rebecca had been an instructor at the Q during Ehud's class a decade ago. She did the math and came up with Israel's current time. It was four a.m. but he had left his message just a half-hour before.

Her call went through immediately. The general was wide awake. "Agent Rose, thank you for returning my call. I am distressed that we have not communicated earlier. But this is no time. Why has not anyone told me of BuDark?"

"I don't know much myself, Ehud. What's up?"

"We have come upon something terrible, something you must have certainly known about. Did we not discuss anthrax, American anthrax, ten years ago at FBI? Now it is here, in Israel, in the hands of Islamic terrorists. They were going to use it on Jerusalem, Agent Rose. *Jerusalem!*"

"Please, General. Tell me what you can."

"Fireworks rockets, brought in on private jet by a group working out out of Iraq and Syria, but they are receiving their supplies from America. Some of the captives are talking. It is an unbelievable story. We are analyzing what we have found. This will take time, because we are using such precautions. How could you allow this? Has America become a gigantic infection, a boil that is bursting?"

"Listen, Ehud, what do you know about the American connection?"

"Some have told us it is a tall man, blond and quiet. He minimizes his contact with others, but some say he is a lady's man. He has one blue eye and one green eye, that he sometimes disguises with contact lenses. He is very careful, and he is no longer in Israel, if ever he was. That is all we have been able to learn."

Rebecca sat on the bed and bent over, feeling as if she were about to be sick. "Can I reach you at this number, any time?"

"Yes. I may never sleep again, Agent Rose."

"Thanks for trusting me, General. Let me do some work here."

"I only hope your FBI and government will trust *us,* Agent Rose. We have of course informed the Prime Minister and Knesset, and they are talking with your State Department. We need answers very soon. We have in custody only one team. What if there are others?"

Rebecca came out of the guest bedroom, her face ashen. Nancy was asleep in the chair. She could hear Hiram still talking in his office.

She slammed her fist on the heavy door.

CHAPTER FORTY-EIGHT
Silesia, Ohio

William hitched a police ride from the tiny local airport. The driver, a young officer from the Ohio State Patrol, had been ferrying officials back and forth for two days now and she looked stretched thin. "They're telling us nothing. Must be pretty big."

Big enough to get him out of a garbage detail.

He quietly observed the neighborhoods of modest homes, trim and clean—except for block after block of overgrown yards. He noticed two or three burned-out houses and wondered if that was above average for a town this size. On the flight, he had hooked up to Web reports about Silesia, famous mostly for grain distribution, bakeries and local German food—as well as for its churches.

He had also read what little was available about Silesia's medical crisis. That made his brain itch. He couldn't fit these reports into a compelling pattern.

A large yellow tent had been set up in the Warren K. Schonmeyer Park. Three patrol cars, two local police cars, a big FBI van, and a CID semi-trailer had been pulled up on the grass next to the tent. Power cables and hoses ran to a brick restroom that had been marked off limits with police tape.

The officer parked. William got out and saw George Matty, the Mississippi agent from his class, standing by an open flap near one corner of the tent. "Thanks," William told the officer. She popped the trunk and retrieved his floppy bag, then backed her patrol car out for more runs to the airport.

William walked across the patchy grass toward the tent. The afternoon air was crisp. He sidestepped a dog turd. Matty grinned. "Scoop your poop, Agent Griffin," he called out. "That one's been lying in wait for some unwary bastard for two days." He held out his hand and William shook it firmly. "I'm case agent. Luck of the draw, I guess."

William suspected it was much more than that. Matty had slimmed down in the months since Quantico. He had also lost some of his drawl. He wore a gray suit and black walking shoes and looked a proper FBI agent, blue through and through. Compared to Matty, William suspected he still looked rumpled.

"How's Cincinnati?" William asked.

"Gritty," Matty said. "Nice town on a long slide. Great work environment. I hate it. Silesia is better, except nobody remembers where they left their keys." He smirked. "That makes interviews a challenge."

"You pulled me out of garbage detail," William said. "I owe you one."

Matty escorted him across the tent. "As soon we got a bulletin about cardboard tubes and traces of polybutadiene, the Patriarch connection came up and we flew out of Cincinnati like bats out of hell. I told the ASAC one of my Academy mates had worked Patriarch fireworks with Rebecca Rose. He doesn't get along with Agent Rose, I guess, so he told me to bring you in."

"Show me," William said. Matty took him to a folding table. Beside a small portable spectrum analyzer, a row of ten clear-top plastic boxes had been filled with fragments of mushy cardboard reassembled on pristine white paper. Pieces were missing but at a quick glance William could see that each cardboard tube, reassembled, would be two or three inches in diameter and about fifteen inches long.

"A sleepless little old lady filed a complaint," Matty said. "She said there were about a dozen bright flashes one morning, very early, right over the park and the town. She was out on her porch and she says she counted them. A couple of months later, an officer scouting for drug use in the park found fragments of fireworks tubes on the top of that very same comfort facility." Matty pointed through a breeze-whipped gap in the tent at the brick restrooms. "All together, we've recovered the remains of ten tubes, scattered from the comfort station to the parking lot of a church just beyond the park."

William peered down at the boxes. "HAZMAT team?"

"Of course," Matty said. "We put the officer and any locals who had touched the fragments under observation and ran tests. I'm sure you're dying to ask . . . Did we find anthrax?"

"Just dying," William agreed.

"Well, we're not, and neither is anybody else. There was perchlorate residue, poly-B, aluminum powder, some glass beads, talc, fine white sand, and . . . this'll sound familiar . . ." Matty looked a challenge.

"Yeast," William said.

"Damn. You're brighter than I remember. So, can you tell me why we're here? Why somebody would bother to shoot fireworks filled with yeast all over a small town?"

"What kind of yeast?"

"Regular kind. I'm no expert. But it's pretty fine."

"Was the yeast killed by the heat?"

"Not according to our analysts. They're growing some right now back in Cincinnati. I'd say most of it blew right out of the tubes and spread out from the point of origin, not far from that curb over there. Are these like the tubes the Patriarch's family was packing?"

William nodded. "They look right," he said. "Any ideas about motive?"

"The Patriarch's kids are rampaging across America, shooting off their damned yeast shells, and thereby telling us they could just as easily use anthrax. Ransom notes to follow."

William frowned. "That would explain a lot, but we haven't heard word one from any of the others."

"Then maybe these were duds. Maybe they didn't work the way they planned. SAC's on my butt about getting a piece of Patriarch pie. Your confirmation could really set me up here."

William walked along the line of boxes. Yeast at the farm, dozens of pounds of it spread over the trees. Yeast in the printer cartridges. Yeast everywhere, but no anthrax—not even BT or some other more suitable anthrax substitute.

"Any guess what altitude they exploded?" William asked.

"Anywhere from five hundred to three thousand feet," Matty said.

"I assume you've already checked up on supremacist churches in town."

"There aren't any. No Nazis, either. Just schnitzel."

"How about you—have you gone to church?"

"Not yet, but there's plenty to choose from."

"Synagogues?"

"Not a one," Matty said.

"Anybody check how far the yeast might have spread?"

"Why? It's yeast." Matty grinned. "Might give our young ladies itchy privates. Is that what you're worried about?"

William shrugged. "My father mentioned Silesia on his hospital bed."

Matty tightened like a race horse at the post. "In what connection?"

"There might have been a map or fragment of a map in the Patriarch's barn. Griff asked us to check out Silesia. It wasn't in the final report because there wasn't any anthrax, nobody could make sense of it, and . . . well, they weren't interested in the fireworks angle. Griff told us there were lots of churches. He seemed to think that might be a motive, that the Patriarch wanted to kill both Jews and mainstream Christians."

"I'm interested, you can bet on that."

"I don't know if anybody kept my father's scrawls. I doubt it."

"Sounds like a bad lapse of judgment," Matty said.

"Well, now it does," William said. "But that's all there was."

"Why didn't you check it out?"

"We were shut down. You know that."

Matty nodded. "Question is, will this be enough to re-open?"

"I'd sure like to know why someone gets his jollies by flinging yeast."

"Could we re-interview your father?" Matty asked.

"You can try. His thinking fades in and out. He doesn't remember a lot of things."

"Doesn't know where his keys are?" Matty asked. "It's a pattern. That's what happened to the deputy who first checked out the Patriarch. He's on disability leave. Happy guy, from what I hear."

I'm telling you, some of it I just don't remember! They're putting stuff in my food. This place is making me crazy.

Jeremiah Chambers, the Patriarch's son—

Griff. And now, the Snohomish County sheriff's deputy, William tried to remember his name—Markham, Kerry Markham.

William stood in front of the table and the boxes, not moving a muscle. He had just felt a sour foreboding, like guilt for a mistake he had yet to make. Matty was watching him. "Can I set up in the trailer . . . or here?" William asked. "I'd like to make some calls."

"As long as you share, and I mean *everything*," Matty said, "you're welcome to join our little circus." He reached in his coat pocket and handed William a green bottle: gingko biloba tablets. "Try some. Whole town's popping them like candy."

CHAPTER FORTY-NINE
Incirlik Air Base
Turkey

Fouad saw his mother standing in the far rocks. His father pointed and smiled. The Jinn swirled around her, whirlwinds of blue and red. "She's making it all up," his father said. "There's nothing to come home to, no blankets, no hot water, no chocolate, no comforts, and neither of us can hide, right? We'll both kill again. No fairy tales. Just a madness for God."

He was dreaming, of course, but even though he felt the bed beneath him and the tape wrapped around his ribs, he could still see his father, his mother, and the rocks. The dark outlines of the small room gradually came into focus through the edgy pall of the painkillers. A picture of a helicopter hung on one wall, and another of an A-10 Warthog hung over his bed. These were his Jinn. They had plucked him out of the desert.

His intercom chimed and he got out of bed to answer. It was David Grange, who had been on the rescue chopper, inviting him to a late night coffee in the mess hall. His chest did not hurt much. He got dressed with only a few twinges.

The mess hall was brightly lit and nearly empty. Two hundred aluminum tables stood in neat rows under a concrete roof that could have covered a football field. David Grange, short and pug-nosed, on the edge of plumpness, shook his hand and asked Fouad if he wanted cocoa or coffee.

"Tea, white, please," Fouad said. Grange went through the long bars before the cafeteria station and brought back two cups. He set one on the table before Fouad.

"You've impressed the hell out of Trune and Dillinger," Grange said. "And me, for what its worth. Who else has spoken to you?"

"The doctors. The officers who debriefed me."

"You did a remarkable thing out there. You helped us put a big chunk of the puzzle together. Do you have any idea what's happening? What's happened in the last few days?"

"No," Fouad said. "I have been pretty dopey. I'm still having dreams."

"Well, that will happen after trauma. We're moving you up a few steps. Right now, everyone's scrambling to get a piece of Iranian nuke pie. But . . ." Grange regarded Fouad through amused eyes. "It was an accident. The Iranians were moving their warheads at Shahabad Kord and one of them got triggered. Right now, that's not the official story, because some of our generals want to play this hand for all its worth. But it's an accident—a wet match fizzle, compared to what we're after. You look a little woozy. Still following me, Fouad?"

Grange pronounced his name perfectly.

"I am okay," Fouad said. "What has happened?"

"Israel may have foiled an anthrax attack. We thought someone was after Jews, maybe Jerusalem, so no surprise there. But Vatican authorities and Interpol have busted a ring of Jihadists preparing to launch a bioweapons attack in Rome. They never got their payload—an interruption in the supply. It's worse than we thought. Someone's after major religious cities. All of them. We don't know why, but now at least we know who—we've ID'd one of the conspiracy, maybe the main guy."

Grange stood. "Drink up. I'll introduce you to some fine young men. They're eager to meet you."

CHAPTER FIFTY
Washington, DC

Rebecca sat next to Hiram in the limousine. Traveling with the director-designate to headquarters would have once made her heart go pitty-pat, but now she was bone-tired and worried sick.

It's going to happen, and this time it's going to be worse.

Something new, some invention or variation nobody could anticipate. Jesus Christ, high schools and junior colleges have gene assemblers now—they can make viruses from scratch.

Her mind raced, trying to go through all the possibilities.

Two young, prime hunks of FBI beef, sitting on the drop seats, gave her their best critical stares. Rebecca had been working the phones and all her connections throughout the day and most of the night before. Her slate chimed.

The call was from Frank Chao at Quantico.

"What's up, Frank?" she said, shoving herself into a seat corner.

"You tell me. Trying to be of service, pulling in a few favors . . . but what I've got is weird. No hits on any criminal database, and I've been through them all. However, I've run some outlandish DNA searches, and your Arizona blood not only proves paternity to the Patriarch's wife's unborn baby . . . but it could be a match to someone who died in 9-11."

"You're joking."

"Not. I scored a hit from a theoretical DNA match list constructed to help people find relatives in the World Trade Center. Fortuitously, that database isn't closed, and obviously it points toward the Memorial Park database from 9-11, but I don't want to go there without solid backup."

"What do you mean, theoretical?"

"Statistical ranges of DNA markers that could represent victims. Relatives of missing persons gave DNA samples to the Medical Examiner's teams working on DM tissue samples held in refrigerated trailers at Memorial Park. Those databases are closed to us, of course."

"I know."

"In those instances where they couldn't retrieve DNA from hairbrushes, tooth brushes, biopsies or whatever to match to victims, a researcher in a contract corporation planned to generate statistical marker links to match living relatives and severely reduced samples. Heat, water, decay—pretty nasty conditions. Some of the bits were recovered from the tummies of raccoons and rats scavenging the Fresh Kills site where they dumped the rubble. They'd trap them and—"

"I didn't need to know that, Frank."

"Sorry."

"You have a hit with a *theoretical* victim of 9-11."

"Right."

"So it could lead us to a relative," Rebecca said, "or to a statistical nobody—a bogus projection."

"Both are possible."

"All right. Let's get Memorial Park."

"Lets us, you mean, or lets me? That's sacred ground, Rebecca. I'd rather continue with every other database, military, hospital workers, whatever, before I tackle Memorial Park."

Rebecca squeezed her eyes shut. Their footing was not good. If they tried something that audacious . . . "How long will it take?" she asked.

"A few days. A week, if I don't get priority time on the computers. And I won't, you know that. I'm just squeezing my searches in between the cracks."

The Arizona trooper's body had been moved away from the rig. The glove was a Hatch Friskmaster.

"Law enforcement, Frank. Narrow it down to recruits and graduates from the last twenty years."

"Any particular reason?"

"More than a hunch, less than a certainty."

"Will do."

She pocketed her slate, then removed it, turned it off, and showed it to the agents flanking Hiram.

"Thanks," said the agent on the left, his jaw muscles clenching. "Is your Lynx active?"

"No," Hiram said testily. "We are off the grid."

CHAPTER FIFTY-ONE
Silesia, Ohio

William walked beside the young doctor through the high school gymnasium. Beds and portable curtains had been erected around the hundreds of patients who had spilled over from the main hospital. The doctor was bleary-eyed from hours of admitting and running tests. William had told him nothing about what he had learned in the last three hours; he was in listening mode, fully aware that everything he thought he knew was wrong.

"It's got to be the biggest outbreak I've ever heard of," the doctor said. "We're getting back diagnosis after diagnosis, and all of them are coming up with the same indicators—CT scans show early spongiform lesions in the brain, we can isolate prions, the prions appear to be able to transform lab tissue cultures—all of which confirms the clinical symptoms, the mental and in some cases physical deterioration. But hundreds of cases in one town? And growing by twenty or thirty every day? Not to mention throughout the county . . . and now, the state."

The doctor pulled back a curtain and let William look in on a middle-aged woman. She was sitting up on her cot, reading an old, tattered *Smithsonian,* and looked up with a puzzled smile and shifting gaze.

"Good evening, Mrs. Miller," the doctor said.

"Good evening."

It was three in the afternoon.

"We met yesterday," the doctor said.

"Yes, I remember."

"This is William, from the government, Mrs. Miller."

"Can he help me find my husband?"

"Your husband is waiting for you at home, Mrs. Miller."

"Oh."

"Can you tell me where you were born?"

"No," she said, eyes piercing. "Have you found my birth certificate?"

"Do you remember your children, Mrs. Miller?"

"I have children, yes." She tracked between William and the doctor, like an actor hoping for a cue from the wings.

"And their names?"

"I've written them down. I know my children's names, of course. Just look." She took a notebook from a metal table and began flipping through it. "Here they are. Nicholas and Susan and Karl."

"Thank you. And your religion? Where do you go to church, Mrs. Miller?"

She referred to the notebook again. "First Ohio Evangelical Lutheran. My husband is a deacon. My youngest son sings in the choir."

"Thank you, Mrs. Miller."

"I'd like to go home soon, Doctor."

"We're working on that. I'll check back in a couple of hours. Do you need more magazines or books, Mrs. Miller?"

"No, thank you," she said, smiling. "These are just fine."

The doctor pulled back the curtain and walked to the double doors at the end of the gym. He held up Mrs. Miller's patient chart and biographical data for William to read. "A lot of our patients began making notes to hide their symptoms from their families. Yesterday, I switched Mrs. Miller's notebook with that from a woman across the aisle. Mrs. Miller is a Southern Baptist, Agent Griffin. And those magazines and books are the ones she was given a week ago. She's re-read them at least three or four times. To her, they're still fresh. Some of our patients have portable DVD players. They watch their movies over and over again—if they can remember how to use the players."

William looked down the aisle and listened to the quiet. For the most part, the patients seemed contented, even happy.

"What we're experiencing here is like nothing I've ever heard of," the doctor said. "It combines elements of Alzheimer's and CJD—Creutzfeldt-Jakob Disease. It strikes all ages, like variant CJD. But it's fast—it acts in weeks or months, not years. And it's epidemic. We may have three or four thousand cases in the next few weeks. They can't go home, they can't work, they just wander off if we don't watch them day and night. That requires twenty-four-hour care, one-on-one nursing. We're already past our breaking point. We're not a rich county, and federal funding for this level of care has become nonexistent. But let's not focus on the money. Where in hell are we going to find that many *nurses*?"

CHAPTER FIFTY-TWO
SIOC
J. Edgar Hoover Building
Washington, DC

Charles Cahill, the outgoing director, was a short dapper man with a cap of prematurely white hair, a short wide nose, and perfect teeth. He firmly shook Hiram Newsome's hand and then Rebecca's and led them down the fifth-floor hallway to the Center. "Congratulations, Hiram. I can't think of a better choice."

Hiram shook his head. "I haven't met with the President yet. And there's still the meat grinder—vetting and confirmation."

"Oh, you'll be confirmed," Cahill said. "Talk radio bastards are already calling you a liberal wienie special-ordered to tear down the agency. That'll endear you to Josephson." He winked at Rebecca. Cahill was younger than Hiram Newsome but looked older. He was renowned for his shoes—he always wore two-tones, white and brown, highly polished.

The Strategic Information and Operations Center at Headquarters—SIOC, or just the Center—had been re-done three years before. Half of its operations had been moved to the sixth floor, reducing its footprint by half on the fourth and fifth floors—and now, once again, the FBI had a command center that actually did look as if it belonged in a high-budget thriller—two stories high, walls of glass and polished steel, floating projections of data and video that circled the room like ghosts, and the ability to access a 24-hour bank of analysts who could look up and process anything available on information networks around the world.

The door to SIOC opened at Cahill's approach. The room beyond was like a dark cave, deserted. "I've got a few minutes before my next meeting and I thought we might spend it in here," Cahill said as he walked around the room, rubbing his hand on the leather chairs. He smiled. "This place can make you believe you know all there is to know."

"Where do you want us? Rebecca's the majordomo on this."

"So I hear." Cahill seated himself in one of the audience chairs, leaving Hiram to assume the Throne—a large black chair mounted on a three-step riser, with the best view of every display. Rebecca stood in a spotlight where the second ring of the circus might have been—the room was almost that large. "Makes you feel like a little girl about to give a recital, doesn't it?" Cahill asked.

"We could move elsewhere," Hiram suggested.

"Wouldn't think of it. Sitting here helps you understand our problems better than anything. We so much wanted to be movie stars. Pretty soon, if we don't do something, and fast, we'll just be extras without any lines. Rebecca, don't get all choked up by the glitz."

"I gave my files to the data logger, sir. They should be coming up shortly."

"And here they are," Cahill said. "My last chance to control the vertical, control the horizontal. News, here you go—the Magic Wand is easy to learn." He raised a small silver remote.

"No, sir," Hiram said. "It's Rebecca's show."

"So it is," Cahill said. "Begin."

"Amerithrax was a punk, gentlemen," she said. "Compared to what we're facing now, what he did to this country was trivial."

On video and slides, sheep, cows, baboons, monkeys, and chimpanzees died awful deaths. She discussed the creation of antibiotics-resistant anthrax in the FSU—the Former Soviet Union—and showed downwind casualty charts from the accidental 1979 outflow of powder-fine anthrax at Sverdlovsk. Next, she flashed the files of U.S. weapons experts who had been the target of FBI suspicions in the years following Amerithrax. She concluded this segment by saying, "Compared to the thousands of tons created in Russia and shipped off to Resurrection Island, the five letters mailed in 2001 were no worse than a mosquito bite on an elephant. But the elephant flinched and it got pretty damned expensive. So Amerithrax was an extremely effective punk, and we never caught him. Now, we think he—or someone with his knowledge and expertise—has surfaced again. We think he and his partners are trying to sell genetically modified anthrax to antagonists in the Middle East. Not necessarily to use against us—though that's a possibility, of course. But to use against each other. The Israelis have recently arrested and sequestered a group equipped with crude but effective bioweapons apparently shipped from the United States—fireworks shells that match the description of those that could have been produced at the farm of Robert Chambers, the Patriarch.

"Our new Amerithrax may be using a particularly seductive lure. He claims that these anthrax shells carry germs modified to attack only Jews. Apparently, he's managed to convince a number of Muslim extremists. They've tested his germs in Iraq at two locations, Baghdad and Kifri. Just off the BuDark wire service," Rebecca added, looking up. "One of our agents, Fouad Al-Husam, was rescued after being shot down in northern Iraq. He delivered autopsy samples to an army assessment unit in Turkey. They came from the bodies of Kurdish Jews exposed to anthrax spores. Weaponized and genetically modified Ames-type Anthrax has been confirmed as their cause of death. We believe the victims were detained and dosed by Sunnis operating in the area, militants connected to a string-puller and money guy named Ibrahim Al-Hitti."

Cahill nodded. "Up-to-the-minute. Continue, Agent Rose."

"While no expert believes it is possible to manufacture a germ that uniquely targets an ethnic group, we can't discount the possibility that the anthrax has somehow been modified to be selective. We've charted a genome from the samples obtained in Kifri."

The diagrammatic ghost of a spiraling and twisted circle of DNA, with two smaller satellite circles, floated to the right and center of Rebecca's position. "In both samples, Baghdad 1 and Kifri 2, they found genes artificially inserted in one of two small circular plasmids—genes that code for bioluminescence. They are triggered by the activation of toxin genes on both plasmids. Our experts say this would have made the lesions on the Baghdad victims glow in the dark—red, then green, just before they died. Oddly, the same genes in the Kifri specimens are not activated. In the Kifri anthrax, a modified Ames strain, there are other, unfamiliar genes inserted in the main chromosome. They may be dummies meant to fool Al-Hitti's scientists, or they may in fact serve a real and destructive purpose. We just don't know—yet."

"Have we got any of these samples, to do our own workup?" Cahill asked.

"No," Rebecca said. "The Baghdad samples are currently being analyzed in Europe. The Kifri samples are in Turkey. The Israeli samples . . . well, relations are icy at the moment, and not just because of Shahabad Kord." She looked up.

"There are many reasons for Israel to be angry," Cahill said. "Their intelligence failures are the equal of our own. Go on, Agent Rose."

"Our prime suspect may have been involved in the murder of a state trooper in Arizona. He left behind DNA evidence, blood, saliva, sweat, and skin cells. We have a description of a tall blond American with one blue eye and one green eye, in both the Patriarch case and the Israeli attempt. Apparently, our suspect fathered a child on one of the Patriarch's wives."

Cahill humphed and buried his chin in one hand.

"We haven't finished our search against available DNA databases to establish his identity." She wasn't about to mention the mismatch between the skin cell DNA and the blood, much less the 9-11 connection, until it was all much more solid.

"How old do we think your suspect is?" Cahill asked.

"Best guess, somewhere between forty-five and fifty-five years old," Rebecca said.

"Experienced sort of fellow," Cahill mused. "Able to move around the Middle East, sell a bill of goods, which means speaka da lingo, Arabic at the very least . . . the gift of bad gab, in Baghdad. That doesn't fit any FBI profile of Amerithrax I've ever read." He sat up and leaned forward. "Hell, if you find him, recruit him. News, what do you want me to do?"

"Give Rebecca the authority to re-open the investigation I authorized in April. The international connection makes this a major hot potato."

"We're a sizzling steak surrounded by hot potatoes. Some are hotter than others. Agent Rose, pardon me for being blunt, but your puzzle pieces are too far apart. They don't join up. Israel doesn't have any evidence for an American connection, other than hearsay from suspects 'under duress.' I've never relied on confessions under torture. I'll go along with evidence of anthrax in Iraq, but hell, maybe someone found Saddam's old stockpiles."

"Saddam never used the Ames strain," Rebecca said.

Cahill shrugged. "We don't even have proof the Israelis have found anthrax in their fireworks shells. No anthrax was detected in Washington state, and none in Arizona. So where's the connection to Amerithrax? If fresh product is being made here, why can't we find even a trace? And how is it being delivered through the tightest security in modern times?"

Now it was Hiram's turn to weigh in. "Diplomatic Security and others are already making a big push overseas, through BuDark. We have agents in the thick of it. FBI headquarters can provide support here. Charles, re-opening this investigation puts us in a good position if BuDark delivers. And BuDark is working on the President's nickel, after both DS and the CIA started tracking anthrax reports in the Middle East. FBI should be seen supporting her initiative. We should be forward thinking."

Cahill was wearing his best poker face, but Rebecca's hopes fell. He wasn't even gumming the hook.

"We're talking inkjet printers, right?" He shook his head. "Even before I was director, I never put much credence in that theory. Last spring, I let Hiram play out his cards and watched you get shot down all over again. Anthrax is bad news in more ways than one, no pun intended, Hiram."

He stood and walked around the circle of seats, then down the short flight of steps, stopping in front of Rebecca. "I worked Amerithrax. I was with the team that bird-dogged Hatfill. I even flew to Zimbabwe in 2003 to investigate a twenty-five-year-old anthrax outbreak. Ten thousand infections, almost two hundred deaths, and the Rhodesian government—Project Coast—might have been involved, but after all that time, we couldn't tell. Hatfill was a cowboy with African connections, a big ego, and a padded résumé. We couldn't hang Amerithrax on him or anyone else—but that doesn't mean we were wrong. Ultimately, it was a heart-breaker." Cahill looked up at Rebecca in the spotlight. "I'll admit, this does sound like something from Project Coast—modifying germs and developing poisons to kill opponents of apartheid, to selectively target blacks or reduce their fertility, to eliminate the black man's food supply. That's still my bet for Amerithrax—some crazy weapons master with South African or Rhodesian training. I'd love to make Hiram happy—maybe he'll increase my retirement. But frankly, I still don't see it. Push the pieces closer together. Find some domestic anthrax. When News comes aboard, formally, he can take all the risk he wants. For now, though, it's still my call. And I say: not proven."

Hiram escorted Rebecca to the parking garage. "Maybe Senator Josephson is right. Maybe we're caught in the same loopy thinking that makes us screw up over and over again."

"What if we don't have a few weeks or a month?" Rebecca fumed. She reached into her purse and switched on her slate, in case Frank called, or anyone else who was still brave enough to work with her.

Hiram slid into the limo and made room for her. "We're not done," he said. He stared at the seat backs. "I'll be betting everything on one roll of the dice. My career, this case, everything."

Rebecca did not feel the need to speak up and add to Hiram's burden. He knew the stakes as well as she did.

"What we know is like a thick fog, but it's real." He leaned forward and told the driver, "Get me Kelly Schein at the White House. Chief of Staff to the President."

The two agents ran to join them in the limo but Hiram waved them aside. "We'll be fine," he announced, and levered the heavy door shut. The agents stood outside, angry and dismayed, visible through the phonebook-thick bulletproof glass.

The limo pulled away.

"I don't think anybody here trusts me, Rebecca," Hiram said. "The President picked me to replace Cahill. They're asking, why? Maybe the droolers on talk radio are right and I'm a traitor."

Rebecca's slate chimed. She swore under her breath and pulled it out.

"What are you, bad news central?" Hiram asked.

She had two messages. The first header said she had a message from Frank Chao at the Academy. *Pretty wild,* Frank had typed in the subject line. *Call ASAP.*

She scanned the second, a voice/text message from William Griffin with accompanying graphic. The text message listed twelve names. She recognized eight—all of them agents and other law enforcement personnel that had been on the Patriarch's farm before or when the barn blew, including Erwin Griffin and Cap Benson. Below the list: *Long-term recall. Some dementia. Exposure at farm.*

The graphic showed what looked like dispersal patterns laid over a town map—of Silesia, Ohio. She arrowed through the entire graphic. Within a grayed parabolic plume almost six miles long and extending outside the town lay hundreds of red dots. Around the plume spread dozens more purple dots. No labels.

"It's from Griff's son," she told Hiram, and showed him the graphic and the list. Then she played back the message.

"*Rebecca, it isn't anthrax. That's just a ploy,*" William said, his voice hoarse. "*It's potentially a lot worse. Whoever he is, he doesn't want to kill. He may not be a terrorist—he probably doesn't even care about the terror.*

"*He's targeting our memories. He wants us to forget.*"

The driver interrupted over the intercom. "I have Kelly Schein, sir."

Three Volvo trucks pulled up at a so-called Hijaz Liberation Force check-point. The twelve-lane highway behind the small convoy was almost empty. Ahead, a tight roiling knot of armed and restive humanity patrolled the road.

Within a week, the highway would be packed with shuttle buses, taxis, pickups filled to overflowing with pilgrims. The invaders were trying des-perately to be prepared for this flood in a time of war. They were, after all, likely to be the new masters of the Hajj. Just the week before, the last of the Saudi royal family had flown out of Riyadh to Paris. King Abdullah had died on the flight . . . of old age, insiders said; others, of a broken heart.

Ragged troops wearing everything from jungle camouflage to modern desert battle gear lined up to witness the inspection, some carrying single-shot rifles or waving pistols, a few bearded men hefting late-model, two-part launcher-assault weapons that must have cost thousands of dollars. All were making at least the pretense of limiting access to the areas they claimed to control: a potential nightmare for pilgrims.

Sam looked at himself in the sunshade mirror. His hair was black with hints of gray. He had tanned his skin with Coppertone Plus and eyelids and cheeks with walnut juice. This gave him a convincing two-tone look. Should they pull him out and thoroughly inspect him—not uncommon in this land of war and fear—they would find him circumcised, and not in a hospital, but cut down with a razor to the sheath, the technique of *es-selkh* or flay-ing leaving no prepuce whatsoever and a naked rod straining like a serpent when erect, something no non-Muslim would ever want or tolerate. He had done this to himself years before. It had gotten him through several tough inspections in circumstances just like this, when he had been employed by NGOs in Iraq, before joining the FBI.

His eyes stung from bits of fine dust that had crept under his contact lenses. He adjusted his *gutra* and loose robes and lounged back in the seat. Let the Israelis handle this. Their Arabic was better than his.

Five guards broke from the rabble and approached, young and tense but displaying big toothy smiles. From the second truck, Sam listened to the irritated, loud exchanges. Soon, the exchanges became friendlier. He had chosen well from among the settlers' children. Who could tell a Sephardic Jew from an Arab, ultimately?

The driver of the lead truck produced the papers Sam had given them all in Tel Aviv, proving association with the Yemeni and Iraqi wings of the rebellion. Ibrahim Al-Hitti had provided those papers over a year ago, for another operation entirely. For a moment, the way the five soldiers passed the papers around and smiled, he wondered if perhaps the passes and permissions were overkill. The soldiers were too impressed, excited even, curious as to who these important travelers might be.

Sam closed his eyes, just listening. *Yes, we are carrying celebratory and medicinal goods for Mecca, thanks be to God for his mercy and bounty. As well, no weapons. We are peaceful supporters of Hijaz Liberation.* The guards appeared to lose some of their respect. He heard the English word *ancillaries* used a few times. The guards asked if these men had ever carried weapons in support of the cause. Sheepishly, humbly, the lead driver answered no. This reduced the excitement even more. As these travelers were not warriors, no exceptional respect need be shown. Arms were waved, hands waggled. Then, the guards moved to the second truck and peered through the lowered window at Sam and his three companions.

Sam wore a pale gray *thobe*, lightly soiled, over loose cotton trousers, *sirwal*. The men with him wore white *thobes* covered with dark cotton *bishts*, and all wore red and white or pure white *gutras* over their *tagiyah* caps, draped around their necks and secured with simple black *agals*. They might be contract workers or laborers, who could know or care; they were not soldiers. At this point nothing was said.

The men got out. All truck compartments were searched. No weapons. Only celebratory fireworks, safely and neatly packed. Men leaped into the backs and squeezed between the plastic-wrapped bundles on their steel pallets, checking the occasional box with a knife, peeling plastic and cardboard to peer inside. They were asked if they had any alcohol. Only medicinal and rubbing alcohol, not drinkable. No, they did not carry narcotics or strong pain relievers. These would come in other shipments. Drinkable alcohol was being confiscated by the insurrectionists, and drugs as well; the fighting was hard and the men needed relaxation.

And what about *qat*?

The Yemenis among the crowd that now surrounded the trucks pressed forward but were disappointed. No, the travelers did not have *qat* or tobacco.

After the inspections, which took an hour, the guards turned them over to three Iraqis, neatly uniformed Sunnis who argued and vacillated for another ten minutes. Of course, the travelers had high authority—but so did the leaders at this checkpoint. Still, ultimate victory was near. All would share in the honor.

Perhaps now was a good time to be magnanimous, even to multinational Muslim aid workers such as these, the first they had seen in weeks. There would be many wounded and sick, and with the Hajj beginning soon, much need for medicines and supplies.

The guards settled their differences in time for sunset prayers. The passengers and drivers joined them, laying prayer rugs in the sand and gravel beside the highway. Sam felt a twinge as he went through the motions. *They're trying to talk to God.*

As the horizon covered the sun, they returned to the trucks and were waved on. Campfires were being lit. Cooking kits were lifted out of red plastic bags.

The mob parted, drew aside the makeshift wooden barricades and empty steel drums, and the convoy passed through on the last leg of the road to Mecca.

CHAPTER FIFTY-FOUR
Temecula, California

Special Agent Brian Botnik caught a ride with a division chief from the Riverside County Fire Department. The slipstream through a crack in the truck window speckled the chief's hair with flakes of gray. "This is more like early summer weather," he was saying. "Big fires put thousands of tons of particulates in the air. We could get more lightning strikes this evening. Damned weird."

Brilliant white clouds towered tens of thousands of feet over the east as the day approached maximum warming. White ash blew off the incinerated land and coated the truck's windshield until they could barely see. A squirt of fluid and the wipers turned it all into a streaked mess. The sky was orange from ash and dust blowing off the hills.

Fuel had built up for six wet years, spawning ten huge fires across five counties: chaparral, creosote bush, sage, and scrub oak on the hills had burned for days. The air was still acrid with fresh char.

The chief peered through a clear band in the smear. "As soon as we got to the barn, I knew we had something peculiar. The main house survived, miraculously—that's what they say, don't they? Miracle, hell—our trucks made a stand at the end of the road and saved it and most of the outbuildings, too."

In Riverside County, the sheriff was also the coroner and he was still attending to burn victims—so Division Chief Clay Sinclair had volunteered to drive Botnik out to the winery. The fires were mostly contained in San Diego and Riverside Counties. The chief's duties now consisted of supervising hotspot control—and escorting congressional looky-loos, as he called them, on fact-finding visits.

"What about the owner?" Botnik asked.

"He must have been living alone for years. They found him inside the house. Big-headed guy. Some sort of mental case. Real sad."

"Did he say anything?"

"Nope, he wasn't talking. A lawyer showed up. I don't think they had met in years. Anyway, the fellow didn't recognize him. The lawyer shrugged and said a few words and drove off. He hasn't come back. Odd. Used to be a winery, I understand. But that barn full of computer printers . . . One of the sheriff's officers got a hit on the KIA trooper in Arizona. A truck full of Epsons, he said. The sheriff thought there might be a connection. Since it's across state lines and could involve drugs or illegal commerce, we both thought the FBI might be interested. We called San Diego FBI and they passed. Only you showed any interest. Here, put this on. It's still pretty bad." The chief handed him a filter mask.

Botnik strapped the mask over his nose and mouth. He had caught a commuter flight from Phoenix that morning, after passing word along—as a matter of courtesy—to Lieutenant Colonel Jack Gerber of Arizona Public Safety. He had very pointedly not contacted Rebecca Rose. He would leave that to the Phoenix SAC if and when the time came. Headquarters politics had grown too fierce for his blood.

No wonder San Diego FBI had ignored this one. All of these fires had been caused by lightning, not arson. Act of God. No crime, nothing worth looking at, plus the fire had flushed a whole bunch of drug labs in five counties and that was keeping everyone busy.

"There's a sheriff's department service officer out there holding down the fort. Making sure nobody loots the place and keeping an eye on the big-headed guy, for his own good, we're saying."

Botnik looked down at the name on his slate. *Tommy Juan Battista Juarez*. DOB: April 27, 1985. Parents deceased, 2000. High school dropout, homeschooled, no college. No criminal record.

"Still got lots of winemaking equipment—and of course, what's in the barn."

"Anyone poke around?" Botnik asked.

"Just our firefighters," the chief said. "We only found the one guy."

The chief turned the truck up a road between a scorched and twisted grove of oaks. "I don't think anyone's been through the whole complex."

Fire had taken out the oaks in a seemingly random fashion. The heat had approached two thousand degrees in areas of high brush, and some of the oaks looked like whitish-gray gnomes—burned down to shriveled stumps. As they approached the Spanish-style rambler, Botnik looked out the truck window and saw the broad parallel tracks of fire trucks, rivulets of water and mud, the trampling of booted feet and sinuous hose lines drawn in the still-damp dirt. This was where the firefighters had made their stand. They had kept Tommy Juarez's place from joining the hell that had consumed the hills—and over four hundred other homes and ranches.

The service officer, a young, earnest fellow in his mid-twenties, met them on the drive. The chief introduced Botnik.

"Owner is still inside," the officer told them. "He's pretty much a human zero. He comes to the window sometimes and smiles. It's what's in the warehouse and the barn that puzzled the sheriff."

They walked up the steps and stood in the shade of the porch. Botnik knocked on the front door. "Federal agent. FBI. Mr. Juarez, I'd like to talk with you about the fire."

Nobody responded. The door was not locked and stood open a crack so he cleaned his shoes on the worn rubber mat, pushed the door wide, and entered. Down a trash-littered hallway with a tiled floor, he saw an archway opening to the living room on the left and another to a kitchen on the right. "Mr. Juarez?"

There was a bump and rustle in the kitchen. Botnik put his hand on his holstered pistol. A shadow like a brief cloud crossed the smoke-tinted light falling through the kitchen arch.

"Mr. Juarez? Federal agent. My name is Botnik. Could I ask some questions?"

A chair on casters squeaked. Botnik approached the kitchen. Through the arch, he could see a refrigerator, then a counter and a nice gas stove, expensive but crusted with food. The chair squeaked again.

Botnik glanced around the corner of the arch.

The man with the large head had sat down at a kitchen table and was staring listlessly over a small stack of scientific journals. He was wearing pajamas. To Botnik he looked like an odd little mannequin trying to hide what had gone missing from its insides.

"Come on in, Sam," the mannequin said. "I've been catching up on my reading. I have to use the dictionary a lot. Take a seat. I've been 'thinking' about you." He fingered quote marks in the air. "I wish I could remember what we were going to do," he added, and looked sideways at Botnik's arm, and then his face. "You *are* Sam, aren't you?"

The service officer and the chief watched from the hall. Botnik asked, "Are you Tommy Juarez?"

The big-headed man lifted one shoulder and smiled.

"Mr. Juarez, would it be okay if we took a look around your property? Just to make sure everything is safe?"

Tommy shrugged again with both shoulders. "I suppose it would be okay," he said, and put on a deep frown. "I can't make anything work. Everything's broken."

Botnik walked with the chief and the service officer to the barn. Fire had charred one side and chewed away at a corner, leaking hot air into the interior. They walked through a blackened door into a melted, ashen nightmare. Curtains of clear Tyvek had shrunk and curled into grotesque shapes all around. Ducts had slumped away from the walls like singed snakes. Over many tables, dozens—hundreds—of inkjet printers perched in incomprehensible rows. Near the fire-damaged wall and corner, the printers had melted into misshapen heads with gaping mouths, trailing wire intestines. Pieces of broken glass plates had fallen or been dunked into plastic tubs of water at one end of the barn. Pools of water from fire hoses had collected across the littered concrete floor.

No paper, no boxes of printed goods—and just the one guy. This was obviously not a hill country porno ring or any sort of publishing outfit.

"Not like any winery I've ever seen," Sinclair said.

The warehouse had suffered scorch marks and bent metal panels along two sides but the interior was intact. Botnik walked between giant steel fermenting tanks to the head of the steps, then looked over his shoulder at the two men standing in the big steel door.

"Stay back," he cautioned.

"I've been down there already," the service officer said. "There's some kind of lab. They have labs in wineries."

"This place hasn't made wine in years," Sinclair said. "There used to be lots of wineries around here. I inspected a few of them."

Rows of respirators and oxygen tanks hung from racks behind the tall steel tanks. A criss-cross of ducting had been suspended from the roof, leading to thick filtration systems—were those HEPA-type filters?—at the rear. At the head of the steps, he stooped to pry open a cardboard box stained by water but untouched by heat or flame. It was filled with plastic gloves. Hidden under a twisted metal panel, two bags held whole-body suits, and piles of disposable booties had been shoved to one side—not generally used in winemaking.

"Just stay there," he said.

He descended the wooden steps into the cool air pooled at the bottom, and passed from the smell of char to a vinegary, flowery scent. There had not been any power down here for days. He switched on his flashlight and waved the bright circle along the rows of old barrels stretching back under the vaulted ceilings.

Carefully, wondering whether the filter mask was sufficient, he walked to the open door on the left. The service officer's footprints stopped here. He shined the flashlight into the mess beyond. Someone, perhaps Juarez, had pulled down and smashed equipment as if in blind rage.

Botnik didn't know much about biology but this had obviously been a well-equipped lab. The field office had received general bulletins about materials, chemicals, and devices that could be useful to bioterrorists, and Botnik recognized a number of listed items smashed on the floor and covered with dust.

He knelt beside a gray enameled box—its sides dented as if it had been kicked—and read the label on the back: *Simugenetics Sequence Assembler*. Plastic tubing clustered and led to jars and jugs on an overturned table. The label on one battered jug read: *Purified Nucleic Acid Residues: Cytosine*. Other jugs had once contained *Tyrosine, Guanine, Uracil,* and *Adenine*—the constituents of DNA and RNA.

A winemaker would not need to assemble or replicate DNA molecules.

Botnik pressed the mask closer to his face. He took out the WAGD marker, uncapped it, tried to hold his breath, and walked to the rear of the underground room. There, a large box with plastic and steel panels and glove holes had been axed open, revealing trays, drawers, rubber tubes, fans, and black gloves hanging from external access ports. A hot box, ingenious and compact.

The ax was still jammed in the right side.

Botnik moved the marker along an exposed panel, making sure not to cut himself on jagged metal or broken plastic. The marker's moist tongue licked at a thin layer of dust.

Then he carefully backed away, stepping around the broken glassware, and paused by the stairs, on the verge of blacking out, still afraid to suck in a much-needed breath.

After two minutes, the WAGD chimed that it had a result.

Then it made a sharp little *squeeeee*, as unwanted and scary as the hiss of an angry cobra. Botnik glanced down. This was not the sound you wanted to hear: a biohazard alarm.

We're All Gonna Die.

"*Positive test result for anthrax spores,*" the device's tinny voice announced. "*Evacuate the premises according to government and training guide-*

lines. *Repeat: positive test result for anthrax spores. Please consult biohazard experts immediately.*"

Botnik ran up the steps and past the two men waiting above. "Get the hell out of here!" he shouted, and then started choking. "Get outside!"

Under the smoky sunlight, pawing at his mask, he remembered who he was and why he was here. His breath returned in agonized whoops and he bent over.

Sinclair and the service officer watched him. "Jesus, what's down there?" the chief asked.

Botnik waved them off and keyed a general alert code into his arm pad, then made the first of two calls. "Don't touch me," he warned the men as they approached. Mechanical voices answered; he keyed in federal Bioshield emergency codes.

"Don't come near me. You," he pointed to the service officer. "Stand back and wait for a HAZMAT team. Understood?"

"What in hell are we talking about here?"

"You're contaminated. Don't leave the area. Call for backup. Don't make contact—don't touch or get close to any other officers or civilians except for medical or HAZMAT personnel. We're going to seal off this entire farm, winery, whatever the hell it is. They'll bring Gamma Lysin and antibiotics, so we'll be okay. But we all have to be tested and treated. And don't let Juarez go *anywhere*. Keep him in that house. Got it?"

The service officer looked as if he might faint. The division chief backed away from both of them with an open-mouthed expression, his hands held out. "Whoa, Nelly," he said.

Waiting for backup and HAZMAT to arrive, Botnik searched behind the warehouse and down a path, trying to keep from hyperventilating, wondering if he was the zeroth man at this site—after the service officer—the man around whom the experts would draw cautionary circles, measuring death and disease at the epicenters of contamination. But screw the training—he couldn't just keep still. He'd flip out.

What in hell had big-headed Mr. Tommy Juarez been doing out here in the brush all these years?

There had been bets laid out in his dorm at the Q as to who would rise the quickest to FBI glory. Agent Trainee Brian Botnik had always stayed in the background, letting the bigger and brasher guys compete for future bragging rights, while he had hoped to do well enough on PT and at the firing range to be allowed to get out of the Academy for the weekend and maybe even find a date.

Forcing his lips and cheeks into conformity to keep the mask's seal, trying to hold back his elation, he shouted hoarsely at the burned stubble: "We got him! We finally got him! Holy Mother, thank you."

He thrust his fist into the air and stamped the ashen ground.

"We got Amerithrax!"

CHAPTER FIFTY-FIVE
Spider/Argus Complex
Virginia

"And who, pray tell, is this for?"

Jane Rowland handed her data request brief to the Chief of FBI Intel at Spider/Argus, Gabe Wrigley, a thick-butted, pasty-faced fellow of forty who wore rumpled brown suits and always seemed distracted. Rowland had landed in the tall corn with her probationary assignment: Spider/Argus, housed on an old Naval station along the Potomac, was the premier Web-tracking agency in the federal system, and she had done very well for a rookie. "Special request from Frank Chao at Quantico, and from Rebecca Rose," Jane said. "They're working with Hiram Newsome."

Wrigley was one of the smartest people she had ever met, social skills aside, but she wondered how he had ever passed PT at the Academy. Perhaps they had given him a special dispensation, like some of the techs and translators in the offices at the back—the Word Forest.

He gave her his best *I'm impressed* face. "And you want . . . what, a more nuanced translation?"

"Something better than what the machines can do. I need more time and resources to work on this. I need priority international Argus access for at least a day. Twenty-four hours. I promise not to sleep."

"Prithee, fair maid, why?"

"Because this is scary stuff," she said. "I can't tell you why, because I'm not sure I know myself."

Wrigley looked at her as if she had gone off her nut, and then smiled—slowly and carefully. They were both known for their eccentricities.

"Rebecca Rose asked me to find something," she continued. "I think I've found it. But I need to double-check that we're not being jived. If this is square, it's major. And if it's skunky, I don't need to waste their time . . . do I?"

Wrigley pushed back his chair. "Is Newsome going to be confirmed?" he asked.

"How should I know?"

"Is he the kind of guy that appreciates the kind of talent and capability we have here? Someone likely to defend us against the incoming barbarian hordes?"

Jane Rowland shook her head. "This is a spooky place," she said. "And it's getting spookier every month. I don't know that, either."

"We can't go back," Wrigley said. "'After such knowledge, what for-giveness?'" He watched her closely. Then he stamped the folder, lifted one hand, crooked a finger, and tugged it down, as if pulling on a train whistle. "What the fuck. Toot toot, Agent Rowland. Track twenty-nine."

"Thanks, Gabe." Jane left the cubicle before he could change his mind.

Back at her desk, she keyed in her new access code, slotted her searches into the top priority Argus queue and watched them move instantly to number five, unleashing ten million little hunters working back through the accumulated hourly records of thousands of split signal pathways to confirm routing through hundreds of servers, all paths ultimately converging on a single ISP, a single user, and slithering in on who and where that user was, no matter the firewalls and other precautions put in place: Argus the thousand-eyed and Spider the master of the Web.

Amazing to think about, and sometimes, it even worked.

With a source confirmed, she would have to get on the horn to the Word Forest, passing her captured pages on to two translators, both female, both familiar with modern Israeli slang.

Jane had two lightly encrypted personal pages relating to an encounter in Kiryat Shimona, three miles from the Lebanese border, with a mysterious, presumably male visitor endowed with many interesting attributes, including one blue eye and one green eye. The roughly one hundred and fifty words of solemn prose conveyed the conflicted but enchanted moonings of an Israeli settler's lonely wife, still traumatized over being moved by government fiat from their house in the Gaza strip; good enough, but the machine translators had undoubtedly garbled something.

According to the machine, with its usual markups and percentages of confidence, the lonely wife had written with admiration and some repulsion about,

> *"A {sl. expl.=*phallus, penis *78%} [*skinned back
> *56%] like a (tribesman's) nomad's naked eel."*

And what in hell did that mean?

CHAPTER FIFTY-SIX
Secure Strategic Support Command (SSSC)
Forward Base DAGMAR
Jordan

Fouad Al-Husam waited nervously at the end of the spare concrete corridor. To his right and left, Forward Team army officers from the UK and the United States stood at parade rest, looking assured in a way he did not feel and possibly would never feel.

Here, in the distant reaches of the Jordanian desert, Fouad had learned just three days ago the details of multilateral logistics support for the insurgents occupying Riyadh, Jeddah, and Mecca. What most of the world regarded as a spontaneous Muslim rebellion against corrupt Saudis now took on the more focused appearance, perhaps even the reality (how could he know how much he was being told?) of a channeled flood of Muslim anger, fed and in some cases incited by other nations in a concerted effort to allow political change while maintaining world oil supplies.

As he had guessed long months ago.

Some called it a controlled burn to prevent much of the world from going up in flames.

Even the Chinese and Indians had secretly signed on, in hopes of maintaining the fuel supplies they desperately needed to keep their white-hot economies growing. The Russians alone, after initial tacit support, had growled back into their caves, angered by this finesse on their plans to marginalize the European Union and the United States.

But the ultimate truth of it was, Muslims were killing Muslims with weapons supplied chiefly by non-Muslims. With the direct aid of Egypt and Turkey—both of whom had once controlled access to Mecca—and to some extent Jordan, a Provisional Hijaz authority was being established in Saudi Arabia, consisting largely of troops from Yemen, Oman, and—fulfilling perhaps the greatest irony of this unpromising century—Iraq.

What Fouad had learned in the last ten days had the effect of both en-lightening and corroding him. Muslims were not in charge of their own destinies. They had lost that option centuries ago, really.

In Iran, Muslim rulers still had a modicum of dignity and control but that meant little: Iran was a nation certifiably going insane, with clerics ordaining the shootings and bombings of thousands of protestors, mostly young students; defying international pressure; and moving their few nu-clear weapons into positions where they could be launched against Israeli, Turkish, or European targets.

The West's best and last hope: that most of those weapons were a bluff, and that the single working nuclear weapon in their possession had some-how been triggered at Shahabad Kord within Fouad's own sight.

The madness that had begun in last century was coming to a head and he was at that head, sitting on an erupting boil of foulness beyond anything even his father or grandfather had conceived of.

"Here come the boys," said the British colonel on Fouad's left, and smiled assurance. "Your best and brightest, I'd say."

"The boys" walked in four ranks of five down the hall with rhythmic step and young, stern faces. They were the first of what some were calling— offensively, in Fouad's opinion—the Janissaries, after the Balkan Christian children who had been raised to serve Turkish masters under the Ottoman empire. All had been selected by BuDark case officers from an original roster of one hundred candidates. When Fouad had heard of the program that had brought these former orphans to the United States, he had not believed such things possible; now he knew their inevitability.

The ranks of handsome and beardless brown faces approached to within ten feet, then paused with something less than military precision and mim-icked the officers before them. Like him, they were officers in BuDark, os-tensibly a non-military operation. They stood at parade rest. A few Adam's apples bobbed. Eyes flicked.

Fouad smiled briefly, then held a frozen expression he hoped conveyed neutral dignity. These men, he was told, would look up to him. He had seen combat; they had not. He spoke many languages. They knew two or at most three. He was blooded. He had killed. They had not. But their combat training exceeded his own. When they realized this, they would be tough to command, and Fouad was not looking forward to such a challenge, but there was no choice.

The die was cast.

Each of these young men had been brought from Iraq or Afghanistan during the Coalition War. They had been hand-selected from orphans found in various cities and in the countryside, adopted by serving military officers into their own families, and raised in special circumstances. They had been educated in schools in Virginia, Georgia, and California. They had earned the equivalent of high school diplomas and then bachelor degrees in many fields, but they had also received training at Fort Benning, with emphasis on special ops.

An even more select few were still in training at elite Strategic Support bases in Turkey and when they were fielded one of them would likely replace Fouad. But for now, for the next five or six months, this team was his to work with. All part of a grand experiment.

Fouad surmised they had an even chance of being sited in Iran to gather HUMINT, human intelligence. But they had an equal chance of being placed in one or two key positions in or around Mecca. He had already been briefed about that option.

The young Muslim men darted their eyes across the line of solemn white faces and then—as predicted—focused on Fouad.

"Welcome to Jordan," Fouad said. They nodded as one but did not express emotion, though their feelings must have been running high. This was the first time they had been close to their homelands in ten years or more. Then, in Arabic, Fouad added—equally for the benefit of the officers around him—"It is our duty to preserve and further the splendid and blessed culture of Islam in a time of cruel trial. God is great."

The young men echoed *Allahu Akhbar.*

"Ultimately we serve no master but God and God willing, Islam will flourish in our modern world and with our help come to new order and power and achieve new heights. Our re-birth has begun."

This had been taught to them all in the foreign schools—that the greatest glory of Islam was imminent, that the West was not an enemy but an ally. These young men, these anti-Janissaries, did not blink or show any signs that they lacked conviction.

The words tasted like gall in Fouad's mouth. But he knew, as his father had known, that this was the only way.

The rigid pale men at his sides who instructed and watched and judged were aware of the fragility. But their time had come, and these experimental weapons in the great cultural war had to be tested to prepare the way for later and even more important operations. Mistakes would be made. Let them be made now, that later they would not.

Fouad Al-Husam finally knew the real names of BuDark.

They were Savior.

And Betrayer.

CHAPTER FIFTY-SEVEN
Private Home
Maryland

White House Chief of Staff Kelly Schein was a plump, homely woman in her late forties with goggling eyes and no chin and an abrupt way of speaking that rubbed much of the fur in the capital the wrong way. That did not matter much in the grand scheme. At the moment she was the second most powerful human being in the world, and still she was not happy.

She walked up the brick steps to the long porch of the Buckler mansion and glanced over her shoulder at a procession of three very serious and alert Secret Service agents, followed by Hiram Newsome and Rebecca Rose, who joined her at the beautiful antique cherry front door. They were among the first to arrive to this peculiar and unexpected soirée.

"I'm sure you'd all rather be at the White House," Schein said. "Unfortunately, it's full of sneaky little bugs. We just found them last week. Nobody's confessed to planting them, big surprise. They're in the paint, for Christ's sake—tiny little flat transducers. Hundreds, maybe thousands. Someone with a debriefer hidden in a magazine could walk in and collect a week's worth of conversation. It's playing hell with the President's schedule." She looked up at Newsome. "I sure hope you didn't know anything about this. Even for a giggle."

Some at headquarters had pointed to Schein as the most serious opponent in the White House to Hiram Newsome's appointment.

Newsome shook his head. "No ma'am. I don't have much time to read paperbacks any more."

Schein gave him a second, dubious glance. "National Security Director is coming with the President. Your cast will assemble before the President gets here. You have half an hour." Schein slipped the key into the large door. "We move randomly from house to house in Georgetown for our most secure meetings. Isn't partisan spirit grand?"

"You're blaming the previous administration?" Newsome asked, his chin developing a few stubborn companions.

Schein smiled, showing large, even teeth, and put on round glasses. "I doubt they were smart enough to know what was happening. Look at all the other messes they left behind for us to clean up."

Rebecca followed Newsome into the spacious living room. The house was quiet and a little chilly. She had pictured a meeting with the President in more formal, glamorous terms: the Oval Office or the Situation Room, stern generals burdened with tons of egg salad—or was it fruit salad? Decorations and campaign medals, anyway—a huge threat board—not a deserted mansion on a ten-acre estate, furnished with exquisite antiques.

A large, striking painting in earth-tones, blues and greens, and gold—an original, she guessed—hung in the foyer above the stairs leading to the second floor. To Rebecca, the emaciated and thoroughly naked woman in the painting resembled a concentration camp victim. She looked at the artist's signature in the corner, *Klimt,* and turned away with a shudder.

Schein removed her coat and draped it over a high-backed chair. "I have five reservations for your party at this clambake," she said. "Besides you two. Four agents and one civilian, I understand."

"Yes, ma'am," Newsome said.

"From all over the country," Schein said. "Some young, some old. I assume they've all pieced together bits of the puzzle."

"Yes, ma'am."

"Is that what FBI does best, put together puzzles?" Schein asked with a straight face.

"Sometimes," Newsome replied, his eyes heavy-lidded.

"Why did the former director fire you, News?" Schein asked as she tried out a large leather chair. She moved up and down and around as if establishing the height and comfort zone of someone taller. Newsome remained standing with his coat on, as if he might be asked to leave. He did not like her use of his nickname.

"Last minute attempt to lighten the lifeboat, I presume," he answered.

Schein smiled again, this time with genuine humor. "The President figured the most self-serving would quickly dump the most useful and dedicated. It looks as if she was right. You're originally a Boston boy, but you moved to Virginia when you were thirteen, correct?"

"Yes, ma'am."

Schein looked at Rebecca. "You're assigned to bioterror at Headquarters in Washington, DC, but you've spent a lot of time as an instructor at the Q, haven't you?"

"I have," Rebecca said. Outside, a big helicopter was landing on the lawn.

"Did you know I wanted to be an agent, long ago?" Schein asked.

Rebecca raised her eyebrows. "No, ma'am."

"Washed out early. Bad eyes. And I can't do a pull-up to save my life," Schein said. "Just wanted you to know, Agent Rose, that Senator Josephson doesn't speak for all of us."

More Secret Service agents poured in through the front door. "Estate perimeter is secure," announced a tall fellow in a long black coat. He glanced at Rebecca. "Marine One is on the ground. Mrs. Schein, we've finished vetting the guest list. The others are waiting in the kitchen."

"Thank you, Ernest. Let's get them in here and seated before the President arrives."

Folding chairs were spaced around the living room in a tight circle. Schein rose from the large leather chair and stood beside it.

Through the back hallway marched Jane Rowland, Frank Chao, and a tall, gray, cadaverously thin gentleman Rebecca had not yet met in person. She assumed this was William's contact, the world's premier expert on yeast, Dr. Daniel Wheatstone, flown in yesterday from Oregon. William himself was still in Ohio, waiting for a flight out through stormy Cincinnati.

They were guided to their chairs and followed Schein's example, standing behind them. All looked nervous. Rowland was actually shivering. There had been no time to rehearse. They were going into this Agatha Christie moment absolutely cold.

Ernest tapped his ear and turned to announce, "Ladies and gentlemen, the President of the United States."

In person, Eve Carol Larsen was shorter than Rebecca had thought, but well-proportioned for her height of five nine. She wore gray, as always, with a red blouse and a black opal pin, its stone mined, as she had told interviewers many times, by a wayward grandfather in Australia before World War 2. In the early eighties, Larsen had served for six years in the Air Force flying support aircraft, then had gone on to law school. After eight years working as counsel to various state agencies, she had been elected Attorney General for the state of Wisconsin, from which role she had moved on to become an effective governor. In politics, she had played extreme conservatives— mostly religious zealots—off against extreme liberals—mostly easy-target academic naïves—with razor wit and a manner of answering questions that

Lou Dobbs had once described as "A look-'em-in-the-eye smile accompanied by a punch in the gut."

Rebecca had not voted for her but was now wondering why—the room was positively energized by her presence. Only after a few seconds did Rebecca see National Security Director Chuck Parsons and the director of Homeland Security, Walter Graham, both younger men—in their early forties.

The President shook hands around the room, then paused before Hiram Newsome and pressed his hand between both of hers. "We need to find time for a heart-to-heart," she said, sharp gray eyes burrowing into his.

"I look forward to that, Madam President," Hiram said.

The President turned to Rebecca. "Congratulations," she said. "I hear the FBI has caught the bastard who mailed anthrax back in 2001. Your case, I understand."

"I wasn't there, but my fellow agents are generously sharing credit," Rebecca said. "And it was Director Newsome's initiative that kept us going."

"That's part of our presentation today, Madam President," Hiram added. "We believe his activities continued until just recently."

Larsen took the large leather seat Schein had vacated. The rest of them sat in a circle around the President.

"They've booted me out of my house. Isn't that a bitch?" the President said. "Let's get started with *Who*. Then we'll go to *What*, *When*, and *Where*. Special Agent Rose, you seem to be at the center. I'd like you to direct this show. Begin."

"Thank you, Madam President," Rebecca said. "Here's the best information we have about our suspect. Agent Frank Chao is a chief analyst at the FBI Academy Crime Lab."

Chao bowed his head briefly. Larsen sized him up, then returned her gaze to Rebecca, unimpressed. Rebecca had testified before female prosecutors many times and recognized The Look.

Chao began, "Madam President, blood evidence and saliva left behind in Arizona at the scene of a patrol officer's murder—"

"Hundreds of inkjet printers spilled all over the highway, right?" the President asked.

Chao nodded and folded his hands in his lap. "DNA taken from saliva on a glove, and additional DNA from a speck of blood, seemed to point to two male individuals, half-brothers with the same mother. I found no matches in CODIS-compliant files in any national criminal database, including NDIS-3—and so I searched DNA records obtained from truck drivers seeking permits to haul hazardous materials, as well as international customs records—and still, nothing. National insurance and medical databases provided to the agency after 10-4 also produced no matches."

Rebecca watched the President closely. Her face had taken on a stony look and she was drumming the fingers of one hand on the arm of the leather chair. Such violations of personal privacy had been a strong part of her campaign.

"I had reached the end of my familiar resources," Chao said, "so I took a stab in the dark and scored an unusual hit—a marker profile in a statistical database used to speed matches for victims of mass terror. That database, of course, would not be usable in obtaining warrants or subpoenas, so we requested access to the actual 9-11 Memorial Park DNA records . . ."

"Goddamn it," the President said. "Did they give them to you without a subpoena?"

Chao looked thunderstruck. "Sorry?"

"Go on," the President said, leaning back in the leather chair.

"We were refused, perhaps rightly," Chao said. "However, I found duplicates of the Memorial Park records retained by a company that had once analyzed DNA for the New York medical examiner. That company had since gone bankrupt. All of its assets, including these records, were in the process of being acquired—in a secret deal—by the Church of Latter Day Saints, and as it happened, were kept on a server that was less than secure. We gained access on a federal warrant and found the actual DNA analysis of the relative's donated sample. This record was still not quite a match—but it was obvious we had a blood relation of someone who had died in that tragedy. Following one of Agent Rose's excellent hunches, we then compared the crime scene DNA and the 9-11 donated record with DNA already on file with the FBI—from police departments, military service medical histories, and so on."

The President had stopped drumming her fingers.

Chao put on a stubborn look. "It is our job to find dangerous criminals. Would you have it any other way?"

"Move on, Frank," Hiram said.

"Law enforcement officers donate tissue samples that we use to rule out contamination of crime scenes—typically, buccal cells—cheek cells. Through patient search of FBI internal records, we found a match—logically, to the half-brother of an FBI agent named Lawrence Winter."

"So you questioned Winter," Schein said.

"Special Agent Winter has been missing for almost five years," Chao said. "He vanished while working undercover in the Pacific northwest. Telomere, viral RT, and epigenetic analysis told us that Winter's half-brother would have to be the same age as he is—a difficulty, since there are no records of his having had a brother and since, in theory, half-brothers cannot be twins. They cannot be born to the same mother at the same time."

The President and Schein looked lost, trying to work through the implications.

"Tragically, Special Agent Winter had suffered a loss in the September 11 attacks. His wife and his daughter had apparently been killed by falling debris outside the World Trade Center. Their remains were never found. Winter did have a sister. Her name was Connie Winter Richards and she was an employee of the state of Washington. She and her father—Winter's father—were murdered on 10-4, along with twenty-two hundred others, as they were riding a ferry in Puget Sound. Their bodies were identified by the mother, who died the next year from an overdose of sleeping pills."

"My God," the President said.

"Lawrence Winter stopped reporting to his chief and his SAC—Special Agent in Charge—shortly after the 10-4 attack."

"Why can't you find him?" Schein asked.

"Some speculate he got lost in his undercover work and was either killed or took his own life," Rebecca said. "He was dealing with domestic and ecological terrorists—Animal Rescue, Earth Liberation Front, Gaia Brigade. Dangerous people. But we should let Frank finish."

"Agent Winter's official FBI photo shows that he has one green eye and one blue. It took creative thinking and extensive research to realize that Winter might be a chimera, of a sort we have not often heard of. Only in the last few years have such individuals been considered possible: an offspring who combines the chromosomes of two half-sibling embryos, fertilized by two separate fathers."

The President looked to her Chief of Staff. Schein shook her head in bafflement.

Before anyone could stop him, Chao enthusiastically added details. "His mother had sex with two men within hours of each other. Two of her egg cells were fertilized by these different fathers, and the early stage blastulas fused perfectly before implanting. Somehow, the resulting single embryo did not miscarry. The genetically disparate tissues worked out an accord—and the embryo's nascent immune system learned to recognize both as self. But this means that DNA from one set of this man's tissues will not necessarily match DNA from his other tissue types. Some of the tissues will have a Y-chromosome from one father, and some from another. His inheritance from each father and from his mother—and remember, we have no samples from any of these individuals—will be statistically muddled. That prevents finding a match in any CODIS or NDIS-3 record search. A very special case of fraternal twins. Therefore, without expert and painstaking analysis, Special Agent Lawrence Winter's DNA, if found at a crime scene, could not be directly matched to any data base—a convenient way of eluding authorities for decades, or even forever. Such fraternal chimeras may suffer from personality imbalances in later life, including schizophrenia. Had we known of this potential, very likely we would never have accepted Lawrence Winter into our agency."

The President looked appalled.

"Based on what we now know, we have determined that Special Agent Winter impregnated the young wife of the Patriarch in Washington state. And we have now matched Winter to multiple samples of DNA taken from the residence of the Amerithrax suspect. We have been led a merry chase," Chao concluded. "But I believe we have finally found our man."

Rebecca picked up the thread. "Based on information from BuDark, we know that Lawrence Winter supplied bioterror weapons to a group of Muslims in Israel. He worked through an intermediary named Ibrahim Al-Hitti, an Egyptian with connections to Hamas, Hezbollah, Al Aqsa Martyrs Brigade, and more. We think Winter convinced Al-Hitti that he could supply anthrax modified to kill only Jews. Apparently, Al-Hitti tested a small amount of this anthrax on Jews in Iraq. Whatever Amerithrax was making in California was shipped to Washington state to be packed into fireworks shells, which were then flown to Gaza City by private jet and driven into Jerusalem. The shells were intercepted by Israeli police. The Israelis have tested them—and surprisingly, these shells contain not anthrax, but yeast. So far, we've only found a tiny supply of anthrax left over in California—but lots of yeast. Three months ago, someone launched twenty similar shells over Silesia, Ohio. As well, these shells apparently contained nothing but brewer's yeast."

"Silesia—loss of long-term memory," Schein said.

Rebecca nodded. "There may have been a similar plot to attack Rome, which we foiled when we disrupted the factory in Washington state."

The President's expression had transformed to stunned wonder.

"We have ten minutes," Schein said, tapping her watch.

Rebecca touched Jane Rowland's shoulder.

Ghastly pale, Jane smoothed her hands on her knees and referred to her notes. "Madam President, I track dating and lonely hearts sites on the Web," she began, "looking for descriptions of possible criminal activity. We resort to this expedient because so much real criminal communication is unbreakably encrypted. We're looking for an entry point, a chink in the encrypted data."

"Let's move quickly, Agent Rowland," Hiram said.

"I found several lovelog chat entries, written by the wife of an extremist Jewish settler living in Kiryat Shimona. She describes having sexual relations with a tall American with one blue eye and one green eye. She says the American is working with her husband on something important for the future of the Jews. She claims her American lover has . . . uh, had experienced an extreme circumcision, all the foreskin removed down to the shaft . . . 'a skinned eel,' as she describes it, 'Bedouin-style.' We have OPM files showing that before he joined the FBI, Lawrence Winter gave himself just such a circumcision, to avoid detection when working undercover in Muslim countries."

"Jesus Christ," the President exploded. "How in hell does a Jewish housewife know what a Bedouin's cock looks like?"

Jane was stricken silent.

Outside, rain from the wet night dripped down a gutter.

President Larsen rose and swirled an accusing finger around the room. "This is more than a nightmare—it's a goddamned *farce*. An AWOL FBI agent gallivants around the world, recruits terrorists, seduces their wives, hell—screws every bitch he can get his hands on—"

"Madam President," Schein cautioned. Larsen was furious and having none of it.

"—Not to mention official privacy violations beyond anything even I could have imagined, at least one murder, and now a clandestine connection between our own beloved FBI and the Amerithrax killer." The President took a glass of ice water from her lead Secret Service agent, drank half, then rolled it across her forehead. "Where is this bastard now? And what in God's name is he up to?"

Another pause.

"Am I next?" asked the sepulchral Dr. Wheatstone, the yeast expert. "I may have an answer to your second question."

CHAPTER FIFTY-EIGHT
Mecca

Lawrence.

Larry.

Special Agent Lawrence Winter.

His memory was definitely not as sharp as it had once been. His energy was also leaking away day by day, and he awoke each morning soaked in a creeping hopelessness that was hard to shake. So many places, so many names . . .

Winter looked through the drawn-back curtains of the hotel room window, across the Al Masjid Haram—the huge, three-story Grand Mosque—at the desert dawn, pallid blue and yellow.

Out on the plain of Mina, five kilometers from the hotel, late preparations for the Hajj were still being made. Fireproof tents were being erected by the tens of thousands, barely in time for the hordes arriving by bus. It was chaos in the broad tent city.

Yigal and Yitzhak entered the room bearing hot coffee in familiar green and white cups. "Wake up, sleepyheads," they called out. When they were in the suite they donned *kipots* embroidered with Hebrew and often spoke Hebrew, in defiance of his orders and of common sense. What if they were heard? Nobody spoke Hebrew in Mecca. They had smuggled the *kipots* in their kits like headstrong kids on a school outing. Months ago, he would have exacted swift discipline. Now, he could barely muster irritation.

Yigal grinned as he handed Winter his coffee. "Have you seen? They are gathering like sardines. There must be a half million already. The war means nothing to them, poor bastards." He began a little dance. "Seventy-two pure and shapely houris for every martyr! Wouldn't you like to wholesale black-eyed virgins? We could make a pile of shekels."

Baruch and Gershon came back to the room, put on their *kipots*, and squatted beside him. "I was out for four o'clock prayer," Gershon said. "The wind is blowing from the west at four to seven knots. I had a long talk with a fine, white-haired gentleman from Ethiopia, full of aches and pains. We spoke of the hardships and glory of those who die on Hajj. He was most interested to hear of what is happening in Palestine. He professed that the world would be much improved if all the Jews were lined up and burned alive."

"He'll surely go straight to heaven and immediately screw all his virgins," Yigal said.

"Tomorrow there will be a million," Gershon said. He saw that Winter had not finished his cup. "What's wrong with the coffee, Mr. Brown? It is fresh from Starbucks downstairs. There is a Kentucky Fried Chicken, even a McDonald's, did you see them?"

Yigal jumped up. "I'll check the trucks. David and Gershon stood guard last but they aren't mechanically minded, so who knows what could be stolen? They wouldn't miss an axle or two."

Gershon scoffed. The trucks had been parked in a secured garage not far from the Grand Mosque.

"Three days," Winter warned as they all removed their *kipots*. "When the pilgrims return to Mina. When they start stoning the devil. Not before."

"Of course," Menachem said happily. "Like sardines. Like fucking shoals of sweet herring."

William rolled his suitcase from the plane, following a young woman dressed in new Bureau trainee casuals—golf shirt, cargo pants and cap, duffel bag—decorated with FBI logos, shooting badges, pins and buttons. She was five-six, in her mid-twenties, with short-cut brown hair and a series of stud holes around her ear but no studs, fingernails painted pink but chipped at the edges, brown eyes bright despite the time—it was eleven p.m. He felt like a wet sock but she was full of energy, arriving for the next class at the Q—the promise of a dream career.

Cop Valhalla.

He had read and re-read Dr. Wheatstone's reports on the plane from Ohio. The last few pages had hit him hard.

The PrPSc prion genes inserted into this transgenic laboratory yeast are easily transferred to other yeast. What is more interesting, the genes have acquired adaptive modifications within the yeast, such that they can also be exchanged with naturally occurring varieties of fungus. Such fungi are ubiquitous in our environment.

Once the modified yeast are released into the wild, there may be no way to cap the genie's bottle. These transformably infectious proteins could become widespread in our environment. The entire world could be exposed to a memory-destroying, brain-wasting sickness as insidious as bovine spongiform encephalopathy—Mad Cow disease.

Rebecca stood by the baggage carousel. William waved a greeting. "Thanks for coming." He tapped the handle of his rolling suitcase. "This is all I'm carrying."

Rebecca surreptitiously stuck out her finger in the direction of the trainee. "Isn't she lovely?"

"Cute," William admitted.

The trainee quickly pulled her luggage from the carousel to the doors.

"Was I ever that fresh, that *new*?" Rebecca asked.

William buttoned his coat. "In my eyes, Agent Rose, you sparkle with morning dew."

Rebecca blinked. "Let's move," she said. "We're going where she's going, but we're not waiting for the bus."

"Why Quantico?" William asked.

"We have an appointment with Pete Farrow."

"Damn," William said.

"You got out of Ohio just in time, I hear," Rebecca said as she drove them down 95 through pouring rain.

William nodded. "They're setting up a Joint Operations Center. EPA is working the hospitals. FEMA brought in their trucks yesterday. Full-blast terror alert. Naturally, they've clamped a lid on everything."

"Looky what you started," Rebecca said.

"How did it go with the President?" William asked.

"Awful," Rebecca said with a grimace. "Nobody in the White House is in any mood to be magnanimous. They're still finding booby traps."

"What?"

"Bugs in the paint, even in the situation room. Can you blame them for being paranoid?"

That left them in silence for a few minutes.

"How did you find Wheatstone?" Rebecca asked.

"I did a search," William said. "Plugged in the words *memory, yeast,* and *dementia*. That brought me to Wheatstone's university Web site. I called—and he told me about the transgenic experiments, then, with a little prodding, about two accidental contaminations, a lab break-in six years ago, and the burgled yeast. He said he had reported all that to Homeland Security and the CDC, as required. Then I tracked down the CDC records. Did our good doctor impress the President?"

"Threat Level Ex-Lax," Rebecca said. "They're still not telling me everything they know, William—not yet. What the fuck happened to this country?"

"We got scared," William said.

"Scared stupid?" Rebecca's tone was pure acid.

"Shall I drive?" William asked.

"I'm *fine*," Rebecca said, her knuckles white on the wheel.

"Congratulations, by the way," William said after another pause.

"Botkin collared Amerithrax," Rebecca said. "Just as well. I'd have shot the bastard." She looked at the highway through underslung eyes. "Did you meet any of the people in Silesia?"

"I visited the hospital," William said.

"What are they like?"

"Like my father. Pleasant. Forgetful. Nothing much left from before a year or two ago. They still have language, habits, skills . . . personality. Just no memory of how they got them. There might be tens of thousands affected already. It got into a bakery."

Rebecca's eyelids fluttered and her lips turned down. Quietly, "A bakery?"

"They shut it down and sealed it off."

"So it's too late, whatever we do?"

"Wheatstone thinks one release won't tip the balance. But two or three, around the world . . . That would be bad."

Rebecca stopped at the red line twenty feet from the guard house and waited for the first stage security inspection. "Are we infected?" she asked.

"I hope not," William said. "It was raining at the farm when we arrived."

The car's radio frequency ID tag met the first guard's approval and the gate lifted. They drove slowly past the concrete gatehouse, then she pulled off to the side and parked and they both got out while the car was examined with undercarriage mirrors, high frequency sonic imagers. One guard checked their stress levels with pong sniffers. "Big meeting today?" he asked with a wry grin.

The young Marine at the gate dropped the concrete and steel barriers across the drive. "Welcome to the FBI Academy," she said.

CHAPTER SIXTY
Hogantown

Pete Farrow walked ahead on Ness Avenue, huge shoulders straining at his knit shirt, loafers silent on the pavement, tapping his folded umbrella. William and Rebecca followed. The rain had stopped at one in the morning and the streets of Hogantown were shiny and empty. Somewhere east, a Hostage Rescue Team helicopter was practicing touch-and-go, turbines alternately whining and roaring, but mostly the Academy was asleep. There was an early morning wakeup.

"We'll talk in the shoot house," Farrow called back, "It's safe. I swept it myself."

William exchanged a glance with Rebecca as they turned into a shallow alleyway. Farrow unlocked the steel door to the command center and pointed them up the long flight of steps to the overlook's bay window. Rebecca went first.

"Still have buck fever?" Farrow asked William.

William smiled.

"All my tricks revealed—shoot house will never play the same." Farrow unlocked the door at the top of the steps and they entered a cool, dark silence.

"I don't think you've met Jacob Levine," Farrow said as a shadow swung around in a chair before the bay window. Farrow switched on the overhead light. Levine was wearing a purple fleece vest and a yarmulke. His face was puffy and stiff. "He knew Griff pretty well," Farrow said.

"Rebecca and I have met," Levine said. "Sorry about your father, Agent Griffin." They shook hands. Levine offered his seat to Farrow, who took it as his due. The rest of the seats in the command overlook were folding chairs. The floor was plywood. Exercise plans on butcher paper had been pasted along the side walls, Xs and Ys scattered around the floor plan

as if in preparation for a game of football. Everything smelled of warm
electronics with a cold tang of concrete powder from the slug-absorbing
walls below.

Farrow sat back in the command chair and folded his hands behind his
head. "Winter was class of '97. I tried to dig up his file." He tapped a small
folder filled with multi-colored sheets of paper. "This is all I got. Someone's
swept the records—I don't need to guess why. Jacob worked with Winter
years later when he was assigned undercover to track bigots in Georgia, and
later on, eco-terrorists in Oregon and Washington state."

"He was a sharp guy," Levine said. "Spoke four or five languages. He
had worked with defense contractors in Iraq and Egypt before joining the
FBI. Real personable. You could trust him. Handsome, quick, strong."

"A couple of weeks after 10-4, Lawrence Winter came to see me again,"
Farrow said. "We had dinner at Pirelli's in town. He filled me in about a few
of his activities in the northwest. He was pretty down. Poor bastard had lost
most of his family."

"So we've heard," Rebecca said.

"I told him he should take some leave—even go on disability. Winter
said he had other plans. He told me that four years after 9-11 he had volunteered to work on a secret project."

"What kind of project?" William asked.

Farrow looked aside and waved his hand at Levine.

"Some of this is rumor and surmise," Levine said. "Starting eight years
ago, Southern Poverty Law Center lost track of some pretty major players in
the old bigot ballgame. They just vanished. Nobody knew where they went.
I had a lunch with three Bureau of Domestic Intelligence types and they
were licking canary feathers off their chops, so I asked a friend of a friend
who knew someone. Nothing is completely secure in the Beltway. Back then,
apparently, the Attorney General had decided that what was sauce for the
goose was sauce for the gander and it was time to exercise a little preemptive
caution against lily-white Americans. He didn't want another Murrow Federal Building—it would take the focus off foreign terror. Some were saying
that even with the National Security Service, the FBI wasn't willing to get
its hands dirty enough to protect America. So they created BDI—the Bureau
of Domestic Intelligence. The AG then instituted a special role for his new
agency—they would work collections."

Farrow said, "Starting six or seven years ago, BDI came to Quantico and
started interviewing agents. Word came down from the AG—cooperate or
get your butts kicked. I voiced strong objections, so I was taken out of the

loop. A couple of years after that, I started hearing rumors about disappearances. I didn't know what to believe.

"At headquarters, some senior executives were being replaced or reassigned—you remember—I presume because they didn't cooperate with the administration and BDI. Later, it became clear that an unknown number of our agents had become involved in pre-emptive arrests. You never heard?"

"I'm little people," Rebecca said. Her cheeks were pink. "So you just sat on your thumbs?"

"Yes and no," Farrow said, shifting his shoulders. "Some senior agents—me among them—just happened to make a special visit to the Southern Poverty Law Center. I worked with Jacob to cross-reference the disappeared. In the interests of balanced government, you understand—these were all major assholes and otherwise I say good riddance. But there were at least two hundred of them, maybe a lot more. And there wasn't a damned thing we could do. Whenever we went to the top, we were shot down. Real eyes of steel. I should have asked more questions, but it just wasn't the right climate."

"We all turned our heads," Levine said. "They were rounding up the Jew-haters and the KKK. It was like a dream. They just vanished. Sometimes, BDI even arranged for a plausible crime scene to explain why they disappeared."

"Then Winter shows up to talk, and he's obviously a broken man," Farrow said. "I tell myself, maybe here's a way in. Maybe he's what I need to keep the FBI from sliding deeper into this pile of manure." Farrow held up a digital recorder. "It was about here that I pressed the on-button."

Winter's voice came out of the tiny speaker with remarkable clarity, soft and regular and certainly lacking in shrillness or sarcasm.

"*. . . What I heard from everybody we dealt with sounded pretty much the same to me. KKK and Aryan Nations guys spoke of their hatred for Jews and Catholics and blacks. Jewish extremists talked about killing Muslims. Muslims spoke of how much they loathed Jews and Christians. The religious wars never ended, Pete. We've been fighting for thousands of years. We're still fighting, still trying to drag everyone in. It's a sickness. And things are different now. You can't believe what I've seen, Pete. Some smart little fanatic with a grudge can unleash something that will kill us all.*"

Farrow paused the recorder. "'Smart little fanatic.' That makes me wonder if Winter had already tracked down Tommy Juarez, and if so, why he wasn't turning him in." Farrow switched the recorder back on.

"*Back in the fifties, it became obvious that nations with nuclear weapons could wipe life off the face of the Earth. Now, it could be five or ten teenagers*"

*in a high school biology lab . . . Or one driven monster. And who's going to set
them off? The big boys build their political careers on suspicion and fear and
hatred . . . But where the rubber hits the road, it always comes down to the
crazy little runts and the monsters—you know that, Pete. We have the profiles
memorized. The big boys rant against the evils of government for years and
then act all shocked when McVeigh and Nichols blow up a federal building. We
squeeze the Middle East, and the monsters blow themselves up and squeeze
back. But what if the runts and monsters get hold of things worse than fertilizer
bombs—worse than* atom *bombs? Who's going to be responsible?"*

The recorder beeped and shut off. "The last of my memory card was
used up," Farrow said. "But I remember where the conversation went. Winter had volunteered to work with a clandestine BDI team. He told them he
was uniquely qualified to do field work—meaning eliminations, I suppose—
because of the way he was born."

"Chimeric," Rebecca said.

William felt utterly lost. *Kidnappings. Murders. Cold cases.*

Farrow nodded. "Genetically stealthy. That was the phrase he used.
Eventually, we got around to talking about 10-4. That's when he fell apart.
He actually started to cry. I was ashamed for him."

"Tough guy, Pete," Rebecca said.

"Yeah, well, Winter said just rounding up the monsters and even killing
them wasn't enough. There would always be more—an endless supply. He
mentioned a plan he was working on. Jujitsu, he called it. Using the money
behind hate to destroy hate."

"Why didn't you turn him in?" Rebecca said.

"I did," Farrow said, watching her closely. "I handed it up to Hiram
Newsome, along with a copy of this recording. News was the only one I
thought I could trust."

Rebecca looked between Levine and Farrow. Levine would not meet her
gaze. "When?"

"That would be what, three years ago. The wave was cresting. The
congressional elections were going the wrong way. BDI was scrambling for
cover."

Rebecca stood. Her chair scraped. "You're a liar."

Farrow rose and went chest to chin with her. "News had it three years
ago," he said.

"That's your story and you're sticking to it," Rebecca said.

"Screw you, little miss."

Rebecca backed off a few inches and cocked her head to one side.

William took Rebecca's arm and held on as she tried to shrug lose. "We're going," he told her.

"Right. Let's climb out of this cesspool," Rebecca said.

"Take your puppy with you," Farrow said. "Ask News how it happened. I've got the paper trail. I made duplicates." His face was red and even his blond-furred forearms were the color of Bing cherries. "Watch out for her, Griffin," he said, his tone ice and mud. "Think about your career. She and Hiram Newsome could get you fried."

"Wait a minute," Rebecca said, and shrugged in just such a way that William let go. She stared straight up at Farrow. "You seem to know everything. Tell me about BuDark—just for old time's sake."

Farrow pulled back, ashamed that he had lost his cool. He brushed his hand through his hair. "Fuck it. I'll tell you what little I know. BuDark is presidential black ops, black budget. Larsen put it into play. They're out to bring us down by gathering international evidence to prosecute BDI, FBI, anyone who opposes the liberals. It's payback time. BuDark is anti-FBI."

"Pete's dirty," Rebecca said as they walked down the long hall filled with art prints of nature serene.

"He's the straightest agent I ever met," William said coolly. "Present company excepted."

"Hiram Newsome is the straightest agent *I've* ever met."

"What reason does Farrow have to lie? He's still confessing to knowing dangerous stuff." William swung his clenched fists in a half-circle and hammered the railing. Rebecca stepped back in surprise. The study lounge was empty. "If any of this is true, what the hell can we do—by ourselves?"

"Nothing," Rebecca said. "We need to reach out and ask questions. But we need to be extremely careful. Some people would kill to keep this big an albatross off their necks."

"Back to Newsome?" William asked.

"Not yet. We need to poke through the cracks in the bricks. Outside confirmation. I know just the guy."

"The one who pissed you off," William said. "What was his name—Grange, from DS. You thought he might be BuDark."

Rebecca looked at William, her eyes both sad and bright. "Simpatico," she said.

They walked past security and through the swinging glass doors to the car. William drove and Rebecca did not object. As they approached the inner gate, they saw several lines of black SUVs and Crown Victorias arranged in zig-zag patterns, marked off with orange traffic cones and blocking the gatehouses and the road beyond.

"Uh-oh," Rebecca said.

William slowed to a stop, then rolled down his window as a man with short-cropped hair and a linebacker's build approached. He wore a dark blue suit and suspiciously thick sunglasses.

"Secret Service," he announced, leaning to peer into the open window. His gaze wavered minutely back and forth; he was comparing their faces to ID photos popping up on the inside of his lenses.

William and Rebecca kept a tense silence.

"We have a match," the agent said. Two other agents in dark suits approached the other side. "William Griffin, Rebecca Rose, step out of the car and keep your hands in plain sight."

"What's going on?" William asked.

"Are you carrying weapons? Irritants? Are you on a grid?"

William and Rebecca answered yes and no and again no, slowly exited the car, and held up their arms. The agents kicked their legs apart and pushed them up against the hood and trunk, bending them over until their cheeks were pressed hard on the painted metal. Their weapons were taken and deactivated. There were no niceties—the agent frisking Rebecca was male. She was cuffed and led away to one car and William to another. She gave him a backward glance, lips tight, dimples etched deep.

Through a long, long evening and into the early morning, they both did exactly as they were told.

CHAPTER SIXTY-ONE
Turkey, Iraq

"Get your Janny boys up and ready to ship out. Let's do it, now!"

Fouad jerked up from a light doze and stared at the bald colonel leaning through the open metal door. The colonel pulled back and Fouad wondered if he had been dreaming, but then he heard the sirens wailing throughout the base.

He quickly slipped into his flak vest and camouflage uniform, then checked his pack.

In the NCO mess hall, he spoke quickly with the twenty-two Jannies under his command. He did not like that name and they did not use it among themselves, but at Incirlik that was what they had been called, and it was now just below the level of official—Jannies or Janissaries.

Outside the barracks, on the runways, dozens of transport aircraft were roaring and fanning thin clouds of sand and dirt as if trying to imitate the recent dust storms.

Another colonel pointed them across the cracked asphalt runway to a truck. They climbed in with what gear they carried. Another truck arrived and soldiers threw some boxes in after them. Nobody knew what was happening. It was six in the morning and dawn gleamed like a sleep-folded eye in the eastern sky.

As they approached their aircraft, another colonel in flight gear ran alongside, pulled himself into the rear of the truck, and called out to Fouad. "They have Turkish troops circling the base. They don't seem to like us right now, so we're pulling out all mobile commands. That includes Jannies and BuDark teams. We'll reconnoiter at a site yet to be determined but way the hell away from here. Questions?"

They had none—for this colonel. They were a tight-knit group now, having trained together for weeks, friendly enough but suspicious of the soldiers, airmen, and officers around them. They were wide awake but not too curious. Life thus far had been boring. Something new was welcome even on such short notice.

The young men around Fouad shook hands and clapped shoulders. Then they passed around a thermos of hot coffee.

"What are they going to do with us?" they asked him, as if he might know.

"Just a guess," Fouad said. "I think the fighting around Mecca is going badly. Wahhabi insurgents are coming in with pilgrims to the Hajj. Someone is losing control."

"Are we?" they asked. By which they meant, "Muslims?"

"We, Americans," Fouad countered softly, "and the people we supply, more likely. Anger among the faithful is burning like a fever. It must be getting particularly bad for Turkey to want us out. Hajj is almost upon us. It is a delicate time."

"When will they brief us? Why don't we fight? What are they saving us for?"

"God only knows," Fouad said. "Living near the heart of the world takes patience."

Early in the morning, their plane landed at another nameless forward mobile air base, a patch of flat rocky terrain, nothing more than a bare airstrip carved from the desert. There were few guards and only light air support so they remained near the aircraft, five transports arranged in a pentacle, and took turns running and timing each other until the breezes subsided and the day became too hot.

Later that afternoon, more sandstorms moved in and they slept and played cards and watched videos inside the hot cargo holds.

After the evening repast of MREs—some containing pork ribs, which they quietly set aside—an Air Force military intelligence officer approached Fouad. "Can we talk?" the older man asked. He was short, gray-haired and big-shouldered, with just the slightest gut which he tried to hide by tightening his belt. "Do you know anything about OWL?" the officer asked. He pulled out a secure slate and calling up a display tagged *Quantum Confirm ACCESS Only. This ACCESS is remotely logged.*

Fouad shook his head. "Owl, O-W-L. No. It is not familiar."

"I have been instructed to give you a tactical briefing on how to call down an OWL strike. Don't ask me why. Neither system has been fully tested, and personally, I wouldn't rely on them, but orders are orders."

OWL, Fouad learned, stood for Orbital Warhead Lancet, an enhanced self-guided kinetic kill weapon designed to pierce deep bunkers. As he listened, Fouad's eyes watered with a hot combination of anger, fear, and exaltation.

Perhaps there would be no bloodshed after all. Blood would not have time to flow.

And there would be no bodies left to bury.

CHAPTER SIXTY-TWO
Mecca

Mr. John Brown had moved most of the settlers' sons into the tent city in Mina. They had kept the hotel room, and two of the young men were staying there to maintain their vigil over the garage where the trucks were stored.

Opening the sealed walls and privileges of the house of Saud had brought chaos and death to the Hajj, as in the times of old, but nothing could stop the hundreds of thousands of pilgrims; their accumulated power and passion had sobered even these sons of Zion, of Eretz Israel, and had turned them inward as they rested in their tent through the long night.

The enormity of what they were about to do had finally subdued Winter's boys.

Once again after decades of tight Saudi control Mecca was dangerous. Thieves and rogue police and soldiers like lost ants worked the outskirts of the crowds. There had been beatings and rapes—of men and women, some said—and even murders. Yet around them now, in a bubble of enterprise and faith maintained by vigilance and a bond between the local merchants and pilgrims, they saw little but brotherhood and joy and a shared passion for God.

The entire city was drunk with God.

The settlers' sons prayed in small groups, seeking a renewal of their strength. Yet not one of his young men asked for forgiveness. They had been raised with equal passion and focus, confirmed in a blood religion rooted in sacred land. They had long since grown inured to the sting of hate, like scorpions immune to their own poison.

The tall American hardly knew what name to use now. John Brown, Sam Bedford, Larry Winter—he could feel his past falling off behind him like the slats of a cartoon suspension bridge. Soon the final slat would drop and he would tumble into a deep chasm of forgetting and all would be peaceful. His grief lost, his reason reduced to a simple matter of day to day, hunger and sustenance . . . should he live to see out the week, which was also doubtful.

I'll return to them their first memory of a blue sky seen by an innocent child. All of them, victims and killers, equal under God.

The only problem was, now that the intense and constant memory of his grief was fading, Winter was less and less convinced any of this was necessary. He had assumed he was acting out of conviction and not hate. Unlike Tommy, he had reason, he had an achievable goal. Now, however, he was like a bullet. Gunpowder spent, the slug moved forward on momentum alone, impeded by the thickening air, slowed by the scent of hundreds of thousands of fellow human beings trying to talk to God.

Trying earnestly, desperately, submissively, to hear His words.

Listening.

CHAPTER SIXTY-THREE
Federal Correction Institution
Cumberland, Maryland
Domestic Security Wing

As Rebecca had commented earlier, no prison was beautiful, but at least they hadn't incarcerated William in a Virginia Department of Corrections facility or in the Marine Corps brig on the base at Quantico.

But then, neither had they told him why he was being held or where they had taken Rebecca or what the hell was going on in the outside world that could explain why two special agents would be treated this way.

After eight hours, guards escorted William to the end of the yellow hall and across a small courtyard with one thin tree to a windowless room on the second floor of a windowless concrete building. The room had a table and two chairs and it was smaller than his cell. Its only other features were a round grill in the wall—some sort of speaker—and higher up two air vents with red ribbons. The ribbons rippled as the two men sat him in the northern chair. William had made sure to keep his sense of direction, if only to have this small bit of knowledge. The rest was a nightmare puzzle.

Even so, he was glad to be out of the cell, and he actually looked forward to this discussion.

"This is Gene, and I'm Kurt with a K," said the taller of the two men. Both were trim and wore golf shirts with alligator patches—one pink, one pale green—and beige pants, and both were shorter than William, less than five ten. The taller one, Kurt with a K, had thinning brown hair and a wisp of mustache. The other, Gene, had thick curly black hair and green eyes. They seemed calm enough. Kurt pulled out the other seat and sat. William could not help but think of the men and women he had interrogated for the NYPD—and of course Jeremiah Chambers.

Gene leaned against the wall under the speaker grill. The east wall. The west wall held the windowless door. There was no knob on the inside of the door. It could only be opened by someone on the outside.

Kurt began. "You graduated from the Academy in April, and right away you were assigned to work with Special Agent Rebecca Rose, correct?"

"It just sort of happened."

"You didn't choose to work with her?"

"She asked the Bureau if I could be temporarily assigned to work with her."

"So she liked you."

"I suppose."

"She usually doesn't work well with others. Is that your evaluation?"

"We got along."

"She's prickly. A loner."

"If you say so."

"Did you know anything about Amerithrax before you worked with her?"

"What we studied in training and read in books."

"She's been working on that case for some time, hasn't she?" Kurt asked. "Crazy theory about inkjet printers."

"She and another agent, Carl Macek," William said.

"Macek is dead. It was a cold case. Why did Hiram Newsome let her continue to work on it?"

"Something like Amerithrax is never really a cold case, is it?"

"Did you know that ten years ago Rebecca Rose had an OPR file opened against her? Sexual harassment. A fellow agent claimed she made inappropriate advances, then threatened to get him demoted and reassigned if he refused her."

"That doesn't sound like Agent Rose," William said.

"It was a scandal, and it took Deputy Ay-Dick Hiram Newsome to cool it down. The charges were eventually dropped. The other agent resigned. He's working as an industrial security consultant in Chicago. Yet here's that same predatory Rebecca Rose, shacking up with fresh young Feeb-eye veal in a Mobile Agent Domicile in Washington state. You tell me how that looks."

"She did not harass me. She didn't make a pass at me. We did not sleep together."

Gene came around and put both hands on his shoulders, then slapped him hard on one ear. His ear rang and then heated up. *Keep it down,* Griff said in the other ear. *You know the drill. There are probably lives at stake. Either that, or these two are dirty. Either way, watch them.*

"Did she ever mention working with an agent named Larry Winter?"

"No."

"Did Hiram Newsome ever mention working with Larry or Lawrence Winter?"

"No."

"What do you know about anthrax?"

"Not much."

"Was Rebecca Rose an expert in the manufacture and production of biological weapons, in your opinion?"

William thought this over for a moment. "She knew as much as an agent should, who's investigating a case," he replied.

"Doesn't it make you suspicious that Hiram Newsome, Rebecca Rose, and Carl Macek—supposedly, but we can't talk to him—that these three were the only agents in the FBI who were pursuing this particular theory?"

"No," William said. "It didn't seem inappropriate."

Gene moved quickly to grab his shoulders and straighten him.

"Don't look at him like that, dickhead," Kurt said. "You have no reason to be afraid if you tell me the truth."

"You asked for my opinion," William said, and despite Griff's best advice, he was getting mad. "I gave you my opinion."

"That makes us think you might have been involved all along. You don't want us to think that, do you? Why don't you tell it all nice and simple, just for the Bureau's sake."

"I don't know of any conspiracy. I don't believe Rebecca Rose or Hiram Newsome were involved in a conspiracy."

"But we *do* know. There *was* a conspiracy. It may have reached to the highest branches of government. Hiram Newsome wanted to cover it up. Rebecca Rose was his partner. Do you think they're fucking each other, William? And maybe they're fucking with *you*, too?"

William pressed his lips together.

"Maybe that doesn't bother you," Kurt said. "Maybe you like that picture. You played queer for vice in New York. Personally, I could never do that. It would make me sick. Maybe you *are* queer. Maybe you secretly want to fuck Hiram Newsome, a real double agent jim-jam, right?" He stood and let Gene take the chair.

Gene resumed the questions. "America is in real danger if we don't stop this shit, Agent Griffin. How did you know so much about transgenic yeast?"

"I did my research."

"Another convenient burst of genius. You found the answer to all these puzzles on a *search engine*, didn't you?"

William nodded.

"Rebecca Rose knows all about inkjet printers, and you know all about yeast. Amazing. Brilliant. You found Dr. Wheatstone all on your own, first guess. Amazing. Brilliant. You knew Wheatstone already, didn't you? Because Hiram Newsome or Rebecca Rose told you who the transgenic yeast had been stolen from . . ."

William looked down at the table. "No," he said.

"You mean, you're admitting you didn't make these discoveries all on your own?"

"No," William said.

"Do you know who we are, William?"

"Secret Service."

"Wrong. I'm Border Security, Kurt here is ATF. We've been tasked to clean up the mess you Feeb-eye agents made, and we're pretty determined fellows. So we're going to be here for a while longer, if you don't mind."

"If it helps get to the truth, I don't mind," William said.

Kurt slapped his other ear.

"Have you ever heard of an operation called Desert Vulture?" Gene asked.

"No," William said.

"Are you absolutely certain it was never mentioned?"

"I'm certain."

"What if I told you somebody was sent to find Amerithrax, and they found him—and didn't turn him in? What if I told you that was Lawrence Winter? And Winter was ordered by somebody high up to use this freak as a source of weapon's grade anthrax that no one could ever trace?"

William felt his stomach tighten. Then, he wanted to be sick. "I don't know anything about that."

"Bullshit, Agent Griffin. You're right in the thick of it. What do you think Winter was going to do with all that anthrax?"

"It isn't anthrax—" William began, but Kurt cuffed him again, and he pressed his mouth shut.

Tight.

Three hours later, after nine rounds of interrogation but not much in the way of physical abuse—a bruised chin, chipped tooth, and two bruised ears—they returned William to his cell. He was none the wiser and neither were they.

But his head swam with bitter possibilities.

What do you really know, son? Griff asked.

The door opened with a mousy squeak. William rolled over on the cot and stared at the two men and one woman standing there. The woman was not Rebecca. It was Jane Rowland. She looked unhappy, and not just for William's plight. One of the two men was the DS agent they had met on the Patriarch's farm, David Grange. He smiled at William. That was good, wasn't it? The other man William did not know. He was big and wore a dark blue suit with a narrow tie. A prison official.

"Let's go," Grange said. "We're getting you out of here."

Jane Rowland had eyes as big as saucers. They escorted him from the cell and down the hall. "Do you remember me?" Grange asked.

"Yes, sir," William said.

Two senior corrections officers in dark brown suits joined them. Grange handed them pieces of paper and they signed without a word. The senior officers did not look happy that William was leaving their care.

"All hell's broken lose in Washington," Grange said. "We're looking for a few good officers and agents, those without significant political baggage. You might have heard—they've arrested Hiram Newsome and two other Ay-Dicks. The Attorney General has been strongly advised to shut down the entire FBI, *statim*. Secret Service is being combed and a lot of nits and ticks are falling out. BDI is down in flames, of course. Border Security—do you believe it?—and DS are about all we have left. And a select few from Quantico, mostly because of the President's Chief of Staff . . . and me. It's an unholy mess."

"What about Rebecca Rose?"

"Rose is traveling in another vehicle. I got her sprung this afternoon. We'll see her in a couple of hours."

"Was she involved?"

"Involved in what?" Grange asked.

"Desert Vulture."

"You know about that? Shit."

"Was she?"

"Absolutely not."

"They were going to attack Mecca, weren't they—if there was a major terrorist hit on the U.S. They were going to cover Mecca with anthrax."

"I'm not at liberty to discuss any of these matters," Grange said.

"You were tracking Winter. He had gone rogue. He was with Desert Vulture, but he changed his mind."

"I didn't learn about Desert Vulture until yesterday," Grange said.

"Then it was real?"

"That's all I can say for now."

They had reached the end of the long corridor. More steel doors and then bars swung wide. The officials peeled off and went their separate ways. William winced at the dark sky. It was night. The stars were out and the air was cold. He embarrassed himself by making a little whooping sound as he sucked in the wonderful freshness.

"Are you circumcised, William?" Grange asked as he showed his badge and signed papers at the first gate.

"Yes, sir," William said. "My parents did it for sanitary reasons."

"As it happens, so am I."

Jane Rowland turned up her eyes.

A black Suburban pulled up to the curb and came to a halt with a slight screech of tires. Two agents inside stared at them with imperious suspicion through the half-open window.

"Where are we going?" William asked.

"We're leaving Cumberland," Grange said. "Other than that, do you care?"

An hour later, they boarded a Coast Guard jet on the runway at Dulles for a flight to Eglin. At Eglin, he showered and shaved in an officer's quiet apartment, wasting twenty minutes under the needle-spray to scrub off the humiliation. Grange brought him a small case with personal items and a fresh change of clothes that almost fit.

From Eglin, they took a C5A military flight to Oman. He heard Rebecca was on the flight, but he wasn't interested in talking or catching up. He was exhausted and he had too many tough questions. William hid himself at the back of the passenger seating area. Outside, the supernal drone of the turbofan engines lulled him into nothing at all like sleep, more like a hop, skip and jump along the nightmare border of death, and it was not pleasant.

Hours later, he came fully awake with a jerk and saw Rebecca sitting across from him. The plane was descending.

He stared at her.

"Jesus, William Griffin. You've got zombie eyes."

William swallowed and looked away. "I don't like being soaked in shit," he said. "Your shit or anybody else's."

"Mm hmm," Rebecca said. Again she made that motion with her up-turned, scissored fingers, as if she really needed a cigarette.

"I have *never* been treated that way," William said. "What other surprises do you have in store for me?"

"It wasn't me. You know that."

"Then what about the FBI? You sucked me into this. What did I do to be tarred with that great big old brush, huh?"

"Nothing," Rebecca said.

"And what about you? What did you do?"

"Nothing."

William grimaced. "I heard a lot at Cumberland," he said.

"So did I. I tend to ignore big tough guys, or haven't you noticed?"

"They wanted to open me up and spill out my brains, Rebecca. They were *scared*. I could smell them even without a pong detector. Somebody told them something that made them want to shit their pants. I think if we had stayed there a few more hours, they'd've started injecting some really cool new drugs, and who cares what they damage? They wanted to turn our brains into alphabet soup and read the little words, Rebecca."

Rebecca looked straight at him, her eyes showing something William had not seen before—real hurt and disappointment. "I didn't do this to you, William."

"What the fuck is Desert Vulture?"

"I don't know. Maybe I don't want to know."

"Did they ask you about it?"

She nodded.

"Did they box your ears?"

She shook her head.

"So with you, they were gentlemen?"

Rebecca lifted her eyebrows and looked down at her hands.

"Why are we here, can you tell me that?"

Her hands were quivering. She took a shallow breath. "How long do you think a sunshine patriot will run around, once you cut off his head?"

"Is that a rhetorical question?"

"No time limit has ever been found," Rebecca said. "They go on for years. The rest of us take up their slack and shovel their shit—or soak in it—and they live to retire and fill their dens with trophies and flags. They get paid hundreds of thousands of dollars to give talks before the American

Eagle Forum or the Red White and Blue Institute of I've Got Mine, Jack, and then they write their memoirs and dangle their grandchildren on their knees. They cram our ears with tales of patriot glory, when all they ever really did was get good people killed. They squander blood and treasure, and then they try to figure out desperate ways to make it come out right. That's what Desert Vulture must be. Some old guy's brilliant idea of how to make the world right again, and to hell with you and me or the grunts on the line, or anybody else."

"It was *anthrax*, Rebecca. Even Lawrence Winter couldn't go through with what they were planning."

"I suppose it was."

"And where are these bastards now? Why are we taking their lumps for *them*? Fuck," William said, and kicked the seat in front of him.

David Grange worked his way to the back, leaning into the seats as the plane banked. "Am I interrupting something?"

"We're done," William said.

"We'll be landing in Oman in an hour."

"Tell William what you've told me," Rebecca said. "About why we were busted."

Grange squatted in the aisle. "There's no way yet of knowing who's involved in what. An executive order went out—it was pretty broad. They decided to detain anyone who had a connection to Winter or Amerithrax. ATF got handed the lead, but DEA and even the Postal Police are involved—it's a real zoo. You two got scooped up in the net. Can't tell the players without a program, and I don't know anyone who has a program."

"David says News may or may not be implicated," Rebecca said. Her expression was fragile, hopeful.

"Newsome may have been stringing some people along, trying to catch up with Winter before any harm was done. BuDark didn't even exist four years ago," Grange said. "Why he wouldn't tell you up front, I don't know."

"He was senior. He had some armor," Rebecca said.

"Yes, and look where that got him. You're out and he's still in," Grange said. "You must have made some impression on the President."

"News was there, too."

"Well, I don't know who the hell impressed who," Grange said. shifting his knees. Then he stood and flexed his legs. "Problems at Quantico and in DC aren't our biggest worries. Jordan and Turkey have refused permission to land. We're going to touch down in Oman, then grab a chopper and transfer to a frigate or something in the Red Sea. After that, there's talk about flying us directly into Saudi Arabia. The insurgency is consolidating its gains, trying to squeeze money out of the Hajj, I suspect, to finance their next moves. We have contacts with what's left of the Saudi General Intelligence Service, *al-Istakhbarah al-A'amah*. They're as interested as we are in preventing a Hajj disaster. So far, we're just telling them it's anthrax—that focuses their attention. We'd let them take the lead, but frankly, they're fuckups when it comes to handling foreign nationals—in their prime, they were best at bullying immigrant workers. Still, I was deputy RSO in Riyadh for a couple of years. I know a few who aren't too bad."

"What good are we in all this?" William asked. Rebecca took a thermos from her travel bag and poured him a cup of black coffee.

"We're short-handed. Desperately so. Most of the career types are covering their asses. After I boosted her from Cumberland, Rebecca volunteered you."

"Thanks, I guess," William said.

"We're bringing along Jane Rowland to handle special communications."

"How about the full scoop on BuDark?" Rebecca asked.

Grange nodded. "BuDark began as an internal DS and FBI response to rumors about Desert Vulture."

"Pete Farrow?"

"Not one of us. Like News, however, probably a good guy—just not in the loop. Some agents tried to dig out facts on their own. Three years ago, we went to the senate and the effort became bipartisan. We found conspirators in just about every branch of government. The last administration tried desperately to shut us down, and then they lost the election—finally, and thank God. Right now, we're a shambles, scattered all over Europe and the Middle East looking for a needle in a haystack. Half the operational directors don't want to believe there *is* anyone in Mecca. The other half—well, we have UAVs watching the city right now, mostly from altitude. But we've dropped some midges into the town to scope out the street scene. Current plan is, we're driving or flying to the outskirts of Mecca, escorted by undercover officers who've bribed their way into Hijaz Liberation. If we get through—and that's a big if—we still need to find the truck or trucks. Based on the equipment captured in Jerusalem, we think there may be as many as three. When we find them, we have to stop them and destroy their contents—and that's where Fouad Al-Husam comes in. He's been made chief of a team of guys they call Janissaries. All American Muslims, orphans from the first Gulf War. Seems to be quite a story. He's going to join us outside Mecca. His team has been trained and equipped but they're not military, they're not CIA—they're not even heavily armed. And none of us is going to carry ID. If we get caught, we're just crazy victims of the Hajj gone wrong—or the revolution."

"Sounds like we're being sent to do the one thing Quantico doesn't train us for," Rebecca said.

"What would that be?" Grange asked.

"Sweep up after the elephant parade."

William snorted coffee through his nose.

CHAPTER SIXTY-FOUR
Mecca

The city was now in the eighth day of the last month of the Islamic calendar, *Dhu al-Hijja*. Islam's year of twelve synodic months, each of approximately twenty-nine days, was ruled by the moon and cyclically fell behind Western calendars. This had pushed the Hajj into October, a relatively pleasant time of year in Mecca. Daytime temperatures rarely exceeded ninety degrees. Many were now dressed in the two white cloths of *ihram,* right shoulders protruding, fat and shining and nut-brown or bony, ancient and withered. They were on their way to Mina, carrying their bags and cases of worldly goods or waiting at the curbs for buses and shuttles. There were no trains or subways in Mecca. Travel to Mina could take hours through heavy traffic. Many simply walked.

Winter felt invisible. He looked poor and sick, not prosperous. Indeed, he was sick. And so he stood on a corner near the Grand Mosque and watched as the pilgrims' mandatory patience—a requirement of *ihram*—was tried by inexperienced police and guards from Oman and Yemen. The air was cool. He struggled to remember and concluded that he had come in search of something—logically, that would have to be God. He had come to listen. He felt as if there had been long years of grief and pain, an unceasing agony of duty and labor, of betrayal and evil—but somehow the details escaped him. Something had been left unfinished.

Along the busy streets, the modern thoroughfares and underpasses and overpasses, the hotels and shops and apartment complexes studded with air conditioners that surrounded the broad plazas around the Grand Mosque, came the streams of travelers and citizens. Down one narrow road lined with bistros and shops and overarched by apartments and neon signs blinking in Arabic and sometimes in English, Winter saw Pakistanis and Palestinians. Along another wider street, shops selling rich fabrics were attended by Indonesian pilgrims who cast suspicious glances at Chinese Muslims. There were old men and young, in some cases handsome but also exotically ugly, even barbaric, as if plucked from ancient centuries—with scars on their glossy cheeks and foreheads, or missing eyes or hands or limbs.

Nervous masses, by the tens of thousands, hundreds of thousands. Troubled or blissful. Sweating and vomiting in the gutters, or walking with heads high, singing the prayerful chant of *talbiyah*. Pilgrims frightened by the confusion, troubled and exalted by what they might find within themselves. Shopping, eating from paper plates and plastic bowls in stalls and at tall round tables set on cracked ochre and red tiles or garish pink linoleum, fueling for the long and trying day ahead.

He could not remember hating these people. He watched them calmly and then felt the lump in his pocket and, right there on the street, reached in and pulled out the vinyl folder and stared at the odd documents and the polished badge. Seeing the English words, he closed the case and returned it to the pocket where it pressed against his thigh.

They would mob him if they saw his creds. They would stone him to bloody pulp. But no one had seen.

What have I done? What have I brought?

Forgetfulness.

But I don't remember why.

He took out his keys and opened the small door beside the battered steel roll-up garage gate. Inside, Gershon stood watch over the second Volvo truck, perched on the edge of a plastic crate, eyes wide at the unexpected entry. Fluorescent lights flickered in the cracked and patched concrete ceiling. Water was leaking from the apartments above. Gershon looked at him with some concern. "Mr. Brown. It's not time, is it?"

The American jangled his key ring and smiled. "We have to keep our powder dry." He opened the back of the truck and climbed up beside the crates. Then he walked the length of the truck bed, caressing the plastic and canvas tarps, tugging at the ropes.

Gershon crammed his hands in his pockets and watched from the rear.

One rope was loose. The American stooped to untie it, then swung it away. "Why do that?" Gershon asked. "We aren't supposed to mess with them yet, are we?"

The American held his finger to his lips and smiled.

Yigal entered from the rear and stood beside Gershon. Together, they asked again what he was doing, voices echoing. He took a crowbar and pried away the side of the middle crate, revealing a launcher within—steel tubes still shrouded in bubble wrap. "They're traveling well," he murmured. "They look fine."

"We aren't supposed to open the crates," Yigal said.

"That's what I told him," Gershon said. "He's going against his own orders."

"Well, he should know." Then, more sharply, "What are you doing, Mr. Brown?"

The crates containing the rockets had been stacked between the larger crates. He knelt and used the crowbar to rip open the wood at a lower corner, exposing the plastic wrapping and foam packing. He jammed the bar into the crate, vigorously punching and whacking at the exposed bottoms of the rockets. Glass beads and white and gray powder dropped in chunks.

"My God, he's gone crazy," Gershon said, pulling himself up onto the truck bed. "Stop it!"

Mr. Brown—that was what they called him, and he could not remember his other names—backed away from the crate as the young men approached.

"Tell us what's happening, Mr. Brown," Gershon said, regarding him levelly.

He shook his head. "It's nothing," he said. "Nothing to worry about. I've been out walking, seeing the sights. Haven't you?"

Gershon called back, "Get Menachem. No, stay here and help me. We have to keep him from doing more damage. Get some rope."

"He's our boss!" Yigal said.

"Mr. Brown, you need to come down here with me. Let's go back to the tent or back to the room. Let's discuss this."

Mr. Brown lifted the crowbar but he did not hate Gershon. He could not strike him. His shoulders slumped. Gershon leaped forward, pulled him down, and jammed him against a crate. Yigal brought more rope. By that time, three more young men had entered the garage. They bunched at the back of the truck, staring at the tall American who had once recruited and led them.

"He's off his nut," Menachem said. They took his arms and legs and dropped him from the back of the truck and let him slump on the floor.

"What should we do?"

The folder fell from his pocket onto the floor. Yigal reached down and flipped it open, examined the credentials with dismay, and then passed the folder around.

"Who is this Lawrence Winter?" Menachem demanded. "This is your picture!"

"Throw him out in the streets," Yigal said angrily.

"Don't go back there!" Gershon yelled at one of the young men who had climbed onto the truck bed. "There's powder all over."

Gershon and Menachem slammed him against the wall of the garage. "Who the hell are you?" Gershon demanded. Menachem struck him several more times with the back of his hand, across the face. His lip cracked open.

He could not answer.

He did not know.

"We have to decide," Menachem said. "Is this some sort of trick?"

CHAPTER SIXTY-FIVE
The Red Sea
U.S.S. Robert A. Heinlein, SF-TMS 41

The helicopter flight from Oman took two hours. William looked through the port beside his seat. Below, the early morning darkness that shrouded the Red Sea was painted by a thin ribbon of silver moonlight. The weather was clear. The new moon would soon be visible across the Arabian Peninsula.

Then, William spotted a long, blunt knife cutting through the ribbon with a glint of sloping sides and a gentle wake that vanished less than a hull length behind. He guessed this was the stealth frigate *Heinlein*.

The chopper descended and described a perfect circle around the Navy ship until clamshell doors opened aft of the two round hillocks of the superstructure. Three ramps folded outward, creating a triangular platform. The chopper was given permission to hover but not to touch down. It dropped a cable to the deck plates to ground its considerable build-up of static electricity. An eerie glow around the rotors and blades slowly diminished in the dry night air.

Grange led his BuDark team to the hatch and they jumped to the platform, ducking in the downdraft. As the helicopter departed, they were met by the executive officer and escorted down a flight of stairs.

"Welcome to the *Heinlein*," the exec greeted them as the noise diminished below a deafening roar. "I'm Lieutenant Commander Stengler. Our skipper is Commander Peter Periglas." Following Stengler, they crossed a lofty hangar beside and beneath dozens of self-guided UAVs stacked in tiers and hung from the bulkheads, wings folded like huge sleeping albatrosses. There were a lot of gaps. Many of the *Heinlein*'s birds were already soaring above the desert and the cities of the Hijaz.

The platform folded, the clamshells closed. Stengler guided them down narrow corridors and more steps to a ready room opposite the Tactical Surveillance Center—what would have once been called the Combat Information Center. "Heads are down the hall and to the right, as well as two staterooms. Do not turn left, or you will be met by some of our fine Marines, and they have no sense of humor. Our ship is small and tidy but our food is excellent. We will be serving an early breakfast at 0700 GMT, to which you are all invited. In the meantime, we've received a secure recorded briefing from Washington which I am instructed is for your eyes only. After you avail yourselves of our facilities, make yourselves comfortable and we will pipe that briefing into the ready room ASAP."

Grange thanked Stengler. They dropped their kits on one side of the ready room. Fifteen minutes later, Grange stood beside the door as it was locked. They all sat in the comfortable high-backed chairs arranged before a wall display on which a sunny ocean portrait of the ship was currently being shown.

The screen went dark. A young, nervous male voice-over informed them that their secure briefing was to be delivered by SAC Quentin T. Dillinger of Diplomatic Security. Dillinger stood behind a White House podium with a map of the Arabian Peninsula half in shadow behind him. He was not at ease and frequently referred to notes on the podium or glanced over his shoulder as areas of the map were highlighted.

"Greetings. David. The rest of you I have not met.

"BuDark was established three years ago as an internal, inter-agency investigation team, by mandate of the Senate Intelligence and Judiciary Committees. I was appointed SAC of the operation, tasked to learn about a covert U.S. plan to respond to a major Islamic terrorist strike, on the order of 9-11. We have discovered that such a plan did in fact exist, targeting Mecca and code-named Desert Vulture, and a version of it may very well be under way. An FBI special agent named Lawrence Winter apparently decided to ignore his original orders and reconstruct Desert Vulture into a scheme of his own, using his own contacts. He traveled throughout Mexico, Central America, and the Middle East, arranging for the transfer of money from several international parties. For reasons still not clear, he expanded the original target list of Desert Vulture to include Ohio, Rome, and Jerusalem—in addition to Mecca.

"Branches of his operation have been located and halted in Washington State, Rome, and in Israel. We could not prevent what may have been a dress rehearsal in Ohio. And one last operation, unfortunately, still threatens Mecca. It is this operation that immediately concerns us.

"We are in the season of the Hajj. Approximately a million pilgrims have entered Mecca, despite unstable conditions caused by the breakdown and departure of the Saudi government. Lawrence Winter and a team of Israeli operatives, hand-picked from the sons of Jewish extremists, are in or near Mecca at this moment. They have more than two hundred custom-made fireworks charges designed to airburst and disperse biological payloads at two thousand feet. The payloads are not anthrax. Winter has substituted a transgenic strain of yeast. In the field, exposure to this yeast has caused rapid onset of memory disorders in civilians and in law-enforcement officers. A small quantity is sufficient to cause illness.

"One of our forensic psychologists suggests that Winter is trying to punish us for killing his family, not with a biblical plague, but something new: a stealth pestilence that causes permanent amnesia. Wipe away the world's memory, and you wipe out hatred—that seems to be his theory.

"Jerusalem and Rome are no longer threatened, so the Muslim world is likely to interpret any strike against Mecca as a call to all-out holy war. I think you can see that any U.S. involvement with Desert Vulture or Lawrence Winter is inexplicable and inexcusable.

"Our only option is to take out these weapons with a series of pinpoint strikes, using a weapon that will cauterize anything within a diameter of fifty to one hundred meters. We cannot use high explosives or even tactical nukes, not just because of collateral damage or the extraordinary political consequences, but because of the potential dispersal of surviving toxic particles. Instead, we have decided to utilize a class of kinetic kill projectiles known as Lancets—essentially guided steel telephone poles tipped with a chemical warhead. They're designed to fall from low Earth orbit and punch a hole in the ground, through several hundred feet of dirt, reinforced concrete, and even steel. They then incinerate anything within the relatively small but very deep impact crater, at temperatures above three thousand degrees Celsius. We've already launched sixty of these bunker-busters into low Earth orbit at intervals, in close-spaced clusters of four. They can be brought down on twenty minutes' notice and will self-guide with an accuracy of one or two meters to obliterate pre-programmed or laser-painted targets.

"We believe there are three trucks involved, and that Winter is going to release the fireworks one the second day of the Hajj, as pilgrims funnel through Mina. That will be tomorrow. One million pilgrims will be tightly concentrated in a small area within the village. Winter's rockets could be launched upwind of Mina, explode, and disperse well over two hundred pounds of uniquely deadly particles.

"We have very little time.

"Sending non-Muslims into Mecca would be considered highly provocative under any circumstance, but we believe the seriousness of our situation renders such concerns irrelevant. It has been determined at the highest level, however, that this operation cannot involve serving military personnel. And so we have selected a team of government officers and agents that we believe are trustworthy and have demonstrably had no knowledge of or participation in any aspect of Desert Vulture.

"If necessary, we will die to protect not only the pilgrims in Mecca, but the citizens of the United States of America and every nation on Earth—the entire human race."

"Who's 'we,' paleface?" Rebecca asked under her breath.

"Your next briefing will take place on the ground in Saudi Arabia. Godspeed."

The screen faded on Dillinger's drawn features.

Having it served up and delivered all at once left William numb. The deck vibrated under his feet as another UAV was RATO-launched into the early morning. Rebecca took his hand and gripped it.

"Goddamn them all to hell," she said.

William returned the squeeze.

Captain Periglas met them in the TSC and dismissed their Marine escorts. "Ladies and gents, this is what we have for you so far." He waved his arm across the darkened room. There was only one display visible; most of the officers and enlisted men in the dimly lighted Tactical Surveillance Center were wearing gogs or helmets. "Currently, there are fifteen UAVs surveilling the sky above and around Mecca, most of them at altitude, that is, exceeding ten thousand meters. They have excellent SAR—fine-resolution synthetic aperture radar—as well as outstanding optics and other sensors. Many of our UAVs are equipped with smaller aircraft that can be dispersed in quantity. We refer to them as 'midges.' Midges have many capabilities. To the untrained eye, they look like sparrows. They even fly like sparrows, for up to twenty hours before they self-destruct. The ones we are utilizing at this moment to search the crowds in Mecca are known as Osmic Mobile Observers or OSMOs. They can zero in on individuals or groups of individuals based on long-term dietary habits.

"Any vegetarian will tell you that meat-eaters stink; I stink, most of my crew stinks. Rich Muslims stink but with significant differences. Poor Muslims stink hardly at all. Three meals a day of eggs, meat, and/or fish, and we can send an OSMO right up to you with the passionate sensitivity of a moth

seeking a hot date. We can also distinguish observant Muslims from drink-
ers of alcoholic beverages, which may or may not be helpful; we are discovering that a disturbing number of security, police, and army personnel have
imbibed spirituous liquors, wine, or beer in the past two weeks."

Grange motioned Jane Rowland forward from the group and Periglas
pointed to a chair beside a Chief Warrant Officer. The chief removed his gogs
and switched on a monitor so that they could all see what he was seeing—a
complicated map of Mecca, spotted with circles and ellipses of pink, purple,
and green. The larger pulsing overlays were accompanied by shifting ranks
of numbers.

"Chief, would you like to explain what we're looking at?"

"Sir, Special Agent Rowland identified an individual in our target group
who may be using a GPS-equipped sat phone to call various females in Israel. Once he switches on that phone, we can pinpoint his position." The
chief handed Jane a pair of gogs, then reached across to switch on her display and tune it to a more specific level of detail. She smiled at the chief,
who returned her smile with technical camaraderie—and barely restrained
male admiration.

"Special Agent Rowland will remain on the *Heinlein* and attempt to spot
and track our cell-phone junky," Grange said.

Jane started to protest, but Rebecca had maneuvered behind her and
put a hand on her shoulder.

"The rest of us will receive deep-canal earphones-slash-wireless nodes
and eyeglass gogs to receive guidance from our remote trackers."

Rebecca squeezed Jane's shoulder, hard, then let go and patted it. Jane
swallowed her disappointment—for the time being—and stared at the display.

In the officer's lounge, Grange sat across from William and Rebecca. "Two
hours nap in the staterooms. Then, a whisper bird picks us up and delivers
us to the rendezvous point."

Captain Periglas entered the lounge and pulled up a chair. "Permission
to register an opinion."

"Of course," Grange said.

"I assume none of you are with the FBI's Hostage Rescue Team, or any
similar organization, correct?"

They nodded.

"Marines from this vessel will volunteer, and Navy Seals could join us
and accompany you within the hour."

"Your offer is sincerely appreciated," Grange said. "But our instructions are explicit."

"Mecca has turned into hell even for the faithful," Periglas observed. "For non-Muslims, discovery means . . . well, having your throat cut would be a mercy. Thousands of pilgrims are already sick and they're not getting any level of medical care. Give this to the Saudis, they kept the Hajj running like a clock for generations. Now the clock has wound down. We may see ten or twenty thousand dead before the week is out."

Grange looked blankly at the deck. "Thank you, Captain. Get us in there, tell us where to go, and make sure we get out. That's all we ask."

Periglas lifted his watch. "We'll have you on your way at ten hundred hours."

William reached to the upper bunk and nudged Grange's shoulder. Grange nearly pranged his head on an overhead beam.

"Showtime," William said.

In the corridor outside, Jane Rowland was arguing with Rebecca. "I've taught the chief everything he needs to know," Jane said, her voice cracking. "It isn't right, not letting me go in—you of all people know that."

"It's not her call," Grange said, still blinking away sleep. "We only have passes and documents for one woman."

Jane looked stunned. "I didn't realize what it meant," she said. "It just hits me. I don't . . . I'm sorry, I don't know what to say to make you change your mind."

"You're our guardian angel," Rebecca said. "If you get any of us killed, you better believe I'll come back and haunt you. So shut up and *focus*."

Stengler guided Jane across the corridor into the TSC.

"Tough lady," William said as they took their seats in the ready room. Rebecca ignored him.

Two pilots in bright green flight suits sat in the front row. They turned and examined their three passengers. "Too old for real baseball, don't you think?" the bald one commented dryly. "Not in the majors, anyway."

The second and younger pilot smiled.

"Stow that crap, Birnbaum," Captain Periglas said to the bald pilot as he came through the door.

"Sir, I'm older than at least one of them."

"As I said . . ."

"Stinking and stowed, sir." He held out his hand. "I'm Birnbaum. This is Higashi. Welcome to Plan B, folks. Nobody *ever* picks us for Plan A."

CHAPTER SIXTY-SIX
Mecca
9th Day, Dhu-Al-Hijjah

Gershon pushed the button and the steel garage door rumbled open. There were no shops on the short street and only a few stragglers. Yigal drove the truck forward. The canvas covers had been dropped and rolled and tied securely and Menachem and Baruch squatted in the back clutching the Chinese AKs they had purchased from a Pakistani arms dealer the day before. In the back, tied and gagged and propped between two crates, Larry Winters kept still, eyes half-closed. They had cinched his bonds tight enough that his arms and feet were insensible.

Have mercy. Let it be over, one way or the other.

The truck lurched. Brakes squealed. They were beginning the journey to the outskirts of Mina. Traffic was heavy on the King Abdul Aziz Road but they had all day. Twelve, fifteen hours, perhaps less, before they pulled back the tarps and opened the tops of the crates, depending on the whim of the breeze blowing across the desert.

The truck rumbled over cobbles, then over asphalt, then dirt, searching for its place.

In the bloody end, surrounded by young monsters, in pain, his memory flickering like a candle in a high wind, he was wracked with fever as he struggled with the knots. They had been wrapped with cord, the cord hidden behind more duct tape. He was still thoroughly bound and he had plucked his fingers raw.

The memory had faded but not the emotion. He did not know why he felt such rage, such grief, or why he was bound. He tried to scream but the tape would not budge. He tried to cry, but the tape had been pressed into his eyes.

He twitched up against the crate and went slack, energy gone.

Then, unexpectedly, there was light.

"You stink," Yigal said. "You've fouled yourself. Look at me! Say something!" To Menachem, squeezed up between the tarp and the crate, he added, "Cut him loose. Let him go off to die. He's disgusting."

The whisper bird, true to its name, came in low and quiet in the early morning darkness over the almost waveless beach. The back of the stealth craft could carry up to twenty troops but now it held only three: William, Rebecca, and David Grange.

"We've got our coordinates from the Jannies," Higashi said to Grange from the cockpit. "A small group will meet us east of Mina. We'll touch down, drop you, hover for just a few seconds, so you'll have to hustle."

"Right," Grange said.

Rebecca turned her head side to side. Right now, she and William were seeing the landing site from the POV of a midge. OSMOs had found the Jannies based on their American diet and zeroed in. Hundreds of midges were zipping back and forth through the mountain passes around Mina and Mecca proper. Soon, UAV mothers would deploy thousands more across the plain of Arafat. They networked like birds or bats, swooping and dispersing through the dark sky, swirling up in little gray tornadoes like starlings, then breaking and scattering to examine suspect scent trails.

Jane Rowland spoke from the *Heinlein,* her voice soft and steady in their earnodes. "We've got hotspots around the richer sections of the tent city. Chief Dalrymple tells me it's chicken, lamb, beef, lots of olive oil, vegetable protein. No surprise. If our suspects are hiding in there, it could take forever to find them."

"No lovesick phone calls?" Rebecca asked, finally mastering the display.

"None so far."

"Someone's taking potshots at our midges," Periglas said. He relayed video clips of men with rifles outside the brilliantly lit Grand Mosque, firing automatic weapons and rifles into the air. Their scent profiles showed they were drunk.

"This town's going to the dogs," Grange said.

"It's getting worse," Periglas said. "Ambulances are trying to get through to the sick and injured. Soldiers are making them pay bribes or grabbing them for joyrides. Not that they can go anywhere. The roads are packed."

Jane tuned their gogs to a midge tracking an old tourist bus. The sides were thick with strap-hangers and a few clung to the roof, trying to keep their parcels from tumbling away at the turns. Two of the strap-hangers fell into the street. The bus did not slow.

"I think that's the Abdul Aziz Road," William said. "There's the Al-Malim Mosque." He had studied maps during the flight.

"Correct," said Dalrymple. "Midge is heading east over the tent city."

"The pilgrims are on the move to Arafat," Periglas said.

"How many so far?" Grange asked.

"We're guessing one point two."

"Million?" Rebecca asked.

"Correct," Periglas said.

Another voice came on. "Is that Agent Grange?" It was Fouad Al-Husam. He did not sound happy. "We were expecting American Muslim soldiers."

"This is Grange. No military. We're sending agents to direct and render assistance."

"What sort of assistance?" Fouad asked. "Without Muslims, we will do well enough on our own. There is no need to—"

"It's already been decided," Grange said. "Is that understood, Agent Al-Husam?"

A few seconds later, "Are your papers in order?"

"All in order," Grange said.

"There are three of us here with a Saudi driver and a minibus. Ten of our agents are already in Mina. They report the main mass of pilgrims are expected at Arafat in five hours. They will return tomorrow to Mina by way of the Jamarat. That could be the best time for pathogen release."

"Agreed," Grange said. "We have to intercept before eighteen hundred hours GMT."

Rebecca faced William across the narrow aisle. The helicopter was eerily quiet. "He's been with his Jannies for how long now, and we're supposed to fit right in, without an introduction?"

Grange said, "He knows William and respects both of you. He'll smooth it over with the others, if there's a problem."

"And how are we supposed to help, exactly?" William asked.

"However we can," Grange said. "My guess, someone in Washington doesn't trust our Muslims to get the job done."

"The ol' FUBAR," Birnbaum called back cheerily. "Plan B with a vengeance."

The whisper bird changed its subtle hum and pitched forward.

"Drop in five," Higashi announced.

CHAPTER SIXTY-EIGHT
Desert, East of Mina

"It is not *fard*, to go on Hajj when there is so much danger," Amir said.

"What I read, if a few pilgrims die, bandits get them or whatever, it's OK. Historically, some danger is inevitable, so it's *fard*." Mahmud stood beside Fouad and watched the lights in the west. They had parked the minibus on a back road leading up and out into an empty, rocky waste of low hills. They were far enough away they could not hear Mecca, but in the dusk they could see its green and orange glow—the lights from the Grand Mosque catching the dust rising from all the trucks, cabs, and cars, forming a low haze in the dry air. The wind in the desert valleys had settled and it was still hot, in the eighties.

"Only God would have told someone to build a city down there," Hasim said.

They were not particularly profane, the young former Iraqis put in his care; but they had too much energy and American attitudes, and so they hid their piety under a layer of banter. Fouad understood. Six years ago he had been like them—unable to believe his good luck at being in America and not Egypt, and yet—

His body and his soul had craved this part of the world. Coming back to Iraq and then to the Hijaz had awakened a deep nostalgia, reminding him of his childhood in the dry air of Egypt. There had been less fear, more variety, more wealth and distraction in America, but also there had been less *life*.

They were still in exile, thirsting.

For them, Hajj was out of the question. They had come to the Hijaz in the wrong frame of mind, with all the wrong intentions—they could not be pilgrims. Yet for every Muslim, even those inclined to an American sense of profanity and joking, simply seeing those lights, knowing how close they were to the House of God, to the Black Stone, to the beautifully and newly woven black and gold *Kiswah* that shrouded the *Kaabah* . . .

What they were about to do—allowing infidels into the Holy City—was necessary to save this sacred place, so that they could return when it was proper, when their time had come to stand before God and shed their earthly confusions with maximum spiritual benefit.

A black aircraft came up over the distant hummock with a sound like an angry wasp—and nothing more. As it approached, all five watched in alert silence, American boys pleased by this marvel.

Fouad stepped down from the bumper of the minibus. Through the windshield, he saw the silhouette of Daoud Ab'dul Jabar Al-Husseini, a rumpled, discouraged-looking man in his sixties, rousing from a pre-dawn nap. Al-Husseini had once occupied a high rank in the Saudi Secret Police. He had probably been a strong man, a pious man, a harsh man not above tormenting other men and their wives in the service of the Wahhabis. Now his eyes were haunted by the privileges and stability he had seen blowing away, the end of a good, cruel dream.

Al-Husseini opened the bus's front door and jumped down heavily to the hard-packed roadbed. He rubbed his nose, then blew it into his fingers and wiped them on his pants. He had become an unkempt, dirty man. "So they're here," he said. "It will soon be over, one way or the other."

The whisper bird circled their position swiftly, little louder than a car but blowing up sand in a thin cloud around the minibus and across the road. The lights of Mecca dimmed.

Then it dropped spindly legs with round pads and set down on the sand twenty meters from the road like a moon lander.

Three people stepped down.

"Shit," Al-Husseini said in English. "They brought a woman? I hope they have excellent papers. These are no more Muslims than I am a Jew."

CHAPTER SIXTY-NINE
The Red Sea
U.S.S. Heinlein

The chief working beside Jane Rowland was named Hugh Dalrymple. He was quick and businesslike as he took control of various midges that had reported interesting results. The video transmitted by the small flying craft was surprisingly clear, the colors almost too vivid—altered to enhance contrast and salient detail. Living things seemed to glow with an inner light in the pre-dawn darkness. Sleeping pilgrims laid out in rows and uneven clumps in the streets of Mina, lying on thin pads or blankets or prayer rugs, or just on the ground in their two towels, stood out like flames against the gray sand and packed dirt and black asphalt. Soldiers and security police had become scarce in the last few hours.

Not a few of the pilgrims that looked asleep were not glowing; they had died in the night.

Wearing the ship's heavier gogs and zooming with Dalrymple through the crowded, noisy streets for the last two hours was taking its toll on Jane; she was almost dreaming awake—the ship's strong coffee was not keeping her focused . . . The whisper bird had yet to report that it had disembarked its passengers . . .

"A person of interest," Dalrymple announced, and nudged her gently with his elbow.

"Midge thinks we have a westerner," Captain Periglas said from the bridge of the *Heinlein*. The midge had been circling at fifty feet over a crowded overpass. Cars and trucks and buses moved in a steady stream, as they had all night, crossing over a pseudopod of tents that had pushed through the formal boundaries of the tent city—if anything could be considered controlled and formal in Mecca now.

"I'm skimming now, sir," Dalrymple said.

The midge descended on a tall, lone man with dirt-colored hair and a staggering, weaving stride. He wasn't wearing *ihram*; he had on flopping socks, boots, shorts and a torn khaki shirt. Cars brushed close, one knocking him with a mirror and spinning him to his knees; buses moved to within a few inches as he stood again and weaved across the lanes. It seemed he'd be struck down at any moment, but there was something charmed about his uneven gait. He glanced up at the sky, face crinkled in a puzzled frown, as if aware he was being watched. He seemed to be listening to something or someone.

Dalrymple dropped the midge to within a few feet of the man. They had a quick close-up, full on, of the mottled face, filthy with sweat, dirt, and dried blood. His eyes were startling in the darker, stained face, staring, childlike and clear.

Green and blue.

Jane paralleled Lawrence Winter's FBI portrait in their gogs. Except for the eyes, the emaciated face was only vaguely recognizable. But Jane was certain. "That's him," she said. "We've found Winter. What in the hell is he doing?"

"Looks pretty out of it," Dalrymple said.

Birnbaum, the pilot of the whisper bird, broke in and reported he disembarked all passengers. "Wind is one or two knots. Standing off at five klicks and setting out biosensors," he said.

A red glow flicked on in the upper right corner of Jane's vision. Frequencies and satellite positions scrolled below the light. Then, beeps and whoops of digital decoding—somewhere in the ship's electronic mind, complicated decrypt was being performed. Within seconds, as she held her breath, she heard . . .

A phone wheedling.

The phone, according to the display, was in the Kiryat Moshe neighborhood of Jerusalem.

The numbers matched.

"Yigal Silverstein is phoning his girl," Jane announced. She was wide awake now like a dog on point.

"Wonderful," Dalrymple said.

The midge rose to ten meters above the wandering man on the overpass.

"Oh, Christ," Periglas said. Jane could see it coming as well. She wanted to turn away, but the image in the gogs followed her head.

A speeding bus, spying a gap in a neighboring lane, had zipped from behind a truck whose bed was thick with pilgrims. Pilgrims leaned inboard where they hung from the slats to avoid being knocked free. The bus accelerated, honking madly—

And the man with one blue eye and one green eye, with dirty hair and bloody face, vanished under its hood and tires. The bus did not even slow. Three more cars rolled over the tumbling pile of meat and rags, lurching on their shocks like kiddy bumper toys.

"Suspect is down," Dalrymple said.

"He's gone," Periglas said.

Jane closed her eyes. For some reason, no time to guess why, former Special Agent Winter had been cut loose to wander and die.

CHAPTER SEVENTY
Mina

Through the open window of the minibus, William felt the wind shift. In a few minutes, it might be just right for an opening salvo of fireworks. He scanned the gray skies. Al-Husseini was driving over the hard-packed dirt trail, not really a road. The minibus was bucking and complaining like a donkey. They were all listening to Dalrymple explain what had just been seen on the overpass.

"Was it Winter?" Rebecca asked.

"We think so," Jane said. "We'll replay—"

"No time," Fouad said. "What else do you have for us?"

"Agent Rowland has picked up one of our settlers," Dalrymple said.

"He's on a cell with his fiancée in Jerusalem," Jane said. "According to our translator, he's sitting in the back of a truck and he's not a happy terrorist. Something about having diarrhea."

"Let me hear his voice, if he is still talking," Fouad said. "I need to hear this man who wants to kill so many Muslims."

Dillinger interrupted from Washington, DC. "Mr. Al-Husseini, we show you coming up on a gated service road outside the tent city."

"Yes, as I have told you," Al-Husseini said. "The gates will be open. I know the guards. That is your point of entry. Papers will be checked. I assume—"

"Fouad, on short acquaintance, do you trust Mr. Al-Husseini?" Dillinger asked.

The two men in the front of the minibus exchanged dark glances. Fouad looked away and grinned. "He is an individual with many fine traits," he said. "What more can I say?"

Al-Husseini smirked. "We are all excellent individuals."

The gate was simple but effective, an opening cut through long straight kilometers of chain link fencing that had been coiled back and staked down.

Five armed men in black berets and olive-green uniforms, trim and professional, stood around a sand-colored military truck open to the early dawn light. They waved their automatic weapons and Al-Husseini pulled to the left and stopped.

Fouad leaned over to listen to the conversation. Al-Husseini spoke rapidly and softly to a thin man with a full black beard. A packet of money was exchanged. The thin man riffled through the bills, then waved the barrel of his gun.

"He will not need to check our papers," Al-Husseini informed them. "I used to be his superior officer. He works now for the provisionals—for Iraqis and Yemenis, so I hear. A true pig among pigs, just like me."

"We've lost the settler's cell signal," Jane said. "We think they were still in Mecca, however. They haven't moved out to Mina."

"There will be time," Fouad said. "The pilgrims are going to Arafat. They'll return to Mina after sunset."

"We should park and drink bottled water," Al-Husseini said. "Patience is all."

CHAPTER SEVENTY-ONE
Arafat, Mina

Having prayed at the Mount of Mercy, where Adam and Eve had found each other after being expelled from Paradise, and where Mohammed (peace be upon him) had delivered his final sermon, pilgrims flowed back toward Mina. Three stone and masonry pillars representing all the temptations of the devil lay in a straight line within the confines of a huge two-story structure that could provide access to thousands at once—yet still, this was the most dangerous moment of the Hajj. Pilgrims, exalted and exhausted from their prayer vigil at the Mount of Mercy, having searched deep within their hearts, having confronted their darkest selves and found God's mercy and forgiveness, had departed at sunset toward Muzdalifa to gather their forty-nine pebbles, then stumbled and stalked toward their final task in such numbers that the crush, even in good times, times of order and control, had left dozens and even hundreds dead. Now there was little or no control. Soldiers and would-be police kept back, standing in groups or sitting on their cars or trucks, rifles slung or raised to the dark sky, dark eyes watching with helpless bemusement. They were surrounded by a sea of human beings clad in towels or long, modest dresses, moving in one direction and with one intention: to rid themselves of the last vestiges of evil and complete their Hajj.

Fouad had instructed Al-Husseini to pull over to the side of the road just north of the King Khalid Overpass. The wind was blowing gently from the southeast. Thousands of cars, trucks, and buses swarmed out of Arafat along all the available roadways, chugging all manner of exhaust fumes. Cook stoves gasped plumes of oily smoke that coalesced into a ragged blanket over Mina, and the slaughter of hundreds of thousands of sacrificial sheep—already underway—added an invisible tang of blood.

The OSMOs were overwhelmed.

Fouad listened to the irritated chatter of security frequencies. All was confusion, even in the electronic caverns of the Navy ship sailing off the coast, but he was still in contact with most of his team.

They might as well be blind. Within the hour, Fouad was sure, the settlers would launch their fireworks. From the minibus, they would look up to see the starbursts and know they had failed. They would share in the fate of all the faithful passing below them.

Yet God was merciful.

William sat by a middle window, scanning the hordes and the traffic. Rebecca sat in the seat opposite, communicating directly with Jane Rowland on the *Heinlein*. They had not recovered the settler's phone signal. Someone in Mecca was jamming across a wide spread of frequencies. The jamming could be penetrated but it would take time.

"They're on to something," Amir told Fouad as they listened. "Someone high up thinks there's going to be trouble."

"If there's anybody actually in charge," Mahmud added. "Doesn't look very organized."

Fouad stared at Al-Husseini's neck and head above the back of the driver's seat. "It is time to join the pilgrims on foot," Fouad said. They were wearing nondescript khakis. Amir pulled black berets from a duffel bag, complete with red and green chevrons, silver pins, and enameled Hajj security medallions. He handed around the insignia, authentic enough to pass at least an amateur inspection.

They finished quickly. Pilgrims overflowing onto the overpass peered through the minibus windows with sleepy curiosity. Al-Husseini glared back. "This is not a good place to begin a search, if you are on foot," he announced. Without warning, he started the bus and honking madly, with little regard for the crowd, he rejoined the flow of vehicles in the center lanes.

Their pace was still agonizingly slow. The entire world moved like thick jam. Outside, the temperature was already ninety-three degrees. The sun burned like a torch and a hot puff through the open windows instantly dried their sweat-damp hair.

Captain Periglas peered over Jane's shoulder. "We must have fifteen thousand midges out there," he said. "Close-up and personal isn't working. We have a UAV at altitude taking some synthetic aperture radar scans—SAR. Let's get clever. We'll shoot ten or twenty high-rez radar images of the entire town, then use our visual search engine to locate every truck in the area above a certain size. That'll narrow it down a little."

"Might work," Dalrymple said when the captain had moved to another section of the TSC. "We're pretty good at pickin' fleas from black sand."

Jane was still searching for the phone signal when Dalrymple switched their gog displays to a fresh SAR scan of Mina. Combined with earlier scans from several angles, resolution was down to twenty centimeters. The ship's computers almost instantly drew more than a thousand red circles on the densely detailed false-color image. Jane focused on the grid defined by the King Abdul Aziz Overpass, then the road of the same name—just a few hundred yards from the boundary that defined Mina to pilgrims—and the King Khalid Overpass.

A fire had started just east of the Mina Mosque. The hotspot and plume of smoke was clearly visible as she switched between an infrared image and the SAR composite. The next IR image came in five minutes later and revealed that the fire had almost doubled in size and more fires had sprung up throughout the tent camp, some creeping to the vicinity of the Al Malim Mosque.

Supposedly the tents were fireproofed.

Something was going very wrong down there.

"Let's track any vehicle longer than ten meters," the captain said. That reduced the number of circles down to a few hundred. "Now compare with the latest scan and see how many of them are moving and how fast."

Twenty-five were on the move. Most were crawling along in the general syrup of humanity and traffic.

"Get me a sat microwave contour of the same region. Let's see who's trying to break through the jamming."

"Watch this," Dalrymple said to Jane.

The display colors abruptly changed to red and green. Purple smudges of radiated microwave energy—minus the normal background for warm objects—spread quickly, combined, threatened to dominate, and then fixed—a huge bouquet covering nearly all of Mina. The computers selected for intensity, reducing the smudges to dots, then cross-referenced with the truck positions and attached five dots to moving vehicles longer than ten meters.

"Let's get some sharp-eyed midges on those trucks," the captain ordered.

"So much for OSMOs," Jane commented.

"It's that damned slaughterhouse," Dalrymple said. "We didn't take that into account. Too much blood and stuff in the air. And there's a lot of smoke. Jesus, look at the fires."

"What's causing them?" Jane asked.

"Not a clue," Dalrymple said.

Periglas leaned over Jane's shoulder again. He pointed to the northern-most expanse of the tents, tens of thousands of them. Jane zoomed in on the latest optical scan until she found herself staring down at blocky images of men with guns—soldiers? Security?—marching in groups of ten or twenty between rows of closely spaced tents, followed by light armored vehicles.

"They're searching for somebody or something, and they don't seem to care what they torch or who they kill," Periglas said.

Jane relayed this immediately to Rebecca.

"We can see them," Rebecca said. "They're not regulars—they're wearing khakis, robes, business suits—carrying every sort of weapon imaginable—we can't tell what the hell authority they're working under."

She turned to William, then to Fouad. Both were sitting on the right side of the minibus, toward the front, keeping an eye on a nearby band of gunmen paralleling their course. Amir and Mahmud took the rear, facing forward, their own guns held low so as not to attract attention. Al-Husseini wasn't able to drive much faster than the armed men could walk.

"Hold on," William said.

"Fighting ahead," Al-Husseini called over his shoulder. "There is a road-block."

Bullets pinged off the masonry of a building to their left. This caused the armed men on their right to return fire—in all directions. The minibus came to an abrupt halt and Al-Husseini turned off the engine. The windows on the right side shattered. Grange crouched and frog-marched behind a seat. Rebecca was already flat on the ridged rubber matting that ran down the aisle. William crawled forward just in time to grab at Al-Husseini. With Fouad, he tried to keep the man from pushing the door open and fleeing. They struggled as more shots blew out the windshield and the remaining windows on their left. Bullets flew from all around. Men and women in the streets were shrieking.

"We must go!" Al-Husseini pleaded. "They are brigands. They are here to disrupt the Hajj. We have guns—we must fight them!"

Fouad pushed him between two seats and he and William hemmed in the Saudi with their bodies. William twisted to stare down the aisle at Re-becca. More fire raked the roof, tearing up the liner and blowing out air conditioner vents. Pieces of plastic rained down.

Rebecca brushed away pebbles of glass and shouted forward, "Fouad, what can you see?"

*   *   *

Jane clearly heard the nightmare outside the minibus. Dalrymple icily worked through his displays as Periglas spoke with Grange about the locations of the rest of Fouad's team. She didn't seem to have anything to do. With half-numb fingers, she resumed what she had been doing earlier—this time using the pinpoint locations of the five trucks they had tracked with the IR and SAR images. She demanded and received access to a high-altitude vehicle and narrowed the UAV and satellite sensors, breaking through the jamming just long enough to catch a burst of Hebrew, or what sounded like Hebrew, she couldn't be sure until the female translator in the United States spoke up.

"You have Yigal again," the translator said. "He's arguing with somebody. They can't communicate with the other trucks."

Rebecca broke in. "There's a truck up ahead. It can't be one of the trucks we're looking for. It's a flatbed, no cargo—but it's being stormed by a mob of armed men. The militia is concentrating fire on the truck and its driver."

Grange spoke breathlessly from the minibus. "I think we've been compromised. They may be looking for the same trucks we're looking for—"

The jamming became more intense and all the digital signals from the Meccan team dropped out.

"That's it," Dalrymple said. "Too much interference. Provisionals are pumping noise all over the valley."

"Somebody doesn't trust us to get the job done," Periglas observed dryly.

Jane stared helplessly at the UAV video feeds of Mina, the mountains, and Mecca itself.

David Grange pinned Al-Husseini with his own body and asked the question that was on everyone's mind.

"You told them we were coming and why we're here, didn't you?"

Al-Husseini, sweating profusely, stared up at Grange and shook his head. "We should get out of here. They are shooting even pilgrims."

"Yes, but there's method in their madness. They're looking for trucks—just like us. They don't know which trucks, so they're going to stop and shoot up every truck they find. Shooting up trucks at random won't solve anything. It could make things worse. You were not supposed to tell anyone."

Al-Husseini grimaced at the pressure on his chest. The noise around the minibus had concentrated ahead of them, outside the blown-out windshield and beyond the makeshift barriers of overturned cars and battered steel drums. Rough-looking soldiers had come in from the side streets to gloat over the destruction. Fouad popped up to look ahead. The truck's driver, from what he could see, had been cut in half and his head was missing. His truck tires were shot-out and smoking.

"There's nothing, he was riding empty," Fouad said. Amir and Mahmud had positioned themselves by the doors, guns ready, in case soldiers tried to board. So far, they were being ignored. The damage to the minibus had been collateral.

Grange placed his hands expertly on Al-Husseini's neck. The unkempt Saudi's eyes began to protrude, but he did not put up a fight—not yet. He could hardly move.

"Let's talk, man to man," Grange said. "We're here to save the Hajj. Bottom line; that's the truth. We told you as much. Did you or someone you worked with . . ."

"Who would believe you?" Al-Husseini said. "All Americans hate Muslims. You feed the soldiers who are rioting in Mecca and Mina, killing pilgrims. They are your soldiers. You want all of Saudi Arabia for America. Kill me, that won't change things."

Grange let go of his throat. "Fuck it. We're compromised," he said.

Fouad leaned over Al-Husseini. "Is that true?"

Al-Husseini stared up at him with bloodshot eyes. "To die in Mecca is a blessing," he said.

"To save Mecca . . . would that not be a greater blessing?"

Al-Husseini was remarkably calm. "Jewish agents are in our city. You have brought infidels with you. It does not matter who eventually rules Mecca, you are not worthy of trust."

Fouad rolled back and chuffed out his breath in disgust. "It is so," he murmured. "Who can deny it? But if we do not find these Jews, Mecca will die. That is also truth. It is not what we want, not what you want."

Al-Husseini looked away.

"Let's hit the road," Grange said, eyes rolling. "Maybe Allah will guide us now."

Rebecca tapped the side of her head. Jane Rowland was back in her ear. William and Fouad could hear her as well. Something was wrong with Grange's earnode and gogs and he heard nothing.

"—rerouting from low altitude. Still there, folks?"

"I hear and obey, oh mighty one," Rebecca said. Then, to Al-Husseini and Grange, she added, "Allah appears to be female today. Sorry to disappoint, boys."

"We have a candidate vehicle," Jane said. "Five young men in a Volvo truck. They're leaving the scene of some major fighting and they can't talk to their other trucks. We're setting up a connection now. Can you follow the street signs?"

Fouad had memorized a map of Mecca. "We can go wherever they are," he said. To Grange, he said, "The rest of you, leave the bus when it is clear." Amir and Mahmud looked distressed, but Fouad waved them on. "To die in Mecca is a blessing. We will all be together soon enough."

Al-Husseini began to struggle. Amir and Mahmud helped Fouad restrain and gag him.

CHAPTER SEVENTY-TWO

Fouad Al-Husam waited a few minutes for the others to make their way across the street and hide in the entries of nearby apartment buildings. He held his finger to his lips and inserted his thumb between the man's cheek and the cloth gag.

"I understand why you did what you did," he said softly. "No matter now that it was wrong. In your place, I might have done the same."

Al-Husseini's eyes were wild but Fouad stroked his matted, thinning hair with one hand. "I do not think anybody knows how we feel. You are like my father in many ways. If I take away your gag . . . will you be quiet?"

Al-Husseini nodded.

"I will shoot you if you make a sound, understood?" Fouad said.

Al-Husseini tossed his head, *Does it matter?*

"Dignity matters. Timing matters. I know that you will do anything to stop us. And we truly are here to prevent an abomination. So . . . I can shoot you now, without dignity, trussed up like a sheep . . . "

Al-Husseini nodded slowly. He had been in bad situations before, Fouad suspected. Close to death, as well; though not so close as he was now.

Fouad loosened the gag.

"This is awkward," Al-Husseini said, his voice low. "I have lost everything—my family is in the Netherlands, the Custodians of the Holy Mosques have fled, and I am guilty of many crimes. If you are to be my executioner—"

Fouad said, "We are not so far from the Mount of Mercy. You have done Hajj?"

Al-Husseini nodded. "My family has lived in Jeddah for many decades. I first went as deputy to an old Hajji when I was fourteen. I performed Hajj myself when I was a young man, just married. My wife went with me."

"I have not," Fouad said, and sat beside Al-Husseini, drawing up his legs. "This will not count, even if I die here."

Al-Husseini regarded his killer with both wonder and growing alarm. "I have always asked others to die with dignity. Now . . . I am weak. Can you not let me return to my family? I will say nothing."

"My father would not have let you. And I cannot," Fouad said. Both were speaking Arabic now.

"Forget our fathers and our history," Al-Husseini said, starting up. Fouad pushed him gently back. "This is no joke, no play-act!"

"The world is sick," Fouad said. "Dignity is the only answer. Here, at the heart of the world . . . God is surely great and most merciful, God understands all and forgives . . ."

Al-Husseini's lips moved in prayer but his eyes were searching for escape. There was no way around it, and no delaying. Fouad brought up his pistol and with one hand turned Al-Husseini's head.

At the last the older man went limp and let loose his water and closed his eyes. Then he apologized and began praying earnestly. Fouad gave him a few more seconds.

"Jesus," William said, cringing at the single shot coming from the windowless minibus. Amir looked at him with narrowed eyes. The streets were almost deserted now and none of the few stragglers seemed to notice his exclamation.

"We're three long blocks from the first truck," Rebecca said. "Jane says there's an underground walkway nearby. Pilgrims are trying to get out of Mina as fast as possible."

The mass of pilgrims had already shifted to the main roads through the center of Mina. Thousands had dropped their supply of pebbles as they fled. Small piles and scatters littered the street. Buses and cars had been abandoned, some blocking access to the smaller roving armored vehicles.

In the distance they heard the rumble of a tank chewing up pavement. A thick, ugly belch of diesel exhaust curled above the square gray blocks of new concrete apartments. The wind had died. Rebecca was watching the tank's filthy plume curl lazily in the still morning air. This would not be the best time to launch the rockets—even if the trucks had survived and were still on the move. But if Jane was right, and Winter had died, the rest of the Israeli extremists might be in disorder, desperate.

Jane directed them down a warren of alleys. William stumbled on a cobble and skidded on some pebbles, nearly falling. He caught himself and slammed up against a concrete wall. The sound of his harsh breath echoed from the gray buildings. Overhead, an old woman threw open a window and stared down on them, but quickly withdrew. Fresh bullet holes had pocked the walls.

"They've all gone mad," Amir whispered as they passed an elderly black man, his *ihram* stained with blood, one leg crushed and impressed by a tire tread.

Fouad spoke to their shipboard guides. "The walkways are almost empty, just bodies. We see no truck."

"We're updating," Dalrymple said. "Fresh UAV image coming in now. You should be seeing our midges. We see *you*."

They all looked up. Four bird-like craft zipped overhead at roof level, then curved out of sight. They heard the distant roar of a crowd on the move, more armored vehicles.

The plume from the tank had shifted. The wind was changing.

Rebecca and William stayed close to a wall of stones set in plaster. Rusted spikes topped the wall. A midge flitted over the wall and down the street. The images in their gogs flickered. Rebecca heard only digital slices of Jane saying, ". . . see you. Next street—heavy . . ."

Grange ran across the street and whipped off his gogs in disgust. "Mine are useless. Getting anything?"

Rebecca shook her head, frowning. "Hold on."

". . . there's a truck that meets . . . —scription . . . street east . . ."

"Maybe something east," William said, "next street over."

Fouad had gone around the corner and now he came back long enough to wave his arm. The cross street, empty moments before, filled with the frontrunners of the crowd they had heard earlier, being harried by an armored vehicle that chugged and veered. A soldier in a green army helmet leaned back from the vehicle's open hatch and fired an automatic weapon into the air.

Rebecca kept close to William, with Grange right behind. They approached the cross street carefully as men in *ihram* and an old woman in gray broke away from the flow and ran back to where they had been, by the body of the old man—turned in confusion—and then ran again, jumping for the sidewalk as an old Mercedes roared along the narrow passage, tires squealing.

Clear as could be, Jane's voice was back in their ears: "Jannies have cornered a suspect truck," she said. "Meets the description. It's a block east."

Periglas broke in. "We can target an OWL. You have a cluster coming up on prime position."

Dillinger added, "If this is the truck, we should take it out now."

They pushed through the last of the pilgrims fleeing northwest. In a roundabout half-circled by new apartments of brick and concrete, opening to the north and affording a view of the shadowed mountains and the tent city, they saw a large white Volvo truck with a canvas cover. The windshield had been crazed by bullets and a body hung from the open driver's side door. Fouad, Amir, and Mahmud were exchanging pistol shots with two young men on the back of the truck.

Dalrymple said, "We see a second vehicle about a klick east of you. It's stopped on a side street. Some of your men are in that vicinity and have called down a strike. That's what you'll hear in three minutes."

William tried to find the tank exhaust. He couldn't, but the wind was increasing and blowing from the southeast. "Where are the pilgrims?" he asked.

"Most seem to be passing the Al Malim mosque," Jane said. "There might be ten or twenty thousand along the Jamarat overpass."

Rebecca and William took up a position behind a low ornamental wall fifty yards from the Volvo truck. Two of the young men—olive-skinned, black-haired, they looked and dressed Arab—had rolled back the canvas covers from the side opposite, trying to keep out of the line of fire. They had revealed three large crates, the wooden tops pulled aside and stashed between.

A matter of seconds. One young man waved a small white rectangle in his hand.

Simultaneously, three bright red dots zipped across the front of the truck—laser pointers from Fouad's men. Across the roundabout, a second group of Jannies emerged from behind a wall and began firing.

Fouad ran and waved his hand frantically for everyone to get back.

"Look away and *cover!*" Grange shouted. "OWL descending."

There was no sound, simply a foreboding, a silent presence like a huge finger pushing aside the air. William felt his breath catch. The ground bucked and an unimaginable noise caught him mid-air and made the flesh of his legs and arms strain back from the bones. Out of the corner of his eye, through the fingers of his right hand and tightly closed eyelids he saw the flashbulb brilliance of the explosion that punched the truck through the pavement and concrete and deep into the earth. The searing heat from the fountain of white fire raised blisters on his face and hand. He hit the ground several yards back. His shirt caught on fire and he rolled and felt Rebecca and Grange slapping down the flames.

"Move back!" they were shouting, and William got to his feet and ran. He could not help but look back—and the image, though much reduced, still half-blinded him. A white-hot smoking volcano had broken through the pavement and buildings and filled the roundabout with simmering waves of heat and light. Showers of burning white metal spewed from the hole and stuck sizzling against the buildings, cracking concrete, stones and plaster.

Another explosion rocked them. Looking east through a gap in the buildings, William half-saw, through dancing voids of after-images, a second column of brilliance ascend over the tent city.

Two down, William hoped, and then realized he had lost Rebecca and the others. He couldn't see them—he could barely see at all. His ears were ringing and he had burns over much of one side of his body.

Fouad came up beside him. "Hey, classmate," he said. "You're injured."

"Sunburn," William said.

Fouad had similar burns across half his face. "When in the desert, wear sunscreen. I do not see the others."

"Neither do I."

"Then it is you and me, bro'." Fouad behaved as if in mild shock; pupils dilated, face pale behind the burn. "One more truck. Did you hear where it might be?"

William shook his head. The earnodes were quiet. He looked down at a small winged thing that lay on the asphalt before them—a midge. It had been knocked from the sky by the blast. He was about to nudge it with his toe when Fouad grabbed his arm. He winced at the touch—he stung all over. They backed off. The midge erupted in white flame and exploded with a sharp pop. "Det cord," Fouad observed.

William heard Jane Rowland, her voice again clicking in and out. "We see you. Can't find others. There's a—"

William bent his head toward the sky, as if that might help, and covered his ear with a cupped hand. "Say again, Jane."

"Now I see both of you."

Midges whistled between the buildings. Fouad was keeping his eye on lines of men in white robes walking with purpose down the broad boulevard. Some had been burned and were moaning. Drivers were returning to their cars and buses but there were loud shouts and the sirens of ambulances and a fire truck nearby, trying to get through.

"Third truck, Jane," William said. "One more to go. Any sign?"

"Something . . . an alley. There are troops between you and the alley.
I'll pass directions to your gogs."

"I'm not seeing anything in my—" But then he did have a map image, as
did Fouad, who touched his glasses with a look of boyish delight. "So fine,"
Fouad muttered. "We must buy her flowers."

An armored vehicle pushed through cars and swung onto their street,
ignoring shouting pilgrims and outraged drivers. William counted twelve
uniformed men on foot following the multi-axle armored vehicle. The troops
were wearing black berets and khakis—similar to their own. They spotted
William and Fouad and immediately the observer in the vehicle held his
hand over one black earphone, getting instructions. Other men aimed automatic weapons.

Crowd sound and the roar of the fire from the roundabout made it difficult to hear. Fouad could not translate. "Wave cheerfully and let's get inside," he said. They waved and smiled and pushed up to a doorway flush in
the concrete wall. The door was not locked. In the holiest city, why would
anyone lock their doors? Just like at the Academy, William thought. Fouad
entered second. "They're not convinced. Hurry."

The darkened hall took them past more apartment doors, some opening
on deserted rooms. No lights. Power was out in the residential neighborhood. They were in an alley when they heard the first door being opened
again and saw sun pouring in from that direction.

The men in pursuit were shouting angrily in Arabic—and then in English. "Give up and you will live!" one called.

"Keep going," Fouad said and pushed him forward.

"—narrow alley—" Jane said.

As the door to the alley swung shut behind them, it exploded in splinters. Slugs slammed into the masonry of an older building opposite. Chips
of brick and mortar whizzed around them, one grazing William's cheek.
William and Fouad ran along the curved narrow alley. Ahead, they heard a
truck engine starting; behind, more shouts and bullets.

Fouad pulled William into a corner filled with old tin garbage cans.
"Listen. They're talking in Hebrew," he said, and pointed down the alley.
William could hear young men shouting but it sounded far away; his hearing hadn't recovered. He could not tell which direction the voices were coming from. Fouad seemed certain, however.

"There's no time," Fouad said. "Nobody speaks Hebrew in the Hijaz . . . *nobody.*"

"We've found it," William said to Jane.

"We have midges behind you," Jane said. "Prepare . . . deorbit . . . two minutes . . ."

William and Fouad moved around the corner and saw the back end of a canvas-covered truck. The canvas had been rolled and tied to the frame on three sides. Three young men in *tholes* stood behind the truck. They were arranging *kipot*s on their heads and chattering nervously, passing instructions. One of the young man wielded a small white rectangle, waving it in the air and calling out instructions. The alley was almost empty. The crating had been pulled aside, revealing the rearmost steel hedgehog launcher.

William could not hear the soldiers. Had they turned right instead of left?

Fouad straightened and removed the pen-sized laser from his pocket. "Tell them."

"Jane, get us an OWL."

"—on its way—" Jane said.

"OWL descending," Dalrymple said.

Then he heard Periglas. "This one's going to take out some buildings. Channeled blast. Get the hell out of there. —brick walls—"

"I will stay and make sure," Fouad said to William.

"Periglas says we need to get away from these buildings. They've got it pinpointed."

"Do they have it targeted precisely? Can we be sure? I don't think we can take that risk."

Soldiers walked cautiously around the curve, gun barrels foremost. That was it. No escape. Plan B with a vengeance. Without hesitation, William brought up his pistol and fired as he had been trained—as Pete Farrow had trained him, without thought. Two men fell back like broken dolls, then more shouting, more bursts tearing up the bricks and stone. Clouds of stone dust drifted down.

The Israelis on the Volvo truck hunkered and returned fire with their own machine pistols. William and Fouad were pinned. They could not escape in either direction. Fouad aimed his shots toward the truck. One of the Israelis screamed. William positioned himself to respond to the soldiers. "I'll keep these guys busy."

Fouad smiled and brushed William's face with his hand, then shined the laser on the back of the hedgehog, creating a brilliant fan of sparkling red.

No time to think. The wisdom of the chambered round. They were all dead anyway.

A young Israeli lying in the back of the truck raised the white control box. Fouad tried to kill him but missed.

Gray smoke poured from the bottom of the hedgehog launcher. They heard an echoing, staccato hiss.

Just one truck would be enough. Millions of pilgrims, spreading around the world, clothes reeking with bad yeast. Goodbye memory. Goodbye history.

William looked skyward as his ears popped. The cloudless blue sky between the apartment buildings shimmered. Was there a white line up there . . . ? Like a contrail, an invisible finger writing in brilliant cloud, descending.

Fouad shouted, *"Allahu Ak—"*

The ground spasmed in rage.

William did not hear the rest.

CHAPTER SEVENTY-THREE

Rebecca helped Grange into a small van commandeered by the Jannies. They had waited in the deserted shop, squatting behind the counter, until Salil, Fouad's second in command, leader of the group that had first entered Mina, returned and gestured for them to come out. The air was hot and still and full of the smell of burning. Three columns of dense swirling black and white smoke rose high over the town and the tent city, but nothing—not the fighting, not the extraordinary pinpoint explosions and volcano-like fires, had stopped the pilgrimage from reaching its inevitable conclusion. From the main road heading west to Mecca, they could see white-clad Hajjis by the tens of thousands streaming into the split levels of pedestrian access to the three stone pillars, *Jamarat-al-Aqaba*, *Jamarat-al-Wusta*, and *Jamarat-al-Ula*.

Rebecca hunkered in the back of the van, crammed beside Grange and ten of the Jannies. There was little to say. Nobody knew the fate of the rest of their fellows, including William and Fouad. Jane and Dalrymple had nothing to report, except that the impact of the third and last OWL had collapsed a section of apartments and shops surrounding the alley. Damage assessment was still being completed, but the judgment of the experts on the *Heinlein* and back in Washington was that all three trucks had been destroyed as planned, punched into fifty-foot holes in the earth and then completely incinerated, and their cargo with them.

Midges capable of retrieval by high altitude UAVs were collecting dust from the air above Mina and from the plumes of smoke to return samples for later analysis.

Salil, driving the van, found the back road through the dry rocky hills to the desert waste. The drive became hot, dusty, and bumpy. Rebecca did not care. She was deep in thought, wondering what more she could have done.

She had lost her students. Sacrificed them. And she did not know for what. Their mission had been accomplished, but she felt no sense of pride for a job well done. All she felt was that deep anger that had propelled her for too many years; the unreasoning, innocent outrage that so many could behave without restraint, with no sense of balance or honor, much less of law, and demand so much of the desperate few tasked to rein them in.

William.

Fouad.

Jane spoke in her ear. "I swear, Rebecca, I'm staying here until the last midge falls from the sky."

"Do you see them?" Rebecca asked.

"I do not. Nothing."

"You stay there and keep watch. You do that," Rebecca said. The others with working earnodes pointedly did not appear to be listening, but their faces were stiff and pale with fatigue and that deadly sense of let-down, of reassessment and shapeless grief that follows combat and killing.

Rebecca wasn't at all sure the world deserved her children.

CHAPTER SEVENTY-FOUR
Arafat

Arafat is the Hajj. So Muhammad had proclaimed.

The final OWL's cataclysm had split the ground beneath their boots and dropped them twenty feet to the dank, dry bottom of a concrete pipe. Brick dust and chunks of concrete had filled the crack above and much of the pipe to either side, leaving only a man-sized gap to the southeast. They had squeezed through the gap and now walked down the slope of the pipe, part of the drainage system that kept these dry valleys from flash-flooding during infrequent rains; a long and straight course through Mina with no openings other than drains too small to squeeze through and manhole covers welded shut by the Saudis before the invasion, to prevent just such excursions as Fouad and William were now attempting.

William held his arm close to his breast. It was broken, that much he knew. He was covered with painful burns and one eye was obscured by proud flesh. He hurt all over but he still looked better than Fouad, the side of whose face was thickly crusted with blood.

They stooped and followed the pipe for long kilometers until both emerged in a culvert that spread a concrete fan into a small wadi debouching into Aramah Valley. From there, they climbed up to a pedestrian road, now almost empty, and removed their uniforms, assuming cast-off robes. Fouad said nothing as they walked, weaponless and naked under the towels of *ihram,* carrying only their forged credentials, to Mount Rahmat, the Mount of Mercy.

William was too dazed and exhausted to wonder what they were up to.

They stood at Arafat for several hours, not the sunrise to sunset required for a true Hajj. Fouad then started walking again, and William followed. They were met by soldiers in a truck, roaring along the pedestrian road and apparently tracking down stray pilgrims to rob them or be bribed to take them through the confusion, back to Mina or even to Mecca, if they had sufficient money.

Fouad convinced them they had been injured by brigands, and the soldiers, impressed by their injuries and solemnity, finally felt some sense of guilt after the orgy of confusion and desecration. They let them be and drove off.

The walk back to Mina took the rest of the day and at nightfall, they stood among the thousands of pilgrims still trying to complete their Hajj, on the top level of the Jamarat Overpass, having both picked up forty-nine pebbles from the scattered little mounds along the road from Muzdalifah.

William was simply following Fouad's example, like an automaton—doing what he thought might be necessary to pass, to survive. For the most part, Fouad behaved as if William did not exist.

With a pained expression, Fouad pushed through the thinning crowds, many of them parting in awe or disgust at the sight of such injuries, such martyrs, and they both threw their pebbles at the pillars, one after the other, walking on stiff legs and staring with dead eyes, like ghosts.

Many things had been thrown at the pillars, piling up in enormous mounds at the bases of each, and not just pebbles: shoes, coins, articles of clothing, and weapons—surprisingly expensive weapons. Perhaps some of the soldiers and brigands had repented as they watched pilgrims die.

Then they moved on to Mecca, another long walk. William did not think they would make it, but they found dropped bottles of water along the way, and more bodies, and Fouad was relentless.

Only as they came within site of the minarets of the Masjid al-Haram did Fouad speak. "I am done with this," he said, stalking backwards ahead of William. "It is over. I am my father's son no more. This is not Hajj, and I can never return for the shame. Who am I now? Does anyone know? *What have they done? What have they done?*"

He spoke these last words in a harsh growl, his swollen face a monster's mask of pain. Tears mixed with blood on his cracked cheeks.

William had no answer.

On the road, a Red Crescent ambulance found them and soon they were surrounded by solicitous doctors and two nurses wrapped head to toe in gray chalabis.

They rode in the back of the ambulance to Mecca, passing trucks filled with soldiers and more bodies pushed to the sides of the road.

Many more bodies.

But the lights of the Grand Mosque burned bright, and they were told that even now, Hajjis were circling the *Kaabah*, the House of God, rejoicing in their fortune. For they had been to Mecca and listened to God, and soon they would be going home.

After Note

The biological weapons and processes in this novel are possible, but not in the way I have described them. I have tried to persuade of the dangers without providing salient details.

The dangers are real, and immediate. Sober judgment, selfless, nonpartisan planning, and sanity are the only solutions.

For those who go in harm's way, there is ultimately no politics. Only pain, loss, death—and hope.